Wolf Among Sheep

Twelve ships in convoy, three escorts. Hechler held the binoculars on bearing as the guns roared out again. He held his breath as a straddle of shells fell across one of the ships. She was instantly ablaze, but it was made more terrible by distance as the fire seemed to spread down from the horizon, like blood brimming over a dam. The convoy was breaking up ... diverging ranks of ships, burning and dying in the spreading flames.

But one ship was not standing away, and coming straight for the *Prinz*. In her dull paint, she still looked huge: the old *Tasmania*. A merchantman, a liner. She wouldn't stand a chance. No plating at all and just a few guns. Hechler stared while she hoisted flags to each mast. They were battle ensigns. They'd sent the poor old girl to fight, and by God she was about to....

Hechler watched, sickened, as the liner rolled heavily on to her side, another funnel tearing adrift. Without realising what he was doing, he removed his cap. A ship had just been destroyed because fools had sent her to war.

JOVE Books by Douglas Reeman

IN DANGER'S HOUR
THE IRON PIRATE

THE IRON PIRATE

PIRATE

DOUGLAS REEMAN

JOVE BOOKS, NEW YORK

This Jove Book contains the complete
text of the original hardcover edition.

THE IRON PIRATE

A Jove Book / published by arrangement with
Highseas Authors Ltd.

PRINTING HISTORY
G. P. Putnam's Sons edition published 1987
Jove edition / December 1990

ISBN: 0-515-10348-9

Jove Books are published by The Berkley Publishing Group,
200 Madison Avenue, New York, New York 10016.
The name "JOVE" and the "J" logo
are trademarks belonging to Jove Publications, Inc.

PRINTED IN THE UNITED STATES OF AMERICA

10 9 8 7 6 5 4 3 2 1

To Dorothy, Frank and Stan —

from us, with love

Contents

1	Charmed Lives	1
2	Faces of War	17
3	And So Goodbye	33
4	Maximum Security	48
5	Rank Has its Privileges	64
6	The Unexpected	79
7	Aftermath	95
8	Flotsam	108
9	Viewpoint	124
10	Beyond Duty	138
11	The Truth Can Wait	152
12	Doubts	167
13	Revelations	182
14	'Auf Wiedersehen ...'	196
15	Middle Watch	211
16	The Signal	223
17	Blood for Blood	238
18	No Hiding Place	254
19	Last Command	268
	Epilogue	289

1

Charmed Lives

The sea's face that morning rose and dipped in an endless formidable swell. There were no crests, and the deep troughs gleamed in the early light like molten glass. A heavy mist drifted above the water, broken here and there into clearings while close by it barely skimmed the surface.

In a few days it would be August, but in the Baltic the dawn air was already like a knife, a threat of the winter which would soon grope down from the Gulf of Finland to torment ships and sailors alike.

Occasionally scattered groups of gulls and other sea-birds lifted on the successive swells like broken wreaths, pale in the dull light, unimpressed by the steepness of the troughs which in happier times could hide one fishing boat from another even when they lay less than half a cable apart. From end to end the Baltic had been one of the busiest waterways in the world where fishermen and coasters, timber ships and colliers created their own patterns and trails. Now, apart from a few wary neutral Swedish vessels, the waters were the hunting ground, and a burial place for friend and foe alike.

It was 1944 and for many, the fifth year of war. The sea noises were muted or dampened by the mist; it was like a wilderness, an abandoned place for a while longer on this particular morning. The gulls which floated silently and waited to begin their search for food were as usual the first to sense they were no longer alone. To begin with it was more of a sensation than a sound, not close enough to be a beat or throb, just a tremor through the water which soon made the birds rise flapping and mewing, disturbed, anxious yet unwilling to quit their territory.

Had there been an onlooker he would have been startled by the suddenness of the ship's appearance. First a great shadow, and then with a contemptuous thrust of her high, raked bows she swept through the mist, parting it, and cleaving the steep swell with impressive ease. Although her three screws were throttled down to reduced speed she threw a sharp white moustache from her stem which spattered against her faded camouflage paintwork to give a hint of her true power. As she thrust across the grey water she grew in size and strength, but her four twin turrets and towering bridge structure did nothing to spoil the perfection of her lines. She was a heavy cruiser, one of the most powerful afloat, yet she retained all the dash and grace of a destroyer.

No figures explored her wet decks, and only occasional movements at gun mountings and on her bridge gave any sign of life. For a few moments she lay fully exposed in a clearing, like a graceful animal crossing a glade in a forest, and the reluctant dawn made her upperworks shine like glass and touched the flag, a solitary patch of scarlet with its black cross and swastika.

Before the mist closed in again the cruiser's secondary armament seemed to come to life, the slender muzzles in their separate mountings around the superstructure training and lifting as if to sniff out a possible enemy. Each gun crew was fully aware of the cost of carelessness, the lack of constant vigilance. In these contested waters there was rarely a second chance.

Closed up at their various action stations, as they had been for most of the night, there were some 950 officers and men scattered throughout her armoured hull. Separated by the needs of safety, and yet welded into a solitary team to fit the demands of their ship, the wishes of their commanding officer.

At the rear of the open bridge, alone for a few more precious minutes in his spartan sea-cabin, Kapitän zur See Dieter Hechler sat at his desk, outwardly relaxed from long practice, but with his mind recording each movement and untoward sound beyond his small refuge. He rarely visited his spacious quarters below except in harbour, for time taken in running to the bridge in any emergency was time lost. He rarely thought about it. This was his world, and had been for the eighteen turbulent months since he had been given the honour of this command, one of the remaining crack cruisers in the German navy.

In a moment or so, Viktor Theil, his second-in-command, would call him on the red handset above the sea-cabin's crumpled bunk. Then Hechler would get to his feet, take a quick look round to ensure he had forgotten nothing, and walk to the bridge.

They would greet him with varied feelings. Relief, doubt, dislike even, but all would accept him as their captain.

He sat back in the chair and stared unseeingly at the chart on his desk, the personal one he kept for his own guidance. When he joined the others of his team he would need to know everything, be ready to answer any question, even the stupidest one. He knew from hard experience that any man rebuked for asking something which in all truth he should have known, would never dare to ask another question, perhaps when it was vital.

His jacket hung from a rail beside the bunk, the four gold stripes glinting dully in the light from the desk lamp. His cap, like the medal ribbons on the jacket, showed his authority and skill at a glance, but any casual visitor would see him now as the man, not the commander. The cap and jacket were necessary trappings, just as banners and flags identified the old sailing men-of-war in the height of battle in another century. But for now, in his favourite roll-necked fisherman's jersey in thick grey wool, and the extra pair of flannel trousers beneath his uniform ones, he looked at ease. Hechler was thirty-six, the youngest captain to command such a ship as the *Prinz Luitpold*, and the responsibility was clear to see in the deep creases on either side of his firm mouth. His hair was dark and had remained unruly despite all the caustic comments of his superiors over the years. His strength, his qualities, the depth of the man himself showed mostly in his eyes. They were blue with the shadow of grey, like the sea itself.

3

In his youth he had discovered that his eyes had made him vulnerable. If they had showed his confidence, so too they had betrayed his doubts. He had taught himself to contain his inner emotions, and had seen the effectiveness of his control when he was dealing with his day-to-day life. A seaman to be punished, or to be promoted with a word of congratulation. A man to be told that his family had perished in an air raid. It was all part of his world, as was watching people die, sometimes horribly, knowing as he did that others would be looking at him to see his reactions if only to gauge their own fates.

Like last month when he had cleared the lower deck and had every officer and man assemble aft beneath the twin muzzles of Turret Dora, to tell them about the Allied invasion of Normandy. To most of *Prinz Luitpold*'s ship's company the other theatres of war had seemed remote and with little meaning. The Pacific, Italy, even the Atlantic, the bloodiest sea war of all, meant little. Their war had been here, or in the Arctic against the Russians. Normandy had changed all that. The official news was optimistic, adamant that the British and their allies would soon be driven back into the sea and in turn leave England ripe for invasion. And anyway Normandy was a long, long way from the Fatherland.

But to many of the listening faces it seemed like a stab in the back, an enemy gnawing away at another front, which would make even greater demands on their own resolution and resources.

The deck gave an unexpected shudder and Hechler had to make himself relax again, muscle by muscle. Perhaps he was too tired. Maybe the war had pared away his resistance without his realising it. He smiled and ruffled his hair with his strong fingers. Then with a sigh he leaned forward and stared at the chart for the last time.

The coastline was familiar enough. It was useless to consider what might have been, to despair over the loss of ground in the past few months. Safe anchorages had come under constant air attack; now they lay in enemy hands. All the time, the Russian armies kept up their pressure along thousands of miles of savagely contested land. Up here in the North, the Finns, Germany's

4

allies, were under terrible pressure, and an entire German army was in danger of being cut off from retreat. Hechler's mouth moved in a wry smile. *Strategic withdrawal,* as the news reports termed it. The heavy cruiser always seemed to be at an hour's notice to get under way even after the briefest respite in harbour. Now, with her escort of two destroyers divided on either beam, she was back in the same fiercely contested waters where she had once been able to rest; where she had been like a symbol to the army ashore.

As he ran his eye along the chart, or checked a measurement with his dividers, Hechler could see the coast in his mind's eye, like a painting, a watercolour. Abeam was the northern coast of Lithuania, the gateway to the Gulf of Riga. During the night they had slipped past the low, sandy point, Kolkasrags, with its wooded darkness beyond, and would soon begin to turn in a wide sweep towards the land once more.

South-east and deep into the Gulf of Riga, where they had been ordered to supply artillery support to the beleaguered German army. Riga was the only point from which the army could retreat if the worst happened, and there had been nothing in the regular signals to suggest that the Russians were losing steam in spite of their horrendous losses in men and tanks.

It was always a risk, a ship against sited shore batteries. Those who gave such orders saw only the overall strategy, the latest necessity, and rarely considered the danger.

It was a task which *Prinz Luitpold* had carried out many times. Originally she had provided covering fire for their own landings, had supported a victorious army through one advance to the next. If winter closed in early there might be some respite on this front at least. Hechler pitied the poor devils who endured the bitter cold and privation, who would face it yet again with the added knowledge that the Allies were nearer their homeland than they were. *Unless.*

Hechler glanced up at the framed picture of his ship. The glass shivered in the frame to the gentle vibration from several decks below his feet. It made it look as if the photograph was alive. *Prinz Luitpold* was a lucky ship, and had become something of a legend in the tight world of the navy. Bombardments, hurling aside air attacks, or matching gun-for-gun with British cruisers of the North Cape, she had sustained only negligible damage, and had lost but two men killed. One of the latter had fallen overboard after slipping on an icy deck. Not a very proud death for his family to remember.

Hechler thought of other ships similar to his own. *Prinz Eugen*, another legend even in the enemy's navy, *Admiral Hipper* which had been rammed in a hopeless attack by a British destroyer early in the war – they were both fine ships. Another of the class, the *Blücher*, had gone to the bottom back in 1940, torpedoed by the Norwegians of all people. One more was still building.

But *Prinz Luitpold* seemed to lead a charmed life. Her launch, shortly after *Blücher*'s end, had been delayed by several fierce air raids. They had played havoc with the Blohm & Voss yard in Hamburg where her keel had been laid. And yet despite the devastation all around her, she had survived, waiting patiently for the smoke to clear and the work to continue.

Hechler had been serving in a small, elderly cruiser when she had been launched by the Führer himself, her name chosen to cement Austrian friendship. He had seen her several times, and as his own advancement had progressed he had set his heart on her, this cherished command.

He stood up, his body balanced automatically to feel the strength of the ship beneath him. Fourteen thousand tons with the machinery to drive and sustain her every need, the weapons to fight anything faster or of equal size, she even carried three Arado float-planes, Hechler's eyes when he needed them.

Hechler was a tall man, with broad shoulders, yet despite this he moved in the confined cabin with the ease of a cat as he slipped into his jacket and patted each pocket without really noticing this regular precaution.

He opened the drawer of his desk and placed the dividers and parallel rulers inside. As he did so he saw her face looking up at him from the worn leather case which he had always carried at sea. He sighed, his eyes distant. *Next to my heart.*

He heard a steel door slam shut somewhere below the cabin. A last bolt-hole sealed for anyone whose nerve might waver?

6

The ship, this ship, had helped him to get over even that, he thought. He could look at her face now, even study it without the old surge of bitterness and despair. Inger was not smiling in the photograph. When he thought about it now he realised that she had never smiled very much.

The red handset buzzed above the bunk, like a trapped insect. Hechler smiled and lifted it. Relieved at the interruption, to be freed from the sudden shadow, the depression. He closed the drawer as he spoke. Shutting her away, until the next time.

It was Theil, as he had known it would be. A man so dependable that Hechler had once found himself searching for flaws and mistakes. He had been in the ship since she had first commissioned at Hamburg and had served under the one other captain before Hechler. A competent officer in every way, one that commanded most people's respect and liking, qualities which rarely went hand-in-hand in a warship.

Theil should have had a command of his own; they were desperate for experienced captains in larger vessels. Each promising junior was snatched up and sent into submarines to combat the mounting toll in the Atlantic. Like cutting down a forest before the trees had had time to mature, as one elderly staff officer had complained.

Theil reported, 'Five minutes to the final change of course, sir.'

It would be. *Exactly*. Hechler replied, 'Very well, Viktor. I shall come up now.'

He put down the handset and reached for his cap and binoculars. A glance in the bulkhead mirror made him grimace as he tugged the cap tightly across his thick hair. He looked calm enough. He examined his feelings as he would a subordinate.

Nothing. It was as if all pointless doubts had been worked out of him. He studied his image in the glass and saw the strain fall away. He was young again, like the day he had stood in church with Inger, had walked beneath an archway of drawn swords of his fellow officers.

The thought made a shutter fall across his blue eyes. Hechler snapped off the light and left the cabin. He never thought that each time might be the last. That too was a waste, an unnecessary burden on his mind.

He waited a few moments more in the deep shadows, his shoulder touching the damp steel plating, his eyes adjusting, preparing for the open bridge, and the sea. For the enemy.

Fregattenkapitän Viktor Theil, the heavy cruiser's second-in-command, stood on a scrubbed grating in the forepart of the bridge. His booted feet were wide apart so that he could feel the ship rising and slithering down beneath him, tasting pellets of salt spray as they lifted occasionally over the glass screen. A new hand aboard ship took days, longer if he was allowed, to grow accustomed to objects and fittings even in pitch darkness. Theil knew them all, just as he could picture the faces of the intent bridge party on either hand and behind his back. Signalmen and petty officers, the massive, oilskinned bulk of Josef Gudegast, the navigating officer. Theil had some reservations about officers who were not regulars, but like the rest of the team he had cause to be grateful that Gudegast was the navigator. In peacetime he had earned his living in the merchant service and had been for much of the time the chief petty officer of a Baltic timber ship. Gudegast knew all the niceties and the perils of these waters like his own considerable appetite.

Theil analysed the captain's voice on the telephone. Calm. Nothing to worry about. Not like the previous captain who had cracked up when the ship had been under constant air attack for three whole days. Theil felt the old hurt like a physical pain. He had taken command, had got the ship back to Kiel when others had been less fortunate. He had dared to hope he would be promoted, and be given *Prinz Luitpold*. He had deserved it. He knew it. Instead, Hechler had stepped aboard to the trill of calls and the proud salutes. A man of excellent reputation who had since proved his worth a dozen times. But he was several years Theil's junior nonetheless.

Theil thought of the other faces, some of which were new to the ship. In the armoured superstructure above the bridge, the conning tower and fire-control stations, the officers he saw each day were waiting for the calm to shatter. Tired faces at the meal table, or flushed with drink after a trip ashore in some port or other. Faces which hid things or revealed too much.

8

Like the youngest officer here on the bridge, Leutnant zur See Konrad Jaeger. A fresh-faced, green youngster of nineteen. He would be perfect on a recruiting poster. Apart from training, *Prinz Luitpold* was his first ship. He had a pleasant manner, and the confidence of one used to authority. His father was a much-decorated captain who had been put ashore after losing an arm and one eye in the North African campaign. Jaeger's father still had influence, Theil decided. Otherwise the youngster would have been a junior watch-keeper aboard a U-boat instead of serving a thoroughbred like this ship. It was rumoured that a junior officer's life expectancy in a combat U-boat was about that of a lieutenant on the Russian Front.

Theil shivered. It was best to leave it as a rumour these days.

He heard the steel gate at the rear of the bridge open, noted the way the dark figures around him seemed to come to life as the captain entered and touched his cap casually to the bridge party at large. Theil faced him, and recalled suddenly how he had resented, hated this man.

From beside the compass platform Jaeger watched the two senior officers, the men who between them controlled the ship and his destiny. They made a complete contrast, he thought. The captain, tall, powerful, yet with a calm unruffled tone. Theil, stocky, with short fair hair, given to angry outbursts if anything slipped below his very high standards.

Hechler could feel the youngster's scrutiny just as he could sense the navigating officer's indifference. The latter knew his charts with an uncanny accuracy; he was often known to scoff at the ship's new navigational aids, the first things to break down when you needed them, he proclaimed.

Beyond his long hours of duty as the ship hurried from one sea area to another, Gudegast rarely mixed with his fellow officers. Another surprise about him was his skill as an artist. Despite his bluff seaman's appearance and colourful language he could paint and sketch everyday scenes with accuracy and compassion. Now he was rising on his toes to watch some circling gulls, one of his favourite subjects, like patches of spindrift against the mist. Another sketch maybe?

Hechler ducked his head beneath the canvas hood which hid

the light of the chart-table and peered searchingly at Gudegast's neat calculations, bearings and fixes. Like his artwork, each pencilled note or figure was clear and delicate. Perhaps a frustrated artist from another age lurked inside his rugged frame. In his shining oilskin he looked like a sea-creature which had unexpectedly come aboard.

Theil joined him by the chart. 'The shore batteries are there sir. Our main armament is alerted and will be kept informed of any change of intelligence.'

From far beyond the hood's shelter Hechler heard the scrape of steel as the aircraft catapult was manoeuvred around ready to fire off the first float-plane. Each had a crew of two, and apart from cannon and machine-guns would today be armed with two heavy bombs.

Thinking aloud Hechler said, 'That is the railway station. We are ordered to destroy it. Ivan will bring up reinforcements by that route. We'll give him a headache.'

He withdrew from the hood and climbed on to the forward gratings to let the salt air sting away any lurking weariness. He thought of his men, sitting and crouching through his command. Some able to see the heaving water like himself, others confined to their armoured turrets, waiting to feed the big eight-inch guns, or down in the bowels of the engine- and boiler-rooms, deafened by the din of machinery and fans, watching dials or each other. Trying not to think of a shell or torpedo changing their roaring world into a merciless inferno.

In the streets of Kiel or some occupied seaport you would not notice many of them as individuals, Hechler thought. It was a pity the people at home could not see them here, in their environment. It might give them heart and perhaps some hope.

Theil said quietly, 'Time, sir.'

Hechler nodded. Glad they were committed. 'Alter course. Full ahead, all engines.' For a second his guise fell away and he added softly, 'Another time, Viktor, but the same enemy, eh?'

Fifteen minutes later the ship surged away from the mist to greet the first weak sunlight like an enraged tiger.

As the four main turrets swivelled soundlessly on to the prescribed bearing, all eight guns opened fire.

'Alter course, steer two-three-zero!' Hechler lifted his eyes from the gyro-compass repeater and tensed as the sea lifted and boiled into a solid cone of white froth some cable's length beyond the port bow.

He felt the deck tilt as the order was passed to the wheelhouse, the instant response as the raked stem bit into the glittering water. The forward turrets swung slightly to compensate for the sudden change of direction and then each pair of guns recoiled in turn, the shock-wave whipping back over the bridge, hot and acrid as the shells tore towards the land.

Hechler waited for the hull to steady and then raised his glasses once more. The land was blurred with smoke, the colour drained out of it by the hard, silver sunlight. Shell-bursts pockmarked the sky where the ship's three Arado float-planes ducked and dived over their targets, and the fall of the cruiser's shells was marked by great smokestains, solid and unmoving. They made the landscape look dirty, fouled, he thought vaguely.

Tracer lifted from the rubble of some dwellings near the water-front, and he guessed that the army were using their fire to retake their old positions, the bitter house-to-house fighting which was an infantryman's lot.

Hechler thought briefly of his father, and the unexpected distraction disturbed him. He was unused to having his mind shifted off-course when he needed it most.

His father had been a soldier in the Great War, and had been wounded several times on the Western Front until he had been badly gassed and sent home, a coughing, broken wreck of a man. In clear moments he had described war at close quarters, and had chilled his family with tales of wiring parties in no-man's-land, raids on enemy trenches armed with sharpened spades, nailed clubs and long knives. No time to load a rifle, and a bayonet was next to useless in a hand-to-hand encounter, he had said. You could smell your enemy, feel his strength, his fear as you tried to kill him with the same methods they had used centuries earlier.

At sea you rarely saw the enemy. Gun flashes, the fall of shot,

11

a shadow against the moonlight or fixed in a range-finder. It was better that way. Cleaner.

A great gout of fire, bright orange and tinged with red, erupted from the shore and Theil, who had a handset jammed beneath his cap, shouted, 'Railway station, sir!'

A seaman nudged his friend and they grinned at one another. The young officer, Leutnant Jaeger, shaded his eyes to look up at the control station with its narrow observation slits, like the visor of a massive helmet. He did not even duck as something whistled above the bridge and Hechler saw a seasoned petty officer glare at him behind his back. He probably wanted him to get down; any fool could die a hero.

'Aircraft, sir! Bearing red-one-one-oh! Angle of sight three-zero!'

The secondary armament were already swivelling round on their sponsons and in their small turrets, tracking the tiny, metallic dots which had suddenly appeared out of the smoky haze.

Hechler thought of Kröll, the gunnery officer, and was glad of his efficiency. Kröll, lean, tight-mouthed and devoid of any sense of humour, was a hard man to serve. Constant drills in every kind of exercise, switching crews around with loading numbers from the magazine and cursing any officer or seaman who failed to respond to his immediate satisfaction, had nevertheless made the ship a living example to many others.

The anti-aircraft guns and then the lighter automatic weapons clattered into life, the bright tracer streaking across the sea and knitting together in a vivid mesh of fire through which the approaching planes would have to fly.

One of the escorting destroyers was turning in a steep welter of foam, an oily screen of smoke trailing astern of her as she headed closer to her big consort, her own guns hammering sharply to join the din.

Prinz Luitpold's main armament recoiled again. Hechler had lost count of the number of rounds they had fired, and he heard the abbreviated whistle of the shells as they ripped towards the target.

'Alter course. Steer due west.' Hechler let his glasses drop to his chest as Gudegast passed his orders through the brass-mouthed voice-pipe by the compass.

'Two-seven-zero, sir.' The rest of his words were drowned by the throaty roar of engines, and the increasing bang and clatter of gunfire as the enemy planes flashed over the water.

Hechler did not see which one straddled the destroyer, but the explosion just abaft her squat funnel made a searing flash and flung fragments high into the air even while the ship staggered round in another turn, her deck laid bare as she tilted over. Another great explosion blasted her from between decks and fire spread along one side like lava, masking her hull in steam and surrounding her struggle with bright feathers of spray from falling debris. Distance hid the sound of her destruction but it was clear enough for anyone to see.

Two of the Russian aircraft were weaving away, their own wounds revealed by smoking trails as tracer darted after them, and the sky around them was filled with drifting shell-bursts.

Gudegast said thickly, 'She's going! God, look at her!'

Hechler watched the destroyer as she began to settle down. One boat was in the water, but was carried away from her side by the swell with just a handful of men aboard. Floats were dotted about, but the first two explosions had obviously taken a heavy toll of life. Hechler had met the destroyer's captain at several conferences. It was a moment dreaded by every commander. *Abandon ship*. Even thinking the words was like a surrender.

Two more Russian planes roared over the listing vessel, and the sea around the solitary boat was torn apart by machine-gun fire. Hechler felt his stomach muscles contract, but made himself watch as the tiny, unreal figures clawed at the air or floundered in the swell before they were cut down.

Theil hurried to his side. 'One of the Arados is finished, sir!'

They looked at each other. Theil's voice was harsh; his words were not just a report. They sounded disbelieving, like an accusation.

Hechler strode across the bridge, his boots scraping on empty cartridge cases from a machine-gun, and watched the pall of smoke beyond the waterfront. The float-plane must have been hit just as she had released her two bombs and had exploded directly above them.

'Signal from escort, sir! Request permission to pick up survivors.'

Hechler glanced at Jaeger's handsome face. He had not yet learned how to conceal his emotions, Hechler thought; his eyes looked wild, full of pain for the men who were dying out there.

It was an additional, unwanted drama. The remaining destroyer's captain knew better, even if the other one was his best friend.

It could have been his ship. The two after-turrets roared out again and sent a violent shock-wave through the bridge as if they had hit a sandbar. *Or it could have been us.* It would be no different. You must not even think about it.

He heard himself reply flatly, 'Denied. Discontinue action.'

He glanced quickly at his watch, aware of the tension around him, the shock at what had happened so swiftly.

His voice seemed to move them again, voices called into telephones and pipes, and Gudegast passed his prearranged course to the wheelhouse. Parts of a pattern. There were things to be checked, not least preparations for another air attack before their own covering fighters flew out to shepherd them to safety.

Hechler raised his glasses and stared at the mounting curtain of smoke where the railway station and surrounding streets had been under fire. It was already falling away as the cruiser swung on to her new course and threw spray over the forecastle like heavy rain. The signal would be sent, the army would be left to use whatever advantage and breathing space the bombardment had offered. Hechler moved his glasses and saw the stricken destroyer hard on her side, the swell around her smooth and stained with oil. A few heads bobbed in the water, but as the distance increased they seemed without meaning or purpose. Two aircraft shot down or severely damaged. A small price to pay for a destroyer and her company, he thought bitterly.

He lowered his glasses and moved to the opposite side to watch the other destroyer increasing speed to take station again. Nearby he could hear the watchkeepers whispering together while the voice-pipes kept up their constant chatter. Routine and discipline kept men from fretting too much. Later they would remember, but their pain would be mellowed by pride. The legend lived on. They had lost one Arado. Two absent faces at the mess table, telegrams to their homes, and later Hechler would write a letter to each family. Now, as he watched the drifting smoke he was dismayed to realise he could barely remember the faces of the dead airmen.

A messenger scrambled on to the bridge, wide-eyed and anxious, the first time he had left his armour-plated shell since the guns had opened fire.

Theil took the signal pad from him and after a quick glance said, 'Priority Two, sir. To await new orders.' Their eyes met.

Hechler nodded and removed his cap. The air felt clammy against his forehead. He thought suddenly of a bath, hot water and soap, an unbelievable luxury. He wanted to smile, but knew he would be unable to stop. It was madness. A helplessness which always followed a risk. He glanced up at his ship, the smoke trickling past her funnel-cap and the shivering signal halliards. She was not built to act as a clumsy executioner, a tool for some general who had failed to outwit the enemy's tactics. He thought of the destroyer which would soon come to rest on the bottom, how her survivors would still be floundering about and dying, but still able to see *Prinz Luitpold*'s shadow fading into the mist. Abandoned. In the twinkling of an eye they had become mere statistics.

He realised that Theil was watching him. Waiting, his features controlled and impassive.

The signal was brief, but said all that was needed. Fresh orders probably meant they would be ordered away from this battleground. The news would flash through the ship like lightning. It always did. Where to? What mission had been dreamed up this time?

Hechler gripped the nearest handrail and felt the ship respond to his touch. Like a great beast whose respect had to be constantly earned and won.

So many shells fired, and each selected target bombarded without damage and without cost to any man aboard. One aircraft was lost, and the others would be retrieved as soon as it was safe to stop the ship and hoist them inboard.

He felt suddenly angry, contemptuous of the fools who had risked the very survival of this ship for a gesture, one which would and could make no difference.

'Perhaps we shall be given bigger game to hunt, Viktor.' He looked at him searchingly and saw him flinch. 'Unless some politician has already thought up some wild escapade for us.'

Theil dropped his voice. 'I am a sailor, not a man of politics, sir.'

Hechler touched his arm and saw Jaeger relax as he watched them. 'Sometimes we must be both!' Then he smiled, and felt a kind of recklessness move through him. 'This ship is a legend. She cannot remain one while she sniffs after fragments left by the army.'

The two Arados flew over the mastheads and rolled their wings. They had already forgotten. Survival was a great tonic.

Theil said, 'Normandy, do you think, sir?'

Hechler walked to the gratings again and rested his hands on the rail below the glass screen. The destroyer was already zig-zagging ahead of them, ready to seek out and depth-charge an enemy submarine, although it was unlikely there would be one in this area, he thought.

He considered Theil's question and pictured his ship charging through the invasion fleets and their supply vessels like an avenger. A proud but short-lived gesture it would be too.

No, it was something else. He felt a shiver run through him. A war on the defensive could not be won. He looked down at the forecastle, at the two pairs of smoke-grimed guns as they were trained forward again.

It was what he was chosen for, and why the ship had been built. To fight and to win, out in the open like *Scharnhorst* or the cruisers of his father's forgotten war.

Hechler nodded to himself. Nobody would forget his *Prinz Luitpold*.

2

Faces of War

Kapitän zur See Dieter Hechler emptied another cup of strong black coffee and glanced around his spacious day cabin. Sunlight shone brightly through the polished scuttles, and he could hear some of his seamen chattering and laughing as they went about their work on deck.

The ship felt at peace as she swung to her cable, and it was hard to believe that they had been in action less than two days back, and had seen the destroyer go down.

Hechler stood up and walked to one of the scuttles. From a corner of his eye he could see Mergel watching his every move, his pen poised over a bulging pad as it had been for an hour or so since they had anchored. Mergel was a petty officer writer and would have made someone a fine secretary had he been a woman, Hechler often thought.

Even the weather was different. He shaded his eyes and looked towards the shore, the high shelving slope of green headland, the clusters of toy houses which ran all the way down to the water's edge. Untroubled – from a distance anyway.

Hechler was moved by what he saw. It was the east coast of Denmark, and the port which was set in a great fjord was named Vejle. He smiled sadly. He had visited here several times during the war, and earlier in a training ship, or to holiday with his parents and brother. Happy, carefree days. It gave him a strange feeling to be here again in *Prinz Luitpold*. Many eyes would be watching the ship, but how would they see her? Would anyone admire her lines, or would they see her only as an extension of the occupation forced on their peaceful country?

He saw a fuel lighter move away slowly from the side, men staring up at the ship, some soldiers with their weapons slung carelessly on their shoulders, a world apart from the Russian Front, he thought. With the taste of good coffee in his mouth he felt vaguely uneasy, as if he should be doing something useful. Another fuel lighter cast off and followed the first one towards the fjord. Stück, the chief engineer, would run him to earth eventually to report on his department. Even in harbour there was no obvious rest from routine. Visitors came and went. Requests, demands, questions – it was like being responsible for a small town.

The thought of going ashore touched something in Hechler and made him eager to leave, if only to smell the land, feel the lush grass beneath his feet.

He sighed. It was not to be. Not yet anyway.

He looked at Mergel. 'Have the letters done first, and I'll sign them.' He tried to picture the faces of the two dead airmen. Did such letters ever help, he wondered?

Mergel gathered up his papers and moved to the door. 'May I ask, sir, will there be leave?'

Hechler shrugged. 'You will probably know that before I do.' He waited for the door to close. In the ship's crowded world he treasured the moments he could be alone. Alone with his ship perhaps?

He poured a last cup of coffee and ran his eyes over the pad of signals and news reports again.

There was some sort of security blanket on Normandy, he decided. Only one thing was certain. The Allies had not been flung back into the sea, but were pushing deeper into France. There was a mention of some possible secret weapon which would soon change all that, and enemy losses were still heavy in the Atlantic due to the aggressive tactics of the U-boats. Hechler bit his lip. Many words, but they said little.

The sentry opened the door and Theil stepped into the cabin, his cap beneath his arm.

Hechler gestured to a chair. 'It will be quite a while before the admiral arrives, Viktor.' He had seen the surprise in Theil's eyes, as if he had expected to find his captain unshaven and still in his seagoing gear.

Theil said, 'The upper deck is washed down, sir, and the boats are being repainted. The admiral will find no fault in the ship's appearance.'

Hechler looked away. There it was again. The defensive, bitter note in Theil's tone. As if the ship was his sole responsibility. Hechler pushed the pad of signals towards him. 'Read these, Viktor. They may amuse you.'

He put on his best jacket and buttoned it carefully. In his mind he could see the admiral very clearly. One of those round, ageless faces with wide confident eyes. He smiled. Unless you knew him. He was only a year or two older than himself and already a rear-admiral. One of Donitz's shining lights, everyone said, highly thought of even by the Führer himself. Or so it was claimed. Looking back it was not so surprising, Hechler thought. He had first met him when they had both been cadets, and then later they had served together in an old training cruiser which had unexpectedly been called to speed to the assistance of a burning cargo-liner in the Mediterranean. The event had captured the headlines, and in Germany had been blown up enormously to cover other less savoury news of attacks on Jews which had been giving the country a bad name abroad.

While others who had once been cadets in those far-off days had progressed or fallen by the wayside, he had always managed to seize the limelight. Now he was a rear-admiral. It would be interesting to see how that had changed him.

Theil said, 'Will there be leave, sir?'

Hechler looked at him and smiled. *You too?* 'I expect so. Our people can do with it. This kind of landfall makes the war seem far away.'

'It's not for myself, sir, you understand—'

Hechler nodded. 'We *all* need a break.'

Theil shifted in his chair. 'I hate not knowing. What is expected of us? I am not afraid of fighting, even dying, but not to know is like a weight on your back.'

Hechler thought again of his father. *Like waiting to go over*

19

the top. Theil was right, but it was not like the man to express it so openly. Perhaps he should have looked for some additional strain earlier?

Hechler said, 'We both know that we cannot go on like this. The *Prinz* was not built to nurse an army. She was designed to fight.' He waved his hand towards the sunlit scuttles. 'In open water, like she did off North Cape.' The picture rarely left his thoughts. It had been the first battle he had fought in this ship. Up there off the Norwegian coast which had been shrouded in day-long darkness. Two British cruisers and some destroyers in a blizzard like the one last year which had covered the end of *Scharnhorst* in those same terrible seas. At the end of the day *Prinz Luitpold* had won the battle, even though her escorts had been sunk, and another cruiser set ablaze. The British had hauled away, their losses unknown, and had left this ship almost unmarked.

Both sides had claimed a triumph, but Hechler knew in his heart that *Prinz Luitpold* was the only victor.

There was a tap at the door and after a small hesitation the executive officer, Korvettenkapitän Werner Froebe, stepped inside. Froebe was tall and ungainly, with huge hands which seemed forever in his way. Next to Theil he was responsible for the running of the ship and the supervision of the various watches and working parties.

Theil glared at him. 'Well?'

Froebe looked instead at his captain. 'I apologise for the intrusion, sir, but there is an officer come aboard from the town.' He dropped his eyes. 'A major of the SS, sir.'

Hechler studied him gravely. 'What does he want?'

'He wishes to load some stores on board, sir.' He held out a piece of paper. 'He has the admiral's authority.'

Hechler took it and frowned. 'It seems in order. Have the boatswain select a party of hands to assist him.'

Froebe said glumly, 'The major has some people, er, workers—'

Theil was looking from one of the scuttles. He said shortly, 'Civilian prisoners, more trouble!'

Hechler saw their exchange of glances. Civilian prisoners

could mean anything in wartime, but with an SS major in charge it probably meant they were from a labour camp.

'Deal with it.' When Froebe had left he added, 'The admiral will be here soon, Viktor. I don't want the ship cluttered up with working parties when he steps aboard.'

Theil picked up his cap. 'I agree.' He seemed suddenly pleased to go, all thoughts of the next mission, even home leave forgotten.

Hechler examined his feelings. Like most of his colleagues he had heard stories of overcrowded labour camps, and the rough handling by the SS guards. But it was not his province; his place was here in the ship, or another if so ordered. It was what he was trained for, what he had always wanted.

He could almost hear himself saying much the same words when he had asked Inger to marry him.

He walked to a scuttle again, but the day was spoilt. It was like having a bad taste in the mouth. Something you could not explain, and certainly something you could do nothing to change.

Somewhere overhead a speaker came to life, followed by the trill of a boatswain's call. The boatswain was already mustering a working party for the unexpected and as yet unidentified cargo. The deck gave a sudden tremble as one of the powerful generators was switched on, while down in the shining galley the chief cook would be ranting and cursing about having to delay the midday meal until the admiral had been piped aboard.

Hechler left the cabin and walked along the starboard side, his eyes on the choppy water, but missing nothing of his men who worked above or around him. They moved aside to let him pass, while petty officers saluted and called their men to attention if he caught their glance.

They respected him, he had brought them back to a safe anchorage, and that was enough.

He saw some seamen by the float-plane catapult, and Brezinka, the massive boatswain, wagging his finger as he explained what he needed done.

Froebe stood slightly apart with the SS major, a man who would have been utterly insignificant but for his uniform and the death's-head badge on his cap.

Something made Hechler pause. He asked, 'Is anything wrong?'

Froebe jerked to attention. 'N-no, sir. These hands will go ashore to man a lighter and bring it alongside—'

The major interrupted. 'They must be under my orders, Captain.'

Hechler glanced at him coolly. 'They are also under mine, Major. I will be pleased if you remember that.' He saw the man's flush of anger, but felt no pity for his embarrassment. He glanced at Froebe. 'Make it quick.' He saw a young acting petty officer who had been placed in charge of the party and thanked God for his gift of remembering names.

'You will be taking your final exam soon, Stoecker?'

The sailor had an open, pleasant face. One you could rely on.

Stoecker smiled. 'Yes, sir. Three weeks' time if—'

Hechler touched his arm. '*If*, a word that carries much weight for all of us, eh?' He walked on, knowing that Stoecker would remember how the captain had spoken to him after snubbing the major. Cheap? Possibly. But it *made* a ship's company.

With the warm sunlight across his shoulders Hechler walked alone right around his ship's upper decks. Past the towering bridge structure and capped funnel, beneath the long guns and over the white-painted anchor cables, his eyes missed nothing.

Germany had broken the treaty made by her old enemies to build the *Prinz* and her sister ships. Ten thousand tons had been the maximum which had been allowed, but secretly they were over 15,000 tons when they had been launched. From her raked stem to her handsome quarterdeck the heavy cruiser would make any shipbuilder proud.

The armament and gunnery controls in each of the class were unmatched anywhere. The ill-fated *Bismarck* had been given the credit for sinking the British battle-cruiser *Hood* early in the war, but it was believed throughout the fleet that *Prinz Eugen*'s guns had fired the fatal salvo.

Hechler looked at the two after turrets and forgot about his irritation over the SS officer.

Just given the chance. That word *if* again.

He smiled at the thought, and two seamen who were polishing the deck plate which bore the ship's name, where the admiral would step aboard, nodded to each other and grinned. There could be nothing to worry about.

Later as the gleaming launch, with a rear-admiral's pendant streaming from it, curved in a frothing wake towards the accommodation ladder, Hechler, with the unaccustomed weight of a sword at his side, felt the same sense of pride.

For a moment at least the war itself had become a backcloth, and only the manned anti-aircraft guns, both here and ashore, gave any hint of possible danger.

The ship's company were dressed in their best blue uniforms, unlike their drab seagoing rig, and all but the duty officers were in ranks, with Theil, unsmiling and grim-faced, at their head.

The launch vanished beneath the rail and Hechler saw the top of the accommodation ladder give a tremble as the boat nudged alongside. He controlled the desire to laugh. All it needed was a band. But as they were always being reminded, there *was* a war on.

Konteradmiral Andreas Leitner lay back in one of the cabin's deep chairs and regarded the glass in his hand.

'Good, eh?' He chuckled. 'I find it hard to admit that only the Frogs can make champagne!'

Hechler tried to relax. Leitner was exactly as he had remembered him, youthful, confident, and so buoyant that it was impossible to imagine him ever being ruffled.

He had come aboard with a bounce in his step and after saluting the quarterdeck and side-party had faced the assembled company and thrown up a stiff Nazi salute which had seemed theatrical in spite of his gravity. An act? It was still difficult to judge. Hechler watched him while Pirk, his steward, refilled the glasses. Leitner must have brought a dozen cases of champagne aboard which his flag-lieutenant was now having stowed for future use.

Leitner had not mentioned their mission or his sealed orders; he was taking his time. In that respect too, he had not changed.

His hair was fair and well-groomed, and his skin had a kind of even tan, although Hechler had not heard of his being out of Germany for a year or more.

The admiral nodded to the steward. 'Well trained, eh? Pours it like a head waiter at the Ritz.' He grinned broadly. 'You have a fine ship, Dieter. I am quite jealous the way you are spoken of in the high command.'

He waited for Pirk to withdraw and said, 'I shall hoist my flag aboard very shortly.' He watched him evenly. 'A private ship no longer, how does that strike you, my friend?'

'I am honoured, sir.'

'You are not. I know you too well to accept that!' He laughed and showed his even teeth. 'No matter. You are the right captain. We shall do well together.'

'Shall we return to the Gulf, sir?'

Leitner became serious. 'I cannot discuss it yet. You and your ship have performed wonders, have given pride where it was lacking, a sense of destiny when some were only thinking of comfort and a quick end to the war.'

He wagged the empty glass at him and added, 'I have often thought of you, and the old days, believe me. Your parents, are they well?'

Hechler replied, 'They are managing.'

'I felt it personally when your brother was lost in *Scharnhorst*. A good ship too. He lies with a brave company, an honour to our country.'

Hechler tried to compose his features and his reactions. It seemed strangely wrong to hear Leitner, or anyone else, speak of his brother like a part of history. He could see him without difficulty, so full of life, excited at being appointed to so famous a ship.

Leitner was saying, 'Young men like Lothar are an example, part of our heritage—'

Hechler refilled their glasses, surprised that his hand was so steady. His young brother's name had come off the admiral's tongue so easily, as if they too had been close, and yet he knew they had never met.

He tried again. 'My people have had no leave, sir, and they

24

deserve it. Whatever we are called to do –'

Leitner gave a mock frown. 'You will be told, but now is not the moment. I can only say that I am here for the same reason. You have earned a rest, albeit a short one, but the needs of Germany rise far above our own petty desires, eh?' He laughed lightly. 'When I watched your ship anchor, my heart was filled, I can tell you.'

Hechler realised he had drained another glass, but Leitner's mood was unnerving. For just a few seconds his pale eyes had filled with misty emotion, then they hardened as he continued, 'We shall have vengeance, Dieter, for Lothar and all the other fine young men who have died for our cause.'

The admiral stood up suddenly and paced about the cabin, touching things as he moved. He said, 'I have arranged some leave, but it will be short, I am afraid. I have my temporary headquarters in Copenhagen. It is not like Berlin, but it must suffice.' He shrugged. 'We do what we can.'

Hechler said, 'You were in America too.'

Leitner swung round, his eyes pleased. 'So you followed my career as I watched over yours, eh? That is good. Friendship is too strong to be parted by events. Yes, I was in Washington as a naval attaché. I learned a lot, mostly about American women. If their men fall on their backs as willingly this war will soon be brought to a successful conclusion!' He laughed and wiped his eyes. 'God, what a country. I was worn out!'

Hechler watched him as he moved about the cabin. Leitner had always excelled in sporting events, but he never recalled any great attachments with girls as a junior lieutenant. He had not married either.

Leitner paused by a bookcase and said without turning, 'I was sorry to hear about your marriage, Dieter.'

It was as if he had been reading his thoughts. Like a single bullet. 'It was a mistake.'

'I can tell by your tone that you blame yourself. I doubt that you have any cause, Dieter. An idealist, yes. A bad husband, I think not.' He sighed. 'Women are admirable. But never treat them as equals.'

Hechler relaxed slightly. Another problem solved. Was that

25

how Leitner had gained flag rank, he wondered?

Leitner said, 'My gear will be sent aboard this afternoon. You have quarters for flag officers, that I do know.'

Hechler nodded. 'Had I known you were coming, sir, I would have had the quarters properly prepared. As it is—'

Leitner shrugged indifferently. 'Castle or charcoal burner's hut, it is the same to me. All I ask is a little luxury here and there.' He did not elaborate. Instead he said, 'Your last mission failed, I believe?'

It was so blunt after his affable chatter that Hechler sensed his own resentment rise to meet it.

'We carried out the bombardment, the objectives were all destroyed. We lost one escort because—'

'I know the hows and whys, thank you.' The smile broke through again like winter sunlight. 'But it was a failure nonetheless. I heard from OKM Operations Division an hour ago that we have at least a whole infantry brigade cut off, surrounded.' He closed his fingers like a claw. 'They will fight to the death of course, but we lost a good destroyer for nothing.'

Leitner looked directly at Hechler but his pale eyes were faraway. 'No matter, my friend. The Führer has ordered the beginning of an aerial bombardment by rocket, the like of which will make Rotterdam, London, Coventry and the rest, seem like mere skirmishes. The first rocket was launched yesterday. I can say no more than that, but you will soon hear of it. There is no defence. The RAF had some success against our flying bombs over London, but against the V-2 there is *nothing!*'

Like most serving officers Hechler had heard about the much-vaunted secret weapons. They never seemed to appear. The fanatical confidence in the admiral's voice made him believe that this one was real, terribly so.

Leitner said, 'I know what you are thinking. War on civilians is foul. Perhaps it is. But to shield Germany from invasion any means are acceptable. God will always congratulate the winner!' It seemed to amuse him and he glanced at his gold wrist-watch before adding, 'We shall dine together tonight. In the meantime my flag-lieutenant will present a brief summary of immediate requirements.' His eyebrows lifted as the sentry's booted feet clicked together beyond the door. 'My aide is not blessed with all the arts, but he is ever punctual.'

There was a tap at the door and Hechler called, 'Enter!'

Kapitänleutnant Helmut Theissen strode into the cabin very smartly, a heavy file under one arm. Like his superior he had fair hair, and the same even tan. Maybe they had both been on a secret mission, Hechler thought, to Spain for instance, whose one-sided neutrality had often proved a great asset.

Theissen was young for his rank, with anxious eyes and a willowy figure which even his immaculate uniform could not disguise. At the sight of the admiral his confidence seemed to melt.

He said, 'I have brought the file, Admiral.'

Leitner glanced at him coldly. 'Don't stand there like a Paris whore, man, prepare it for the Captain.'

He looked at Hechler and winked. 'A mother's gift to a war-starved nation, yes?'

Hechler heard the harsh echo of commands and the clatter of the main winch. The mysterious lighter was about to leave. Froebe's men had done well. They had hardly made a sound.

He would escort the admiral to his quarters or wait until he was ready to go ashore again. He glanced briefly in the bulk-head mirror then looked away quickly. It was like uncovering a secret – worse, sharing it.

In those brief seconds he had seen Leitner and his anxious-eyed aide looking at each other behind his back.

There had been no animosity. Affection was the nearest description he could think of. He was surprised and troubled to discover how the possibility left its mark.

Later at the gangway before they exchanged formal salutes, Leitner said, 'I shall send my car to the pier tonight, Captain.' He glanced at the side-party and rigid guard of helmeted seamen. 'We shall speak of *old times*.'

Then he was gone, and Hechler saw his aide staring up from the launch, something like relief on his face.

Hechler nodded to the duty officer. 'March off the guard, Lieutenant.'

He watched them clump away, doubtless thinking of their

27

delayed meal. It was a pity that life could not be that simple for us all, he thought.

When he looked again, the launch had vanished around an anchored freighter with the Swedish flag painted on her side. Her only frail protection against bomb or torpedo.

Life would not be quite the same again, he decided grimly.

A muffled explosion echoed against the superstructure and made several seamen come running, their faces taut with alarm.

Froebe panted along the deck and saluted. 'Captain, the lighter is on fire, an explosion in her engine, I think!'

Hechler thought suddenly of the young acting-petty officer's face. 'Call away the accident boat at once! Send help.'

It had been on the way back to the shore after unloading the mysterious cases.

Froebe watched men running for the main boom beneath which the duty boat was already coughing into life.

Then Hechler glanced at the placid shoreline. 'I want to know immediately what happened. Everything.' He strode away and wondered if the admiral's launch had seen the explosion, which must have been near the fjord's entrance.

In war you never accepted even the smallest disaster as an accident.

Hans Stoecker walked abreast of the lighter's long hatch-covers and turned to watch the cruiser, his home for about a year, as she drew astern, and her details and personality merged like a misty photograph.

Astern, *Prinz Luitpold*'s motorcutter kept a regular distance, her crew relaxed and unconcerned about the brief break in routine.

Stoecker was twenty-five and very conscious of his small authority. Even this rusty lighter represented *his* ship until he could gather the small working party together and return in the motor-boat. He watched the SS major, hands in pockets as he chatted quietly with two of his men, machine-pistols crooked under their arm and not slung on their shoulders.

Stoecker glanced at the wheel, aft by the low guardrail. Künz was the helmsman. They had had a few rows since his acting rank had been awarded by the captain. Now he seemed to accept him. And he was a reliable seaman despite his foul mouth.

Stoecker walked along the side and kept the hatch covers between himself and the SS men. Locked down below there were ten prisoners who had carried the heavy steel boxes to the cradles to be hoisted up the cruiser's side. They had needed careful watching, for Stoecker knew that if just one tackle had been allowed to scrape the paintwork he would have felt Froebe's wrath.

He smiled and thought of his father who had been recalled to the navy after a few years' retirement. Too old for active duty, he was in charge of some naval stores in Cuxhaven. How pleased his mother would be after he qualified and they both went home in the same uniform!

Something touched his ankle. He glanced down, and saw a wiry hand reaching for him.

He looked quickly around the deck. The SS men were in deep conversation and peering at their watches, the few seamen who had not transferred to the motorboat were sitting on the hatch-covers, looking up at the sun, their eyes slitted with pleasure. Stoecker crouched down and peered through a narrow air vent at an upturned face.

He had mixed feelings about the prisoners. He did not after all know what they had done – they must have done something. They were dressed in clean, green, smocklike overalls, unnumbered, unlike some he had seen. They had been very docile, even cowed, and any sort of contact with the sailors had brought a scream of anger from the little major. There was one naval officer aboard, a pale, listless, one-striper who was said to be on light duties after his E-boat had been blown up in the North Sea. Stoecker and his companions had watched the young officer until his indifference and his sloppiness had made them bored.

He was up in the bows, his back to all of them, shutting them out.

Stoecker lowered his face. 'Yes, what is it?' He tried to be clipped and formal.

The man gazed at him, his eyes almost glowing in the gloom of the hold.

'I have a letter.' His German was perfect. 'Could you give it to my family?' He paused and licked his lips. '*Please!*' The word was torn from his mouth.

'I can't — I don't see why —'

A dirty, folded letter was thrust through the hole, and Stoecker saw the man's thin wrist and arm beneath the green smock. It was raw, and covered with sores. Like something diseased.

The man whispered, 'I am going to die. We all are. In a way I am glad.'

Stoecker felt the sweat break out on his neck like ice. The address on the letter was Danish.

The weak voice said, 'I am, *was* a teacher.'

'Ah, *there* you are!' The major's boot glinted in the sunlight as he came round a hold-coaming.

Stoecker snapped to attention, his eyes on the sea alongside as the boots clicked towards him.

He knew that the prisoner's hand had vanished, just as he was sure that nobody had seen him in conversation. But he felt something like panic, the prickle of sweat beneath his cap.

He was a good sailor, and was secretly proud of the way he had behaved in the actions and bombardments which had been the cruiser's lot since he had joined her. His action station was high up above the bridge in the Fire Control Station, one of the gunnery officer's elite team. Kröll was a hard and demanding officer to serve, but Stoecker had noticed that he was rougher on his officers than the rest of them. Perhaps because he had once served on the lower deck and had had to build his own standards.

Stoecker knew what he should do, what he should already have done. But he could feel the grubby letter bunched in one hand, and anyway he disliked the major with his snappy arrogance. He doubted if he had ever been near the front line in his life.

The major snarled, 'The motorboat is falling too far behind. Tell it to draw closer!'

Stoecker climbed on to the hold cover and raised his arm until the boat's coxswain had seen his signal. What was the matter with the man? The boat was at exactly the right distance.

The coxswain would not hold the job otherwise, Froebe would have made certain of that.

The major watched as the motorboat's bow-wave increased and said sharply, 'See that it keeps up!'

Stoecker saw the two SS men watching, the way they were gripping their machine-pistols. Afterwards he recalled that they had looked on edge, jumpy.

The explosion when it came was violent and sharp, so that the side-deck seemed to bound under Stoecker's feet, as if it was about to splinter to fragments.

The dozing sailors leapt to their feet, and even as the motorboat increased speed and tore towards them, the lighter's engine coughed, shook violently and died.

Künz shouted, 'No steerage way!' He stood back from the wheel, his eyes fixed on a billowing cloud of smoke which was spouting up through a ventilator.

The major shouted, 'Get that boat here!' He glared at Stoecker. 'What are you gaping at, you dolt?'

Stoecker stared at the hatch coaming. Smoke was darting out as if under great pressure, and he could hear muffled screams, and the thuds of fists beating on metal.

The major flipped open his pistol holster and added, 'Sabotage! There may be another bomb on board.'

The motorcutter surged alongside, but when some seamen tried to climb aboard the major screamed, 'Get back, damn you! It's going down!'

Stoecker looked at the pale-faced naval officer and pleaded, 'We could get them out, sir!'

Over the officer's shoulder he saw one of the SS men swinging the clamp on the ventilator to shut off the dense smoke.

The officer stared at him glassily. 'Do as you are told. Abandon *now*!'

Stoecker felt his eyes sting as the smoke seared over him, and he peered at the little slit where the prisoner's arm had been. Only smoke, and even the cries had stopped. Like a door being slammed. He felt Künz grip his arm and hiss, 'Come *on*, Hans! Leave it!' Then all at once they were clambering into the motorcutter, and when he looked again Stoecker saw that the lighter was already awash and sinking fast in the current.

The major said, 'Take me ashore.'

The boat turned towards the land again and Stoecker saw a naval patrol launch and some other craft heading towards the smoke at full speed.

He looked down at his fingers, which were clasped together so tightly that the pain steadied him. Some of the seamen sighed as the lighter dived beneath the surface, and one said, 'Lucky it didn't happen when we was alongside the old *Prinz*, eh, lads?'

No one answered him, and when Stoecker again lifted his eyes he saw the major was watching him. He appeared to be smiling.

They barely paused at the pier before turning and heading back at speed for the ship. It seemed important to all of them that they should be there, with faces they knew, and trusted.

There had been a black car waiting for the major and his men. He apparently offered a lift to the young naval officer, but the latter merely saluted and walked away.

Stoecker put his hand inside his jacket and touched the letter. The man had known he was going to die. He remembered the SS men looking at their watches. Most of all, he remembered the major's smile.

He looked up as the heavy cruiser's great shadow swept over them. He had expected to find comfort in it, but there was none.

3

And So Goodbye

One day after the admiral's visit to the ship the news of leave was announced. It was little enough of an offering and brought a chorus of groans from most of the mess-decks and wardroom alike. Only seven days' leave would be allowed, and first preference for married men only. The rest of the ship's company, by far the greater proportion, was confined to local leave on Danish soil, with no sleeping-out passes below the rank of petty officer.

For the lucky ones seven days would be precious but pared away by the time taken to reach their destinations and return to the ship. It was rumoured that rail transport was always being delayed or cancelled due to day and night air raids.

As the men were lined up and inspected in the pale sunshine before rushing ashore to the waiting buses and trucks, Fregatten-kapitän Theil reminded them of the seriousness of careless talk and the damage it could do to morale. Anyone who witnessed bomb damage or the like would keep it to himself, nobody would gossip about the ship, the war, anything.

Viktor Theil left the ship himself as soon as the others had departed. His home was in Neumunster on the Schleswig–Holstein peninsula, so he had less distance to travel than most.

As he sat in a corner of a crowded compartment in a train packed to the seams with servicemen and a few civilians, Theil reflected on the choice of a home. Not too far from Denmark. Now it seemed ironic, something to mock him.

The train crossed the frontier and clattered at a leisurely pace through the Hans Andersen villages, and the green countryside with its scattered lakes and farms. It was a beautiful part of the country, especially to Theil who had been born and brought up in Minden. At least, it should have been.

He thought of his wife Britta, their nice house on the town's outskirts, the perfect retreat for a naval officer on leave. He was known there, and certainly respected, especially when he was appointed to the *Prinz Luitpold*.

But he sensed people watched him, wondered what he really thought, if he cared. For Britta was Danish, and marriages from across the border were common enough before the war. It was often said that the Germans on the peninsula were more like Danes than they were. That too had a bitter ring for Theil.

When the German army had invaded her country Britta had tried to discover what had happened to her parents. Her father was a printer in Esbjerg, but he also managed a local newspaper. It had begun with letters and telephone calls, none of which had been answered. In despair she asked Theil to make enquiries but he had met with a stone wall of silence from the security offices. Eventually, when he was on a brief home leave, a plain-clothes police officer had called to see him. He was fairly senior and eager to be friendly and understanding.

'Your wife probably does not understand the need for security in these matters –'

Theil had tried to delve deeper and the policeman had said, 'You are a well-respected officer, a fine career ahead of you. Why spoil things, eh?'

When he had departed Theil had explained as well as he could to his wife. Perhaps her father had been in some political trouble, and was being kept out of circulation until things settled down. It had been the first time which he could recall when she had turned on him.

She had shouted, '*Settle down!* Is that what you would call it if the Tommies came here and started locking people in jails for wanting their country, their freedom!'

That leave had ended badly, and Theil had returned to his ship, which unbeknown to him was about to be called to action when the captain finally cracked under the strain and he himself by rights should have been promoted and given command. If not of the *Prinz Luitpold* then another of similar status. Instead, Hechler came.

Then Theil had received a message from a friend in Neumunster. He had not said much, but had sounded frightened, and it had been enough to make Theil hurry home after giving a vague explanation to his new captain. The ship was to be in the dockyard for a week, and anyway he knew that Hechler wanted to come to terms with his command on his own, and at his own speed.

The news had been worse than he had imagined. Britta had gone to her parents' home alone. In spite of the strict travel restrictions, the impossibility of moving about in an occupied country without permission, she had managed to reach the port of Esbjerg.

When Theil had confronted her he had been stunned by her appearance. She had been close to a breakdown, angry and weeping in turns. That night when she had finally allowed him to put her to bed she had shown him the great bruises on her arms. The military police had done that to her when they had dragged her from the house where she had been born.

When he had tried to reason with her, to calm her, she had pushed her away, her eyes blazing, and cried, 'Don't you see? They've killed my mum and dad! Don't you care what those butchers have done!'

The doctor, another old friend, had arrived and had given her something.

When she had finally dropped into a drugged and exhausted sleep he had joined Theil over a glass of brandy.

Theil had asked desperately, 'What should I do? There must be some mistake, surely? The authorities would never permit—'

The doctor had fastened his bag and had said crisply, 'Keep it to yourself, Viktor. These are difficult times. Perhaps it is best not to know all the truth.' He had fixed him with a grim stare. 'You are a sailor. Be glad. At sea you *know* your enemies.' He had gone, leaving Theil with his despair.

As time wore on Britta withdrew more and more into herself.

The local people tried to be friendly but she avoided them for the most part. She had been a pretty girl when he had married her; now she seemed to let herself go. Theil always regretted that they had no children, preferably boys to grow up in his footsteps and serve Germany. Once it had distressed her that she could not give him a child. The last time it had been mentioned Theil had found himself almost wanting to strike her.

'A *baby*! What would you give it? A black uniform and a rubber truncheon to play with!'

Theil walked the last part of the journey from the railway station. It had always been a pleasant little town but he noticed that the queues of people outside the provision shops seemed longer, and the patient women looked tired and shabby.

And yet the town had escaped the war apart from a few stray bombs from homebound aircraft. The sky was empty of cloud as it was of the tell-tale vapour trails of marauding aircraft. It was almost like peacetime.

Theil was too deep in thought to glance at the bulletin boards outside the little church, and the people who were studying the latest casualty lists which like the queues were longer than before.

He thought of the case which he shifted from one hand to the other to return the salutes of some soldiers from a local flak battery. It was heavy and contained among other things, cheese and butter, Danish bacon and eggs which might bring a smile to her lips. She had enough to worry about without the damned shortages.

He had written to her several times since that last, unnerving leave. She had only replied once, a loose, rambling letter which had told him very little. Britta was never a great writer of letters. Their leaves spent together had always made up for that. He quickened his pace. This time it would be all right again. Just like all those other times. It *must* be.

Whatever his personal worries might be, Theil was a professional to his fingertips. He had noted all the recent happenings, not least the arrival of the rear-admiral, an officer whose face and reputation were rarely absent from the newspapers.

It might be his chance. The *Prinz Luitpold* was obviously

earmarked for something important. That meant dangerous, but you took that for granted.

Perhaps he had been hard on Britta, or had written something in a letter which had upset her without intending it.

She had to understand, and be seen to be with him, no matter what. It was bad about her parents, but then he had never really got to know them. They should have considered her before they became involved with some political or subversive activity.

It was so unfair that because of it, his future might be endangered and her health also.

He thought of the ship lying up there in Danish waters. He knew the *Prinz* better than any of them. They would all need him when they were really up against it.

He turned on to the quiet road which led to his house; it was the last one in a line of five. Nothing was changed, and the flowers and shrubs in every garden made a beautiful picture after grey steel and the Gulf of Riga.

They would have three, maybe four days together. Then he would go back to the ship. As second-in-command he must be on time even at the expense of losing a day or so. But the leave would be just right. Like a reminder and a memory. A hope too for the future.

He thought he saw a woman in the neighbour's house, bending perhaps to pick up some flowers. When he looked again she had gone. He was glad. He did not want to loiter and discuss the war, rationing, and all the other complaints.

Theil reached the gates to his own garden and shifted his grasp on the heavy case. He squared his shoulders and wondered if anyone was watching. 'He's back.' He could almost see himself in his best uniform with the decorations and the eagle across his right breast.

He looked at the garden and hesitated. It was not like Britta to allow it to become so neglected. It was dry, and dead flowers drooped over the neat driveway, running to seed. It was unheard of. He held back a sudden irritation and strode to the main door. He fumbled with his key, expecting at any moment for the door to open and for her to stand there staring up at him. Her flaxen hair might be untidy but he would see it as before.

37

Her dress would be for doing jobs about the house, but to him it would be like the silk one he had once brought her from France.

The house was so quiet that he stood stock-still within feet of the open door. Without looking further he knew it was empty. The sunlight which streamed through the back windows was dusty, and there were dead flowers in a vase near the framed picture taken on their wedding day. He paused by it, off-balance, uncertain what to do. He stared at the photo, her arm through his, the faces in the background. That one was Willi, who was lost in the Atlantic two years back.

Theil put down his case and flexed his fingers. What did he feel? Angry, cheated, worried? All and none of them.

Perhaps she had gone away? He stared at the dead flowers. Where? He turned away, a sick feeling running through him. She had left him.

He walked about the house, opening doors, shutting them again, then went upstairs and looked out at the neighbours' house. So quiet and deathly still.

He opened a wardrobe and touched her clothes, remembering her looking up at him as he had undressed her.

What was she thinking of? He tried to contain it, as he would aboard ship when some stupid seaman had made a mistake. Did she think it could do anything but harm to behave like this? He touched a curtain which was pulled aside. Untidy. Again, out of character, or was it deliberate?

Theil went slowly downstairs and then saw some letters neatly piled on a hall-table where she kept her gloves.

He recognised the official stamps, his own writing. Unopened. She had not even read them.

He looked fixedly at his case by the front door. Abandoned, as if someone else had just arrived, or was about to leave.

What the hell had she done? There was no point in calling the police or the hospital. He would have been told long ago. An army truck rolled past, some soldiers singing and swaying about on the rutted road. How sad their song sounded.

He thrust the letters into his pocket and after a momentary hesitation picked up the heavy case once more.

He would ask the neighbours; they were decent people and had always liked Britta.

But he hesitated in the doorway and looked back at the silence. He thought of the future, the ship lying there waiting for him, for all of them, and was both apprehensive and bitter.

He *needed* her, just as she had once needed him, and she was gone.

Theil slammed the door and locked it and walked down the drive and then round to the next house.

Once he glanced over at his own home and pictured her in a window, laughing and waving. It had all been a joke, and now she wanted him.

The doorbell echoed into the far distance and he waited, knowing somehow that nobody would answer. But as he walked down to the road again he felt someone was watching him.

What should he do? He thought of his friend the doctor and walked all the way to his house, ignoring the weight of his case, his mind snapping at explanations like an angry dog.

The doctor was pleased to see him, although he had to leave for an urgent visit almost immediately.

He listened to Theil's story impassively and then said, 'I think you must face up to it, Viktor. She has left you.' He raised one hand as Theil made to protest. 'She will be in touch, be certain of that, but she has to sort things out in her own way, d'you see? Women are like that. All these years, and they still surprise me!'

Theil made to leave. Britta had some other relatives somewhere. He would check through his address book. He looked at the heavy case. 'You take it, Doctor. For old time's sake, eh?'

The doctor opened it and gazed at the array of food.

'Thank you, Viktor. Some of my patients—'

Theil nodded and tried to grin. 'Of course.'

Outside, the shadows of evening were already making purple patterns on the road. Theil did not look towards his house. If he went back now he knew he would go crazy.

She had left him, had not given him a chance to make things right. He compensated by telling himself that she had no warning of his coming.

But all this time? Another man? He hastened towards the main road and did not even see two saluting soldiers as they went past. Never, not Britta. No matter what. Then back to Denmark? He looked at his watch. What should he do?

He felt his fingers touch the black cross on his jacket; like his other decorations it had always given him pride and confidence. For a few moments longer he stared unseeingly around him, hurt and then angry when he thought of what might have been, *could* have been. Because of Britta's anguish over her parents his own advancement and career had been scarred for all time. He had lost the *Prinz* because of it, because of her.

When she did come back, pleading for understanding, what would he do?

Theil turned towards the railway station. There was nowhere else he wanted to go now.

To some members of *Prinz Luitpold*'s ship's company the seven days' leave were as varied as the men themselves. To many of the lucky ones it was a lifeline, something precious and yet unreal against the harsh background of war. For others it might have been better if they had stayed with the ship, men who eventually returned from leave with the feeling they had lost everything.

Amongst those who remained aboard there was one who, after a quick visit to a dockside telephone, made the most of each day and night in Vejle.

Korvettenkapitän Josef Gudegast, the cruiser's navigating officer, not only knew the ways of the sea and the landmarks which he had used in peace and wartime, he also hoarded a comfortable knowledge of harbours and what they could offer. When he had earned his living in timber ships he had often visited Danish ports, and Vejle was one of his favourite places for a run ashore.

On the last day but one of his leave he sat in a big chair, his reddened face tight with concentration as he completed a charcoal sketch of the woman who lounged opposite him, on a couch, her naked body pale in the lamplight.

The small house was quiet, more so because of the shutters

and dark curtains across the windows. The place had always been his haven, stocked with food and drink, some of which he had carried with him from the ship to which he returned every morning, keeping an eye on his department and the work done by his assistants.

The room was very hot, and he sat in his shirtsleeves, his jacket with its three tarnished gold stripes hanging carelessly from the door, a reminder, if he needed it, that his time of freedom was almost over.

'There.' He sat back and eyed his work critically. 'Not bad.'

She got up and stood beside him, one arm around his massive shoulder. He could feel her body against his, her warmth and the affection which they had shared with passion and quiet desperation in turn. Soon they would lie together again and later they would sleep, wrapped around one another like young lovers.

Gudegast was forty, and felt every year of it. He tugged at his ragged beard and murmured, 'You're still a bloody fine woman, Gerda.' He gave her a squeeze. 'I've never forgotten you.'

She touched his hair. It was getting very thin, and without his uniform cap he looked his age, she thought. She could remember him as the bright-eyed mate of a visiting ship, the way that they had hit it off from the start.

She said, 'Get away with you. I'm sagging everywhere.' She peered at the picture. 'You've made me look nice.'

He covered it with some paper and said abruptly, 'It's yours.'

She stared at him. 'But you've never given –'

Gudegast stood up and glanced towards the bedroom door. 'I'll be off soon. Something to remind you of old Josef, eh?'

She gripped his arm, disturbed by his mood. 'It'll be all right, won't it?'

'*All right?*' He took his pipe from the mantelpiece and filled it with slow deliberation. It gave him time.

He was surprised that he cared that much. At the same time he did not want to alarm her.

He said slowly, 'No, I don't think it will, as a matter of fact.'

She sat on the couch and dragged a shawl over her naked

41

shoulders.

Gudegast added, 'Did you see the way they buggered us about in the café this afternoon?'

She replied uneasily, 'They said they were full up.'

He frowned. '*Said.*' He lit his pipe and took several deep puffs. 'Little bastards. I had to put my foot down.'

She watched him and smiled. 'You got us a lovely table.'

'Not the point.' Puff, puff. 'They're more scared of the bloody Resistance now than they are of us, don't you see?' He studied her full mouth and barely covered breasts. She had been such a pretty girl. He should have married her, instead – he turned his mind away from his wife in Hamburg. It was all a mess. Like the bloody war.

He tried again. 'What will you do, Gerda, when it's all over?'

'I – I shall be here –'

He moved to her side and ruffled her hair. 'We're losing. Can't *you* face it either?'

'You mustn't say things like that, Jo! If anyone heard you –'

He grinned, his whole face crinkling. 'Christ, you care, don't you?'

'You know I do.'

'All these years.' He stroked her hair with one big hand while he gripped his pipe with the other. 'I know you're Danish, but there'll be plenty who'll remember you had German friends when it's all over.' He felt her stiffen and almost regretted saying it.

A few more days and he'd be off again. Probably for good, if the mad bastards at headquarters had anything to do with it. What sort of a war was it becoming? He was not even allowed to see his new charts. He felt angry just thinking about it so that when he spoke again his voice was unexpectedly hard.

'You must get out, girl. You've relatives in Sweden, go there if you can.'

She clung to his arm. 'Surely it won't come to that, Jo?'

He grinned, the rumble running through his massive frame. 'I expect our high command have it all worked out, some sort of treaty, a compromise. We've only wiped out half the bloody world, so who cares?'

She stood and looked up at him, her eyes misty. 'I never thought –'

He smiled at her gently. Too many German friends. No, they'd not forget. He had seen it in Spain after the Civil War. All the *heroes* who showed up after the fighting was finished. Brave lads who proved it by shearing the hair and raping girls who had backed the wrong side. It would be a damned sight worse here.

He held her against him and ran his big hands across her buttocks. Neither noticed that his fingers had left charcoal marks on her bare skin.

Their eyes met. He said, 'Bed.'

She picked up a bottle of schnapps which he had brought and two glasses. Gudegast stood back and watched her march into the other room with a kind of defiance. She would not leave. Perhaps she would find a nice officer to look after her when the Tommies marched in. He felt sweat on his back. God, you could get shot for even thinking such things.

He pushed through the door and stared at her, the abandoned way her legs were thrown on the crumpled sheets, unmade from that morning, and probably from all the rest.

He would do another sketch tomorrow. If he got time he might try and paint her in oils when he was at sea again. He shivered and then stepped out of his trousers.

She put out her arms and then knelt over him as he flopped down on the bed. He was huge, and when he lay on top of her it was like being crushed.

He watched her and said, 'I wish we'd wed, Gerda.'

She laughed but there was only sadness there. She took him in her hand and lowered herself on to him, gasping aloud as he entered her.

It was as if she knew they would never see each other again.

The cinema screen flickered and with a blare of trumpets yet another interminable newsreel began.

Hans Stoecker tried to concentrate but it was difficult to see anything clearly. The air was thick with tobacco smoke. The cinema had been commandeered from the town, and he guessed it had once been a church hall or something of the kind. Between him and the screen were rows and rows of square sailors' collars, broken only occasionally by the field-grey of the army.

The newsreel was concerned mainly with the Eastern Front and showed thousands of prisoners being marched to the rear of the lines by waving, grinning soldiers. The commentator touched only lightly on France, but there were several good aerial shots of fighter bombers strafing a convoy of lorries, and some of burning American tanks.

The major part of the reel was taken up with the *Bombardment of London*. The usual barracking and whistles from the audience faded as the camera panned across the great rocket, the V-2, as it spewed fire and dense smoke before rising from its launching gantry and streaking straight up into the sky.

The commentator said excitedly, 'All day, every day, our secret weapon is falling upon London. Nothing can withstand it, there is no defence. Already casualties and damage are mounting. No people can be expected to suffer and not break.'

There were more fanfares, and etched against a towering pall of flame and smoke the German eagle and swastika brought the news to an end.

Stoecker got up and pushed his way out of the cinema. Several voices called after him. There must be half the ship's non-duty watch here, he thought.

Outside it was dusk, with the lovely pink glow he had first seen in these waters. He thrust his hands into his jacket and walked steadily away from the harbour. There were plenty of German servicemen about, and they seemed carefree enough.

He thought again of the sinking lighter, the terrified screams of the prisoners trapped below. He had passed the place in one of the cruiser's motorboats when he had been sent on some mission ashore. It had been marked by a solitary wreck-buoy, but as one of the sentries on the jetty had told him, there had been no investigation, nor had any divers been put down. *Prinz Luitpold* carried her own divers but had not been asked to supply aid.

It was obvious, whichever way you looked at it. It was not sabotage. He thought of the SS major's face. It had been murder.

44

Stoecker crossed the street automatically and paused to peer into a shop window. He had done it merely to avoid three officers whom he would have had to salute. It was childish, but like most sailors he disliked the petty discipline which the land seemed to produce. He thought of the captain, how he had spoken to him, called him by name, from a company of nearly a thousand men. Hechler never laboured the point about discipline. He had his standards, and expected them to be met. Otherwise he was a man you always felt you could speak to. Trust.

A hand touched his sleeve. 'Hans! It *is* you!'

He turned and stared at the girl who was smiling at him. It all flashed through his mind in seconds, the brown curls and laughing eyes, school uniform, but now in that of a nursing auxiliary.

'What are you doing here, Sophie?' At home she lived just three doors from his mother. 'A nurse too, eh?'

She fell into step beside him, the pleasure at seeing him wiping away the tiredness from her eyes.

'There is a big hospital not far from here.' She glanced away. 'Mostly soldiers who were in Russia.'

Stoecker thought of the jubilant newsreel, and of the ship's superstructure shaking like a mad thing when they had fired on the enemy position.

Later he had heard the deputy gunnery officer, Kapitänleutnant Emmler, say angrily, 'Ivan still smashed through and decimated a whole brigade! When will we hold the bastards?'

He said quietly, 'They are lucky to be in your care, Sophie.'

She put her hand through his arm. It was so simply done that he was moved.

She said, 'They have been in hell, Hans. Some of them are —' she shrugged and smiled, but there were tears on her cheeks. 'Now look what you've made me do!'

He guided her from the main stream of people and traffic and together they entered a narrow street, their footsteps their only company.

They talked about home, people they had known, and the last time they had seen some of them.

He said suddenly, 'I'd like to see you again.'

She looked at him gravely. 'I have every evening off unless –'

He nodded and gripped her hands. 'Tomorrow. Where we just met. I have to get back to the ship now.' His mind was unusually confused. If he had not gone to the cinema he would have missed her, would never have known.

'I'll be there.' She touched his face. 'You've not changed, Hans.'

She saw his expression and asked quickly, 'What is it?'

Stoecker stared past her, his hand on her arm as if to protect her. The street name was faded and rusty and yet stood out as if the letters were on fire. It was the same street as the one on the letter. Almost guiltily he touched his pocket as if to feel it there. He knew it was the house even though he had never been here in his life. There was a shop beneath the living quarters, but the windows, like the rest of the building, were burned out, blackened into an empty cave. But on one remaining door post he saw the crude daubs of paint, badly scorched but still visible. The Star of David, and the words, *Dirty Jew!*

The girl looked with him and whispered, 'Let's get away from here.'

They walked down the narrow street towards the main road again. Who was it, he wondered? Parent, wife, girlfriend? He tightened his hold on her arm and could almost hear the man whisper. *I am going to die. We all are.*

'Are you sick?'

He smiled, the effort cracking his lips. 'No. It is nothing.'

They looked at each other, sharing the lie as if it was something precious and known only to them.

'Tomorrow then.'

He watched her hurry towards a camouflaged van with red crosses painted on it.

Perhaps he had imagined it all. There was only one way he would find out and he knew that he was going to read that letter, no matter what it cost.

As darkness closed in over the anchorage, the boats which plied back and forth from the shore ferried the returning sailors to their ship. The duty officer with his gangway staff watched as each returning figure walked, limped or staggered away to the security of his mess.

Like a resting tiger the *Prinz Luitpold* was blacked-out, with only the moonlight glinting on her scuttles and bridge-screens.

Almost the last launch to head out from the shore made a broad white wash against the other darkness, her coxswain steering skilfully between anchored lighters and a pair of patrol boats. Hechler seemed to sense that his ship was drawing near. He climbed up from the cockpit and stood beside the coxswain, the collar of his leather greatcoat raised around his ears, his cap tugged firmly down. Spray lanced over the fast-moving hull, but he did not blink as he saw the great shadow harden against the pale stars, and he felt a strange sense of relief. He saw the bowman emerge from forward, his boathook at the ready, heard the engine fade slightly as the helmsman eased the throttle.

The proud talk, the dinner parties, the uniforms and gaiety – he had had enough in the past few days to sicken his insides. Only here was reality. His ship.

A voice grated a challenge from the darkness and the coxswain shuttered a small hand-lamp.

The ship's raked bows made a black arrowhead against the sky and then they were turning towards the long accommodation ladder.

The captain is back on board. Maybe there will be news.

Hechler ran lightly up the ladder and folded back his leather collar so that the faint gangway light gleamed dully on the cross around his neck.

Prinz Luitpold's captain felt as if he had never left her.

4

Maximum Security

There was a tap at the door to Hechler's day-cabin and then Theil stepped over the coaming and closed the door.

Hechler was glad of the interruption. His table was covered with intelligence files, packs of photographs and even vague news reports. In a matter of days he had soaked up everything he could find about the war so that he felt his mind would explode. It was the first time he had seen Theil since he had returned from leave, other than for the brief requirements of reporting aboard.

Theil looked paler than usual, and tight-lipped. Hechler had felt a change of atmosphere throughout the ship when the married men had returned from their brief escape. They might make laws about spreading gloom and despondency, but they could never enforce them, Hechler thought.

Several men had requested extra leave on compassionate grounds. Relatives killed or missing in the constant bombing. Unfaithful wives and pregnant daughters. The list was endless.

He waited for Theil to be seated and for Pirk to produce some fresh coffee.

Theil said, 'Everyone is aboard, sir, except for two seamen. I have posted them as deserters.'

Hechler frowned. A tiny fragment set against the war, and yet in any ship it was distressing, a flaw in the pattern.

Pirk opened one of the scuttles and Hechler saw some trapped pipesmoke swirling out towards the land. Gudegast the navigating officer had been one of his visitors; in fact Hechler had seen all of his heads of departments.

Gudegast never actually complained, but his dissatisfaction over the charts was very apparent. It was useless to tell any of them that he did not know the ship's new role or mission either. Nobody would have believed him. *Would I in their place?*

'They may have their reasons, Viktor. They won't get far.'

He thought of the news from the Russian Front. The enemy were making a big push, perhaps to gain as many advances as possible before winter brought its ruthless stalemate again.

Theil said, 'We sail this evening, sir.' It was a statement. 'The escorts have already anchored as ordered.'

Hechler looked at him casually. Theil sounded almost disinterested. It was so unlike him and his constant search for efficiency.

'Is everything well with you, Viktor?'

Theil seemed to come out of his mood with a jerk. 'Why, yes, sir.'

'I just thought – how was your leave?'

Theil spread his hands. 'The usual. You know how it is. A house always needs things.'

Hechler glanced at the papers on the table. So that was it. An upset with his wife.

'Anything I can do?'

Theil met his gaze. It was like defiance. 'Nothing, sir.'

'Well, then.' Hechler looked up as the deck trembled into life. It was a good feeling. He never got tired of it. The beast stirring after her enforced rest.

He said, 'Norway. We shall weigh at dusk and pass through the Skagerrak before daylight.' He studied Theil's reactions if any. 'I want to be off Bergen in thirty hours.'

Theil grimaced. 'I doubt if the escorts will be able to keep up.'

'So be it.' He pictured the jagged Norwegian coast, the endless patterns of fjords and islands. It would give Gudegast something he *could* grumble about.

'After that we shall keep close inshore and enter our selected fjord to await further intelligence.'

Theil nodded. 'Another fjord.'

Hechler guessed he was thinking of the great battleship *Tirpitz* which had been hidden in her Norwegian lair many miles from the open sea. Safe from any kind of attack, and yet about a year ago they had reached her. Tiny, midget submarines with four-man crews had risked and braved everything to find *Tirpitz* and to knock her out of the war by laying huge charges beneath her as she lay behind her booms and nets.

Hechler thought of his young brother again. *Scharnhorst* had been sunk a month later, the day after Christmas. The seas had been so bitter off North Cape that only a handful of survivors had been found and saved by the victors. His brother had not been one of them.

Hechler tried to push it from his thoughts and concentrate on what his ship would be required to do. The North Russian convoys again? Any pressure on the Russians and the destruction of much-needed supplies from the Allies would be welcomed by the army. Or was it to be still further north, and round into the Barents Sea itself before the ice closed in? Attack the Russian navy in its home territory. Hechler tightened his jaw. It might be worth a try.

Theil said, 'I had expected to see an admiral's flag at the mast-head when I returned, sir.'

Hechler smiled. 'The admiral intends to keep us guessing, Viktor.'

He thought of the mysterious boxes which had been taken below. All the keys of the compartment where it was stowed had been removed from the ship's office. The admiral had one key, and Hechler had locked the other in his cabin safe. He was determined to get the truth about them out of Leitner.

He recalled Leitner's temporary headquarters in Copenhagen where he had been driven that first evening and almost every day since. Copenhagen was still beautiful. A war and occupation could not change that, he thought. The green roofs and spires, the cobbled squares, even the huge German flags which hung from many commandeered buildings could not spoil it.

Leitner seemed to have created another world of his own there. His HQ had once been an hotel, and the people, men and women, who came and went at his bidding seemed to treat it as one.

There was always good food and plenty to drink, with a small orchestra to entertain his official guests with music either sentimental or patriotic to suit the occasion.

If Leitner was troubled by the news from the Russian Front he did not reveal it. He was ever-optimistic and confident and seemed to save his scorn for the army and certain generals whom he had often described as *mental pigmies*.

If any man was enjoying his war it had to be Leitner.

Theil watched him across the table, half his mind straying to the shipboard noises, the preparations for getting under way once more. But Hechler fascinated him far more. Was he really as composed as he made out? Untroubled by the weight of responsibility which was matched only by its uncertainty?

Theil thought of the rumours which had greeted his return. The arrival of piles of Arctic clothing on the dockside had added fuel to the fires of speculation even amongst the most sceptical.

He should feel closer to Hechler now. *His* wife had left him, although no one had ever discovered the whole truth. Did he fret about it and secretly want her back again? He watched Hechler's grave features, the way he pushed his hair back from his forehead whenever he made to emphasise something.

Theil tried not to dwell on Britta's behaviour. Perhaps she only wanted to punish him, as if it had all been his fault. He felt the stab of despair in his eyes. It was so unfair. Just when he needed her loyalty, her backing. If only –

Hechler said, 'I wonder how many eyes are out there watching us right at this minute, eh, Viktor?' He walked to a scuttle and rested his finger on the deadlight.

He looked more relaxed, more like a spectator than the main player, Theil thought desperately.

Hechler felt his glance, his uneasiness. It was not time for Theil to be troubled. Their first loyalty was to the ship, and next to the men who served her. After that – he turned, hanging from the deadlight like a passenger in a crowded train.

'We're going to fight, Viktor. I feel it. No more gestures, no more bloody bombardments with barely enough sea-room to avoid being straddled.' He looked at the nearest bulkhead as if he could see through it, to the length and depth of his command. 'Have you ever read about Nelson?'

He saw from Theil's expression that the change of tack had caught him off balance.

'No, sir.' He sounded as if he thought it was somehow disloyal.

Hechler smiled, the lines on either side of his mouth softening. 'You should. A fine officer.' He gave a wry grin. 'Misunderstood by his superiors, naturally. Nothing changes in that respect.'

Theil shifted in his chair. 'What about him?'

'The boldest measures are the safest, that's what the little admiral said. I believe it, never more so than now.' He eyed him calmly, weighing him up. 'We'll lose this war if we're not careful.'

Theil stared at him, stunned. '*Impossible!* I – I mean, sir, we can't be beaten now.'

'Beaten – I suppose not. But we can still lose.' He did not explain. Instead he considered Norway. The first part of their passage should not be too dangerous. Air attack was always possible, but the minefields should prevent any submarines from getting too close. He thought of the new detection gear which was being fitted. As good as anything Britain and her allies had. Kröll, the gunnery officer, had shown rare excitement, although he obviously disapproved of having civilian technicians on board telling him what to do. They would still be in the ship when they sailed; it was that sort of priority.

The unseen eye, one of the civilians had described it. The *Scharnhorst* had been tracked and destroyed with it even in a dense snowstorm. *Prinz Luitpold*'s was supposed to be twice as accurate, and they were the first to have it fitted.

Hastily trained men had been rushed to the ship, new faces to be absorbed, to become part of their world.

There was also a new senior surgeon, the original one having been released because of ill-health. It had been something of a cruel joke amongst the sailors.

Hechler considered discussing the surgeon with Theil but decided against it for the moment. The man's name was Stroheim; he was highly qualified and a cut above most naval doctors. The best were usually in the army for all too obvious reasons.

Hechler had skimmed through his confidential file, but only one part of it troubled him. There was a pink sheet attached to it. Hechler hated political interference. It was like being spied on. Nevertheless, Stroheim had come to him under a cloud. You could not ignore it. He held a mental picture of Oberleutnant Bauer, the signals and W/T officer. On the face of it a junior if important member of his team. Bauer too had a special form in his file. He was the ship's political officer, a role which even as captain Hechler could not investigate.

Hechler shook his sudden depression aside. 'I would like us to walk round the ship before the hands go to their stations for leaving harbour.' He forced a smile. 'To show a united front.'

Theil stood up and grasped his cap tightly to his side.

'It will be an honour. For the Fatherland.'

For a moment Hechler imagined he was going to add 'Heil Hitler' as Leitner would have done. He said, 'No one goes ashore from now on.' He thought suddenly about the explosion which had sunk the lighter. It was always unexpected when it happened. Vigilance was not always enough. *Sabotage.* They were out there watching the ship, the same people who had placed the bomb aboard the lighter. To damage the ship or to destroy Leitner's boxes, the reason made little difference. It could have been serious.

In London, quaking under the new and deadly rocket bombardment, a telephone would ring in some Admiralty bunker. *Prinz Luitpold is leaving Vejle.*

A brief radio message from some Danish traitor was all it took. He smiled again. Or patriot if you were on the other side.

Another more persistent tremor came through the deck plating from the depths of the engine-room.

He looked away from Theil's strained face. Like me, he thought. Eager to go.

The *Prinz Luitpold*'s swift passage from the Baltic into Norwegian waters was quieter than Hechler had anticipated. They logged a regular speed of twenty knots and passed Bergen within minutes of Gudegast's calculations.

For much of the time, and especially for the most dangerous

period in the North Sea when the Orkney Islands and later the Shetlands lay a mere 200 miles abeam, the ship's company remained closed up at action stations. Every eye was on the sky, but unlike the Baltic the weather was heavily overcast, with low cloud and spasms of drizzle which reduced visibility to a few miles. They were able to test some of the new radar detection devices, and Hechler was impressed by its accuracy as they plotted the movements and tactics of their escorts even though they were quite invisible from the bridge.

Further north and then north-east, still following the wild coastline which Hechler knew from hard-won experience. Past the fortress-like fjord of Trondheim and crossing the Arctic Circle until both radar and lookouts reported the Lofoten Islands on the port bow. To starboard, cut into the mainland itself lay Bodø, and an hour later the cruiser's cable rattled out once more and she lay at anchor.

A grey oppressive coast, with sea mist rising around the ship like smoke, as if she had just fired a silent salute to the shore. They were not alone this time. Another cruiser, the *Lübeck*, was already anchored in the fjord, and apart from their escorts there were several other big destroyers and some supply ships.

Some if not all of the tension had drained away on the passage north. To be doing something again, to accept that a sailor's daily risks put more personal worries into their right perspective, made Hechler confident that his ship was ready for anything.

With the ship safely anchored behind protective nets and booms, and regular sweeps by patrol boats, Hechler found time to consider the wisdom of his orders. Bodø was a good choice, he thought, if only for the enlarged, military airfield there. Bombers and fighters could supply immediate cover, as well as mount an attack on enemy convoys or inquisitive submarines.

Routine took over once again, and after the fuel bunkers had been topped up from lighters, they settled down to wait.

Less than twenty-four hours after dropping anchor Hechler received a brief but impatient signal. He was to fly immediately to Kiel. After the uncertainty and the mystery of his orders it was something of an anti-climax. But as he was ferried ashore and then driven at reckless speed to the airfield in an army staff car, the choice of Bodø as a lair for his ship became all the more evident. Everything was planned to the last detail, as if he had no hand in anything. He did not even know what to tell Theil before he left. He might even be going to Germany only to be informed he was relieved, that perhaps Theil was taking command after all.

The aircraft, a veteran Junkers three-engined transport, arrived at Kiel in the late afternoon.

Hechler had been dozing in his seat, not because he was tired but mainly to avoid a shouted conversation with an army colonel who spent much of the four-hour flight fortifying himself from a silver flask.

As the plane tilted steeply to begin its final approach Hechler got his first glimpse of Kiel through a low cloud bank. He had not returned there for about a year and he was unable to drag his eyes from the devastation. Whole areas had been wiped out, so that only the streets gave any hint of what had once been there. There was smoke too, from a recent air raid or an uncontrollable fire, he could not tell. He had seen plenty of it in five years of war. Poland, Russia, even in the ship's last bombardment he had watched the few remaining houses blasted into fragments.

Smoky sunlight glinted momentarily on water and he saw the sweeping expanse of the naval dockyard before that too was blotted out by cloud.

It was hard to distinguish serviceable vessels from the wrecks in the harbour. He saw fallen derricks and gantrys, great slicks of oil on the surface, black craters instead of busy slipways and docks.

In such chaos it was astonishing to see the towering shape of the naval memorial at Laboe, somehow unscathed, as was the familiar, gothic-style water-tower, like a fortress amidst a battlefield.

The drunken colonel peered over his shoulder and said hoarsely, 'We'll make them pay for this!' He wiped his eyes with his sleeve. 'My whole family was killed. Gone. Nothing left.'

The plane glided through the clouds and moments later bumped along the runway. Here again was evidence of a city under siege. Sandbagged gun emplacements with grim-faced helmeted crews lined each runway. Parties of men were busy repairing buildings and filling in craters. It seemed a far cry from *Prinz Luitpold*'s ordered world and Leitner's luxurious headquarters.

It felt strange to be here, he thought. More so to be amongst his fellow countrymen, to hear his own language in every dialect around him.

A camouflaged staff car was waiting and a tired-looking lieutenant seemed eager to get him away from the airfield before another alert was sounded.

No wonder some of his returning ship's company had seemed so worried and anxious. If all major towns and cities were like this – he did not allow his mind to dwell on it.

Naval Operations had been moved to a new, underground headquarters, but before they reached it Hechler saw scenes of desolation he had not imagined possible. There were lines of men and women queuing at mobile soup-kitchens, their drawn and dusty faces no different from those he had seen on refugees in Poland.

They drove past a platoon of marching soldiers who carried spades and shovels instead of rifles. They were all in step and swinging their arms. Some looked very young and all were singing in the staccato manner of infantrymen everywhere. But their faces were quite empty, and even their NCO forgot to salute the staff car.

The lieutenant saw his expression and said dully, 'It's been like this for weeks.' He dropped his eyes under Hechler's blue-grey stare. 'I – I'm sorry, sir.'

Another small cameo came and went as the car picked its way around some weary-looking firemen.

A stretcher was being carried from a bombed house, the front of which had tumbled out on to the street. Hechler caught a glimpse of some torn wallpaper and a chair hanging from the upper floor by one leg. An old man was being led to safety by a nurse, but it was obvious even at a distance that he wanted to remain with the blanket-covered corpse on the stretcher.

Hechler said, 'Night raids?'

The lieutenant shrugged. 'The Yanks by day, the Tommies by night.'

Hechler wanted to ask about Kiel's air defences but said nothing. *I am a stranger here.*

The lieutenant gave a sigh and wound down a window as some armed sentries blocked the road. The new headquarters was like a slab of solid concrete, not much different from the outside to one of the great U-boat pens, he thought.

But once inside, with the huge steel doors shut behind them, it was more like a ship than anything else. Steel supports, shining lifts which vanished into the ground like ammunition hoists, and even the officers and seamen who bustled about with brief-cases and signal folders looked different from the embattled people he had just seen on the streets outside.

The lieutenant guided him into a lift and they stood in silence as it purred down two or maybe three levels. More doors and brightly lit passageways where the air was as cool and as fresh as a country lane.

Hechler had the impression that the lieutenant was taking him on a longer route than necessary in spite of his haste, perhaps to show him the display of businesslike efficiency. Hechler had not been in the bunker before and he looked into each room and office as they hurried past. Teleprinters, clattering type-writers, and endless banks of switchboards and flashing lights. There were several soldiers about too, and in one map-covered room Hechler saw that the Luftwaffe was also represented.

He felt his confidence returning, the dismal pictures he had seen on the street put momentarily aside. It was just that when you were involved in the fighting you never thought of those at home who had to stand and accept whatever was hurled at them. He thought of his parents and was glad they lived well away from the city.

The lieutenant pressed a button and another steel door slid to one side.

Several uniformed women were busy typing, while an officer was speaking intently on a telephone.

All of them jumped to their feet as Hechler appeared in the bright electric glare, and stared at him as if he was from another planet.

The lieutenant was relieved. 'The Admiral is waiting, sir.'

Two more doors, and each new room became less warlike. There were rugs, and pleasant lamp-shades, and the desks were of polished wood and not metal.

Leitner was sitting in a comfortable chair, a glass in one hand, his uniform jacket unbuttoned. He looked fresh and untroubled, as if he had just had a swim or a shower.

'Right on time, Dieter.' He gestured to another officer, a captain who was vaguely familiar.

Leitner said, 'Perhaps you know Klaus Rau? He commands *Lübeck*.'

They shook hands, and Hechler recalled the other captain who had once commanded a destroyer during the attack on Narvik.

He was a stocky, dark-jowled man with deepset eyes which seemed very steady and unblinking. Hechler sat down and pictured the cruiser which lay near to his own ship. *Lübeck* had been in the thick of it from the outbreak of war. The Low Countries, France and then in the Baltic against the Russians, she too had a charmed life despite being heavily damaged by gunfire and bombs alike on several occasions. *Lübeck* was an old ship, built in the early thirties and about half the size of *Prinz Luitpold*.

Leitner put down his glass and looked at them blandly.

'We shall be working together, gentlemen, just as soon as I hoist my flag. It will be a small but crack squadron, and the enemy will have cause to remember us.'

Rau glanced at Hechler. 'My ship has already given them reason enough.'

Hechler kept his face impassive. There it was again. Like Theil. He wondered briefly if it was coincidence or an accident that Rau had arrived here ahead of him. He had not been aboard the old Junkers. He smiled inwardly. It was unlikely that Leitner would ever permit a coincidence.

The rear-admiral added, 'You will receive your final orders when you return to your commands. This is a maximum security operation.' He gave a quick grin, like an impish schoolboy. 'If it leaks out, I shall know where to come looking, eh?'

A telephone buzzed, and the flag-lieutenant appeared as if by magic through another door and snatched it up before his superior had time to frown.

Hechler could not hear what he said, but saw some dust float down from the ceiling; he would not have seen it but for the lights.

Leitner listened to his aide and said, 'Air raid. They are going for the harbour again.' He gestured for his glass to be refilled. 'Our fighters have brought down four already.'

Hechler looked at the ceiling. Was that all it meant down here? A tiny trickle of dust, and not even a shiver of vibration. He thought of the drunken colonel on the plane, his despair. How could a man like that lead his troops with conviction? He had been damaged as much as any man who loses a limb or his sight in battle. It was dangerous to cling to the past merely because he imagined he had no future.

Leitner glanced at his watch. 'We must see the head of Operations.'

Rau stood up. 'Until tomorrow then, sir.' He glanced at Hechler. 'A pleasure meeting you again.'

Hechler watched the door close. A man without warmth.

Leitner smiled. 'He is jealous of you. Nothing like envy to keep men on their toes.'

He walked to the other door. 'Come with me, Dieter. The time for cat-and-mouse with men like Rau can keep.'

Admiral Manfred von Hanke was an impressive figure by any standards. He was standing straight-backed in the centre of a well-lit map-room, his heavy-lidded eyes on the door as Leitner and Hechler were ushered in by another aide.

Hechler knew a lot about the admiral, although he had not found many people who had actually met him.

Von Hanke had been a captain in the Great War with a distinguished career ahead of him. He had been in the United States attached to the German Embassy where he had been engaged for several years in organising a powerful intelligence and espionage ring. In the final months of the war when America had abandoned her umbrella of neutrality, he had found himself arrested as a spy. Even that, and the possibility of summary execution, had not broken him, and despite his aristocratic family background, something frowned on in Hitler's New Order, he had survived and prospered. Today he was second only to Donitz, while his grasp of strategy and naval operations took second place to no one.

He had iron-grey cropped hair, and because he had just come from an investiture was wearing his frock-coat uniform and winged collar. He could still be one of the Kaiser's old guard, Hechler thought.

Leitner began brightly, 'This is our man, sir –'

Von Hanke raised one hand in a tired gesture and Leitner fell instantly silent.

Von Hanke said, 'Be seated. This will not take too long, but of course if you have any questions?' He gave a dry smile. 'In that case –'

He pressed a button on his deck and several long wall panels slid away to reveal giant maps of each of the main battle areas.

Hechler stared at one of the Baltic and the Gulf of Finland where his ship had been mostly employed. It all seemed so long ago instead of weeks.

His eyes fastened on some red flags where one of von Hanke's staff had marked the various army units.

Von Hanke watched him steadily, his hooded eyes without expression. 'You have seen something, Captain?'

Hechler hesitated. 'The Twenty-First Division, sir. It is still shown south-west of Riga.'

'Well?' Not a flicker of emotion although Hechler could sense Leitner's irritation behind his back.

'It no longer exists. It was decimated weeks ago.' The admiral's silence was like an unspoken doubt and he added, 'I was there, sir.'

Leitner said, 'I expect it has been regrouped –'

The admiral clasped his hands behind him.

'I am glad you show interest as well as intelligence, Captain.'

Von Hanke gestured to the adjoining map which showed Norway and the convoy routes from Iceland to North Cape. It was pockmarked with pointers and flags, and Hechler felt a tightness in his throat when he saw his own ship's name on a metal pennant placed on Bodø. Pictures leapt through his mind. Theil's anxiety, the straddled destroyer heeling over in a welter of fire and steam. Men dying.

The straight-backed admiral said in his slow, thick tones, 'The Allies are throwing everything they have into France. Even now there are advance units within miles of Paris, others breaking out towards the Belgian frontier. Our forces will blunt their advances of course, and already the army's pincer movements have taken many prisoners and valuable supplies. But the advance goes on.'

Hechler glanced at the flags nearest to the Belgian frontier. It was said that the new rocket-launching sites were in the Low Countries. The Allies would use every means to reach them before they could do their maximum damage in England.

Von Hanke continued calmly, 'Intelligence reports are excellent. The British intend to do something they have not attempted before and have two convoys in Northern waters at the same time. A loaded convoy routed for the Russians in Murmansk, and an empty but nonetheless valuable one on the reverse route to Iceland. The Normandy campaign has made the Royal Navy very short of escorts, that is their only reason.'

Hechler could see that too in his mind. The endless daylight, the convoys drawing further and further north towards Bear Island to avoid air and U-boat attack. It had always been a murderous battleground for both sides.

He examined his feelings. It was what he might have expected. An attack on two convoys when Allied warships were deployed in strength in the English Channel and Biscay. If they destroyed one or both of the convoys it might give a breathing space. Even as he considered it, he sensed a nagging doubt. Just to look at those probing red arrows, the British and American flags, made such an operation little more than a delay to the inevitable.

Much would depend on the army's counter-attacks in France. They had to hold the line no matter what if they hoped to gain time to break the enemy's determination with an increasing rocket bombardment.

Von Hanke said softly, 'You look troubled, Captain.'

Hechler faced him. 'I think it can be done, sir. My ship –'

'Your *ship*, Captain, is possibly the most powerful of her kind afloat, and she is one of half a dozen major units left in the fleet.' He glanced absently at the maps. 'Others are supporting our troops in the Baltic, as you will know better than most. Some are marooned in ports on the Biscay coast. And there are those which are damaged beyond repair by air attacks.' He turned again and fixed his eyes on Hechler. '*Prinz Luitpold* is the best we have. If she is not properly employed, she may end up like her less fortunate consorts.'

Hechler glanced at Leitner. He looked bright-eyed; inspired would be a better description, he thought.

'At the right moment you will leave Bodø and seek out one of the convoys as directed by OKM.' His eyes never left Hechler's. 'And then, Captain, you will take full advantage of the disruption caused and –' He walked towards him and then gripped his hands in his. 'You will take your ship into the Atlantic.'

For an instant longer Hechler thought he had misheard or that the admiral was about to add something.

The Atlantic. A ship like *Prinz Luitpold* could create hell on the sea-lanes until she was run to ground.

Von Hanke said, 'You do not question it?' He nodded slowly. 'That is good. I would not like to give the ship another captain at this stage.'

Leitner exclaimed, 'It is a perfect plan, Dieter!' He could not contain his excitement. 'A tiger at large, with all the chain of supplies to make it possible!'

Von Hanke frowned. '*Later*.' He looked at Hechler. 'Surprise will be total. It will show the world what we can do.' He gripped his hands again. 'You will do it for Germany!'

A door opened and Hechler knew that the interview was at an end.

It was so swift, so impossibly vast he could barely think of it as a feasible plan. At the same time it was like a release, perhaps what he had always been looking and hoping for.

Von Hanke folded his arms. 'Nothing will be said beyond these walls. Only the Führer knows, and he will let nothing stand in your way.'

Hechler thought of the colonel on the plane, the frightened-looking people he had seen in the bombed streets.

Perhaps this *was* a way. Maybe it was all they had.

Outside the map-room Leitner said, 'Return to your ship. I will fly up in two days.' He shrugged. 'After that, who knows?'

Hechler found the tired lieutenant waiting for him and the car was ready to take him to the airfield.

He barely noticed the journey and was astonished that he could accept it so calmly.

The Atlantic. The vast Western Ocean. *The killing ground*, where every ship would be an enemy.

Leitner's words stuck in his mind. *A tiger at large.*

He touched the peak of his cap to a saluting sentry and walked out to the smoke-shrouded runway.

The waiting was over.

5

Rank Has its Privileges

Dieter Hechler opened his eyes with a start and realised that his face was pressed on to his forearm. Two other facts stood out, that he had been writing a letter to his parents, but had been awakened by the clamour of alarm bells.

He jumped to his feet, his mind still refusing to grasp what was happening. He was in his day cabin, his jacket hanging on a chair, an empty coffee cup nearby. Normally the sound of those alarm bells would have brought him to instant readiness and it was likely he would have been in his tiny sea-cabin, or dozing in the steel chair on the bridge.

The telephone buzzed through the din of bells and running feet with the attendant slamming of watertight doors.

It was Theil. 'Red Alert, sir. Air attack.'

Hechler slammed down the handset and snatched his jacket and cap even as Pirk scampered past him to screw the steel deadlights over the scuttles.

On deck the ship seemed deserted, and only abandoned brooms and paint brushes marked the sudden alarm.

He climbed swiftly to the upper bridge, aware that the anti-aircraft guns were already traversing towards the land, and men were putting on helmets and dragging belts of ammunition to the short-range weapons.

It was still a bright afternoon with just a few jagged clouds towards the open sea.

Hechler barely heard the quick reports from the officers

around him but stared instead at the long stretches of camou-flaged netting which hung between the masts and above the main armament. It was the same aboard the *Lübeck*. It did not hide a ship from an inquisitive aircraft, but it acted as a disguise and broke up a ship's outline.

Theil took a pair of binoculars from a messenger and then handed them back with a terse, 'Clean the lenses, damn you!'

Hechler looked across the starboard screen. The airfield was invisible from here, but there ought to be some fighters scrambled by now, he thought.

He hated being at anchor. Like lying in a trap. The bait. The ship had been at short notice for steam since his return from Kiel, but not that short. It would take an hour to slip and work out to some sea-room.

He turned his attention to the other cruiser. All her secondary armament was at full elevation, and in his mind's eye he saw Rau, watching the heavy cruiser and probably comparing the times it had taken for both ships to clear for action.

Theil muttered irritably, 'Come on, get those planes airborne!'

He must be thinking much the same. Too many warships had been caught in enclosed fjords and damaged beyond repair by daring hit-and-run raids.

An inland battery had opened fire and every pair of glasses scanned the clouds as the shells left their familiar dirty brown stains in the sky.

Theil exclaimed, 'I can't see a bloody thing!'

The young one-striper, Konrad Jaeger, called suddenly, 'I see it! One aircraft, sir, at red four-five!'

Hechler sensed Theil's annoyance but concentrated on the bearing until sunlight shone like a bright diamond on the plane's cockpit cover.

Another voice hissed, 'Nowhere near the thing!'

Hechler watched the shell-bursts gathering in an untidy cluster while some earlier ones broke up and drifted downwind.

Hechler had to agree with the unknown sailor. The shooting was very poor and the tiny sliver of metal in the sky did not even alter course.

It was not a bomber anyway, and seemed to be quite alone.

Bodø was described as a safe anchorage and better protected than most. It was likely that enemy agents would know of *Prinz Luitpold*'s presence here, just as her departure from Vejle would be known and plotted in London. However, there was no need to invite some reckless reconnaissance plane to confirm everything.

Theil said between his teeth, 'Our Arado replacement is expected, sir.' He sounded anxious. 'I hope to hell that headquarters have ordered it to stand away.'

Hechler looked over the screen and past the nearest gun-crews as they tried to track the aircraft, their anti-flash hoods making them look like members of some strange religious order.

The aircraft derrick was already swung out, the tackle prepared to hoist the new Arado inboard as soon as it landed in the fjord.

'Gunnery officer requests permission to use main armament, sir.'

'Negative.' Hechler knew that Kröll would shoot at anything just to exercise his men. But it was a waste of ammunition and with as much hope of hitting the reconnaissance plane as a bow and arrow. In fact the solitary aircraft was already heading away, flitting between the clouds, the shell-bursts too far away to catch it.

Theil said, 'Here they are! *At last*. Late as bloody usual!'

Two fighters streaked from the land, the echo of their engines roaring around the fjord with a throaty vibration. The sun shone on their black crosses as they tilted over and then tore towards the sea.

Hechler lowered his binoculars and glanced at Theil and the others. Theil was furious, too angry perhaps to notice the coincidence. The anti-aircraft battery had been haphazard, just as the fighter cover had been far too late to do anything.

It was as if they had been ordered to hold back. If that was so, it meant just one thing. Headquarters wanted the enemy to know they were here. It was like being in the dark. Being told only a part of von Hanke's strategy. Hechler tried to shrug it off. It was not the first time that air defences had been caught napping. He pictured the admiral in his winged collar, the dry grip of his hands. Von Hanke of all people would know each step before it was made. Just as he had known about the army division which existed only on his map. How many more divisions or battalions were represented only by coloured markers and flags? A million men lay dead from the last campaign. How many more were there now? He tried to dispel the sudden apprehension, the sense of danger.

'Aircraft at green one-one-oh, angle of sight one-oh!'

The gunnery speaker snapped into life. 'Disregard! Aircraft friendly!'

Some of the seamen grinned with nervous relief, but Hechler crossed the bridge to watch the float-plane as it left the land's protection and followed its own reflection across the flat water.

He snapped, 'I want to see that pilot as soon as he comes aboard! We may be short of a plane and the man to fly it, but by God I'll send him back double-quick unless he can explain himself!'

All the smiles were gone now. Even young Jaeger had enough experience to realise the cause of the captain's cool anger. If there had been a proper air attack, especially by carrier-borne torpedo bombers, the Arado replacement would have been right in the middle of it, and Kröll's flak gunners would have had to hold their fire or shoot it down with the attackers.

'Fall out action stations.' Hechler controlled his anger.

Moments later the guardrails were thronged with men again as the new float-plane made a perfect landing and then taxied towards the anchored cruiser.

Theil dropped his glasses. 'Extra passenger, sir.' He bit his lip. 'It looks like the rear-admiral.'

Even as the plane glided towards the side Hechler saw Leitner grinning up at them, before removing his flying helmet to don his oak-leaved cap.

He said, 'I don't care if it's Christ Almighty. That was a damn stupid thing to do!'

Hechler was as much concerned at his own anger as he was about the admiral's unorthodox arrival. Was it because there were so many questions still unanswered? If they engaged one of the British convoys for instance. Would Rau's *Lübeck* be able to withdraw safely? That, almost more than the mission itself, had filled him with uncertainty.

Followed by Theil he hurried from the bridge and down to the catapult, where a side-party had been hastily assembled.

Leitner pulled himself up from the Arado without waiting for it to be hoisted aboard. He was flushed and excited, and could barely stop himself from laughing aloud at Hechler's grave features. Together they watched the plane being hoisted up the side, water spilling from the floats as the handling party used their guy-ropes to sway it round. The Arado was brand-new, and bore no camouflage paint. As it came to rest on the catapult before being manhandled inboard Hechler saw the bright red stripe on the side. Like something from the Great War, he thought grimly.

Leitner stood with his arms folded, still dressed in a white flying suit, his cap at a rakish angle as he had appeared many times in the newspapers.

Hechler watched the pilot and observer climb down to the deck and then said, 'I'll see *you* later. You might have got your arse shot off!'

The pilot turned and stared at him and then pulled off the black helmet goggles.

Hechler stared as a mass of auburn hair tumbled over the other man's shoulders.

The admiral made a last effort to contain his amusement and said, 'Captain, may I introduce Erika Franke. One of the finest pilots in the Third Reich, I believe!'

She eyed him without curiosity, her lips slightly parted as she shook out her hair from her flying suit.

'Quite a welcome, Captain.' She did not offer her hand.

Hechler could feel the side-party's astonishment giving way to broad grins, and Theil's pink-faced disbelief that this had happened.

Hechler looked at the admiral. 'What I said still goes, sir.'

She was watching him, amused or merely bored he could not tell.

Erika Franke, of course. Her father had been an ace pilot who had died in attempting a lone flight across a desert in Africa.

She had won several prizes within a year of obtaining her licence. And she had even made her name in the war when she had flown into an encircled army position in Italy to rescue one of the Führer's top advisers before the whole place had been overrun.

He said, 'I am not used to –' It sounded defensive, foolish.

She turned away to watch as the two fighters came roaring back across the water.

'Evidently, Captain. We must try to change that, mustn't we?' Leitner clapped him on the shoulder.

'It will be a different war, Dieter.' He became serious again. 'For all of us, yes?'

The girl turned and looked at them calmly. 'I'd like to change and have a shower, if I may.' She touched her upper lip with her tongue. 'Even at the risk of getting my, er, arse shot off, eh?'

Hans Stoecker in his best uniform with a holstered Luger at his belt stood nervously outside the wardroom. He felt on edge, unable to concentrate on anything, even the prospect of meeting Sophie again.

It was all so strange and unreal, he thought, after the patrols and bombardments, the wild elation of watching from his position high above the bridge when the main armament had fired on the enemy.

The wardroom throbbed with music, and was packed from side to side with officers and visitors alike. Like the peacetime navy must have been, he thought, without fear of a sudden air-attack or torpedo.

With the rear-admiral's flag hoisted over the ship everyone had expected things to move swiftly, that the *Prinz* would head out to sea again.

He recalled seeing the girl pilot as she had climbed down from the catapult. Like most of the company he had read of her exploits, especially the last one when she had flown through enemy flak to lift off an important politician. Stoecker did not really like the idea of women in the firing line, but after meeting Sophie he was not certain of anything. She was not a schoolgirl any more. She was a woman, and had probably seen more results of war than he had.

Now he had two secrets to hold. One was the letter, still unopened. He had nearly destroyed it several times but something made him hold back. The other secret was what Sophie had told him.

She was ordered to a hospital in Norway. Suppose it was where they were based? They would meet again. Like that last time when they had kissed and clutched each other, hearts pounding while they had tasted a new and delicate love.

A curtain swirled back and Leutnant zur See Konrad Jaeger stepped over the coaming. He took a pistol from the rack and clipped it around his waist.

He grimaced as a great burst of laughter came from beyond him.

'Time for rounds, Stoecker. Others have all the luck.'

It would take all of an hour to go round the flats and messes, to check padlocks and magazine and to sign all the log-sheets. By the time they had finished some of the guests would have left.

Stoecker nodded to a boatswain's mate and messenger who were waiting to accompany the young officer on his rounds. There was a faint smell of schnapps in the damp air, and he hoped Jaeger had not noticed it. He was a good officer, for a one-striper that was. But he'd come down on Stoecker if he found someone had been drinking on watch.

Jaeger was not aware of the acting petty officer's wary glance. He was thinking of the wardroom party, the first one he had ever attended in a real combat warship. The *Prinz* was famous; you could see the excitement, even awe, on the faces of the guests, and especially the women. The admiral must have a lot of influence even in that direction, he decided. There were lots of women aboard, and most appeared to be German except for the wives of some local officials.

Preceded by the boatswain's mate, Jaeger and his little party climbed to the cooler air of the quarterdeck, where Korvetten-kapitän Froebe was waiting by the accommodation ladder to welcome guests below the shaded police lights.

It was a rare sight, and Jaeger paused to watch as two women in long, colourful dresses with some officers from the airfield stood by the guardrails, their hair moving in the evening breeze, their eyes exploring the ship.

Jaeger thought of the young girl he had met in the wardroom. It was unlikely he would get a look-in there, he thought. Hampe, the torpedo officer and a well-known womaniser, had been watching them, waiting for rounds to be called. For him to leave.

A figure moved from the shadows and Jaeger called his men to attention.

The captain touched his cap and smiled. 'Hard luck, Jaeger, but rank has its privileges, you see.'

Jaeger grinned. He could recall standing like a ramrod at attention for minutes on end in his last ship, where he had completed his training. That captain had been a tyrant, a bully you would never want to speak to even if it had been allowed.

Hechler was so different. Did he never have any worries or doubts?

Hechler saw the youngster's glance in spite of the gloom. He had also noticed the faint tang of schnapps. That would be the boatswain's mate. His mother and sister had just been reported killed in an air raid. He would let it pass. Hechler strode on, half-dreading the party and Leitner's exuberance. *This* time, he would say nothing.

Theil was waiting to meet him outside the wardroom and Hechler asked, 'All going well?'

Theil nodded. 'Like old times.'

Hechler stepped into the wardroom and moved through the packed figures. It was hard to see this place as it usually was, or used as a sickbay for wounded troops brought offshore from the fighting.

He sensed the glances and the occasional bold stares from some of the women. Why should he feel so ill at ease? This might be the last time for a long while that they could relax and drink too much. It could just as easily be the last time ever.

He heard a woman laugh and saw the auburn hair shining beneath a deckhead light.

Erika Franke wore a neither gown nor a uniform, it was something in between, dove-grey which set off her hair and her skin. She was speaking with Zeckner, a quarters officer, so that Hechler made to step aside before she saw him.

He was still uncertain what to do. Leitner had explained that the orders came from von Hanke and even higher. Erika Franke was to stay aboard. Incredibly, there was also a camera team. That in itself was not unusual in major warships, but with the prospect of immediate action it could put their lives at risk. Leitner seemed to treat the whole matter like a personal publicity operation.

She called, 'Why, Captain, so you have come amongst us after all!'

He faced her, surprised and angry at the way she got under his skin and made him feel clumsy.

He said, 'I hope you are being looked after?' She had long lashes and eyes which seemed to change colour as he watched. Hazel and then tawny.

She smiled. 'You are staring, Captain.'

Hechler took a glass of champagne which someone thrust into his hand.

'Yes. I'm sorry.' He raised the glass and lowered it again. 'And I apologise for the way I greeted your arrival on board.'

She touched her lip with her tongue as she had when she had faced him at their first meeting.

'That must have cost you a lot, Captain.' She nodded, her eyes grave. 'I suspect you are not used to bending your knee.' The smile moved into her eyes again. 'Especially to a mere woman.'

Leitner joined them before Hechler could answer. He said, 'Good party. It will make everyone believe we are here as a part of a local squadron.' He beamed and showed his perfect teeth. 'Let them all relax and enjoy themselves, eh? Who cares about tomorrow?'

Theil was making signals from the door and Leitner remarked, 'A night full of surprises. As it should be.'

Hechler glanced past the noisy, laughing figures and saw her as she stepped over the coaming. He felt as if his breath had stopped, that even his heart was still.

Her hair was quite short so that her small, perfectly shaped ears were visible, as were the pendant earrings as she turned to look around.

Several officers stopped talking to stare, questions clear on their faces.

Hechler put down his glass. Inger had always commanded a lot of attention, like the first time he had seen her and lost his heart.

She had an escort, a much older man in an olive-green uniform, a political officer of some kind and obviously quite senior. That too was pretty typical, he thought bitterly.

Leitner was watching him, one eyebrow cocked. 'She asked to come.' He spread his hands with mock gravity. 'What must I do? How could anyone refuse her?'

'Your wife, Captain?'

Hechler looked at the girl with auburn hair. He felt suddenly lost. Trapped.

He said, 'Yes.'

'She is very beautiful.' But she was studying him, her eyes quiet with interest. 'You seem surprised?'

Leitner smiled. 'It is only right, Dieter.'

Hechler said, 'She has no place here.'

But she was coming across, men parting before her or trying to catch her glance.

She wore a red silk gown with thin shoulder straps. It was cut very low both front and back and Hechler guessed that she wore little if anything underneath it.

She presented her hand for him to take and kiss. Even that was perfectly done. The perfume on her skin, it too he could recall as if it were yesterday.

Leitner was shaking hands with her escort, but Hechler did not even catch his name. It was as if nothing had happened, that the fire still burned. The touch of her hand, the movement of her breasts which were barely concealed by the red silk, seemed to render him helpless.

He knew Theil and some of the others were watching. They were learning more about their captain every day. Why had she come?

She said softly, 'You look tired, Dieter. Doing too much.' She observed him calmly. 'As always.' Her eyes moved to the girl. 'And who is this?'

Erika Franke met her gaze, unruffled by the casual but faintly imperious tone.

She replied, 'I work here.' She gave a quick smile. 'I shall go and enjoy myself.'

Inger watched her leave and said, 'That's the flier. I thought I knew her.' She seemed to relax. 'She's been in some bother, I believe.'

Hechler did not want to discuss it. 'I was not expecting –'

'*That* is evident.' She smiled and touched his cheek but her eyes were quite cool. 'No matter. You are a man, a *hero*, some say.'

Leitner had moved away and was in deep conversation with her escort. The latter was staring across, unwilling to be shelved so soon.

Hechler felt the old anger again. Why should he have to put up with it?

Theil was watching too, although he was at some pains to cover it.

He heard himself ask, 'Why here and now, Inger? It's over.'

'You think so?' She rested one hand on his sleeve and touched the four gold stripes. 'You need me. You always will. Nothing's changed.' She seemed to become impatient and thrust her hand beneath his arm. 'Can we talk? In private?'

Hechler heard the lively dance strike up as another record was put on the gramophone and was grateful for the interruption. Voices grew louder and some of the guests began to revolve although there was barely room to move. Perspiring stewards and messmen pushed amongst the throng with laden trays of glasses. This evening was going to cost the wardroom a small fortune.

She said, 'Your cabin?' She looked up at him, her eyes steady, her lips shining, inviting.

They walked along the deck, the noise growing fainter as if the ship was reasserting herself, rising above them, grey steel and hooded guns.

Once she turned and looked across at the darkening water, the thin white line of a motor-launch's wake.

He asked, 'What about your friend?'

She shrugged. Even that motion stabbed him like a knife.

'Ludwig? He is head of a mission here, something to do with fisheries, I think. Don't worry about him.'

The cabin was quiet, with a tidiness which showed Pirk had been busy clearing up from the last official visitors. But there was some champagne and two glasses, as if it had all been planned. She saw his expression and said, 'Thank you, I should like some.'

He could feel her watching as he opened the bottle and wiped it free of ice. She never looked tired; he could not recall her ever refusing an invitation to a party or a reception. Like the time he had returned home with the knowledge he was being given *Prinz Luitpold*. He had been in bed reading when he had heard her come into the house, then the sound of men's voices.

When he had gone down he had found her in the arms of an artillery major, while another officer was on his knees beside a girl who had obviously passed out with drink. The man had been tearing the clothes off her, stripping her naked while Inger and her friend ignored what he was doing.

Somehow, he could barely recall how, they had made it up. She had even been excited when he had thrown the others out of the house, had pleaded for his forgiveness and then given herself to him with such wild abandon that he had surrendered.

Looking back he must have been mad. But he had loved her then. Hechler turned with the glasses. He still wanted her. Was that the same thing?

He sat beside her, feeling the longing and the pain of it as he studied her face and her mouth. When she took his hand and put it around her breast he could feel the drumming in his mind, could think of nothing but taking her, here and now. As Leitner had said, who cares about tomorrow?

She stretched out and put down her glass so that one shoulder strap slipped away and her breast was almost lying bare in his hand. She watched his face as if to test each emotion there and said, 'You are sailing soon. Why else would Andreas invite me?'

He should have guessed that Leitner was behind it. It was a game to him. He used people with little thought for what might happen.

'What do you want, Inger?'

She touched his mouth with her fingers. 'I need you to love me.'

It made no sense, but he wanted to hold her, tell her everything. Hopes, fears, all the things which were bottled up inside him ... The telephone shattered the silence and she smiled as he reached out to take it.

It was Theil, his voice hushed and troubled. One of the guests had fallen down a ladder. It was someone important. He thought the captain should know.

Hechler watched her, the way she smiled as she slipped the other strap from her shoulder and allowed the red silk to fall about her waist. Her breasts were lovely, and she touched one, her lips parted, knowing it would provoke him.

He said quickly, 'Get the senior medical officer, Viktor.' He had not met the newcomer yet and as he watched the thrust of her breasts he could barely recall his name. 'Stroheim.'

He put down the phone and looked at her. She was staring at him, her eyes full of disbelief. 'What name?'

Hechler said, 'Karl-Heinz Stroheim. He's new on board. I—'

She struggled into her dress and knocked over her champagne without seeming to notice it.

Hechler stood up while she looked around the cabin like a trapped animal.

'You know him?'

She faced him, her eyes hot. 'Don't you *dare* question me! I'm not one of your snivelling sailors!' She recovered slightly and glanced at herself in the mirror. 'Take me back. I must go.'

He blocked her way. 'Tell me! For God's sake, you said you wanted me!'

She stared at him, and he could see her self-control returning, like a calm on the sea.

'What will you do, Dieter? Knock me down? Rape me?' She tossed her short curls. 'I think not—your precious Andreas would

76

not care for *that*!'

Hechler could not recall walking back to the wardroom. More curious stares, her bright laugh as her escort lumbered over to claim her. He heard her say something about a headache, and then as she turned to look towards him she said, 'It will be a relief to be alone.'

Leitner watched as she followed Theil towards the door. He asked softly, 'Not going with her, Dieter? Tch, tch, I am surprised.'

Hechler turned his back on the others, his voice dangerously calm.

'You did it deliberately, sir. For one moment I thought –' He shook himself angrily. 'I don't know what I thought.'

Leitner glanced towards his willowy aide who had just entered, his eyes everywhere until he had found his lord and master.

Hechler saw the brief nod. Nothing more.

Leitner picked up a fresh glass and watched the busy bubbles rising.

'I shall set an example and retire, Dieter.' He looked at him for several seconds as if making up his mind. 'First-degree readiness.' He shook his head as Hechler made to speak. '*Not yet*. People are watching. We shall weigh tomorrow evening. As soon as the guests have departed, pass the word to the other commanding officers.' Some of his self-control slipped aside. 'You will brief your heads of departments as soon as we clear the anchorage.'

Hechler watched the crowd of guests thinning soon after Leitner had followed his flag-lieutenant outside. It was like an unspoken command, and he walked to the guardrails opposite Turret Caesar to watch the boats and launches queuing at the accommodation ladder to collect their passengers.

Perhaps he hoped to see the red silk gown. He did not know any more. But he could picture her sitting beside him, her lovely body naked to the waist. Then her anger – or was it fear?

Some of the departing guests were singing. The ship, deep in shadow, must look quite beautiful from the boats in the water, he thought.

First-degree readiness. Like the opening of sealed orders. Page one.

The squadron would slip away unseen in the darkness, but not a man in any of the other ships would know *Prinz Luitpold*'s true purpose. When they did there would be few who would wish to change places with them.

As one of the duty officers, Jaeger, with Stoecker standing close by, stood by the gangway and watched the visitors being guided and helped down the long ladder. The sailors were taking much greater care with the women than the men, he noticed.

He saw the girl pause and look up at him. She had waited until he returned from rounds, and he had spent the rest of the time speaking with her.

He raised his hand in salute and saw her blow him a kiss.

He did not see the pain on Stoecker's face as he spoke her name aloud. *Sophie.*

By midnight as the watchkeepers changed round for the next four hours Hechler still walked the decks alone.

When he eventually went to his cabin he saw that the glasses and ice-bucket had gone, the stain of her champagne all but mopped up from the carpet.

A light burned beside his bunk, some coffee in a thermos nearby.

He thought suddenly of the new medical officer, and her expression when he had spoken his name.

There was so much he wanted to know, so much more he dared not ask.

When Pirk entered silently to switch off the light he found the captain fast asleep, still fully dressed.

Pirk sighed and then swung Hechler's legs on to the bunk.

He thought of the newly installed admiral and what he had heard about him and his flag-lieutenant. If the other stewards knew, it would soon be all over the ship.

Pirk smiled with satisfaction and switched off the light.

The captain would see them all right. He always had.

Hechler slept on, and with his ship waited for the dawn.

6

The Unexpected

Hechler slid from his steel chair on the port side of the bridge and stamped his feet on the scrubbed gratings to restore the circulation. One of the watchkeepers jumped at the sound, and Hechler noted the tense backs of the bridge lookouts as they peered through their powerful glasses, each man to his own allotted sector.

Hechler glanced at the armoured conning-tower and past it to the fire control position. Beneath and around him the ship vibrated and quivered but the motion was steady, and even some pencils on the chart table remained motionless.

He tried to dampen down his own anxieties. It was always like this when a ship left the land. For him in any case. Now, with the additional knowledge of what might lie ahead, he had to be certain of everything. *Confident*.

There had been no flaws, nothing serious anyway. He looked past two signalmen and saw *Lübeck* following half a mile astern, her faint funnel vapour streaming out abeam like her flags. The destroyers too were exactly on station, as if they were all on rails. They dipped their bows occasionally and Hechler saw the sea creaming over their forecastles before cascading down through the guardrails again. A small but powerful force, he thought, with air cover to make it easier. Every few minutes, or so it seemed, they sighted one of the big Focke Wulf Condors which acted as their eyes and escorts.

Two bells chimed out from below the bridge and the men

relieved from watch would be having their lunch, the main meal of the day. It had been sixteen hours since they had weighed and with little fuss had steamed out of Salt Fjord, soon to lose Bodø in the gathering dusk.

Hechler had been on the bridge throughout that time, watching the cable clanking inboard with the usual chipped paint scattering to each massive link.

Westward to skirt the Lofoten Islands and then north, the ships closing in protectively on either beam.

All the captains had come aboard just prior to sailing, but Leitner had kept his comments on a general level. They all knew about the enemy convoys, each captain had an intelligence pack as big as a bible. The British might have a change of heart, or perhaps one of the convoys would be re-routed at the last minute.

Sixteen hours at a relatively gentle fifteen knots, although the destroyers were finding station-keeping hard work.

It was a strange feeling to be heading out into an ocean instead of sighting land every so often as in the Baltic. Now as *Prinz Luitpold*'s raked bows ploughed across the seventieth parallel nothing lay ahead unless you counted Spitzbergen or Bear Island. Scenes of other sea-fights, Hechler thought, before every eye had turned to Normandy and the Eastern Front.

He walked to the chart-table to give himself time to glance at the men around him. Most of them were warmly dressed, for despite the fact it was August, the air had a bite to it. Soon there would be no escape from the ice.

Their faces looked normal enough, he thought. That morning he had sensed the silence throughout the ship when he had spoken on the intercom to the whole company.

Leitner had been ready to make a speech, but Hechler had bluntly asked permission to speak to his men, in his own way.

He had pictured them as his voice had echoed around each deck and compartment like a stranger's. Gun crews and engineers, the damage-control men and those who cooked and served the hundreds of meals it took to feed the *Prinz*'s people.

'We are going out into the Atlantic—' There should have been rousing music, cheering; instead there was a silence which meant

80

so much more to him, no matter what Leitner might believe.

Some had tried to tell him privately that they would not let him down. Others, like the huge Gudegast, had merely joked about it. *Good a place as any to lose a ship!*

He wondered what Rau would say if he knew.

Hechler shaded his eyes to look at the horizon. It was so eerie. A great, unbroken swell which roamed on and on for ever. And the sky, which was salmon-pink, painted the ragged clouds in a deeper hue, like copper. The ship's upperworks too were shining in the strange glow. Endless daylight, empty seas.

Another Focke Wulf droned overhead; a lamp winked briefly to the ships below.

The camera team had been on the bridge for much of the forenoon, but they seemed to have exhausted their ideas, and even the big four-engined Condor did not lure the cameras on deck again.

Oberleutnant Ahlmann, who was officer-of-the-watch, put down a handset and said, 'The lady flier wishes to come to the bridge, sir.'

Hechler thrust his hands deep into his pockets. He had not seen her since they had left Bodø, except once when she had been on the admiral's bridge with Leitner. Like the two girls who were in the camera team, her presence gave a sense of unreality. According to Leitner, they would be transferred before the ship headed deep into the Atlantic. Their films would be invaluable, he had said with all of his usual enthusiasm. A tonic to the people at home. It all depended on the first move. Von Hanke would decide after that.

Hechler had the feeling that the rear-admiral intended to use von Hanke as an excuse for almost everything.

He said, 'Very well.' He might get to the bottom of it by asking her what exactly she was doing aboard, in his ship.

Her voice came up the ladder and he pictured Inger, as he had a hundred times since the party. Her anger, her contempt, were so different from that earlier seduction. If it was to happen again...

He turned to face her as she was ushered into the bridge.

She wore a black leather jacket with a fur collar turned up

over her hair. Her skin was very fresh from the wind and he guessed she had been exploring the upper deck.

'A wonderful view, Captain!' She climbed on to the gratings and peered through the salt-blotched screen. 'I should love to fly right now!'

Hechler watched her profile, her neat hands which gripped the rail as the deck tilted slightly to a change of course.

Ahlmann looked up from a voice-pipe and reported, 'Steady on Zero-Two-Two, sir. Revolutions one-one-zero.'

He turned and saw her watching him.

She shrugged. 'So different.' She gestured towards the upper bridge and radar, Leitner's flag leaping stiffly to the wind. 'So huge. You feel as if nothing would stop her, as if she could run away with you.'

Hechler nodded. 'When I was a young watchkeeper I often thought that. Especially during the night, the captain asleep, nobody to ask. I used to look at the stars and—'

'Gunnery Officer requires permission to train A and B turrets, sir.'

Hechler replied, 'Yes. Ten minutes.'

'It never stops for you, does it?'

He looked at her. 'I hadn't thought about it.' Together they watched as the two forward turrets swung silently on to the same bearing.

Kröll never missed a chance, which was why he had given him a time limit for this, another drill. At any moment, any second, the alarms might scream out. Men had to be clear-minded and not confused by too many exercises.

He thought of what Inger had said about this quiet-eyed girl. In some sort of trouble.

She said, 'Seeing those great guns makes me realise what your kind of war is all about.'

'Are you afraid?'

She seemed to consider it. 'I don't think so. It's like flying. There are only certain things you can do if the plane gets out of control.' She shrugged again. 'I don't feel I have any hold on things here.'

Then she laughed and one of the lookouts tore his eyes from

his binoculars to glance at her.

'I *know* you are going to ask me, Captain, but like you, I am under orders. I am on board your ship because I have been so ordered. I am a civilian but I fly for the Luftwaffe.'

'I heard what you did.' Hechler tried to adapt to her direct manner. 'It's more than I'd care to do.' He scraped the gratings with his boot. 'Give me something solid...'

Theil appeared at the rear of the bridge and saluted, although his eyes were on the girl.

'The admiral sends his compliments, sir, and would you see him.'

'Yes.' Hechler was annoyed at the interruption. Being captain usually gave him all he needed, but he craved a conversation with someone who was not committed or involved with the same things. Leitner had probably seen them chatting, and was merely calling him away although it could hardly be from jealousy.

The thought made him smile and she said quietly, 'You should do that more often, Captain.' She turned away as the two forward turrets purred back to point fore-and-aft again.

Theil stepped forward so that he seemed to loom between them.

Hechler said, 'If there is anything I can do while you are aboard...'

She watched him, her eyes tawny in the strange light. 'Attend your ship, Captain. Her needs are greater than mine, I feel.'

Hechler turned away. The brief contact was broken. And why not? His own self-pity was a poor enough bridge to begin with.

He found Leitner on his armoured bridge, leaning with his arms spread wide on the plot-table.

Leitner glanced up, his neat hair glossy beneath the lights. 'All intelligence reports confirm my own thinking, Dieter. Tomorrow, we shall meet with the eastbound convoy. The British will know we are on the move. No matter, they will expect us to strike at the westbound one, to protect their friend Ivan's supplies, eh?' He nodded, satisfied. 'All working out. There are six U-boats in this area, and round-the-clock air patrols.' He stood up and clasped his hands at his sides. 'I can't *wait* to begin. Into the Atlantic, all that planning and von Hanke's preparations. God, it makes one feel quite humble!'

Hechler watched his emotion. It came and went like the wind. He thought of the reams of orders, the methods of fuelling, rendezvous, and alternatives. This would be a million times different from previous raiding sorties.

Leitner said, 'I know it is important to you, Dieter, the close comradeship amongst your people. I heard it in your broadcast this morning. Saw it on their faces. Just boys, some of them, but the older ones who can be so hard and cynical –' he gave an elaborate sigh '– you had them eating out of your hand.'

Hechler replied, 'Comradeship is everything.'

'I *knew* it.' Leitner looked down at his plot-table again. 'Your second-in-command. I had a private signal about him.'

'Viktor Theil?'

'His wife has gone missing.' He sounded almost matter-of-fact. 'Of course I'm certain it will be all right. After all, ration books, identity cards, a civilian can't just vanish, eh?'

Hechler recalled Theil's face, the way he had parried questions about his leave.

Leitner said softly, 'I know what you're thinking, Dieter. *Don't!* He is a good officer, I'm sure, but he *is* the second-in-command. Should anything happen to you, well . . .' He shrugged.

'I trust him, sir.'

'Good. I shall remember it. But if he trips up on this mission, he goes, do I make myself clear?'

Hechler nodded. 'Very.'

Leitner yawned. 'Pretty girl, that Franke woman, eh? I wonder if she's as good in bed as in the cockpit.'

Fortunately a telephone rang and the flag-lieutenant appeared again like magic to answer it.

Hechler returned to the bridge. He felt strangely disappointed to find she was no longer there. Theil had gone too. For that at least he was glad.

He climbed into his steel seat and listened to the deep throb of engines, the occasional clatter of a morse lamp as signals were exchanged between the ships. Tomorrow that would all cease. He glanced over the screen at the same heavy guns. Moving targets, not rubble and houses, or a position on a range map.

He tried not to let Inger into his thoughts, to recall how she had looked, and shifted uneasily in the chair. He was getting rattled just when he needed every thought honed to a knife-edge. Tomorrow they would engage the enemy. Right now, at this very moment the convoy was being attacked by U-boats. Like sheepdogs gone mad who were driving the convoy on a converging course.

He thought of Theil, then of himself. Two deserted husbands. It was laughable when you considered it. Was that all it meant? Voices muttered in voice-pipes, while guns moved in their mountings as the faithful Condor droned past the formation yet again. No, it was anything but laughable. He gripped the arms of his seat. Men would die, cursing his name, ships would burn.

Wives and petty squabbles were as nothing.

The bows dipped and he saw his reflection in the smeared glass. No, that too was a lie.

Hans Stoecker slammed yet another watertight door behind him and wedged the clips into place. Below the ship's waterline where one compartment was sealed from another the air felt cool and damp, the motion more pronounced. He passed the massive circular trunk of B turret, Turret Bruno, and paused by a brightly lit door to the forward starshell room.

He had been carrying a message from the gunnery officer for one of the lieutenants but had purposely taken a roundabout route, and had parried not a few questions from sentries who guarded some of the vital bulkheads which in an emergency might prevent serious flooding. Stoecker glanced at the studded rivets and rough steel. It was best not to think of it, of those who might be trapped on the wrong side to face a terrible death by drowning.

He heard the familiar whistle and saw a grey-headed petty officer rummaging through a box of tools. Oskar Tripz was probably the oldest member of the ship's company. He had served in the Kaiser's navy, and when you got him going over a quiet glass of brandy or schnapps, would dwell with relish on the Battle of Jutland, and clashes with the Grand Fleet off the Dogger Bank. Even when he had quit the service he had been unable or unwilling to leave the sea and returned to it in the merchant marine and eventually in the famous Hamburg–Amerika Line. There again he could open the eyes of young sailors with his yarns of great liners, rich widows and randy passengers who chased the girls and sometimes the stewards with equal enthusiasm.

He was a rough, self-made seaman, and one of the gun-captains, despite his great age, great to younger men like Stoecker anyway. Stoecker was never bored by his stories of that other navy, another world, and was ever impressed by the man's knowledge of the sea. Tripz had even managed to teach himself at least three languages, with enough of some others to get him around in ports all over the world.

Tripz looked up and squinted at him questioningly. He had a round, crumpled face, as if that too had been carved from old ship's timber.

'You're a bit off-course, young Hans?'

Stoecker sat on a steel chest and eyed him awkwardly. Of all the people he knew he probably trusted the old petty officer the most. It had been due to his patience and private coaching that he had risen this far, with the hope of confirmation to petty officer in the near future.

With Tripz it was not learning. It was more like listening to well-told history.

'A job for the gunnery officer.'

Tripz wrinkled his nose. 'Oh, him.'

They both glanced up as the sea, muffled but ever-present, boomed along the outer hull. Thick steel and one of the great fuel bunkers separated them from it, but they both knew it was not enough to withstand a torpedo.

Tripz asked casually, 'Bit bothered, are you?'

Stoecker shrugged. Straight to the point. As always. This rough, outspoken man was respected by almost everyone, even if some of the young recruits made fun of him behind his back. God help them if his wintry eyes saw through them.

'It's the first time I've been in a battle with other warships.'

'Huh. Maybe it won't come to that. The Tommies might have other ideas.'

'When I heard the captain explain what we're going to do, I—'

Tripz grinned slowly. 'The Old Man knows more than *we* do, Hans.'

Stoecker bit his lip. It was useless to go on like this. He could barely sleep even when he got the chance, and he had been off his food since that day at Vejle.

Suppose he was wrong? Tripz might go straight to his divisional officer. He had been known to pass the time of day even with the captain, the Old Man as he called him, though Stoecker guessed that Tripz was old enough to be his father.

But he couldn't go on. He would certainly fail his exams and let down his parents unless—he made up his mind.

'I found a letter.' He hesitated as the petty officer's faded eyes settled on his. 'Somebody told me that—'

'Show it to me.' He held out one calloused hand. He saw the lingering hesitation. 'I'll make it an order, if you'd prefer it?'

Stoecker passed it across and momentarily the prospect of action, even death, faded into the background.

Tripz prised open the much-folded envelope and scanned the letter with great care.

He said, 'It's in Danish. But then you'd know that, right?' He did not look up to see Stoecker nod. 'One of those prisoners.'

'Yes.' He was surprised the admission came out so easily. 'Just before he was killed.'

Tripz eyed him grimly. 'Before the explosion.'

'Yes.'

'Told anyone else?'

Stoecker shook his head and thought of the others he had almost confided in. Even the young one-striper Jaeger. Until he had discovered about him and Sophie. That moment still gnawed at his insides like teeth.

'Good.' He folded the letter with great care. 'This is hot stuff.'

Stoecker found himself blurting out about the SS officer, then the ravaged shop.

Tripz grunted. 'Jews, eh.' He added vaguely, 'Well, they started it all, you know.'

Stoecker waited; at any moment Tripz might put him under arrest, take him to Korvettenkapitän Kröll. He could face detention barracks or much worse.

Tripz said, 'Best leave it with me.' He looked at him strangely. 'Just between us.'

'But I don't even know . . .'

'Better that way, my son.' Tripz placed the letter inside an oilskin pouch and buttoned it in his tunic.

He added, 'It could get both of us shot. Do I make myself clear?'

Stoecker nodded, glad to have shared his secret, moved by Tripz's confidence in him.

'When I've fathomed it out, I'll tell you.' His battered face split into a grin. 'Feel better?'

Stoecker gave a shaky smile. 'Much. I—I'm just sorry I got you mixed up in it.'

Tripz looked up quickly at the deckhead as if he had heard something. It was like an inbuilt sixth sense for at that moment the air cringed to the strident clamour of alarm bells.

Tripz was thickset, even ungainly, but he was through the steel door and on the rungs of a ladder before Stoecker had grasped fully what was happening.

Tripz peered down at him. 'Move it, boy! No time to hang about! You'll get a wooden cross, not an iron one, if you do! Remember what I once told you, one hand for the Führer, but keep one for yourself!' Then he was gone and would doubtless be in his turret before the bells had fallen silent.

Stoecker ran after him; he had further to climb than anyone. And yet despite the crash of steel doors he felt as if a great weight had been lifted from him.

'Ship at action stations, sir!'

Hechler returned Korvettenkapitän Froebe's salute and glanced briefly around the bridge. In war what a short time it took to know their faces, to forget them after they had gone.

Everyone stiffened as Leitner entered the bridge and strode

unhurriedly to the gratings.

Hechler watched him curiously. The whole scheme might go badly wrong from the outset. There had been plenty of examples like *Graf Spee* and *Bismarck*, he thought. But Leitner looked very much at ease, even theatrical with a pure white silk scarf tossed casually around his throat, his rear-admiral's cap set at a rakish angle.

Leitner remarked, 'The stage is set, eh?'

Hechler could picture his men throughout the ship, as he had when he had told them their mission. Theil as second-in-command was down in the damage-control section, as far from the bridge as possible. Not too many eggs in one basket, as his father would have said. Did he ever hope a shell might fall on the bridge and give him the command he craved so desperately?

'I assume the engine-room is warned for full revolutions?'

Hechler nodded. It was almost amusing if you knew Wolfgang Stück, the taciturn senior engineer. He had been like a midwife to the *Prinz*, had been with her within weeks of her keel being laid, had watched over every tube and wire, valve and pump until her birth, when she had slid confidently into salt water at Hamburg.

So many miles steamed, thousands of gallons of oil, and a million day-to-day details. Stück would need no reminding. They got along well, allowing for the unspannable gap between bridge and engine-room, he thought.

Leitner was saying, 'Looking back, it all seems worthwhile now. Remember breaking the ice on those buckets with your head aboard the training ship before you could wash in the morning, eh? It would make some of these mother's boys puke!' His eyes were almost dreamy. 'And the electric shock treatment to test your reaction under stress at Flensburg Naval Academy. I'll bet we know more than those old has-beens ever did!'

Hechler raised his glasses and studied the nearest destroyer. 'Signal the first subdivision to take station ahead.' He glanced at Leitner. '*Now.*'

A lamp clattered and Hechler saw a young signalman staring at the admiral with something like awe. He had probably never been so close to a god before.

Hechler asked sharply, 'What are those people doing here?'

Leitner smiled. '*My* orders, Captain.'

The camera team huddled by a flag-locker, the two women looking ill-at-ease in their steel helmets.

Leitner added smoothly, 'A record. We must all take risks in war.'

Hechler watched the camera being mounted, the way Leitner was adjusting his scarf. But he thought of the battered streets in Kiel, the faces of his men who had lost their relatives and their homes.

The flag-lieutenant hurried across the bridge and handed Leitner his signal pad.

He took his time while the camera purred into life and all eyes watched as the scene was recorded.

Hechler thought for an instant it was an act, but Leitner said briskly, 'The attack on the convoy was a success. The one escort carrier was hit by torpedoes. She is out of the fight.' He returned the pad to his aide. 'Two U-boats were destroyed, but they carried out their orders. Brave men, all of them.'

Hechler tried to shut him from his thoughts. Voice-pipes and telephones kept up their muted chatter and he saw the two forward turrets turn slightly, the four big guns lifting and lifting until they appeared to be trying to strain themselves from their mountings.

The first subdivision of destroyers were tearing ahead and heeling over in a great welter of spray as they formed into line abreast, well ahead of their big consorts. The others were on either beam, with one solitary vessel lifting and plunging across *Lübeck*'s wake as she followed like a spectator. To sniff out any submarine, to pick up survivors, to stay out of trouble.

Leitner had made his name in destroyers; he was probably remembering it right now.

Froebe, the executive officer, tall and ungainly, his huge hands gripped around his binoculars, stood in Gudegast's place by the gyro-repeater. The navigator and his small team were up there in the armoured conning-tower, waiting to plot every manoeuvre and change of course, to advise, to take command even, if the main bridge was demolished.

Hechler could feel the youngster Jaeger standing as close as he dared to the steel chair. His action station was here too, and unlike the other junior officers he was privileged to hear and see everything. He was also more likely to be hit if the Tommies got too near.

Hechler thought suddenly of their sister-ship the *Admiral Hipper*. She too had carried out a raiding cruise in the Atlantic, and after a successful attack on a convoy and other ships had returned in triumph to her Norwegian lair.

But that had been in 1941. Things were different now.

Hechler examined his feelings again. What were their chances? His ship was the best there was anywhere. If skill and audacity counted they stood every chance of success.

It was strange to realise that *Hipper*, powerful though she was, had been rammed and severely damaged by the little destroyer HMS *Glow-worm*. A brave, hopeless gesture which had cost her captain his ship and most of his men. He smiled to himself as he thought of Theil's expression when he had mentioned Nelson. It was exactly what the little admiral would have done had he lived in this century.

The flag-lieutenant returned with his pad and Leitner said quietly, 'The British are concentrating on the eastbound convoy, Dieter. Von Hanke is a shrewd old devil. They have a battleship and two heavy cruisers as a covering force, but well to the north as expected.'

Hechler put one hand in his pocket and felt the familiar shape of his favourite pipe. It was somehow comforting, and he would have dearly liked to smoke it. It reminded him of Inger again. She had wanted him to give it up, change to cigars. Like Leitner who usually appeared in press photographs with a jaunty cheroot, although he had never seen him actually smoking one. Just for the record.

He walked to the rear of the bridge and peered aft past the funnel. The new Arado looked bright and incongruous beside one of the camouflaged ones. Was she really going to fly it as Leitner had vaguely outlined? He never gave the whole story about anything. Again, that was exactly how he had been as a junior lieutenant. A touch of mystery. He thought of the photographs Leitner had shown him prior to weighing anchor. The fjord at Bodø, shot from several thousand metres up. Even the camouflaged nets had looked the same. It could have been *Prinz Luitpold* lying there. But Leitner had explained, two old supply ships had been preparing for weeks. After this sortie they would be moored together in such a way that any reconnaissance aircraft would imagine the *Prinz* had returned to her anchorage. It was so simple, it was almost ridiculous. But if it worked it might give them the extra hours they needed.

Ahlmann, the lieutenant in charge of bridge communications, handed him a telephone.

'Gunnery officer, sir.'

Even the telephone could not disguise the satisfaction in Kröll's voice.

'Enemy in sight, sir. Bearing Green one-oh. Range two-one-five.'

Hechler wanted to turn and look up at the fire control station. The unseen eye reached beyond the empty horizon so that Kröll could already watch the enemy formation at a range of over 21,000 metres.

Leitner jabbed his sleeve. 'I am going to my bridge.' He grinned. 'This is a great day!' He brushed past the bridge party and Jaeger said, 'They are almost within range.'

Froebe watched him over the gyro-repeater and muttered, 'So will we be soon.'

Hechler raised his glasses and stared past the leading destroyers. Even their wakes were salmon-pink, their shining hulls like coloured glass.

Intelligence had reported a dozen merchantmen in the convoy. Probably twice that number had originally set out for Murmansk, he thought. Homeward bound, and with all the heavy support groups to the north of them waiting for an attack on the other precious array of supply ships. He listened to the regular ranges and bearings coming over the bridge gunnery intercom and pictured the two converging formations in his mind as he had studied it on the chart and had planned for such a moment. As Leitner had said, all that training was bearing fruit now. *Observation, method, conclusion, attack.*

The forward guns shifted slightly, the muzzles high-angled for the first salvo. Astern, *Lübeck*'s gun crews would be ready too, but they would have to be patient a while longer.

He wanted to glance at his watch, but knew such a move might be mistaken for doubt, anxiety.

Above the whirr of fans and the surge of water against the hull he heard the dull thud of an explosion. Far away, like someone beating an old drum. Another torpedo hit, one more ship gone to the bottom. Leitner did not seem to care about the cost in U-boats. To him nothing mattered but this moment.

Ahlmann asked, 'Permission to open fire, sir?'

'Denied.' He pictured the convoy again. Liberty ships for the most part. It would be a fast one, probably about fifteen knots. They would scatter if they fired too soon. It would be harder, and there was always the covering force to consider. A battleship and two heavy cruisers.

'*Aircraft*, sir!' Several of the men gasped aloud. 'Red one-five! Angle of sight one-oh!'

Froebe said between his teeth, 'Torpedo bombers, for Christ's sake!'

Orders rattled out from every side and the short-range weapons swung instantly on to the bearing.

Hechler stood in the corner of the bridge and levelled his Zeiss glasses, surprised that he should feel so calm, almost detached.

Two aircraft, so they had to be from the crippled carrier. They must have been flown off just prior to their being torpedoed. He considered it, weighing it up. Each pilot would know he had no chance of returning to his ship.

Like the little *Glow-worm* all over again, the unexpected factor. It would be the worst kind of attack – bravery or cold-blooded suicide, you could take your pick.

One of the aircraft might even be radioing a sighting report. So much for radar.

The British senior officer must have outguessed von Hanke, or was it just luck?

He tightened his jaw. 'Short-range weapons stand by. Secondary armament –' his eyes watered in the powerful lens as he saw the two small dots heading towards the ships. They were so low now they appeared to be scudding across the water. He knew their outdated silhouettes well enough. Swordfish, twin-winged torpedo bombers, like relics from the Great War.

He cleared his mind and shouted, '*Open fire!*'

The line of destroyers were already firing and the sky soon became pockmarked with shell-bursts. It would be tracer and cannon-shell soon, and then—

Ahlmann said thickly, 'The Admiral, sir.'

Leitner sounded faraway. 'The convoy may scatter. Increase speed. Signal the group to engage the enemy as ordered.'

Hechler saw the signalmen bending on their flags and said, 'Full ahead. Prepare to take avoiding action.' He saw Froebe nod. Then he forgot him and the others as the power surged up through the bridge like something unleashed until the whole structure quivered around them.

He had to shout above the sharp bang of the secondary armament, which poured acrid fumes over the bridge as the ship swept forward, faster and still faster.

'Main armament. *Open fire!*'

He barely had time to adjust his ear plugs before both forward turrets blasted the air apart to fire upon the target which was still invisible, below the horizon.

He looked for the two aircraft and saw them weaving amongst the shell-bursts while bright tracer lifted from the destroyers and crossed their path in a fiery mesh. One of the Swordfish was trailing smoke and it seemed impossible that either of them could survive the barrage.

One thing was obvious. *Prinz Luitpold* was their target.

7

Aftermath

Neither of the Swordfish torpedo bombers stood any chance of survival, and each pilot must have known it. As they pounded past the line of destroyers, the one trailing smoke seemed to stagger as tracer and cannon-fire tore into it.

Hechler jammed his elbows below the screen and stared at the weaving silhouettes as pieces of the damaged plane splashed into the glistening swell. Seconds later it exploded in a vivid orange flash. When the smoke drifted clear there was nothing to be seen. But the second aircraft was dodging the flak, and even as he watched Hechler saw the torpedo drop from the plane's belly and make a small feather of spray as it hit the water.

The plane continued towards them, shell-bursts, tracer, everything which would bear hammering into it. Perhaps the pilot and crew were already dead, but the Swordfish rolled over and then dived into the sea with a dull explosion.

'Torpedo running to port!'

'Hard a-port!'

At thirty knots the cruiser seemed to lean right on her beam, men falling and clutching anything for support as she thundered round.

'*Steady*. Hold her!' Hechler thought he saw the thin thread of white as the torpedo streaked towards the port bow.

The ship was steadying up, and Froebe croaked, 'Two-eight-zero!'

Leitner's voice broke through the din, distorted and wild on his intercom.

'Signal *Hans Arnim* to –' He got no further. The destroyer received the torpedo halfway down her port side even as she dashed protectively between it and the flagship.

At full speed the effect was instantaneous and terrible. Half of the forecastle collapsed and then rose in the air as the ship broke in two, the thrust of her screws driving her on and down as they watched.

Hechler said, 'Bring her back on course.' From one corner of his eye he saw the *Lübeck* surging past to take the lead into battle. He could picture Rau laughing as he watched the *Prinz* reeling from the line in confusion. His guns suddenly opened fire, and moments later he saw the tell-tale flash-flash on the horizon to mark the fall of *Lübeck*'s salvo.

Gudegast's voice intruded from his armoured conning tower.

'On course, sir. Zero-two-zero.' He sounded calm, even disinterested, even though the destroyer was turning turtle in a welter of smoke and foam.

The intercom reported dully, '*Hans Arnim* has sunk, sir.'

Hechler snatched up the gunnery handset. 'This is the Captain. I am turning to starboard. Bring the after turrets to bear on the enemy!' They had a better chance with four turrets in action.

He said, 'Alter course. Steer Zero-seven-zero.'

He raised his glasses again and winced as the fire-gong preceded the violent crash of the main armament. Kröll was using each turret in sequence, so that the bombardment seemed unbroken and deafening.

Jaeger wiped a smokestain from his cheek and gasped, 'The Admiral, sir!'

Leitner strode across the bridge, his silk scarf no longer so white.

He snapped, 'Can't see a damned thing up there. Too much bloody smoke.' He gritted his teeth as the two after turrets fired, gun by gun, the great shells shrieking past the ship and lifting towards the unseen enemy. They sounded like express trains.

Leitner shaded his eyes to look for the destroyer. If there were any survivors they were left far astern, forgotten.

Hechler waited for the guns to shift slightly and asked, 'Can I signal *Lübeck* to take station again?' He grimaced as the guns thundered out once more, their long orange tongues showing that Kröll was using semi-armour-piercing shells.

The intercom shouted, '*Straddling!* Two hits!'

Leitner scowled. 'Get up there, Theissen! I want to know what we're hitting today!' He seemed to realise what Hechler had said. 'No. Let Rau have his fun. He can take the lead.'

Flash-flash. Flash-flash. The blink of gunfire, partly masked by a mist along the horizon. It looked like copper-coloured smoke. The screeching hiss of a falling salvo and then the tall waterspouts which betrayed the fall of the enemy's shells made every glass turn towards the *Lübeck*.

Leitner said, 'Not even a straddle.'

The intercom shouted again. 'Another hit!' Somebody sealed behind thick steel was actually cheering. Or going mad.

'Gunnery officer, sir.' The lieutenant named Ahlmann looked pale, and was biting his lower lip as another salvo screamed out of the sky and burst into towering columns of spray. They seemed to take an age to fall, as if they were solid.

'Captain?'

Kröll said between explosions, 'We've sunk a wing escort and have hit two merchantmen. One ship is leaving the convoy, range closing. I would say it's a cruiser by her size and speed.'

More waterspouts shot from the sea, changing from white to copper in the weird light.

Hechler stared at the *Lübeck*, which was almost stern-on, her turrets trained hard round to bear on the enemy. Where his own ship should be. The bridge quivered again and yet again and Hechler could feel the din of gunfire probing into his ears like hot wires.

'Enemy in sight, sir! Bearing Red four-five!' Hechler lifted his glasses and scanned the distant mist. No longer empty. A dull, blunt silhouette suddenly wreathed in smoke as her guns fired at extreme range.

Hechler did not lower his glasses. 'Tell the Gunnery Officer to concentrate on the cruiser.' The forward turrets fired instantly, but it was too far away to see the results.

He heard the gunnery intercom mutter, 'Short.' Then Kröll's voice. 'Four hundred metre bracket!' A pause. '*Fire!*'

'Straddling!'

Leitner clasped his hands together. 'Signal *Lübeck* to go for the convoy. We'll take care of this upstart!'

'Two hits!' The rest was drowned by a violent explosion and as Hechler twisted towards *Lübeck* he saw smoke and flame burst from below her bridge and spread upwards and outwards in a fiery scarlet mushroom.

Lübeck was altering course again, her forward guns firing and recoiling as she concentrated on the convoy as ordered.

The British cruiser had been hit too, but there was no let-up in her gunnery or its accuracy.

The next salvo straddled the *Lübeck* as if she was smashing through columns of ice, and another fire had broken out aft, the smoke trailing astern in an oily screen.

Hechler saw a boatswain's mate start with shock, his eyes glow like twin coals as the *Lübeck* received another direct hit. She was slowing down, her bow-wave dwindling.

The speaker intoned, 'A hit!'

Hechler tried to keep his glasses steady. It was as if they were all struck by some terrible fever. Nothing would hold still, only the guns which fired again and again until thought became impossible. He saw the glow of fires amidst the smoke and knew that the enemy too had been badly hit.

Kröll announced, 'Convoy's scattering, sir. Cruiser's disengaging.'

Leitner snapped, 'What about the other escorts?'

'Some destroyers, I think, sir.' He sounded guarded, aware that he was speaking with his admiral.

The first merchantmen were now in view, ungainly and pathetic as they tried to head away from the oncoming warships.

The damaged cruiser was standing off with two of the destroyers closing around her to take her in tow if need be, or to make a last stand against *Prinz Luitpold*.

'Shift target! *Open fire!*'

The merchantmen had no hope of survival. One by one they were straddled and set ablaze until smoke stretched across the horizon like a dense curtain.

'Cease firing.' Hechler glanced at the conning-tower, knowing that Gudegast would be watching the helpless merchantmen burn and die. Would be recalling his own life in a peaceful timber ship. There were others in his command who would see beyond the destruction, who would feel disgust as their mindless companions cheered and slapped one another on the back.

The enemy cruiser had been outgunned from the start, but it only took a lucky shell. That was different. But merchant ships were vital to the enemy, who knew that each convoy route had to be kept open, no matter at what cost.

Hechler said quietly, 'In my opinion we should return to Norway, sir.' He stood his ground as Leitner stared at him. '*Lübeck* is down by the head. Even under tow –'

Froebe called, 'Signal from *Lübeck*. *Unable to make more than six knots. Request assistance.*'

Hechler watched his admiral. That must have cost Rau a lot, he thought.

Leitner shrugged. 'Signal the senior officer, destroyers, to escort *Lübeck* back to base.' He watched the lamp stammering, the young signalman's face white as he shuttered off the signal. The aftermath of battle. A convoy destroyed; God alone knew how many had died in the twinkling of an eye, or so it seemed.

Lübeck's signal lamp flashed again, almost hidden by the dense smoke which billowed from her lower bridge. Through his glasses Hechler could see the splinter holes in her funnels, the great crater left by a direct hit. But the fires were under control.

'From *Lübeck*, sir. *I require a tow.*'

Leitner said, 'Has the destroyer leader acknowledged?' He sounded more impatient than concerned.

'Acknowledged, sir.'

'Very well.' Leitner seemed to take a long breath. 'Discontinue the action, Captain. Phase Two, *if* you please.'

He turned as the smoke-grimed camera crew emerged from where they had been hiding.

Leitner went to the prettier of the two girls and pinched her chin.

'Warm work, eh, my child?'

She stared after him, still too dazed to understand any of it.

'Fall out action stations.' Hechler picked up the damage control telephone. 'Viktor? This is the Captain. Come up, will you. We have disengaged.'

Gudegast already had his orders. He spoke on his own intercom. 'On new course and speed, sir. Revolutions for twenty knots.' It was all he said, or had to say.

Even the men who had appeared on deck as they were stood down from first-degree readiness must have felt it, like a sickness as their ship turned away from the others, the strange light playing into shadows through upperworks and guns, leaving her wake in a wide, crisp arc.

Rau would be watching. Cursing them and their ship, Leitner most of all. But he was too good a sailor to speak out even with a bitter signal as the sea opened up between them.

Left to the wolves. The British would be out for blood, and every aircraft which could be flown from the nearest carrier would be after Rau's *Lübeck*. And he would know it. In the same way that the captain of the *Glow-worm* had known, or the pilots of the two elderly Swordfish. Death or glory. It was no choice.

Gudegast came to the bridge and waited for Hechler to see him.

Hechler said, 'In ten minutes I'll join you in the chart-room.'

Gudegast nodded, his beard on his chest. He knew what Hechler meant. In ten minutes *Lübeck* and the others would be too far astern to matter.

He watched Hechler's grave features and did not know whether to pity him or to thank God he was in command.

He had seen one of the merchantmen die. A big freighter, high out of the water, in ballast. That feeling. *Going home.*

Gudegast decided to make a sketch of the unknown victim.

For the first time in his life he was suddenly afraid.

That evening as *Prinz Luitpold* steamed south-west into the Norwegian Sea she was greeted by a thick mist which cut down the visibility to two miles.

All signs of the brief attack on the convoy were cleared away, and ammunition racks and magazines were refilled and ready for instant action.

Every turn of the great triple screws carried them further and further from land, paring away the safety margin should they have to turn and run for home again.

Hechler had to admit there was some value in Leitner's confidence. Every radio message and intercepted signal was checked and plotted by Gudegast and his team, while high above all of them their new, triumphant radar kept up a constant search for unwelcome visitors. A pack of U-boats had forced home an attack on the big eastbound Russian convoy, and every available British warship was apparently engaged. The flimsy plan might just work, he thought, and *Lübeck* would reach Norwegian waters where she could carry out her repairs. Hechler could not accept that part. It stuck in his throat like a bitter taste. To leave *Lübeck* to her fate had been part of the plan, but at no time had Leitner allowed for such a spirited defence of the convoy by the lone British cruiser.

When he had voiced his opinion to Leitner the admiral had given him a dry smile.

'*You*, Dieter, of all people? I thought you had the stomach for this mission!'

There was no point in pressing the argument. It was said that an open row between the captain of the *Bismarck* and his admiral had sealed her fate as much as enemy gunnery.

Hechler considered it. They had destroyed the convoy, just as the enemy had tried to finish them in return. It was war. He thought of the radar and was glad of it. Apart from its vast superiority over anything else they had used, its range meant that they had some warning of possible attack by sea or air forces. It meant that the company need not stand at action stations all day and night. They could sleep for four hours at a time off-watch. It was little enough, but they were used to it. To lie down, even for a few moments, made all the difference. Escape.

Despite the frantic manoeuvring to avoid the torpedo, there

101

had been no damage in the ship, apart from some broken crockery in the main galley.

There had been plenty of minor injuries, two men scalded in the boiler-room when they had been hurled from their feet, another with a broken leg after pitching down a ladder to the deck, and several other casualties.

One of the latter was Erika Franke, who had suffered a severe sprain to her wrist.

The medical report had been handed to Hechler with all the other items from the various parts of the ship. It was customary for the doctor to report in person, but he had sent a brief message to say he had too many casualties. Nervousness at meeting him, or a kind of arrogance, Hechler did not know. Yet.

Theil joined him on the bridge, his coat glistening as if it had been raining. The mist was wet and made everything shine in the failing light.

Hechler said, 'We seem to be clear, Viktor.' He spoke quietly. The men on watch were obviously straining their ears. Perhaps this lull after the roar of gunfire seemed like an anti-climax, or intimated that they had the sea to themselves.

He looked up at the sky, at Leitner's flag curling damply above the ship. 'We shall stand-to tonight.'

Theil looked away. 'Do you still intend to run south of Iceland, sir?'

Hechler nodded. 'Unless we're challenged, yes. At this time of year there's no advantage in taking the northern route through the Denmark Strait. Too much daylight, too many air patrols. If we head between Iceland and the Faeroe Islands it will give us 150 miles on either beam to play with.'

Theil grunted. 'Do you think we'll get through, sir?'

Hechler watched two seamen carrying an empty stretcher into the shelter of the forward turret. It made him think of the girl. Theil was right to question him; he would be required to execute Leitner's wishes should anything happen to him. He looked strained, anxious. He was not worried about their mission, it would be out of character. He was a book man, and rarely trusted personal opinion. Maybe that was why he had never been recommended for a command. No, he was worried about his missing wife. That was bad. You could not afford that kind of diversion when you were at sea. It could be fatal. For all of them.

Hechler listened to the steady vibration, felt the confident power of the great engines. They had been doing thirty knots when they had made their turn. She could manage thirty-five if need be. Even a destroyer would find her a difficult one to outpace.

It seemed to get darker as they hurried to the south-west, the night an ally, their only friend in this hostile sea.

Hechler tried to contain the excitement. It was like heady wine. After the stark pictures of battle and burning ships, the prospect of actually getting into the Atlantic seemed suddenly real and clean.

Theil saw the lines at Hechler's mouth soften and wondered how he would have felt in his place.

Like all the senior officers in the ship Theil had studied their orders with great care. The plan was marked both by its audacity, and its very scale. The naval staff under von Hanke must have been working on it for many months just in case the chance presented itself. Perhaps too many people were already involved? Secrecy was vital; without it they might as well give up now.

Von Hanke's son was a U-boat commander, or had been until he had been lost in the Atlantic. Maybe he had first given the old admiral the idea. For two years at the beginning of the war, U-boats had been hampered by the length of time it took them to reach their patrol areas in the Western Ocean, with the same delay in returning to bases in France to refuel and rearm.

To counteract this a building programme had started to produce a flotilla of huge submarines which could stay at sea for months. Their sole duty was to carry fuel and stores for their smaller, operational consorts. In prearranged positions on a specially charted grid, a rendezvous could be made or rejected according to the needs of each U-boat commander. It more than trebled their time at sea, and the enemy's losses had mounted accordingly. Nobody ever mentioned what this extra time on active service did to the morale of the submarine crews.

Now, these same supply submarines, milch-cows, were to be

employed as tankers for the *Prinz*. Daring it certainly was. Practical? Nobody knew, as it had never been done before.

None of the others had voiced any doubts, and after today they might be glad they had not shown any lack of confidence. Once again the ship had come through unscathed. It was a pity about the *Lübeck*, but if it had your number on it, there was not much you could do. *Lübeck* had got off lightly, Theil thought. While she was in port, licking her wounds and enjoying all the glory, the *Prinz* would be in the Atlantic, in the thick of it. It was some comfort to know that a pin's head laid on a chart of the Western Ocean represented as far as a man could see in any direction.

Hechler said suddenly, 'I was sorry to hear about your wife.'

Theil stared at him and then at the nearest of the watchkeepers. He lowered his voice. 'The admiral?'

'He had to tell me, Viktor. I would have been informed anyway if Leitner was not aboard. What's the matter, did you think I'd see you as a lesser man?'

Theil felt the colour draining from his face. 'It makes no difference to my ability. None whatever, and anyone –'

Hechler slid from his chair and moved his legs to get rid of the stiffness.

'I'm going to the sick-bay while it's quiet. Take over.' He eyed him calmly. 'Shake the load off your back, Viktor. I just wanted you to know that I am concerned for you, not your bloody ability!'

Theil was still staring after him as he clattered down the internal ladder.

It felt strange, wrong to be off the bridge while the ship was at sea. Hechler saw the surprise on the faces of his men when he passed them while he made his way down two decks to the sick-bay. As a boy he had always hated hospitals, mostly because he had had to visit his gassed father in one; that was when they had promised there was still a good chance of a cure.

His poor mother, he thought, facing up to those daily visits, passing all the other veterans. No legs, no arms, gassed, blinded, some would have been better off lying in the mud of Flanders.

And always the bright cheerfulness of the nurses. *Coming*

along nicely. As well as can be expected. It had all been lies.

He wondered how his father was managing now. He would soon be reading about the *Prinz* and their exploits.

His father, so sick but quietly determined to stay alive, was beyond pride. Love would be a better word, he thought.

The sick-quarters were white and brightly lit. Two medical attendants were putting bottles into shelves, and there was a lot of broken glass in a bucket. The same violent turn had done damage here too.

Some of the injured men were dozing in their cots, and one tried to sit to attention when he saw his captain enter, his plastered arm sticking straight out like a white tusk.

Hechler removed his cap and forced a grin.

'Easy there. Rest while you can, eh?'

The new doctor was not at all as he had expected. He was forty years old but looked much older. He had a heavy, studious face with gold-rimmed glasses. A lawyer, or a school teacher, you might think if you saw him as a civilian.

He made to stand but Hechler closed the door of the sick-bay and sat down. Then he pulled out his pipe and said, 'Is this all right?'

Karl-Heinz Stroheim watched him warily, one hand plucking at the three gold stripes with the Rod of Aesculapius on his sleeve.

He said, 'I have dealt with all the casualties, Captain.'

Hechler lit his pipe. A good feeling, almost sensuous, after being deprived on the bridge.

'I thought we should meet, so –' He blew out some smoke. 'So, Mohammet and the Mountain, you see?'

'I'm honoured.'

'You'll find this a different appointment from your last. The barracks at Wilhelmshaven, right?'

The man nodded. 'Before that, well, you know about it too.'

'You were in trouble.'

A flash of anger came and went in Stroheim's brown eyes. 'I was too valuable to be thrown out. They put me in uniform instead.'

'No disgrace in that.' Hechler tried not to listen to the engines' beat. So much closer here.

He asked casually, 'Abortions, wasn't it?'

Stroheim's jaw dropped. 'How did you know?'

'I didn't. I guessed.' He smiled gravely. 'And I shall put down your lack of respect to the suddenness of your appointment, right?'

Stroheim thrust his hands beneath the table. 'I – I am sorry, Captain. I went through a lot. One day they will accept my views. Too late for many, I fear. But I have always believed –' he hesitated, as if he expected Hechler to stop or reprimand him – 'a woman must have the right to choose.' His voice was suddenly bitter, contemptuous. 'There should be a better reason for having a child than producing soldiers and more mothers for Germany.'

Hechler stood up, his eyes on a bulkhead telephone. 'We'll talk again.'

Stroheim got to his feet. 'I'd enjoy that.'

Hechler glanced round the little office. A pile of records and a portable gramophone, some books, and a box of chessmen.

Hechler said, 'Don't make this too much like home. Mix with the others. It's not good to be cut off.'

Stroheim took off his glasses and held them to the light.

'Like you, do you mean, Captain?'

Hechler turned away. 'I don't need a consultation just now, thank you!'

He paused by the door. 'Take good care of my men. *They* did not ask to be here, so you see, they are like you, eh?'

He made to leave and almost collided with Erika Franke, her left hand bandaged and in a sling.

She gave a wry smile. 'Next time you change direction, Captain, please let me know. I need both hands for flying, you know!'

He looked past her at the doctor. 'I was sorry to hear of your injury.'

She laughed. It was the first time he had seen her really laugh.

He said, 'Can I see you to your quarters?'

She became serious, and gave him a mock scowl.

'So correct, so proper, Captain.' She relented. 'I shall walk with you. I find the ladders a bit difficult at the moment.'

They reached the upper deck, the passageway in shadows, the steel doors clipped shut.

She said, 'I would like to visit the bridge again. I hate being shut away down here. I feel trapped.'

'Any time.' He watched her, the way she moved her head, the colour of her eyes. He had hoped to see her. The doctor had been an excuse.

A messenger skidded to a halt and saluted. 'There is a message from the bridge, Captain.'

Hechler strode to a handset which was clipped to the grey steel and cranked the handle.

He heard Theil's voice, the muted sound of the sea and wind.

Theil said in a hushed voice, 'The admiral had a signal, sir. *Lübeck* was sunk.'

Hechler replaced the handset very slowly.

She watched him, her eyes concerned. 'May I ask, Captain?'

He looked at her emptily. '*Lübeck*'s gone.'

He could see it as if he was there. As if it was now.

She said quietly, 'You didn't want to leave her, did you?' She saw the question in the brightness of his blue eyes.

She shrugged and winced; she had forgotten her injury. 'I was told. Everyone knew. They're very fond of their young captain, you know.'

He rested his hand on one of the door-clips. 'There are no secrets in a ship, no matter what they say.' He faced her again. 'Yes, I wanted to stay with her. Now she's gone.' He thought of the burning convoy.

They had had their revenge. He touched the girl's sound arm. 'Later, then.'

He opened the heavy door and stepped out into the damp air. *Lübeck* had been sacrificed. He quickened his pace to the first ladder, oblivious of the watchful gun crews.

It must not have been in vain.

8

Flotsam

The South African naval base of Simonstown was packed to capacity with warships of every class and size. It was like a melting-pot, a division between two kinds of war made more apparent by the vessels themselves and their livery. The darker hues of grey and garish dazzle paint of the Atlantic, at odds with the paler hulls of ships from the Indian Ocean and beyond.

Powerful cruisers which had the capacity and range to cover the vast distances beyond the Cape of Good Hope seemed to make the greater contrast with a cluster of stubby Canadian corvettes which had fought their convoy all the way from Newfoundland.

Freighters and oilers, ammunition vessels and troopers. There was even a cleanly painted hospital ship.

The largest cruiser in Simonstown on this particular afternoon lay alongside the jetty, her White Ensign hanging limply in the harsh sunlight.

She was HMS *Wiltshire*, a big, 10,000-ton vessel, typical of a class which had been constructed in accordance with the Washington Treaty in the late twenties. She was heavily armed with eight, eight-inch guns in four turrets, with many smaller weapons to back up her authority. An elderly Walrus flying-boat perched sedately on the catapult amidships, and her three tall funnels gave the ship a deceptively outdated appearance. She stood very high from the oily water, and because of her comparatively light armour plating her living quarters were both airy and spacious when compared with other men-of-war.

It was Sunday, and apart from the duty watch and men under punishment *Wiltshire* was deserted. Officers and ratings alike took every opportunity to get ashore, to visit Cape Town and enjoy the colourful sights, untouched by war.

In his day cabin Captain James Cook Hemrose, Distinguished Service Order, Royal Navy, sat beneath a deckhead fan and regarded his pink gin while he wondered if it was prudent to take another. On one chair lay his best cap which he had worn for Divisions and prayers that morning. Beside another stood his golf clubs, a reminder of the match he had had to cancel.

He was a heavy man, and in his white shirt and Bermuda shorts looked ungainly. There were dark patches of sweat at each armpit despite the fans and he hated the oppressive heat.

He was in his late forties, but service life had been hard on him. He looked older, much older, and what was worse, he felt it.

The door opened and the ship's commander entered quietly.

Hemrose gestured heavily to the sideboard. 'Have a pink Plymouth, Toby. Do you good.'

The commander looked at the signals on the table and said, 'It's all true then, sir?'

'Pour me one while you're at it. Not too much bitters.'

The commander smiled. As if he did not know his ways. He had been with him over a year. The Atlantic, convoys round the Cape, Ceylon, India. It suited the commander. Routine, and often boring. But you could keep the Atlantic and Arctic runs. Let the glory boys do them if that was the war they wanted.

'Yes, it's true.' Hemrose's eyes were distant. 'The Jerries have put one of their big cruisers to sea. They think it might be *Prinz Luitpold*.' His eyes hardened into focus. 'I hope to God it is.'

The commander sipped his gin. Just right. 'She won't get down here. Not at this stage of the war.' When Hemrose remained silent he added, 'I mean, it's just not on, sir.'

Hemrose sighed. The commander, Toby Godson, was a well-meaning fool. He ran a smart ship, and that was enough. Until the signal had arrived anyway.

Hemrose recalled his excitement, although he would die rather than display it. The war might indeed end soon, maybe even next year. Being captain of a big cruiser, a ship well known as any of her class, was some compensation. But he had seen himself, still in command when the war ended. Then what? Passed over for promotion again, or merely chucked on the beach like his father before him.

They had some saying about it. 'God and the Navy we adore, when danger threatens, but not before!'

He looked at the lengthy signal from the far-off Admiralty. As from today he was promoted to acting commodore, to take upon himself the command of a small squadron. To take all necessary steps to seek out and engage the German raider should she manage to penetrate the defences and come to the South Atlantic.

It was unlikely, as Godson had said. But it had given him a well-needed boost. *Acting commodore*, a temporary appointment at the best of times. But it was his chance. The all-important step to flag-rank. It was not unknown in this war. Harwood, who had commanded the little squadron which had run the raider *Graf Spee* to earth, had made flag-rank immediately afterwards. It was something to think about.

One of his new squadron was already here in Simonstown. She was the small Leander class cruiser *Pallas* of the Royal New Zealand Navy. She looked like a destroyer compared with the *Wiltshire*, but her captain and her ship's company were well trained, and had been together since she had commissioned.

He heaved himself up and walked to one of the scuttles, one which faced away from the glare.

He thought vaguely of his home in Hampshire. His wife Beryl would be pleased when she heard. There were too many naval officers' wives who lived in the county whose husbands seemed to have been promoted ahead of him.

Acting commodore. He nodded. It sounded good. Old world; he liked that. He was distantly related to Captain James Cook and was proud of it, although it did not seem to have helped him over the years.

The commander asked carefully, 'I'd forgotten, sir. You crossed swords with *Prinz Luitpold* before. North Cape, wasn't it?'

'*I* don't forget.' He stared through the scuttle. Two sailors in a dinghy were calling up to some black girls on the jetty. A bit of black velvet, as his father would have said.

The commander ignored the warning signs. 'They say that Rear-Admiral Leitner's in command.'

Hemrose glowered. 'I don't give a bloody damn about *him*. Her captain's the man – Hechler. He was in command at North Cape, when –'

The commander said, 'She's a miniature battle-cruiser, sir. Makes our armour plate look like cardboard.'

Hemrose ignored him. 'Came out of the snow like a cliff. It was gun-for-gun.' He looked around the pleasant cabin, remembering it as it had been. 'This place was riddled, like a bloody pepper pot.'

The commander had lost his way. 'She made off anyway, sir.'

'Aye, she did that. Just as well. It was a right cock-up, I can tell you.' He saw the sailors paddling away. They had probably seen him looking at them. 'I hope it *is* Hechler in command. I'll get him this time.' He gave a rueful grin. 'Now he's like I was at North Cape.'

'How so, sir?'

Hemrose laughed out loud. 'He's got his fucking admiral breathing down his neck, that's why!'

The commander downed his gin. He was used to the captain's coarse speech and blunt manner. Perhaps his temporary promotion would mellow him. But it could not last. The fleet would catch the German raider before they got a look-in.

Hemrose rubbed his hands. 'Recall all the senior officers. I want 'em aboard by the dog watches.' He eyed his golf clubs. 'See how *they* like it.'

The commander nodded. 'I see –'

'You don't, Toby.' He became grave. 'I meant what I said. For the first time in my life their bloody lordships have given me a free hand, and by God I intend to use it.' He clapped him on the shoulder. 'Make a signal to *Pallas*. Captain repair on board.'

Godson said unhappily, 'He's playing cricket with the South Africans, sir.'

Hemrose beamed. 'Good. I want us out of harbour by this time tomorrow and I'll need you to form your own team to monitor all despatches and signals. Every damn thing.' He slammed his fist into his palm. 'So get that Kiwi aboard, *chop, chop*!' He bustled to the sideboard and groped for some ice, but it had all melted. He slopped another large gin into his glass.

'*Lübeck*'s gone to the bottom anyway. That's one less. Scuttled herself when our lot were almost up to her.' He frowned. 'I wonder if Hechler knows?' He turned. 'Somehow I doubt it.'

But he was alone.

Kapitän zur See Dieter Hechler closed the conning-tower's steel door and pushed through the fireproof curtain.

Outside it was dusk, but in here it was like night, with only the chart-table lights and automatic pilot casting any glow on the thick armour plate.

Hechler could sense the tension as well as the controlled excitement. Gudegast was leaning on the vibrating table, his face in shadow, only his beard holding the light. His team stood around him, boys most of them, in various attitudes of attention as Hechler joined them.

Hechler looked at the chart, the neat calculations and pencilled fixes. Then at the plot-table which told him all the rest. Course, and speed, time and distance, variations, fed in by a dozen repeaters from radar, gyro and log.

'We're through.'

Gudegast nodded. Then he pointed his dividers to the chart where the course had crossed the Iceland–Faeroe Rise, where the seabed rose inexplicably like a hump. To U-boats and blockade-runners alike it was known as the *meat grinder*. Not a good place for a submarine to run deep to avoid a depth-charge attack, and no scope for a surface vessel to manoeuvre.

And yet they had made it. This great ship had passed through the 300-mile gap without opposition. Not a ship, not even a distant aircraft had been sighted.

Luck, a miracle, or a direct result of von Hanke's decoy, it was impossible to tell.

The curtain swirled aside again and Leitner strode in with his aide behind him.

He stared unwinking at the chart and said, 'We did it. As planned.'

He looked at the darkened figures around him. 'Two days since the convoy, and now we are here!' He slapped the chart with unusual fervour. 'The Atlantic, gentlemen! They said it could not be done!'

Some of the men were shaking hands and grinning at each other; only Gudegast remained unmoved and grim-faced.

He said, 'I should like to alter course in fifteen minutes, sir.'

Hechler nodded. 'I shall come up.'

A seaman called, 'From the bridge, sir.' He held out the telephone.

Hechler shook himself. Fatigue or anxiety, which was it? He had not heard it ring.

It was Froebe, who was in charge of the watch.

'Radar has reported a faint echo at Red one-oh, sir. About five miles.'

That was close. Too close. Hechler calmed himself. 'What is it, man?'

He could picture Froebe shrugging his gaunt shoulders. 'Very small, sir, barely registers.' Someone shouted in the background. 'It will be dark very soon.'

Hechler said, 'Alter course to intercept.' He felt Gudegast brush past him to adjust the chart.

Leitner muttered, 'Something small, eh? God damn them, it might have been a submarine's conning-tower. At five miles anything might happen!' Another flaw. The unseen observer.

Froebe spoke again, relieved. 'We've identified it, sir. It's a boat.'

Hechler hurried from the conning tower, not caring if Leitner was in agreement or not.

On the main bridge it was quite cold, and the clouds had thickened considerably.

He raised his glasses and felt the deck tilt very slightly as the helm went over.

Then he saw it and felt his taut muscles relax. There would be no attack from this lonely boat. It was a common enough sight on the Atlantic, but new to most of his company, he thought.

Theil had arrived on the bridge, panting hard as he snatched some binoculars from a messenger.

He said, 'A boat full of corpses.' He sounded angry, as if the drifting boat had wronged him in some way.

Hechler watched the boat. Would their journey ever end, he wondered?

'Slow ahead, all engines.'

Theil was peering at him with disbelief. 'You're not going to stop?'

Hechler said, 'Boatswain's mate, call away the accident boat.'

The boat would automatically have an experienced petty officer in charge. He glanced at young Jaeger. 'You go. Keep your wits about you.'

Theil said between his teeth, 'In the name of God, sir, we're a sitting target.'

Hechler said quietly, 'Keep your voice down, Viktor.' He gripped his glasses more tightly. A trick of the fading light, or had he seen a movement amongst the silent, patient figures in the listing boat?

'Stop engines!' He hurried to the side as the motorboat hit the water and veered away on the dying bow-wave. Jaeger had only just clawed his way aboard in time.

He remarked, 'Someone's alive out there.' When Theil said nothing he added coldly, 'Would you have me fire on the boat?' He raised his glasses once more, sensing the rift between them. He saw the motorboat speeding across the swell, Jaeger looking astern at the cruiser and probably wondering what would happen if there was an attack.

He knew Leitner was beside him, could smell his cologne. But he kept his eyes on the little drama as the motorboat hooked

114

on and Jaeger with a petty officer scrambled over the gunwale. The petty officer was old Tripz. He was used to this kind of work. He saw Jaeger lean on the gunwale with a handkerchief to his mouth. Jaeger was not.

A signalman lowered his glasses. 'Two alive, sir.'

'Call the sick-bay.'

More feet on the ladder and he heard her thank a seaman for helping her through the gate. She was wearing her black leather jacket again, her hair ruffling in the breeze.

Theil moved aside so that she could stand between Hechler and the admiral.

How huge the ship looked as the long forecastle lifted and then fell again very slowly, the motion increasing as the last of the way went off the hull.

She asked, 'Just two?'

Hechler nodded. She was probably thinking of its futility.

Ships sunk and men killed, two aircraft shot down, and we stop because of these living dead. The unwritten law of the sea perhaps? Or to make up for those they had already left to die.

He saw her right hand grip the rail beneath the screen so tightly that her knuckles were white through the tanned skin.

When he glanced at her he saw moisture in her eyes, or were they tears?

Leitner remarked, 'Flotsam of war, my dear.'

She said huskily, 'My –' She tried again. 'I knew somebody who died at sea.'

Hechler glanced down at her. She looked sick. The motion was getting worse as the *Prinz* rose and dipped like a huge jugger-naut.

'Sit in the chair.' He took her elbow. 'Take some deep breaths.' Then, so that the others should not hear he added quietly, 'Stay in the air, little bird. The ocean can be a dirty place.'

He glanced across her head. 'Take over. I'm going to the sick-bay.'

Someone yelled, 'Boat's hooked on, sir!'

The motorboat rose swiftly on its falls, and Froebe asked, 'The lifeboat, Captain? Shall I have a shot put into it?'

'No.' He raised his glasses once more and knew she had turned in the chair to watch him. 'They have found their harbour. Leave them alone.'

A great tremor ran through the deck and he felt the men sighing with relief as the great screws began to beat out their track of white froth again.

Leitner called sharply, 'Find out what you can, eh?'

Hechler ran down the first ladder and paused, gripping it with both fists.

What is the matter with me? Is it that important?

He found Jaeger and Petty Officer Tripz already outside the sick-bay.

'All right?'

Jaeger made an effort, but he looked ghastly.

'All the rest were dead, sir.' He was reliving it. 'Bobbing about together as if they were really alive. The gulls had got to some of them –' he retched and old Tripz said, 'Easy, sir. You'll get used to it.'

Jaeger shook himself. 'We brought two of them aboard.' He stared at the deck for a long moment until he could continue. 'One of them is an officer. The other –' he shook violently. 'He wouldn't leave without the cat.'

'Cat?'

Tripz said, 'The animal was dead, sir. We left it in the boat.' He looked despairingly at the young officer. 'Must have been adrift for weeks.'

Hechler said, 'You did well.' He gave Tripz a meaning glance. 'Both of you, go to my steward. He'll give you something to warm you up.'

Tripz gave a sad grin. 'It was worth it then, sir.'

The doctor was wiping his hands on a towel, and Hechler saw that both blanket-wrapped survivors were lying in bunks inside the office and away from the injured sailors.

An armed seaman stood outside but it seemed unlikely their passengers would create any problems.

One, the young officer with two tarnished stripes on his sleeve, was conscious, but only just. Hollow-eyed and filthy, he was staring at the white deckhead with shock and disbelief.

The other man was much older with a white beard. Perhaps

116

he had already seen and done too much when his ship had been blasted from under him. He had his arms wrapped into a cradle, as he had been when Jaeger had found him, clutching the ship's cat to his body to protect it.

The doctor said, 'I've given them something, Captain. They'll sleep. I shall get them some hot soup later on.' He nodded to the pathetic belongings on the glass table. 'They were aboard the *Radnor Star*, a freighter.'

The officer was probably the second mate. He was too young for much else, Hechler thought. In charge of a lifeboat, perhaps the only officer to get away when the torpedo struck. Watching them die, one by one, until he was alone but for the old man with his dead cat. Some last thread of discipline had made him hold on. He had been in charge. What else could he have done?

The doctor took off his glasses and polished them as he had done at their first meeting.

He said, 'So this is the Atlantic, the *killing ground* they warned me about?'

Hechler looked at him. 'Don't be clever with me, Doctor!' He jerked open the door as the sentry snapped to attention. 'Report when they recover enough to speak.'

He waited outside, breathing hard, angry with the doctor, more so with himself for dropping the guard he had built up so carefully. When he reached the bridge he was greeted in silence. He looked for the drifting lifeboat but it had already disappeared into the darkness astern.

He walked to the gratings, and with a start realised she was still sitting in the tall chair, wrapped about with somebody's heavy watchcoat.

She did not say anything and he was grateful. He saw Jaeger return to his place on the bridge, the way Gudegast moved across to pat his arm. That would mean more than anything to Jaeger just now. He was accepted. One of them.

And what of me? The captain without a heart? Do they imagine I have no feelings?

He stared down with surprise as she placed her hand on his wrist. She did not move it or grip with it. It lay there, separate, as if to listen.

117

She said quietly, 'I am here, Captain. I shared it with you. I saw it through your eyes.'

Hechler looked at her neat hand and wanted to seize it, press it against himself. She had understood, as if he had shouted aloud.

He said, 'I would like to talk –' He felt her hand move away very slightly. 'Later, afterwards –' He was lost for the right words.

She said, 'Afterwards may not be ours, Captain.' She slid from the chair and handed the coat to a seaman with a quick smile. Then she melted into the shadows and he heard one of his men assisting her on the ladder.

He touched the chair; it was still warm from her body. He climbed into it and wedged his feet against the voice-pipes.

She would probably laugh in his face if he even laid a hand on her. What about the man who had been lost at sea? She had nearly said something else. 'My lover' perhaps?

Afterwards may not be ours. Her words seemed to linger in his mind. His head lolled and he was instantly asleep.

The *Prinz Luitpold*'s petty officers' mess was in complete darkness apart from shaded blue lamps and one light above one of the tables. A different story from an hour before when the men off watch had been watching a film in the other part of the mess, one of the luxuries which went with their status. The film had been a noisy display of German armed strength, backed up between the excited commentary by rousing music from *Tannhäuser*.

The air had been electric, and had remained so since the intercom announcement from the bridge that they were forging deeper and deeper into the Atlantic, unchallenged as they were unbeaten.

Hans Stoecker sat in the pool of light, sipping a mug of bitter coffee, restless, unwilling to sleep although he had only just come off watch.

Opposite him, his grey head nodding in a doze, was old Oskar Tripz. His chin was covered in grey stubble so that he looked almost ancient.

His eyes opened and he stared at Stoecker, his gaze searching. Trying to discover something, to make up his mind.

'Why don't you turn in?' Tripz sniffed at the coffee and shuddered. 'What do they make this muck from – acorns?'

A dark shape shrouded in blankets called irritably, 'Hold your noise! Think of the watchkeepers!'

Tripz grinned. In harbour the mess housed a hundred petty officers, the backbone of the ship, as of any other. Now, with many of them on watch it seemed quiet, deserted by comparison.

Stoecker lowered his voice. 'I keep thinking about *Lübeck*.'

'You're always thinking about something. You should keep your mind on your exams. Do you more good. Let the bloody officers think. It's what they're paid for.'

Stoecker persisted, 'I mean, *Lübeck* should have been with us surely? Together we'd have made a stronger force.'

'Easier to find too.' Tripz rubbed his chin with a rasping motion. 'I reckon she was meant to return to base.'

Stoecker stared at him. 'We wouldn't just leave her!'

Tripz shrugged. 'Who knows anything any more? They'd sell their mothers for a bit of glory.'

'You don't mean that.'

Tripz became impatient. 'I've got more important things on my mind at present.' He leaned across the table until their faces were only a foot apart. 'Those boxes, for instance.'

They both glanced along the silent bunks like conspirators, then Stoecker asked, 'Do you know what's in them?'

'It's all in that letter. If half of it's true, and I see no reason why that prisoner should lie about it, our gallant admiral is carrying a bloody fortune with him, though I can't imagine why.'

Stoecker blinked. 'What kind of fortune, I – I mean, how much?'

The man watched him grimly. 'Do you know how much the *Prinz* cost to build?'

Stoecker smiled. 'You're joking –'

Tripz tapped his arm with a thick finger. 'You could build three ships like this one with what he's got tucked away.' He dropped his voice again to a hoarse whisper. '*If* that letter tells the truth.'

119

Stoecker thought of the man's face in the air vent, his despair. He often thought about it, also the man's quiet courage in the shadow of death. *Murder*. The word was fixed in his mind.

Tripz seemed satisfied with the young man's acceptance; he had never doubted his sincerity.

He said, 'It seems that the prisoner was writing to some friends. To warn them that the boxes were being moved.'

Stoecker recalled the burnt-out shop, the crude insults.

Tripz continued, 'His friends were Jewish, right enough. One of them was a jeweller. Probably why he was still at large.' He dropped his eyes. 'Or was.'

'I still don't understand.'

Tripz's gaze softened. 'You wouldn't, Hans.' He hurried on. 'All I do know is that we're probably carrying a bloody great fortune. If so, my guess is that Rear-Admiral Leitner's no more entitled to it than we are.' He changed tack before Stoecker could speak. 'What will you do when this lot's over, Hans? Always assuming you're still in one lump, of course?'

Stoecker hesitated. 'The navy. A career, I thought –'

The finger jabbed his arm again. 'Suppose we lose? D'you ever think about that?' He did not wait for an answer. 'Me? I'll be good for nothing, no matter who wins. I saw it after the last war. You couldn't even sell your bloody medals for a crust of bread. No, peace will be hard, even for the kids.' He shook his head. 'They'll toss me out like so much waste.'

Stoecker felt vaguely uneasy. 'Anyway, we'll probably never know. The boxes are locked away, under guard.'

'I know. The admiral's got one key, the captain's got the other.' He tapped the side of his nose. 'But there's a duplicate, my young friend.' He saw his astonishment and grinned, showing his uneven teeth. 'You've caught on. It's mine.'

A figure, naked but for a lifejacket, lurched past on the way to the heads.

Tripz stood up. 'Say nothing, or we'll both end up on the wrong side of a firing-squad. And that would be a pity, eh?' He leaned over and patted his shoulder. 'Thought you should know. In case I stop a bit of the Tommies' steel. After all, we're partners, right?'

He walked away, leaving Stoecker alone beneath the solitary light.

The *Prinz Luitpold*'s senior medical officer looked up from his book and saw the girl standing in the open door.

'Can't you sleep either?'

She walked to a chair and glanced at the two motionless survivors, swaying gently in their white cots.

'My wrist. It's bothering me. If I lie on it –'

He took her hand and reached out for some scissors. The girl was very attractive. It was hard to think of her as the professional flier, as good as any Luftwaffe ace, they said. It seemed wrong that she should be here, in this iron machine.

'You're new aboard the ship?' She had a direct way of asking. As if she was telling him.

He looked at her. She seemed strained, and there were shadows under her tawny eyes.

'I am. Lost amongst strangers.' It seemed to amuse him.

She said, 'Call me Erika. If you like.'

He cut the last of the bandage. 'I do like.'

Her skin felt hot, feverish. He remembered all those other women. The scandal which had almost got him into prison, a ruined man. But the women who came to him 'in trouble' were people of influence, or those who had powerful friends. Curious that such power could be smashed because of an unwanted baby, he thought.

Like the captain's wife, for instance. Well-bred from an old family, she was always in the centre of society, that jungle which was safe only for the privileged few. It was strange how the high party members, *men of the people* as they liked to be known, were so in awe of women like her.

He wondered if the captain really knew what she was like. One of his colleagues had once described her as a thoroughly delectable whore. That doctor had been indiscreet in other ways too. Then one day he had simply disappeared.

He said, 'It is a bit stiff, er, Erika.'

She watched him, unsmiling. 'I have to fly in a day or so.'

'It will be all right by then.' What were they thinking of?

121

Flying? They would meet up with the enemy at any time now. The British would not give up until they had brought them to action.

She glanced at the gramophone and the pile of well-used records. She raised her eyebrows. 'Handel? You surprise me. Is it patriotic?'

She smiled then, at some private joke perhaps.

'I like it.'

'You always do what you like?'

'I try to.' He looked at her, and tried not to think of her on his examination couch, naked.

She said, 'I wanted to talk. I knew you would still be awake. It's not like a ship down here.'

He chuckled. 'I suppose not. I shall attempt to keep it that way.'

'I was with the Captain when these survivors were brought aboard.'

He said nothing and waited. So that was it. There was certainly nothing wrong with her wrist which could not wait until day-light.

She said, 'He is different from what I expected.'

'An enigma perhaps?'

She smiled at him. 'You are leading me.' She added, 'He seems to care so much about people. How can he do his work?'

Stroheim spread his hands. 'Perhaps it is tearing him apart. I do not know him that well. Yet.'

'But you know his wife, don't you?'

He started. 'How do you hear these things?'

'A friend told me.' She had been going to say *a little bird told me*. But at that instant she remembered his face, the concern in his voice as he had said so quietly to her, 'Stay in the air, little bird.' To use the expression loosely would seem like a betrayal, like sharing a secret.

Stroheim said vaguely, 'She is very beautiful.'

'I met her.' She thought of the other woman's searching stare, her arrogance giving way to caution when she realised who Erika was. Because she was a flier and had carried out a mission for the Führer, people often thought she too had influence. Yes, she recalled that stare, her perfect body, so carelessly displayed in the cutaway gown. Try as she might, she could not see her and the Captain together. Maybe they had both changed.

'Well, you know what she's like.'

'Are they still married, or anything?'

He warmed to her. '*Anything* would be closer, I believe.'

She opened and closed her left hand, her face expressionless as she tested the pain, the discomfort.

Stay in the air, little bird.

'I'll say goodnight then.' She looked at the two sleeping figures. Flotsam, Leitner had called them. 'Or, good morning now, I believe?'

He watched her leave and then reopened his book.

Every so often, even in the midst of danger and death there was one small light. Like a flower in a forest, a lone star.

He sighed and crossed his legs. She had made him feel human again.

9

Viewpoint

Apart from the regular swell the sea's face was like glass, blinding bright in the sunshine. There was a fine haze which never seemed to get any closer, so that there was no break between sea and sky. For the Atlantic it was unusual, even this far south.

The two ships stood close together as if for support, which was true, and at a greatly reduced speed appeared to be almost motionless above their quivering reflections.

The SS *Port St Clair*, a freighter of some 8,000 tons outward bound from Sierra Leone, had the second vessel in tow. It was a slow, painful passage, with the other ship yawing out clumsily until she seemed to be overtaking, before veering back again with all the maddening alterations of course and speed until they were under command once more.

The first mate of the leading ship watched his captain, who was standing out on the bridge wing, staring astern at their companion. It was almost funny, when you thought about it. Both the captains were rivals of many years, and yet that same rivalry seemed to join them more persistently than any tow-line.

The other ship, the SS *Dunedin Pioneer*, had joined the convoy with them at Freetown, but after a few days had broken down with engine trouble. It was hardly surprising, the mate thought, she was probably older than he was.

The convoy escorts had been unwilling to leave them astern of the main body of twelve ships on passage for Liverpool. At any other time the senior naval officer would have ordered the

Port St Clair, with her precious cargo of rice, New Zealand butter and meat, to keep station and leave the other ship to fend for herself until a tug could be sent from somewhere, or a hungry U-boat had found her.

But the rivalry, which over the years had often been akin to hatred, had carried the day.

The mate considered the news. A German raider at large in the Atlantic again. The navy had probably got it all wrong. The enemy warship had either returned to base, or had already clashed with Allied patrols.

It was a strange feeling to be out here, alone, on such a fine day. Soon the Atlantic would show its other face, but by then they would have turned round, and be on their way back to the sunshine and New Zealand.

He walked out on to the bridge wing and waited for the master to notice him. The latter had his stained cap tilted over his eyes as he watched the tow lift from the water, hesitate and then dip into it again.

He remarked, 'Bloody old cow.'

The mate replied, 'What about the raider?'

The master rubbed his bristled chin. He would not shave until they crossed the Liverpool Bar. There was no point in shaving while there was a chance of being blown up.

They had passed the Cape Verde Islands to starboard in the night, and tomorrow, or maybe the next day, would meet with ships of the screening squadron. Cruisers from Simonstown, it was said.

Half to himself he said, 'Should have left the old bugger.' He turned and eyed the mate cheerfully. 'If there *is* a raider, and that I doubt, it's a comfort to know that the convoy will run smack into it before we do! Justice for leaving us behind!' He chuckled.

The mate agreed and rested his hands on the rail, but withdrew them instantly with a curse. The bridge was like an oven. But you could keep Liverpool. A sailors' town, they said. Blackouts, air raids, and tarts outside the clubs who looked as if every one of those sailors had had a go at them. You could keep it.

Steam spurted from the ship astern, wavered around her poop and then faded away.

The master said unfeelingly, 'If his Chief can't get her going. I'll tow the sod all the way. That'll give him something to bite on!'

A whistle shrilled and the mate walked into the wheelhouse and hauled a little brass cylinder up the tube from the radio-room.

He returned to the glare and said sharply, 'Intercepted a signal. Convoy's under attack. German raider.' They stared at each other and the master hurried to the chart-room abaft the wheelhouse and snapped, 'Give it here. Where the bloody hell are they?'

He did not speak again until he had plotted the convoy's approximate course and bearing on the chart. 'Call up *Dunedin Pioneer*.' He held him with a grim stare. 'On the lamp. Tell him. He may not have picked it up on that relic he calls a receiver.'

Alone in the chart-room he stared at the chart. It was worn and stained. So many convoys, too many risks, and always a target for torpedoes and bombs.

It must be serious, he thought. He pictured the other ships as they had weighed anchor and had formed into two lines with the destroyer escorts bustling around them like sheep dogs.

The mate came back, breathing hard. They were all used to danger, and both the master and mate had already been torpedoed in other ships and knew the margin of survival. The U-boat, the most hated and most feared of any war machine. The unseen killer.

The master looked at his second-in-command. 'Rouse the lads, Bob. Have the gun manned, and set two more lookouts.'

The gun was mounted aft on the poop, an elderly four-inch weapon from another war.

This was something else, he thought. A raider, one of their bloody cruisers. How could she get through the patrols at this stage of the game, he wondered? The invasion was said to be going better than anyone had dared to hope – a newspaper in Freetown had proclaimed big advances all along the front. No longer beachheads, not just another wild hope; they were going all out for a grand slam.

He heard some of his men clambering up ladders and protesting at the call to arms. He gave a tight smile. They might soon have something to moan about.

He looked at the sky. A few clouds, but it was clear, washed-out blue. And it was another eight hours to dusk. He glared at the ship astern through the chart-room scuttle. Six knots. Without her dragging along like a sick elephant, they could increase speed, go it alone if need be. They would stand a better chance.

The mate and the second mate entered the chart-room and watched him without speaking. The second mate was just a kid, wet behind the ears, but he was learning.

'Look.' The master eyed them gravely. 'This bugger might come our way. But she's more likely to stand off before the screening squadron comes down on 'em like a ton of bricks. He stared hard at the chart. 'It's like being blind and deaf.'

The mate asked, 'Can't we make a run for it?'

'Is that what you'd do?'

The second mate said, 'We could turn back, sir.'

The master smiled. *Sir*. That showed how green he was.

He said, 'Can't leave the *Dunedin Pioneer*. He wouldn't cut and run if it was us.'

They looked at each other for support while the ship noises intruded. Usually they gave confidence. Now they seemed to represent their sudden vulnerability.

The master exclaimed angrily, 'No, sod 'em, we'll keep going as we are.'

There was a clang from aft and he strode out to the sunlight again to watch as the four-inch gun trained round on its mounting. Fat lot of use that would be against a bloody cruiser, he thought. But some of the seamen saw him and grinned up at the bridge. For some peculiar reason the old captain wished he had shaved, that his cap cover was crisp and white like those bloody RN characters.

The second mate clambered on to the bridge and said, 'Call from the tow, sir. Will be getting up steam in fifteen minutes.'

They all breathed out and the master said, 'Tell the silly bugger to get a move on.' He hid his relief from the others. 'And about bloody time!'

It was just minutes later that a seaman called, 'There's a plane, sir!'

'What? Where away?' The master strode through the wheelhouse and out on to the other wing. 'Why can't you learn to report the thing properly?' He ignored the lookout's resentment and raised his massive binoculars.

An aircraft. Out here. Hundreds of miles from anywhere. It could not be hostile. Maybe they were looking for them? To tell them to alter course, or to rendezvous with a tug. They'd get a surprise when the other ship cast off the tow and began pouring out her usual foul smoke, the bane of every escort commander.

He saw the sunlight glint on the little aircraft and stared at it until it misted over.

He said flatly, 'It's a Jerry.'

The second mate said, 'But it's too far—'

The master turned away. 'From the raider. Call up *Dunedin Pioneer* right now. Then tell Sparks to prepare the emergency signal—'

But it was already too late even for that. As the little toylike aircraft cruised back and forth against the pale sky, the horizon's mist seemed to raise itself like a frail curtain.

They saw the blurred flashes, almost lost in the fierce sunlight. The master waited, counting the seconds, until with a terrifying screech the salvo fell close astern, the white columns bursting high above the ships before cascading down in a torrent of spray and smoke.

The old captain shouted, 'Send that signal! Plain language, tell the bloody world! *Am under attack by German raider!*'

The next salvo shrieked down from the sky and he felt the hull shake as if it had run aground. He staggered to the rail and peered aft. It was almost impossible to see anything through the smoke, but the other vessel was still there, standing away at right-angles. The tow must have been slipped, or had parted in the explosions.

128

Then he stared incredulously at a solid, black shape as it rolled over and began to sink. It was their own stern, the useless four-pounder pointing at the sky, its crew nowhere to be seen.

He seized the rail and yelled, 'Sway out the boats! Abandon ship! What the hell is Sparks doing?'

Glass shivered from the wheelhouse windows and men fell kicking and screaming under a fusillade of glass and wood splinters. The ship had stopped, her holds already flooding as bulkheads burst open and turned the engine-room into an inferno of scalding steam.

Another earsplitting screech, and the shells burst alongside and on the foredeck.

The master slid down the bridge wing, his eyes glazed with agony while he tried to call out. His mind recorded the crash of falling derricks, the savage roar of water through the hull below, and the fact he could not move for the pain. He was still staring at the top of the bridge canvas-dodgers when the sea boiled over the edge and swamped the wheelhouse as the ship plunged to the bottom.

Then there was silence, as if the whole world had been rendered speechless.

Aboard the other ship, the men on the bridge and along her rust-streaked decks, stared dumbly across the empty sea towards the horizon. Like beasts waiting for the inevitable slaughter. for their own execution.

But nothing happened. Even the tiny aircraft had disappeared.

The master crossed the bridge and peered at the carpet of oil, the rising litter of fragments which spread across the swell in a great obscene stain.

Around him his men stood like statues, shocked beyond words or movement.

Then the master said, 'Lower a boat, Mister. Fast as you can.' He made himself stare at the floating pieces, all that was left of his old enemy. His best friend. He added brokenly, 'Seems they've no time for us, the bastards!'

As if to mock him the engine began to pound again.

'Stop engines!' Acting-Commodore James Cook Hemrose sat

stiff-backed in his bridge chair and surveyed what was left of the convoy. A battlefield. A junk yard.

The commander stood beside him as the way went off the ship, and the endless litter of wreckage, bodies and pieces of men parted across the *Wiltshire*'s high stem.

Half a mile astern, her signal lamp flashing like a diamond eye, the New Zealand light cruiser *Pallas* followed reluctantly amongst the remains.

The convoy had scattered at the last moment when the first salvoes must have come crashing down. Hammers of hell, Hemrose thought bitterly.

'Stand by to lower boats!'

Hemrose trained his binoculars across the sea, hating the stench of escaping fuel oil and burned paintwork. A few figures floated or splashed amongst the filth, their bodies shining and pitiful in the oil. There were more corpses than living, but it was worth a try.

'Signal *Pallas* to cover us, Toby.'

The lamp clattered again. Even it sounded subdued.

A distant voice called, 'Lower away!' That was one of the whalers. The motorboat was all ready to slip from her falls, the surgeon in the cockpit with one of his SBA's.

He looked long and hard at a black line which lifted and dipped above the water like a crippled submarine. It was the keel of one of the escorting destroyers. Of a corvette there was no trace at all.

Another destroyer had escaped without a scratch and was now lashed alongside a listing tramp-steamer, hoses dousing some fires while men passed back and forth with stretchers and inert bundles. An oil tanker was awash, but still afloat, her engines and pumps working manfully to keep her going. Some wag had hoisted a Union Flag on the stump of her remaining mast.

The commander returned and watched the light cruiser increasing speed to circle around the scene of pain and death, her pale hull streaked with oil like an additional waterline.

Hemrose said savagely, 'Whole convoy wiped out except for these pathetic remnants!' He pounded the arm of his chair with his fist. 'All they needed was another day. The escort group was on the way from Gib, and three destroyers from Bermuda. And us.'

The commander stared at the drifting filth and spreadeagled corpses. Some of them wore naval uniforms, or bits of them. It was like being with them, part of them. He resisted the urge to shiver. Even Hemrose must know that they would have stood no chance either.

The Admiralty had confirmed that the raider was *Prinz Luitpold*, and fresh details came in every hour. He watched his superior, suddenly glad that he did not share his responsibility.

Hemrose watched the boat coxswains signalling to one another with their shortened, personal semaphore. He knew what the commander was thinking. It made it worse. If *Wiltshire* had been on the spot, she might have scored a lucky hit, enough to cripple the bastard, or at least slow him down.

Now the German could be anywhere. He thought of the signals, and the information from the lone freighter *Dunedin Pioneer* which had been left untouched. Somebody aboard that poor ship, a spectator to the total destruction of the one which had been towing her, had kept his head. Had reported seeing the enemy's faint silhouette as she headed away at full speed to the south-west.

The commander had asked, 'Give chase, sir?'

Hemrose had studied his charts with the navigating and cypher officers for an hour while they had steamed at full speed towards the convoy's last position.

The raider had steamed away without sinking the *Dunedin Pioneer*. There had to be a reason. Now as he watched the oil-streaked boats picking their way amongst the human remains, he went over it again for the hundredth time.

Give chase. To where? To the coastline of Brazil, or back along the same course?

It had certainly put the cat amongst the pigeons, he thought. Every available ship was under orders. A nightmare for the Admiralty and the Allied Command. There must be no let-up in the lines of supply to the armies in France. The Channel was filled with vessels of every kind, carrying fuel and ammunition, transport and the precious cargo of men to replace the convoys which passed them on the way back. The wounded and the dying.

According to the latest intelligence there were seventeen major convoys at sea. Well escorted for the most part, but to resist U-boat and bombing attacks, not a bloody great cruiser like *Prinz Luitpold*.

Hemrose still could not fathom how it had happened. The RAF recce boys had reported that after the battle near Bear Island, *Prinz Luitpold* had been seen and photographed back at her lair in Bodø. It did not make any sense. Somebody's head would be on the block over it, but it offered no satisfaction for all this horror. He pictured the pandemonium in Whitehall. It made a change for them to be under siege. First the flying-bombs, then the massive V-2 rockets. The Allied HQ which controlled the Normandy invasion would be worried too. You could not ignore a raider, any raider. Convoys had to be diverted, held up, cancelled altogether.

Hemrose glanced around the open bridge, the intent figures and anxious faces. A midshipman was retching into his hand-kerchief as he stared at the bobbing remains which surrounded the tall hull.

Hemrose rasped, 'Get off my bridge, damn you, until you can act like a man!'

It was cruel and unfair. Hemrose knew it but did not care.

There was a third cruiser coming at full speed to join his little group. They should meet up with her in two days, unless ... He said to the commander, 'I want a full team on this, Toby. The paymaster-commander, even the bloody chaplain. See to it.'

The man's words came back to him and he heard himself say, 'Give chase – I don't think so, Toby. He had a reason for letting the *Dunedin Pioneer* stay afloat. He wanted her to see him steam away, to report his course.' It felt easier now that he had decided. 'No, I reckon he changed direction as soon as he was clear of all this. Get the convoy lists, and we'll study the chart. Outguess the bastard.' He eyed him grimly. 'It's up to us. As I see it, Toby, we'll get precious little advice from their lordships just now.' He wrinkled his nose. 'Signal a recall to the boats and we'll get under way. That destroyer can stand by the survivors until the escort group turns up.'

He heard one of the boats creaking up to the davits and felt the commander let out a sigh. No U-boats were reported in their vicinity. But if they could miss a big cruiser there was no point in adding to the risks.

The deck began to tremble and the *Pallas* headed round to take station astern again.

When the third cruiser joined them it would make all the difference. He looked down from the bridge and saw the first survivors being led away, wrapped in oil-sodden blankets. There did not seem to be many of them, he thought.

'Resume course, cruising speed, Toby.' He settled back in the chair. 'Send for a brandy. I need to *think* about this one.'

Astern, the listless ships, and the great span of oil and fragments seemed to fill the horizon.

For Hemrose the war had suddenly become a personal one.

It was like fighting free from a nightmare, only to discover that it was real. Even the overhead light, although it was partly screened by some kind of curtain, had a hard, unreal shape. Cold and still. Like death.

The man lay motionless, his hands balled into fists at his sides while he waited for his senses to return, or to fade again and leave him in peace.

In tiny fragments his mind recorded that he was suspended in some kind of cot, high-sided and white. He felt the surge of panic. A coffin.

He tried again and groped for clues, explanations, like piecing together parts of a puzzle.

He made his taut limbs relax but kept his hands pressed against his sides. His body was naked, but warm beneath a sheet and a soft blanket. Again, he felt the surge of hope. A nightmare after all. He could feel the pulsating tremor of engines through his spine, the gentle clatter of unseen objects. But he felt despair close over him once more. It was not his ship. He closed his eyes tightly as if to shut out the stark, leaping pictures, the great fountain of searing flames, exploding metal as the torpedo, maybe two, had exploded into them. He tried again, and in his reeling thoughts seemed to read the vessel's name, as he had once seen it at the dockside. The *Radnor Star*. An old ship, then part of an eastbound convoy from St John's to Liverpool, packed to the gills with engine spares, bridge-building equipment, armoured vehicles, all heavy stuff. The poor old girl must have gone down like a stone afterwards.

He opened his eyes wide and stared at the solitary light. *Afterwards*. What then?

It was almost painful to work it out. He had been in the open, something in his hand. Had to see the captain. Then the explosion, wild faces, mouths open in silent cries, smoke, dense choking smoke which he imagined he could still taste.

Then the boat, water swilling over his feet and thighs as someone had fought it away from the ship, the terrible suction as she had dived for the last time. Why had nobody seen them? It was coming back, sharp and hard, like heart-beats, the panic of a child who wants to hide under the blankets.

It had been at night. That was it.

He felt the sweat break over his chest and stomach. The lifeboat then. Why did his mind refuse to examine it?

He heard a distant bell, the clatter of feet somewhere. *Where the hell am I?*

He tried again. *My name is Peter Younger*. He wanted to laugh, but was closer to weeping. He had a name after all. He could not be dead.

It was difficult not to cry out as another picture loomed through the mist.

Men bailing and working at a handful of oars, a great sea which lifted and flung the boat about like a sodden log. Later still, the deathly quiet, the silent figures, some seared by fire, others who had died of exposure, a few eyeless, victims of sea-birds. *They were all dying*. He vaguely recalled the hoarse voice of Colin Ames, *Radnor Star*'s second mate, close against his ear. He must have been dying too. The whole bridge had collapsed, and it was a miracle he had made it into a boat.

'Take the tiller, Sparks.' That was all he had said. Sparks? It was coming back. He had been the radio officer. Had been on his way to the bridge with a signal when the world had exploded. He recalled the other man wrapping his jacket around him. He must have lost his own. Younger examined his body limb by limb without moving a muscle. He ached all over, but he was whole. Then more distorted faces, alien voices, hands hauling him into another boat, a huge ship away in the distance. He tensed. This must be the one.

He remembered that he had been too weak to protest or struggle, but knew that in some strange way he had not wanted to leave his dead companions, and the boat he had steered until the last oar had drifted away.

All dead. Like the old ship, nothing left.

Another twist of terror as he pictured his mother reading the telegram. God, there had been plenty of those in their street. He could not remember its name, or that of the town. A seaport. Pictures of his father and uncles, all in uniform. Sailors.

Feet scraped on metal and he tested his strength, tried to raise his head above the side of the cot.

His eyes would not focus at first. All glaring white, bottles and jars on neat shelves, like a hospital, while nearby lay a pile of gramophone records.

Perhaps he had gone mad?

Bit by bit, section by section, like a complicated, coded message over the receiver.

He stared uncomprehending at two uniform jackets which hung from a brass rail. One with three stripes, the other with two, with some odd insignia above them, and – he caught his breath – the Nazi eagle on the right breast. He had seen enough of those. Again the urge to laugh. But only in films.

Then he saw the other cot, the untidy white beard, the ancient face creased with pain or some terrible memory.

He held on to what he saw. Like a life-raft. It was Old Shiner. A bit of a character in the *Radnor Star*, listed as boatswain but one who could do almost anything. He had been at sea since he was twelve. *A bit of a character*.

He caught a brief picture of him in the boat, his pale eyes wild while he had clutched the cat against his scrawny body.

Younger attempted to bridge the gap between the boat and

here. All he could remember was warmth, the fact that he felt no urge to hold on, even to live.

He imagined he had heard a woman's voice too, but that was impossible. A part of something else maybe.

So he and Old Shiner were in a German ship. Prisoners. Survivors. But not a U-boat. He recalled the misty silhouette of the ship. He also remembered a needle going into his arm, oblivion, but not before the world had begun to shake and thunder to gunfire. He had wanted to scream, to escape; instead there had been nothing.

He winced as a shadow fell across the cot and he saw a man in gold-rimmed glasses looking down at him.

'Well, now, Herr Ames, are you feeling better?'

Even his voice made him shake with silent laughter. Shock.

The man must be a doctor, and he spoke like one of those Germans in the movies.

He prised his lips apart, or so it felt, and tried to explain that his name was Younger. Then he saw the crumpled, oil-stained coat with the two tarnished stripes lying on a table. Ames's jacket, the one he had used to shield him from the wind and drenching spray. It flooded through him like fire. Anger, hatred, and an overwhelming sense of loss.

The doctor leaned closer and took his wrist. 'You had a narrow escape, young man.'

Younger moved his dry lips again. 'What ship?'

'*Prinz Luitpold.*' He lowered the wrist. '*Kriegsmarine.*'

Younger was not sure if the name meant anything or not.

'How is Old Shiner?'

'Is that his name?' The doctor gave a sad smile. 'He will live, but I fear his mind may be scarred.'

Younger heard himself shouting, but the words sounded wild, meaningless.

A door opened and he saw an armed sailor peer in at them, his eyes questioning. *Just like the movies*, a voice seemed to murmur. It must be his own, he thought despairingly.

The doctor waved the sailor away and said, 'You must try to eat something soon. You are young, it will pass.'

Younger could feel his strength draining away, and twisted

his face to the pillow to hide the tears which spilled down his cheeks. They were all dead. He saw the needle glinting in the overhead light and tried to struggle, but the doctor's grip was like steel. 'You killed them!' He saw the needle hesitate. '*Bloody murderers!*'

Stroheim felt the fight go out of the young officer and stood back to watch his face lose its anguish, its hate.

He moved to the other cot where the old man still cradled his lost cat in his arms.

They had no part in their ship's destruction, but the fact gave no comfort.

He thought of the guns thundering and shaking the ship from deck to keel, the muffled shouts of the intercom as one by one the convoy had been decimated.

Karl-Heinz Stroheim examined his hands. They were surprisingly steady.

He had been sent to the *Prinz Luitpold* as a punishment or a reprieve. All things considered it seemed likely they would come to rely on his skill.

The twist of fate which had brought these two strangers to his care was like an additional challenge. The oldest and the youngest in the lifeboat had survived.

He put on his jacket and gestured to the sentry. If hate was a reason for survival, the young officer named Ames would outlive them all.

10

Beyond Duty

Hechler wriggled his shoulders deeper into his watchcoat and felt the damp air exploring his bones. By leaning forward in his tall chair he could see much of the *Prinz Luitpold*'s long forecastle, which glistened now as if from a rain squall. But there was no rain, and as the high bows sliced through the Atlantic swell he saw the spray drift over the anchor-cables and breakwater to make the angled gun turrets shine like glass.

It was afternoon, and the sky was almost hidden by dark-bellied clouds. He heard Gudegast's rumbling tones as he passed another helm order before checking his ready-use chart again. How many times had he done that, Hechler wondered?

He saw the rear-admiral appear around Turret Anton, head high despite the misty spray, his face flushed and youthful in the distance. He was walking in step with Oberleutnant Bauer, the signals and communications officer. They could be brothers, he thought. Bauer was also the political officer and had been having a lot of private conversations with Leitner. What did they discuss? The *Prinz*'s captain probably.

Gudegast called, 'New course, sir. Two-one-five.'

It was a strange relationship, Hechler thought. Leitner had been as good as his word for the most part, and had let him handle the ship in his own way.

As they had steered south-west away from the broken convoy and the additional freighter which the radar had plotted with unnerving accuracy, Leitner had only once questioned his judgement.

Hechler had answered, 'The British will look for clues. By heading south-west in view of that ship which was under tow, they will assume it was a ruse, and expect us to alter course immediately to throw them off the scent. I think I would.'

Leitner had considered it, his eyes opaque, giving nothing away.

'But if *not*, Dieter? Suppose the British admiral thinks as you do?' Then he had nodded and had given his broad grin. 'Of course, that other convoy – they will think we are after it.'

OKM Operations Division had signalled more information about a vast troop convoy which was scheduled to head around the Cape of Good Hope en route for England. Commonwealth soldiers with all their equipment and vehicles, life-blood for the armies in France. A prize which would draw every U-boat pack in the Atlantic, and which would have a massive escort to match it.

Heavy units of the Home Fleet would be hurrying at full speed to meet it and swell the defences. Suicide for any attacking surface raider, but with such high stakes, the end might justify the means. Because of that risk no admiral would dare leave the convoy underguarded.

It was one of the biggest of its kind, too large to turn back, too vital to stop.

So the *Prinz Luitpold* had carried on as before. Nothing further had been sighted. If anything showed itself now they would have to forego their first rendezvous with a milch-cow. They had plenty of fuel, and Leitner intended it would remain like that. A little and often, as he had termed it.

It was too early to expect enemy submarines in their path. The simplicity of von Hanke's strategy had worked perfectly, and there had been no time to deploy submarines from their normal inshore patrols in the Baltic and the North Sea.

Hechler watched the two windswept figures until they vanished beneath the bridge. He thought of Leitner's broadcast that morning to the ship's company. Rousing, passionate, compelling. It was all those things, if you did not know the man.

Hechler had watched him as he had stood with the handset

139

close to his lips in the armoured admiral's bridge. The flag-lieutenant and Bauer had also been present while Leitner's clipped tones had penetrated the ship above and below decks.

He had spoken of *Lübeck*'s loss at some length. Her sacrifice. 'We must not fail her, can never forget they fought for us, to give us the freedom to break out into the Atlantic! For *us* and our beloved Fatherland!'

Hechler had watched as one hand had darted to his cheek as if to brush away a tear. An act? He was still not sure.

Of one thing he was certain, however. There were two faces to the youthful admiral. After the attack on the convoy Leitner had walked around the upper deck, chatting to the jubilant gun crews, lounging against the mountings or slapping a seaman on the shoulder to emphasise his satisfaction.

Then, on the bridge, almost in the next breath, he had snapped complaints about this man or that, and had ordered Theil to deal with their slackness. So the reprimands would come from the bridge, not from their popular and untiring rear-admiral.

Then there had been the flash of anger over Leitner's mysterious boxes.

Hechler had requested permission to move them deeper in the hull, so that their space could be used to store additional short-range ammunition.

Leitner had snapped, 'They belong to me! I will not be questioned! I am entrusted to this mission, to carry it out in *my* way!' He had been almost shouting, his voice trapped inside the armoured bridge. 'It is a mark of my trust in this ship's ability, surely? If we are crippled or sunk in battle, my boxes will go to the bottom too!'

So they were that valuable, Hechler thought.

He heard Theil's footsteps on the gratings and shifted round to look at him.

'All well, Viktor?' Things were still strained between them, although Theil had shown his old pride and excitement when the enemy convoy had been destroyed.

Hechler had thought about that often enough. It had been so easy, he had found no satisfaction from it. It had been slaughter, the careering merchantmen and their escorts falling to their massive bombardment like targets in a fairground.

He had told himself that they would have done the same to *Prinz Luitpold*, would have cheered like his own men, if they had been left to burn and drown.

It was their war. What they had trained for. What they must do.

Theil shrugged and stared moodily at the grey ocean, the lift and dip of the raked bows.

'Yes, sir. I have just questioned the prisoner, the officer named Ames.' He shrugged again as if to sum up his irritation. 'The other one is raving. I can't imagine how he ever got to sea.'

Hechler eyed him thoughtfully. The old sailor should have been ashore with his grandchildren, not fighting for his life in an open boat. They had been adrift for five weeks. How could the human body stand it? But it was pointless to say as much to Theil. It would sound like one more disagreement. Perhaps he was more worried about his missing wife than he would admit.

Hechler tried not to let his mind stray to Inger, but even in distance her will seemed too strong to resist. In that low-cut gown, when he had held her, had seen her perfect breasts. In another moment – he sighed. She could never be kept out of his thoughts for long. Her betrayal and her contempt were like deep scars.

He had felt clumsy by comparison, and she had scorned his reserve as being stuffy, and dull.

Maybe she had been right?

Theil said abruptly, 'The Englishman knows nothing. Just that the torpedoes hit his ship in the forward hold. She sank in minutes, apparently.'

Hechler glanced at his watch. The rendezvous was in twenty minutes' time. If it happened at all. It seemed impossible that two such diverse vessels could meet on a pinpoint in this ocean.

There was a coughing roar from amidships and Hechler stirred uneasily in his chair. He wanted to walk aft and watch the brightly painted Arado as it was tested on the catapult. Leitner had told him that it would be launched without further delay. The camera team would be down there too, waiting to record their audacity as they flew off their new aircraft, indifferent to the enemy and what they could do.

Hechler had seen the girl when he had left the bridge to visit the various action stations while the ship had steamed away from the last fall of shot. She had been in the hangar, where her new Arado had been housed throughout the bombardment, its wings detached and stowed separately rather than folded, like a toy in a crate. They had faced one another awkwardly like strangers; perhaps each was out of his or her depth.

Hechler had heard himself enquiring how she had accepted or endured the din of salvoes, the hull's shaking to each ear-shattering crash of gunfire.

She had watched him as if to see her own answers without asking the questions. How small she had seemed against the wet, camouflaged steel, and the smoke-blackened gun-muzzles.

Now she was down there with the aircraft-handling party. Ready to fly off, so that some lunatic's desire for patriotic realism could be filmed.

Theil said dourly, 'I think it is madness to put that plane in the air. Suppose—'

The word hung between them. There were no enemy carriers anywhere in this part of the ocean if the OKM's reports were to be believed. Submarines, then? Even the hint of a plane would be enough to make them increase speed and head away. The Arado might fly after them, like a fledgling abandoned by its parents, until it ran out of fuel.

Theil whispered, 'He's coming up, sir.'

Leitner strode on to the bridge, the familiar silk scarf flapping in the keen air, but otherwise unprotected by a heavier coat. He smiled at the bridge-party and then returned Hechler's salute.

'According to my watch—' He frowned as Gudegast called, 'Permission to alter course for take-off, sir?'

Hechler nodded. 'Warn the engine-room.'

Leitner's good humour returned. 'See, the sky is brightening. It will do our people at home a lot of good to see these films.' He glared at his willowy aide as he clambered on to the bridge. 'Well?'

The flag-lieutenant eyed him worriedly, hurt by his master's tone. 'The camera team would like you to join them, sir.' He glanced shyly at Hechler. 'I have a list of the questions you will be asked.'

Leitner clapped one hand across his breast and gave an elaborate sigh. 'What we must do in the name of duty!'

Gudegast lifted his face from the voice-pipe as the helmsman acknowledged the change of course. He watched Leitner march to the after-ladder and then looked over at Jaeger, who shared the watch with Korvettenkapitän Froebe.

He said softly, 'Does he fill you with pride, young Konrad? Make you want to spill your guts for your country?' He grimaced. 'Sometimes I despair.'

He thought of the painting he had begun of Gerda. Just imagining the softness of her body, the heat of their passion, had helped him in some strange fashion to endure the massacre of those helpless merchantmen. Bomber pilots who nightly released their deadly cargoes over Germany did not care about the suffering they created; the U-boat commander did not see ships and sailors in his crosswires, merely targets. Any more than an escort captain spared a thought for that same hull being crushed by the force of his depth-charges as the sea thundered in to silence the submariners' screams.

Hechler heard him, but let it pass. Gudegast was releasing the tension in his usual way.

'Ready to fly off aircraft, sir!'

'Slow ahead all engines.'

Hechler walked from his chair and leaned over the screen, the damp wind pressing into his face.

He saw the camera team down aft, some sailors freshly changed into their best uniforms, outwardly chatting to their admiral. Hechler looked at the vibrating Arado on the catapult, trained outboard ready to be fired off.

He saw the girl's helmeted head lowered to speak with one of the deck crew before she closed the cockpit cover and waved a gloved hand.

He felt his stomach contract and was stunned by the sudden concern. There was nothing that they could do or share. What was the *matter* with him? Was it Inger's fury or his own loneliness?

He tensed as the shining Arado roared from the catapult and without hesitation climbed up and away from the slow-moving cruiser.

Leitner returned to the bridge, his eyes squinting as he watched the little plane weaving and circling over the water.

He said, 'I hope she flies nearer than that. It's a camera down aft, not a bloody gunsight!'

Hechler lifted his binoculars and watched the weak sunlight lance through the clouds to pick out the plane's thin silhouette.

'Five minutes, sir!'

Gudegast's voice made him pull his thoughts together.

Leitner remarked, 'Now we shall see, eh?'

It was more like a shoal of fish than a surfacing submarine. Long flurries of spray and frothing bubbles, so that when the hull eventually appeared some half-mile distant it rose with a kind of tired majesty.

Jaeger exclaimed, 'God, she's *big*!'

Leitner heard him and turned to look. 'Another idea with vision and inventive skill!'

The huge submarine surfaced and lay on the heaving water like a gigantic whale. Unlike an ordinary combat U-boat she lacked both menace and dignity. Even as they watched, men were swarming from her squat conning-tower, while from her casing, untidy-looking derricks and hoses were already rising from hidden compartments like disturbed sea-monsters.

The tannoy blared below the bridge, and men ran to the prepared tackles and winches, ready to haul the fuel lines to the bunkers. Hechler saw the men waving to each other across the water. It must be a heartening sight to see such a big warship at large in enemy waters, he thought.

There would be no news from home as yet, but his own men could send their letters across while the two vessels lay together. It might be many weeks before those letters were read by wives, mothers and girlfriends. He wished now he had a letter written for his own parents. But they would understand. Without effort he could see the photographs of himself and his dead brother in the neat, old-fashioned house where he had been born. His mother preparing the evening meal early, in case there was an air raid, although they had been mercifully spared most of those where they lived. His father, reading the newspaper and coughing quietly at painful intervals.

A telephone buzzed and Jaeger called, 'Chief engineer reports hoses connected, sir.'

'Very good. Warn the wheelhouse to hold her steady.' It was probably unnecessary to warn anybody. Severed hoses might take hours to replace, and every minute exposed like this was too much.

Hechler watched the oily hoses jerking busily as the fuel was pumped across the gap of heaving water. What a strange war it was becoming. He glanced down at the deck below as an armed seaman walked past beside the captured English officer. The latter was downcast, and did not appear to be looking in any direction as men scurried to tackles to release the strain or to take up the slack.

A victim and a survivor.

Theil said, 'I think it unwise to let him walk about like that.'

Hechler smiled. 'He is hardly a threat, Viktor.'

He looked up to seek out the Arado, but the sky seemed empty. She would be feeling free right now, he thought. Unlike the sad-faced prisoner who walked alone despite all the seamen around him.

But the young officer who wore another man's uniform jacket was anything but despairing. On his way to the upper deck, with his guard sauntering beside him, a machine-pistol dangling from one shoulder, he had heard the one sound which was so familiar that it pulled at his reserve like claws.

The urgent stammer of morse and waves of hissing static. The radio-room with at least three headphoned operators at their bench was like a laboratory compared with anything he had been used to. But the idea had formed in his mind even as they had passed the open door.

It was his one chance. His life would be forfeit, but he found it surprisingly easy to accept that. He had died back there in the open boat with his gaunt, eyeless companions.

When the time was right. It would take just one signal to

bring the navy down on this bloody German like a force of avenging angels. He looked up and thought he saw the captain framed against the low clouds.

It would all be worth it then, even if he was dead when the first great salvoes came roaring down on the raider.

The armed guard saw him give a wild grin and sighed.

It could be no joke to be adrift in this ocean, he thought.

The girl named Erika Franke adjusted the clips of her safety harness and peered to starboard as she eased the Arado into a shallow dive. She had flown several of these float-planes when she had worked for a while as a delivery pilot, before she had been asked to serve with the special section of the Luftwaffe.

She watched the grey wastes of the Atlantic tilt to one side as if it was part of a vast sloping desert, the occasional white horses where the wind had broken the swell into crests.

The cruiser had already fallen far away, and it was hard to picture her as she had first seen the ship. Huge, invulnerable, and somehow frightening. But once aboard it had seemed so much smaller, the great hull broken up into small intimate worlds, faces which you sometimes saw only once before they were swallowed up again. She watched the ship in the distance, her outline strangely broken and unreal in its striped dazzle paint. Beyond her was the austere shape of the great supply submarine which Leitner had described to the ship's company.

She saw the perspex screen mist over very slightly and adjusted her compass accordingly. They were too high for spray. The looming clouds said *rain*.

She bit her lip. If the visibility fell away she must return to the ship immediately.

She touched the microphone across her mouth. 'Rain soon.' She heard the observer, Westphal, acknowledge her comment with a grunt. A thickset, bovine man, he obviously resented being in the hands of a woman. She ignored him. It was nothing new in her life.

She deliberately altered course away from the ship and the motionless submarine. If only she could fly and fly, leave it all behind, until – she checked herself as Hechler's grave features

146

intruded into her thoughts.

A withdrawn man, who must have been badly hurt and not just by the war. She remembered his voice, his steady blue eyes when he had visited her after the encounter with the enemy convoy. His presence had calmed her, like that moment when you fly out of a storm into bright sunlight.

During the bombardment she had felt no fear. There had been no point in being afraid. Her father had taught her that, when he had first taken her flying, had given her a taste for it. If you could do nothing, fear had no meaning, he had often told her.

But the feeling of utter helplessness had been there. The ship, powerful though she was, had shaken like a mad thing, with every plate and rivet threatening to tear apart, or so it had felt. Then Hechler, his voice and his quiet confidence had covered her like a blanket.

The Arado swayed jerkily and she quickly increased throttle until the blurred propeller settled again into a misty circle. The plane was unarmed, or at least it carried no ammunition. Just as well, she thought. That was one kind of flying she had not tried.

She thought of the two survivors who had been brought to the ship by the young officer, Jaeger. He was a nice young man, she thought, and she had seen him looking at her when she had joined the others in the wardroom for meals. It made her smile within the privacy of her flying-helmet. She was twenty-eight, but far older in other ways than Jaeger would ever dream. Why did they have to be so predictable? Those who saw her only as an easy victory, a romp in bed. Others who saw her reserve as a coldness, like something masculine.

When she glanced down at the endless, heaving water, she recalled another face with sharper clarity. Claus had loved her, and she him. He had been married, but the war had brought them together in Italy.

Had they ever really decided to take a step beyond the endless anxiety of being lovers? He had promised; she could almost hear his voice in her hair as he had held her, had pressed down to that delicious torment when he had entered her.

147

She had learned of his death through a friend. After all, she had no *rights* to him.

His ship had been torpedoed, lost with all hands. It was over.

She came back with a start as Westphal's surly voice intruded into her memories.

'Time to turn. Visibility's down.'

They would fly back now, she thought, and the camera crew would film her landing near the ship, and again as she stepped aboard to be greeted by Andreas Leitner. Strange how people of his kind always professed to be such men of the world, with an eye for every pretty girl.

She had met plenty like Leitner. It was surprising that the war machine attracted so many who might have been happier as women. She considered Hechler again. Dominated by his wife? Hardly. What was it then with women like Inger Hechler? She had seen her occasionally at those staid parties in Berlin which so often had changed into something wild, repellent.

She moved the controls sharply so that the plane tilted over to port. She could feel the pull of her harness, the pain in her breast as the Arado went over even further until it appeared as if the wingtip was cutting the water like a fin.

The changing light, the endless procession of unbroken waves, or was it a shadow?

'Dead ahead!' She eased the throttle with great care. 'Do you see it?'

Westphal had been deep in thought, watching her hair beneath the leather helmet, imagining how she would fight him, claw at him, when he took her.

He exclaimed, startled, 'What? Where?'

She found that she could watch the submarine quite calmly, for that was what it was. It looked dark, blue-grey, like a shark, with a lot of froth streaming from aft, and a faint plume of vapour above the conning-tower.

Westphal had recovered himself, his voice harsh as he snapped, 'Enemy boat! Charging batteries and using her *schnorchel!*'

He reached forward to prod her shoulder. 'Back to the ship, *fast!*'

The girl eased the controls over to port. Westphal had seen what he had expected to see, but had missed something vital. The submarine was trimmed too high – most of them would be almost at full periscope depth to charge batteries, and in their own waters it was unlikely they would submerge at all.

The submarine must be damaged, unable to dive.

Thoughts raced through her mind, and in her imagination she could hear Hechler's voice, then see the cruiser and the supply submarine lying somewhere back there, totally unaware of this unexpected threat.

Damaged she might be, but her commander would not hesitate when *Prinz Luitpold*'s silhouette swam into his crosswires.

Erika Franke had learned quite a lot about the navy, and one of the things which stood out in her mind was something which Kröll the gunnery officer had said about his new radar. That a submarine on the surface nearby could interfere with accuracy, and that was exactly what was happening right now.

She thrust the controls forward and tilted the Arado into a steep dive. She felt the plane quivering, the rush of wind rising above the roar of the BMW engine.

Westphal shouted wildly, 'What the hell are you doing? They'll see us!'

Sure enough there were tiny ant-like figures on the submarine's deck. They might have picked up the supply boat's engines on their sonar, or even the heavier revolutions of the *Prinz Luitpold*, but the sight of a brightly painted aircraft must have caught them on the hop.

She laughed. 'Scared, are you?' The Arado's shadow swooped over the water like an uneven crucifix, and then tumbled away as she brought the nose up towards the clouds.

It was responding well; she could even smell the newness in the fuselage and fittings.

She shouted, 'By the time we made contact with the ship it would all be over!'

Then she winced as several balls of livid green tracer floated past the port wing, and the plane danced wildly to shell-bursts. The clouds enfolded the aircraft and she peered at the compass, her brain working coolly but urgently as she pictured the other vessels, the enemy submarine's bearing and line of approach. She was probably American, one of their big ocean-going boats, which she had studied in the recognition books. She held her breath and pushed the stick forward, and felt the floats quiver as they burst out of the clouds into a great span of watery sunlight.

Just right for the camera team, she thought vaguely. Then more shell-bursts erupted on either side, and lazy balls of tracer fanned beneath her, so that she instinctively drew her legs together.

The plane jerked, and she heard metal rip past her body. But the engine was behaving well. It was time to turn back. They must have heard the shooting. There was still time.

She twisted round in her seat to yell at Westphal, but choked on a scream as she saw his bared teeth, his fists bunched in agony at the moment of impact. His goggles were completely filled with blood, like a creature from a nightmare.

The plane rocked again, and she almost lost control as more bursts exploded nearby. She felt as if all the breath had been punched from her body, and when she looked down she saw a tendril of blood seeping through the flying suit and over her belt.

Then the pain hit her like a hot iron, and she heard herself whimpering and calling while she tried to find the compass and bring the plane on to the right bearing.

She felt the pain searing her body, so that her eyes misted over. She dared not turn her head where her hideous companion peered at her, his teeth set in a terrible grin.

Nor could she call up the ship. Dared not. The submarine would know instantly what he probably only suspected.

'Oh, dear God!' The words were torn from her. 'Help me!'

But the engine's roar drowned her cries and every vibration made her swoon in agony.

There were no more explosions, and for a brief moment she imagined she had lost consciousness, was dying like the men in the lifeboat. Clouds leapt towards her and then writhed aside again to bathe the cockpit in bright sunlight.

She cried out, then thrust one hand against her side as blood ran over her thigh and down into her flying boot.

There was the ship, the supply submarine almost alongside, with tiny lines and pipes linking them like a delicate web.

She saw the ship begin to turn anti-clockwise across the wind-shield, revolving faster and faster, blotting out everything until it seemed she was plunging straight for the bridge.

Her mind recorded several things at the same time. The lines between the two vessels were being cast off, and a great frothing wash was surging from beneath *Prinz Luitpold*'s bows as she increased to maximum speed.

The girl fought to control the spin, to bring the aircraft's nose up and level off.

All she could think of was that she had warned him. She would never know if she was in time.

11

The Truth Can Wait

Hechler joined Gudegast at the compass platform. It was going well, but any sudden cross-wind might bring the unmatched vessels too close together.

'Alter course to two-two-zero degrees. Signal the submarine's commander yourself.' He touched the big man's arm. 'Don't want oil spilled all over the ocean.'

He walked back to the gratings and imagined he could feel the fuel coming through those long, pulsating hoses.

His ship was the best of her class for performance, and with the additional bunkers she had been given last year could cruise over 7,000 miles unless she was called to offer full speed for long periods.

He thought of the girl in her brightly painted plane. It worried him more than he cared to admit to have her aboard. At the same time he knew he would miss her when she was ordered to leave. Maybe she did not have a genuine mission? Perhaps after all she was only a piece of Leitner's public relations puzzle.

Theil lowered his glasses. 'The Arado's a long time, sir.' He eyed him worriedly. 'Completely lost sight of it.'

Hechler peered over the rear of the bridge wing. One of the regular float-planes in its dappled camouflage was already standing on the catapult, the handling party lounging around with nothing to do.

Hechler contained his sudden impatience. One thing at a time. It was the only way. The collection of charts with their plotted rendezvous marks were all in the future. Nobody could say how much future they still had.

Leitner strode on to the bridge, his mouth set in a tight line. 'Where the *bloody hell* is that woman?' He moved this way and that, almost blindly, so that men on watch had to jump out of his path.

Theil suggested, 'Perhaps we should send up another aircraft, sir?'

Leitner stared at him. 'Don't be such a bloody idiot!'

Hechler saw the seamen nearby exchange glances. Some worried, others pleased that a senior officer was getting a choking-off for a change.

Hechler said, 'I agree with him, sir.'

Their eyes met. Hechler felt very calm and relaxed even though he wanted to yell at Leitner. *Go on, tell me I'm a bloody idiot!*

Leitner recovered his composure somewhat. 'It's taking too long,' he said mildly.

Hechler looked at Theil and winked. The admiral had climbed down. For the moment anyway.

Then Hechler moved to the opposite side of the bridge to watch the fuelling operation. In the Great War, German raiders had been tied down to coaling stations, built up in readiness for such a dangerous form of sea piracy. He smiled in spite of his anxiety for the girl. *Piracy. Is that what we have come to?*

He glanced at his team, the watchful faces, the occasional padding of an order for helm and engines.

And yet, in spite of the quiet discipline, or perhaps because of it, there was something not quite right. Like a fault in a painting. He knew it was not Leitner's outburst, or Theil's embarrassed confusion at being reprimanded like a first-year midshipman in front of the watch. You got used to the petty whims of superior officers. *Maybe I am like that myself now?*

No, it was a feeling of uneasiness.

He made up his mind. 'Warn the milch-cow, then sound off action stations.'

Leitner heard him and glared from the other corner of the bridge.

'It'll make them jumpy!'

Hechler forced a grin. 'I *am* jumpy, sir.' He heard the clamour of bells, muffled and far away beyond the thick plating.

To Theil he said, 'You stay here.' He shrugged. 'It's just in case.'

Leitner climbed on to the bridge chair and tugged his cap down over his eyes. When one of the camera team requested permission to come to the bridge, Leitner snapped, 'When I'm ready, damn him!'

Hechler lowered his voice. 'Pass the word to the catapult, Viktor. Prepare to launch aircraft.'

A telephone buzzed and seconds later the Arado's engine spluttered, then bellowed into life.

Leitner swung round. 'Of all the bloody useless –'

He got no further as the gunnery control intercom filled the bridge.

'Gunfire to the north-west!'

Hechler moved like lightning to the compass platform. 'Discontinue fuelling!' He snatched up the red handset and waited, mentally counting seconds. Then he heard Stück's voice from the depths of the engine-room, machinery sighing in the background like some insane orchestra.

Stück began, 'I'm sorry about the delay, Captain, but we're almost topped-up. I –'

Hechler said, 'Stop immediately, Chief. Maximum revolutions when I give the word.' He slammed down the handset. There was nothing to add. Stück better than most knew the narrowness of their margin.

He waved his arm. '*Cast off!* Take in those wires!'

Leitner was beside him, peering at him wildly. 'What the hell's going on?'

'Gunfire means an enemy, sir.' He swung round as a lookout yelled, 'Aircraft, Red four-five, angle of sight four-oh!'

'Stand by, secondary armament!' Without looking Hechler pictured the twin turrets along the port side already lifting and training. But for what?

He levelled his glasses and found the Arado almost immediately. It was rolling from side to side, but apparently intact.

He felt his heart throbbing as he followed every painful movement.

Theil called, 'Clear that breast-rope, damn you!'

Hechler lowered his glasses and saw the remaining wire dragging the heavy submarine dangerously close alongside.

'Cut that line! *Now!*'

He turned back again but the plane had plunged into some low clouds.

The gunnery intercom intoned, 'Submarine on the surface, bearing Red two-oh. Range four thousand!'

Leitner was almost beside himself. 'How can it be?' He peered over the stained screen. 'In the name of Christ!'

Hechler called, 'Full ahead all engines!' He felt the sharp tremble through the deck plates. Now or never. If that wire refused to part they would take the milch-cow with them.

The port lookout was leaning against his mounted binoculars, his legs braced behind him as if he was taking the whole weight of the ship.

'Aircraft in sight again, sir. Closing. Shift bearing to Red six-oh!'

Hechler gripped the rail as the deck seemed to rise and then surge forward beneath him.

'Line's parted, sir!'

'*Open fire!*'

The three twin turrets along the port side opened up instantly, their sharper explosions making men grope for ear-plugs, others crouch down away from their savage back-blast.

Theil called, 'Supply boat's diving, sir!' He sounded breathless.

Great fountains of spray shot from the milch-cow's saddle tanks as water thundered into them, and her wash indicated a frantic increase in speed.

Hechler tore his eyes from the Arado as it reeled over the ship and then appeared to level off on an invisible wire. Not before he had seen the bright, starlike holes in the paintwork, some of which appeared to cross the cockpit itself.

'Port twenty!' He wrapped his arms around the voice-pipes with such force that the pain seemed to steady his mind, the ache which that last sight had given him.

She had drawn enemy fire. There was no other possible reason but to warn the ship.

He felt the deck going over. Like a destroyer. '*Steady!* Hold her!'

Voices yelled on every side and then the secondary armament recoiled in their mountings yet again, their shells flinging up thin waterspouts against the horizon where the enemy lay hidden in the swell.

'*Shoot!*' Again the urgent cry, and again the sharp, ear-probing crashes.

'Torpedoes running to port!'

Theil jumped to the voice-pipe but Hechler snapped, 'As she goes!'

He looked quickly at the supply-boat. Her bows were already under water, her squat conning-tower deserted as she prepared to run deep and head away. She would not even be a spectator, let alone wait around to pick up survivors.

The explosion was like one great thunderclap which rendered men blind and deaf in a few seconds, as if shocked from every known sense.

Dense black smoke billowed across the water, so thick it seemed solid, then it rolled over the decks and through the superstructure and masts, and for a while longer it was like the dead of night. Through it all the intercom kept up its continual babble.

'Short!' Then, 'A straddle! Got the bastards!'

Hechler groped to the forepart of the bridge and almost fell over a young signalman. He could barely remember the boy's name as he was their newest addition. Logged as seventeen years old, Hechler guessed he was a good deal less.

He dragged him to his feet by the scruff of his tunic and shouted, 'Hold on, Heimrath!' He could hear his gasping and retching in the foul stench and dense smoke. 'It's not us this time!'

The torpedoes must have hit the big submarine just as she made to lift her tail and dive. There could be nothing left. Fuel, ammunition, spare torpedoes, they had all gone up together, scattering fragments for half a mile, while some had clattered across *Prinz Luitpold*'s forecastle and maindeck.

'Target is diving, sir.'

156

Diving or sinking, it made no difference now. That last salvo would put her out of the fight. It was far more likely that she was falling slowly into the depths, blacker than any death pall, until the weight of water crushed her and her crew into a steel pulp.

'Slow ahead.' Hechler dabbed his mouth with his sleeve. The smoke was streaming over and around them, and men were peering for one another, dazed and with eyes running while they sought out their friends.

Hechler gripped the rail with both hands. 'Tell the accident boat to stand by.' He saw Theil's disbelief, his eyes bulging in his smeared face. 'Lower to the waterline. Now!'

Reluctantly almost, training and discipline reasserted themselves. Like a great beast, rising and shaking itself before it had time to consider the fate which had taken one and spared another.

Leitner wiped his binoculars and glared through the fading smoke.

'Another minute and we'd have shared the same end, Dieter.'

Hechler steadied his glasses as the Arado's bright paintwork gleamed through the smoke. It was settled on the water, and rocking like a wild thing in the powerful rollers.

He said, 'Stop engines. Slip the boat!'

He raised his glasses once more, thought held at bay while he searched for the aircraft, made himself ready for what he might find.

A voice murmured on the intercom, 'Sounds of ship breaking up, sir.'

It must be the enemy submarine. There was not enough of the milch-cow to disturb their sonar.

He flinched as he saw the horrific face in the rear of the cockpit. Eyes of blood, hands in raised fists behind the slumped figure at the controls.

'Get the doctor on deck!' There was a new harshness in his tone.

Jaeger looked up from the voice-pipes. 'He's already there, sir.'

The motorboat ploughed into view across the lens, familiar

faces he knew and respected leaping past his vision.

Leitner seemed to speak from miles away. 'It's afloat anyway. Good thing.'

Another voice said, 'The boat will tow it to the hoisting gear, sir.'

Was that all Leitner cared? Was it perhaps unimportant to him when so many men had died horribly just moments ago?

He gripped the binoculars harder as the motorboat's bowman clambered on to one of the plane's floats and hauled himself on to the fuselage. He wrenched open the cockpit and faltered. It must be a hundred times worse close to, Hechler thought despairingly.

Then he saw the man turn and signal. One dead.

She was alive. *Alive.*

He lowered his glasses to his chest and made himself walk slowly to the chart-table.

Around him, smoke-grimed and dazed by the cruel swiftness of destruction, the watchkeepers watched him dully.

Hechler said, 'As soon as the boat is hoisted inboard, get under way and alter course as prearranged.' He saw Gudegast nod. 'I want a complete inspection of hull and upper deck. We could have sustained some minor damage.' He touched the rail again. Even as he said it, he sensed that the *Prinz* would be unscathed.

He looked at Theil. 'Take over.' He half-turned to the rear-admiral. 'With your permission of course, sir?'

Leitner looked away. 'Granted.'

Bells jangled softly and the ship gathered way again.

Hechler hesitated at the top of the ladder to watch as the Arado was swung over the guardrails on its special derrick. The doctor and his assistant were there, and some men with stretchers. He hesitated again and looked into the bridge. His world. Now he was sharing it. Hopeless? Perhaps it was. But she was alive. Because of what she had done, they had all survived. He glanced at the admiral's stiff shoulders. He had made an enemy there, but it no longer mattered.

He nodded to Theil and then hurried down the ladder. This world could wait.

The *Prinz Luitpold*'s spacious wardroom was almost deserted. It was halfway through the first watch, and the officers who would be called to stand the middle watch were snatching all the sleep they could. Then the hand on the shoulder, the unfeeling voice of boatswain's mate or messenger, a mug of stale coffee if you were lucky, and off you went to the wretched middle watch.

A few officers sat in deep armchairs, dozing but unwilling to leave their companions, or quietly discussing the explosion which had destroyed the supply submarine and everyone aboard. One man suggested it was lucky they had pumped off most of the fuel. Otherwise both ships might have been engulfed in the same inferno. But most of them, especially the older ones, were thinking of the miles which were hourly streaming away astern. The ship had made a violent turn and was now heading south-east, further and still further from home. If they continued like this, even at their economical speed of fifteen knots, they would cross the Equator in two days' time, and into the South Atlantic.

Viktor Theil as the senior officer in the mess stood with his back to the bar, a glass of lemon juice in his hand. He was conscious of his seniority, the need to set an example at all times in a wardroom where the average age was so low. His immediate subordinate, Korvettenkapitän Werner Froebe, tall, ungainly, and unusually solemn, clutched a tankard of something in one of his huge hands and asked, 'Do you think it went well today?'

Theil eyed him warily. An innocent enough question, but the delay in casting-off from the doomed milch-cow had been his responsibility. It could have been a criticism.

He replied, 'We saved the new plane anyway. Only superficial damage. Pity about the observer.'

Froebe grimaced. 'And the woman. Caught a splinter, I'm told.'

Theil swilled the juice around his glass. 'Could have been much worse.'

He looked at the red-painted bell on the bulkhead. Like an unblinking eye. As if it was watching them, waiting for them to relax, lose their vigilance even for a minute. Then the clamour would scream out here and in every watertight compartment throughout the hull. You never really got used to it.

Even in his bed at home, sometimes in the night – he gritted his teeth. He must not think about it. It would all solve itself. He tightened his jaw. But Britta would have to come to him. She had been in the wrong. He could see it. In the end he would forgive her. They would be reunited as never before.

Froebe watched him dubiously. 'I just hope they know what they're doing.'

'Who?' Theil wanted to finish it but something in Froebe's tone made him ask.

'I don't know. The staff, the high command, OKM, everybody who doesn't have to pick up the bloody pieces!'

Two of the very junior officers hovered closer and one said, 'At home, our people will know about us, and of *Lübeck*'s great sacrifice!'

Theil smiled. 'Of course. We are honoured to serve in this way.'

A figure moved heavily into the light. It was the doctor, jacket unbuttoned, his tie crooked.

He looked at them each in turn, his eyes tired. To Theil he said, 'There are ten casualties below. All doing well.'

Theil nodded. They were the men who had been cut or injured by falling debris on the upper deck after the explosion.

The same young officer exclaimed, 'They are lucky to be free of standing their watch!'

The doctor looked past him. 'The *Lübeck* didn't go down gallantly with guns blazing, by the way.' He returned his gaze to Theil. 'She was scuttled.'

Theil felt as if his collar had suddenly become too tight. Figures in nearby chairs were stirring and turning towards the small group by the bar. From torpor between watches the air had become electric.

Theil exploded, 'What are you saying? How dare you tell such lies in this mess!'

Stroheim gave him a sad smile. 'I was in the W/T office. One of the operators broke a finger when he lost his balance as the supply boat blew up. They were monitoring an English-speaking broadcast, from Bermuda it may have been. But that was what they said.' His voice hardened and he leaned forward, his eyes on Theil's outraged face. 'And something else to fill your pipe with. The Tommies and their allies are up to the Rhine, *do you hear me?*' He swayed and glared around the wardroom at large. 'Ivan is coming at us from the East, and *they're* up to the Rhine!' He looked at Theil again. 'Don't you see, man? We're on the bloody run!'

Theil snapped, 'Keep your voice down! How dare you spread –'

Stroheim made a sweeping gesture. 'What is the matter with everyone? It was in the W/T office! What are they in there, a separate navy, or something?'

Froebe interrupted unhappily, 'Easy, Doctor – this won't help!'

Stroheim removed his glasses and massaged his eyes savagely. 'Then what will, eh?' He stared at the sideboard at the end of the bar, Adolf Hitler's profile in silver upon it with the ship-builder's crest and launch-date underneath.

'All lies. Raised on them, led by them, and now going to hell because of them!'

Theil said sharply, 'I must ask you to come with me.' He could feel his grip returning, although his anger was matched by a sense of alarm.

The doctor laughed, a bitter sound. 'Follow you? Of course, *sir*. Does the truth disturb you that much?'

Froebe saw another figure rise from a chair and then slip through a curtained door.

It was the flag-lieutenant. He suppressed a groan. In about three minutes the admiral would know all about this.

The doctor moved after Theil and said mildly, 'Don't any of you get sick until I return!'

Froebe leaned on the bar and stared at the steward. 'You didn't hear that.'

The man bit his lip. 'No, sir.'

Froebe saw the curtain sway across the doctor's back. The poor sod was drunk too. God, what a mess.

Suppose it was true. If it was, would it make any difference

161

if they held up another convoy, or two dozen of them, *really* make a difference in the end?

He thought suddenly of his wife and two children. Near the Dutch frontier.

He felt like a traitor as he gave silent thanks that the Allies and not the Russians would reach there first.

Hechler clipped the door behind him and stood inside the admiral's bridge. It was illuminated only by the light immediately above the main table against which Leitner was leaning, his hands flat on the chart.

'You sent for me, sir?'

Leitner glanced up. 'I like to know where you are. At all times, eh?'

Hechler watched him as he peered down at the chart again. He had expected Leitner to lose control, to scream at him. It was obvious that he must know about Theil and the doctor.

Hechler had been in his quarters when Theil had come searching for him, his eyes ablaze with anger and indignation. Hechler had closed the door to his sleeping cabin where the girl lay drugged and unconscious after being treated by the doctor. One of Stroheim's attendants had sat nearby, and Hechler had stood beside the bunk, not moving, hardly daring to breathe as he looked down at her. She had seemed so much younger, like a child's face, eyes tightly shut, beads of perspiration on her upper lip and forehead.

A splinter had hit her in the side, just above the left hip. Stroheim had explained that she had lost a lot of blood, and a bone had been chipped, how badly he did not yet know.

Hechler had turned down the sheet and stared at the neat bandages, a small red stain in the centre. She was dressed in a pyjama jacket, and he pulled it across her breast, one of which was exposed in the bunk light.

He remembered the touch of her skin against his fingers as he did so. Burning hot, like some inner fire, or fever. Otherwise, apart from bruising from her harness when she had made a desperate attempt to steady the aircraft as it had smashed down in a deep trough, she was unmarked. It was a miracle.

He thought of Theil's outrage, and Stroheim's apparent indifference. He was still not sure what he would have done, but the telephone had called him here. It might give him time.

Leitner was saying, 'Leutnant Bauer just brought me a new batch of signals. I have been working on them, plotting what we shall do.'

Hechler studied his glossy head and waited. So it was Bauer.

He said abruptly, 'He is one of my officers, sir, and as captain I expect to be informed of every signal which affects this ship.'

Leitner looked up, his eyes cold. 'His first responsibility is to me. I will decide –'

Hechler could feel the armoured sides of the bridge closing in, just as he could sense his rising anger and disgust.

'So it's true about *Lübeck*?'

Leitner straightened his back, his face moving into shadow as he snapped, 'Yes, I knew about it. What had happened.'

'You told our people she had gone down in battle.'

Leitner replied, 'Do not adopt that tone with me. It was the right decision. Afterwards, they can believe what they like!'

'I can't believe it.'

Leitner smiled gently. 'Because Rau was another captain, is that it? Death before dishonour? I can read you like a book. You've not changed, you with your outdated ideals and fancies!'

Hechler met his eyes. '*Graf Spee* would have fought back. Her captain was ordered to scuttle too. It did more damage than losing the ship to the enemy. It was madness.'

Leitner banged his hand on the table. 'I believe he shot himself after that, eh? Hardly the act of a *gallant captain*!'

He moved back into the shadows, his voice barely under control. 'I will not be questioned. I command here, so remember it. And if that idiot Theil cannot keep order in his own wardroom, and shut the mouth of any foul, defeatist rumour, I will have him removed!' He strode about the small bridge, his shadow looming against the grey steel like a spectre. 'God damn it, I could order a man shot for such behaviour!' He swung round and said, 'After all I did for him, the ungrateful bastard!'

Hechler said, 'He brought the doctor to me, sir.'

'And I suppose you gave him a pat on the back! He can do

no wrong, not one of *your* officers, oh no! Ingratitude, that's what it is. I am betrayed on every side –'

'I'm sure he acted as he thought right, sir.'

'Not before half the ship's officers heard what Stroheim said.' Leitner paused by the table, his chest heaving with exertion. 'I should have known, should have overridden your belief in the man, damn him. No wonder his bloody wife was taken away –'

He paused at that point, his eyes staring, as he realised what he had said.

Hechler pressed his hands to his sides. 'When was that, sir?' He leaned forward. 'I must know!'

Leitner ran his fingers through his hair and replied vaguely, 'When we were at Vejle.'

All that time, while Theil had gone around the ship like a man being driven mad by some secret worry, Leitner had known.

'What had she done?'

Leitner took his calm voice as some kind of understanding. 'She had been making trouble. Her parents were arrested. Terrorists, I expect.'

'Is she in prison, sir?'

Leitner's gaze wavered. 'The Gestapo took her.' He looked at the chart without seeing it. 'That's all I know.'

Hechler thrust his hand into his pocket and gripped his pipe. He felt sick, unable to believe what he had heard. *Gestapo.*

Leitner picked up a telephone and added, 'Well, you wanted the truth, Dieter. Sometimes not an easy thing to share, is it?'

'Does Bauer know about it?'

'Yes.' It sounded like *of course.*

'Anyone else?'

Leitner smiled very gently. 'Only you.'

Leitner spoke into the telephone and asked for the navigating officer to be awakened and sent to the bridge.

He put down the telephone and said, 'The war goes on, you see. Within the week we shall carry out an attack which will throw the enemy into utter confusion.'

'Are you going to tell me about it, sir?' He was surprised that he should sound so level. If he had had a Luger in his hand instead of a pipe he knew he could have killed him.

'When I have decided.'

'Then I should like to leave, sir.'

Leitner watched him by the door. 'It is up to you whether you tell Theil about his wife. The ship comes first, you told me so yourself. If Theil is told, what good can it do? He is like the rest of us. A prisoner of duty until released, or killed. As it stands, stupid as he may be, he is a competent enough officer. I will not tolerate interference with my plans because of him, or anyone else, do I make myself clear?'

'Perfectly, sir.'

'Then you *are* dismissed.' He bent over the chart again.

Hechler opened the door and groped his way through the darkness, the night air clammy around him.

On the forebridge all was quiet, the men on watch intent on their various sectors, although Hechler guessed that Theil's confrontation with the doctor would by now be common knowledge.

He thought of the men he commanded. The ones who had trusted him, who had listened to Leitner's passionate speech about the *Lübeck*. Her sacrifice, he had termed it. Rau must have been ordered to scuttle his ship by no less than the Führer. Was there no room left for honour?

He knew Theil was waiting for him, could see his dark outline against the pale steel.

Theil said in a fierce whisper, 'I have sent him to his quarters, sir.'

'Good.' Hechler walked past him. 'I will have a word with him in the morning.'

Theil persisted angrily, 'He was raving about the *truth* all the time! Why should we be told everything, when security must come first! I did not believe him anyway – we would have been informed if –'

Hechler did not hear the rest.

What would you do with the truth, I wonder? If I told you here and now that your wife had been taken by the Gestapo?

He looked over the screen and allowed the spray to refresh

his face. She was probably in some terrible prison. She might even be dead. God, it did not bear thinking about.

Theil finished, 'Duty first, I say. The truth can wait.'

Hechler slipped into the chair and touched his arm. 'If you say so, Viktor.'

It was as if Theil had decided for him.

12

Doubts

Konteradmiral Andreas Leitner appeared to shine as he stood in the entrance of the conning-tower and waited for Hechler to receive him.

'All present, sir.' Hechler touched the peak of his cap and noted that Leitner was dressed in white drill, with a freshly laundered cap-cover to set it off.

Inside the conning-tower it was already stiflingly hot despite the fans, and the sunlight which cut through the observation slits seemed to add to the discomfort of the ship's heads of department who were crowded around the chart-table.

Leitner stepped over the coaming and nodded to his subordinates. For the next few moments at least *Prinz Luitpold* would be in the hands of her junior officers.

They were all there, Theil, beside the towering Gudegast, Froebe, and Kröll, even Stück, immaculate in a white boiler suit and somehow out of place. Oberleutnant Meile, the stores officer, who could at any time tell you how many cans of beans or sausages were being consumed per every nautical mile steamed, and of course Bauer, the smooth-faced communications officer.

Hechler saw the new doctor's shape wedged in one corner, as if he was trying to stay out of sight.

Leitner cleared his throat and glanced at his aide. 'Very well, Helmut, we will begin.'

Hechler saw Gudegast raise an eyebrow at Froebe, and the

latter's brief grin. Leitner's familiarity with his flag-lieutenant was unusual in public.

Hechler felt their interest as the aide laid a new chart on the table. It was covered with arrows and estimated positions where Leitner had plotted the ceaseless stream of information gathered by the W/T office.

He thought of the hasty Crossing the Line rituals that morning as the ship had reached the Equator, the makeshift ceremony on the forecastle while the anti-aircraft guns had sniffed at the clear sky, and every lookout had scanned his allotted piece of ocean. There was no carrier within a hundred miles, nor had any more submarines been reported. But the spies and the intelligence network which had been built up into an efficient worldwide machine during the past ten years or so, could not be expected to have all the answers.

Hechler had been on the bridge and had watched the boatswain, Brezinka, dressed in a false beard of spunyarn and a flowing robe made of bunting. His cropped head had been topped by a convincing crown, as he had challenged the cruiser's right to enter his domain. The rough ceremony was like a tonic after the strain and uncertainty, and even the young officers who were subjected to the 'bears'' rough handling and ducked in a canvas bath, took it all in good part.

He thought of the girl who was confined to his own quarters, of his last, short visit there. She had been propped on a bank of pillows, dressed in another pyjama jacket which Stroheim's assistants must have found somewhere. She had greeted him with a smile; once again it had been an awkward greeting. Not as strangers this time, but like those who have been parted for a long while. 'Are they taking care of you?' Even that had sounded clumsy. He had wanted to tell her how he had touched her, had later sat on the bridge chair and thought about her, when the words had flowed so easily through his mind.

She had smiled and had tried to struggle up on her elbows. He had seen the sudden pain in her eyes, and helped her to be comfortable again.

She had said, 'You came to me when I got back.'

'Yes. We were all so proud of you.' He had looked at his

hands. 'I was very proud. I thought when I saw the damage –'

She had reached out and their hands had touched. 'I knew you'd wait for me. Somehow I thought you'd pick me up.'

She had lain back, her hand still against his. 'How is the plane?' she had asked.

Then they had laughed together. As if it mattered.

Hechler looked up as Leitner's voice brought him into the present.

'It has been confirmed that the major convoy of enemy troops is going ahead.' He waited for his aide to rest a pointer on the chart. 'Around Good Hope, then escorted all the way to Gibraltar to change to an even larger protective screen with all the air cover they need.' He eyed them calmly, and Hechler wondered if the others were thinking of the doctor's outburst about the *Lübeck*, the Allied successes in France and Holland. Equally, if Leitner was searching for doubt or disloyalty amongst them.

Hechler glanced at Theil. He looked very calm, but the hands which gripped the seams of his trousers made a lie of his composure.

Leitner continued, 'If the British have a weakness it is their overriding interest in protecting life rather than the materials of war. They do not seem to realise that without such materials, they can lose everything, including the lives of those they intended to defend. It is a false equation, gentlemen, and we shall prove just how futile it is.'

The pointer moved on past the Cape, where the Atlantic met the power of the Indian Ocean.

'In moments of crisis, whole armies have been forced to a halt by the inability to keep up a supply of fuel. Even our own forces in Russia have often been in a stalemate because of hold-ups, flaws in the supply-line.'

Hechler thought of the great battleship *Tirpitz*, confined in her Norwegian fjord while her fuel had been earmarked for the tanks on the Eastern front. Because of her inability to move, the British midget submarines had found and crippled her. It was unlikely she would ever move again. Hechler still believed that the precious fuel would have done far more good in *Tirpitz*'s bunkers than in a squadron of snow-bound tanks in Russia. She was the greatest warship ever designed. If she were here now, they could have taken on the troop convoy and destroyed it, no matter what escorts were thrown against them.

Leitner said, 'There is just such a convoy, two days behind the troopships. A fast one, of the very largest tankers.' He allowed his words to sink in as the pointer came to rest on the Persian Gulf. 'It was assembled here. Twelve big tankers. Think of them, gentlemen. The life-blood of an army!'

Then his tone became almost matter-of-fact, bored even, as he said, 'Except for any unforeseen factor there would be little chance of surprise. My information –' his gaze rested only lightly on Hechler '– is that the enemy has no idea where we are at present, nor how we are obtaining our own fuel supply.' He nodded slowly. 'Planning, gentlemen – it far outpaces sentiment and outmoded strategy.' He jerked his head at his aide. 'Show them.'

The pointer rested on a mere dot in the Atlantic, just north-west of Ascension Island.

Leitner watched their faces as they all craned forward. 'The island of St Jorge.'

Gudegast said, 'A rock, nothing more. Like a pinnacle sticking up from the ocean bed.'

Leitner gave him a thin smile. 'I shall ignore your scepticism. You are, after all, more used to trading your wares around the sea ports than practising the arts of war, eh?'

Gudegast flushed, but when he opened his mouth to retort, Froebe touched his arm.

Hechler saw it, but doubted if anyone else had noticed the warning.

Leitner said, 'There is a Cable and Wireless station there which was built just before the outbreak of war.' His eyes flashed. 'Before we were forced as a nation to defend ourselves against British Imperialists and the dictates of Judaism!'

His aide said nervously, 'The wireless station has a powerful transmitter, more so even than those in the Falklands.'

Hechler asked, 'Shall we destroy it, sir?' He felt he had to say something, if only to snap the tension, to release his officers

170

from being addressed like unreliable schoolboys.

'I spoke of *surprise*.' Leitner was very relaxed. Only the eyes gave away his triumph, the sense that he had them all in the palm of his hand. 'Provided we are not detected or attacked by some untoward enemy vessel, I intend not to destroy that radio station, but to capture it!'

They all stared at each other, their incredulity giving way to surprised grins as Leitner explained, 'We will *fly* our landing party ahead. By this method the enemy will have no chance to warn their patrols and raise the alarm. Down here, in mid-Atlantic, it would be the last thing any sane man would be expecting.' He turned his face very sharply to Hechler. 'What do you say?'

Hechler pictured the lonely Cable and Wireless station. An outpost in the middle of nowhere. No real loss to the enemy if some long-range U-boat surfaced and shot down the radio masts. But absolutely vital if they could signal the *Prinz*'s where-abouts.

Hechler said, 'Capture it and make a false signal.'

Leitner said, 'Yes. When – er, we are ready.'

He sounded irritated, disappointed perhaps that Hechler had not waited for a full explanation of his plan.

Hechler said, 'It is a wild chance.' He looked at Theil's blank face. 'And I think it might just work.'

What did it matter now anyway? Any risk, almost, was justi-fied this far from base. Keep the enemy guessing, leave no set or mean track, and then they would continue to hold an advan-tage. A final confrontation could be avoided if their luck held out.

Leitner said, 'We will have another conference tomorrow.' He eyed them for a few seconds. 'Early. I will not abide laggards in this command!'

He swung on his heel and left the conning tower.

Gudegast exclaimed, 'Aircraft? Better them than me!'

Theil crossed to Hechler's side. 'What do you really think?'

Hechler looked at the chart. If they failed to mount a surprise attack it would be an open invitation to every enemy squadron and patrol to converge on the tiny island of St Jorge. Hechler

171

pictured the *Lübeck* as she must have been, heeling over, her guns silent while the enemy watched her final moments.

Suppose a signal was handed to him? The order to scuttle rather than meet an honourable fate; what should he do? What *could* he do?

He said, 'It is a daring plan, Viktor. It would mean leaving some volunteers on the island. For them, the war would be over, but we will cross that bridge when we come to it. After the war they might be heroes.' He watched for some sign of a smile or even disagreement. But Theil said fervently, 'For Germany. *Any* man would volunteer!'

'Perhaps.' He heard Gudegast give a snort of anger at something Froebe had said and when Theil turned to listen he watched his profile. Did he suspect, he wondered? Surely no man could love someone and not feel her anguish, her need?

For all their sakes, the ship had to come first. And yet, had he been informed earlier, when Leitner had not been aboard, would he have told Theil about his wife?

Suppose it had been Inger?

He saw the doctor making for the door and called, 'I want to talk to you.'

The doctor faced him warily. 'Sir?'

'Come to the bridge. I should like to ask you something.'

Theil watched them leave and ground his teeth. Thick as thieves, even after what had happened.

It was because of that girl. How could the captain behave so stupidly? Any officer, let alone one given command of a ship like this, had to be above such things. He stared after the others as they hurried away to their various departments. It was all so unfair. *I should have command here.* Perhaps it had all gone wrong a long time ago without his knowing? Britta may have said or done something indiscreet. It would go on his record, not hers. He clenched his fists together until he felt sick with the realisation. It had been her fault. When the war was over, he would be overridden by younger men; he might even be discharged! He thought of the friendly way Hechler had spoken to the doctor.

A new strength seemed to run through him. This was his

chance to show Hechler, to prove to everyone what he could do, how much he was worth.

Gudegast rolled up his chart and watched his superior grimly. What was the matter with everybody, he wondered, if they could not see that Theil was cracking up?

He glanced at his watch. He would work on his charts and then retire to his cabin. The painting was coming along well. He gave a great sigh. Gerda was probably fixed up with another man already. He grinned. The painting would have to do instead. But for once he was unable to lift his apprehension.

Hechler felt the arm of his chair dig into his side, remain there, and then slowly withdraw as the ship swayed upright again. They had reduced speed to twelve knots and the *Prinz* was finding it uncomfortable. She was more used to slicing through every kind of sea with her cutaway Atlantic bow.

Despite the clear blue sky it was chilly on the open bridge after the heat of midday. The sun looked like a solid bronze orb, and was already laying a shimmering cloak down from the hard horizon line. Hechler turned up the collar of his watchcoat and saw his reflection in the glass screen. Hat tugged over his forehead, the old grey fisherman's sweater protruding through his heavy coat. Not everyone's idea of a naval officer, he thought.

A seaman handed him a mug of coffee and another to the doctor who had joined him, somewhat uneasily in that corner of the bridge. Hechler said, 'It will be another clear day tomorrow.'

'Is that good, sir?' He watched Hechler's strong profile. A face with character and determination. No wonder Erika Franke was so interested. She had not said as much, nor had he asked her directly, but Stroheim knew enough about women to recognise the signs.

Hechler sipped the coffee. It must have been reheated for a dozen watches, he thought. But it was better than nothing.

'It could make things easier for our pilots.' He thought of the girl in his bunk. It might have been Leitner's intention to send her with the others, perhaps with a film camera as her sole protection. She had at least been spared that. He thought too of his answer. Another clear day might also bring an unexpected ship or aircraft, detection and the beginning of a chase.

Hechler added abruptly, 'You were stupid to speak as you did in the wardroom. I should punish you, but –' He turned in the chair and glanced at the doctor curiously. '*But*, that word again.'

Stroheim smiled awkwardly. 'Perhaps I was wrong. I'm sorry. But I was angry at the time, incensed. Not that I could do anything.'

Hechler turned away to watch the horizon as it began to slope to the opposite side once more. *In another moment he will ask me what I think, if what he heard is true.*

He said, 'You are a non-combatant, but out here you are at risk like the rest of us.'

Stroheim made himself look at the ocean and shivered despite his thick coat.

He would be glad when night fell. The ship became more dominant, invulnerable, just as his own quarters and sick-bay had become personal, an escape.

He watched the bronze reflection and knew he would never be at home on the sea. Up here, on one of the highest points in the ship, it was all the more obvious. A vast, shark-blue desert, endless in every direction, horizon to horizon, so that the great ship seemed to shrink to something frail and unprotected. He thought of Gudegast, a man he liked although the navigator fought off every kind of close contact. He was at home out here, could find his way as others might grope through a city fog.

A man of peace, no matter what he proclaimed openly. A true sailor, not a professional naval officer like Theil and most of the others. He glanced at Hechler again. And what about the captain? One who was not of any mould he knew. A loner, who accepted leadership without question.

Stroheim asked, 'Do you ever have doubts?' For a moment he thought he had gone too far, that the small contact was broken.

Hechler swung round in the chair, his eyes very blue in the

174

strange light.

'Doubts? What do you think? You are the expert, surely!' He became calm again, angry perhaps that his guard had been penetrated so easily. 'My day is full of them. I must question the weather, my resources, the strength and weakness of every man aboard. The ship is like a chain. A weak link can cause disaster.'

He forced a smile. 'Satisfied?'

Stroheim grinned. 'I am glad you are in command. I hate the sea, but if I must be here, then so be it.'

Hechler did not look at him. 'You are a man of the world. While I have been at sea, learning my profession, you have seen and done many things. You must have found the war very difficult.'

Stroheim replied, 'I thought at first it was the end of life as I had known it. You on the other hand would have seen the war as a culmination of things, a suitable theatre to practise the arts of battle, to exercise all that training.' He looked at the captain's profile again. 'But I learned to live with it. People always need doctors.'

Hechler heard the bitterness. 'I know you were in trouble with the authorities.'

Stroheim grimaced. 'The whole world seems to know that.'

He recovered himself and added, 'But I am a good doctor, surgeon too. Otherwise I would be in field-grey on the Russian front instead of here on a cruise.'

'You see, I am ignorant of that kind of life.' Hechler waved his hand over the screen. 'This is what I know best.'

Stroheim's eyes gleamed behind his gold-rimmed glasses. The captain was working round to something which was troubling him. He had experienced it many times, the patient in his plush consulting room, the roundabout approach to what was really the problem.

Hechler glanced round at the watchkeepers, familiar faces, men and boys who trusted him.

He lowered his voice. 'I knew someone who got into trouble, too. He was arrested, in fact.'

Stroheim held his breath. 'Easy enough to do.'

175

Hechler did not seem to hear. 'I was wondering, what sort of process does it involve?' He changed tack immediately. 'Here, in my command, justice is swift but I hope fair. I would never punish a sailor just to prove my authority. I am the captain, that is all the proof they need. The rest is up to me.'

Stroheim made himself look abeam where some large fish were leaping from the swell and flopping down again. He could feel Hechler watching him, could sense the importance of his casual questions. 'It depends on which security force is involved.'

Hechler said, 'Suppose it was at the top, the Gestapo. I mean, they have a job to do, but they must surely tread carefully too?'

Stroheim clenched his hands in his pockets. Gestapo. The *bottom*, he would describe them.

He said tightly, 'They are scum.' He felt the same recklessness as when he had spoken to Theil of the British broadcast. 'They are a machine for creating terror.' He faced Hechler suddenly and said, 'If your friend is in their hands, he can expect as much mercy as a heretic facing the Spanish Inquisition!' He turned away and stammered, 'I – I am sorry, sir, I had no right –'

He started as Hechler gripped his arm. 'Do not apologise. I asked for your help. You gave it.' He retained his grip until their eyes met. 'I have been in the dark.'

Feet clattered on ladders, and the watchkeepers shifted their bodies about, impatient to be relieved so that they could go below to their other world.

Stroheim flinched as Hechler said, 'I will not *ask* you this other question.' He tried to smile, but his eyes were very still and cold. 'You knew my wife. She had come to you for an abortion before, but this time you could not help.'

Stroheim stared at him. 'You knew?'

'*Guessed*. She came to my ship as you know. I should have realised why she had come, I ought not to have had *doubts*, eh?'

Stroheim said quietly, 'You would not be the first one to be deceived, Captain. She would have claimed that the child was yours.'

Hechler looked away. How could anyone hate the sea?

He said, 'Thank you for your company.'

Stroheim moved away as Kapitänleutnant Emmler, the assistant gunnery officer, clumped on to the bridge to take over the First Dog Watch.

As he reached the internal companion ladder he heard Hechler call after him. He turned and said, 'Captain?'

Hechler merely said, 'Between us.'

Stroheim nodded, suddenly moved by the man's quiet sincerity. 'Of course. Until the next time.'

Hechler faced the ocean again and wondered why he had spoken so freely with the doctor.

He had not needed to demand an answer from him about Inger, it had been plain on his face. But in his heart he had also known it, and that was what hurt the most.

The tiny cabin was more like a store or ship's chandlery than a place to live and sleep. There were shelves, jam-packed with wire strops, spare lashings and blocks. Mysterious boxes were wedged beneath the bunk, and the air was heavy with paint, spunyarn and tobacco smoke.

Rolf Brezinka sat cross-legged on the bunk, a huge pipe jutting from his jaw. The cabin was very hot, the air ducts switched to a minimum flow, and he wore only his singlet and some patched working trousers. As boatswain he stood alone, between wardroom and petty officers' mess. One of a dying breed, he often said, a man who could turn his hand to any form of seamanship, who could splice wire or hemp with equal skill, and who knew the ship's hull like his own battered face.

Opposite him, a cigar jammed in one corner of his mouth, was Oskar Tripz, the grey-haired petty officer. They were old friends, and although both had given most of their lives to the navy, they had each served in the merchant service between the wars, and more to the point in the crack Hamburg–Amerika Line.

When Brezinka had been drafted to the *Prinz Luitpold* he had pulled strings to get his old comrade and fellow conspirator posted to her too. The strings he pulled were unorthodox, but carried no less power than the brass at headquarters.

'It's asking a lot, Oskar.' *Puff, puff.* The big, crop-headed boatswain eyed him grimly through the smoke. 'We've taken a few risks, but I don't know about this one.'

Tripz grinned. At first he had thought of ignoring it, of telling young Stoecker some cock-and-bull yarn to set his mind at ease. Then, the more he had thought about it, the less of a risk it had become. Those cases contained loot, there was no other word for it. Tripz had served in a destroyer in the Norwegian campaign and had seen senior officers shipping their stolen booty back to Germany. They came down like an avalanche on any poor sailor who so much as lifted a bottle of beer without permission. It was all wrong. Leitner must be in it up to his neck, although a ship was the last place Tripz would have stored it, unless he could not trust anybody.

He said, 'Suppose we're wrong? Maybe all the boxes are full of papers, secret files and the like.' He could see that Brezinka did not think so either. 'If we are, we'll drop it right there.'

Brezinka removed the pipe and shook it at him. 'You bloody rogue!' He grinned. 'How *could* we have a look-see? The place is guarded, day and night, and we don't want half the ship's company getting involved. I'm an old bugger, but not ready for the firing party just yet, thank you very much!'

'Nor me.' Tripz rubbed his chin. 'The only time the place is left without a sentry is –'

The boatswain frowned. 'I know. When the ship is closed up at action stations, you in your turret, and me in damage-control. No, mate, it just won't work.'

Tripz sighed. 'What about Rudi Hammer?'

The boatswain stared incredulously. 'Mad Rudi? You must be as crazy as he is!'

Hammer was a petty officer with the damage-control party and on the face of it, the obvious choice. He was no boot-licker, not even a Party member, and although he said very little, was liked by almost everyone, perhaps because of his eccentricity. His hobby was glass. He was determined to retain his skills as a glazier, in spite of all his mechanical training, and nothing could deter him. His divisional officer had had him on the carpet several times about scrounging glass and cluttering his mess with it; he had even taken him in front of Theil because of it. Glass was dangerous in a confined space, especially if the ship was suddenly called to action.

It made no difference. Some hinted that Rudi Hammer's apparent dedication was his way of staying sane, not the other way round.

Brezinka persisted, 'You couldn't rely on him, Oskar, he might blow the whole plan to the executive officer.'

Tripz shook his head. 'He hates officers, you know that, Rolf.'

'But, but –' Brezinka grappled for words. 'It makes me sweat, just thinking about it. No, we'd best forget the whole idea.'

Tripz said, 'If Rudi has any doubts, you know who he goes to?'

The boatswain swallowed hard. 'Well, *me*.'

'Exactly.' He leaned over to stub out the cigar. 'I'll put it to him. The rest is up to you.' He knew that his friend was wavering. 'Look, Rolf, we've been through a lot together. Remember the time we sold that fishing boat to a Yank, when it belonged to the harbour master?'

The boatswain grinned sadly. 'It would have meant jail in those days, not the chop.'

'They'll dump us when this lot's over. Like last time. I don't want to end up on the scrap heap, begging for bread, do you?'

Brezinka nodded firmly. 'No. You're bloody right, old friend. Let's just have a peep at the boxes.' He winked. 'Just for the hell of it.'

They both laughed and then solemnly shook hands.

'Mad Rudi it is.'

She lay as before propped up on pillows, her face pale in the bunk light.

Hechler heard Stroheim's orderly leave the cabin and after a slight hesitation sat down beside the bunk.

She watched him and said, 'You look tired.'

He saw that she had placed her hands under the sheet. In case he might touch one, he thought.

'How are you feeling?'

She smiled. 'The motion is awful. I was nearly sick.' She saw his concern and added, 'I'm feeling better. Really.'

Hechler heard the dull clatter of equipment, the buzz of a

179

telephone somewhere. Perhaps for him. No, the red handset by the bunk was silent. Mocking him.

He explained how the ship was moving slowly to reach their rendezvous at the right time.

She listened in silence, her eyes never leaving his face.

'Don't you get tired of it?' She reached out from beneath the sheet and gripped his hand. 'It never ends for you, does it?'

He looked at her hand, as he had on the bridge that first time. Small but strong. He found he was squeezing it in his own.

'You know about the plan to fly off our Arados ahead of the ship?'

She nodded. 'Yes. The admiral came down to see me.' She seemed to sense he was about to withdraw his hand and said, 'No. Stay like this, please.'

Hechler grimaced. 'I am behaving like an idiot again.'

She returned his grip and smiled at him. 'A nice idiot.'

He asked, 'Can it be done?' He had pictured the two pilots missing their way, flying on and on before they fell into the sea.

She seemed surprised, touched that he should ask.

She replied, 'Yes, they could find it. After that –'

Hechler pushed it from his thoughts and said, 'I want you to be well again very soon.' He studied her face, feature by feature. 'My little bird belongs up there, where she is free.' He smiled and added, 'I wish –'

She saw his hesitation and asked softly, 'You wish I was not here, is that it? You are going to fight, sooner or later, and you are afraid for me?' She tried to raise herself but fell back again. 'Do you think I cannot tell what is going on in that mind of yours? I have watched you, listened to what your men say, I gather fragments about you, because it is all I have!' She shook her head against the pillow. 'Don't you *see*, you stupid man, I want you to *like* me!' She was sobbing now, the tears cutting down her cheeks and on to the pillow. 'And I look a mess. How could you feel more than you do?'

Hechler placed his hand under her head and turned it towards

180

him. Her hair felt damp, and he saw a pulse jumping in her throat, so that he wanted to press her tightly against him and forget the hopelessness of it, the drag of the ship around them. He dabbed her face with the corner of the sheet and murmured, 'I dare not use my filthy handkerchief!' He saw her staring up at him, her lips parted as he continued quickly, 'You do not look a mess. You couldn't, even if you wanted to.' He touched her face and pushed some hair from her eyes. 'And I do like you.' He tried to remain calm. 'More than I should. What chance –'

She touched his mouth with her fingers. 'Don't say it. Not now. The world is falling down about us. Let us hold on to what we have.' She pulled herself closer to him until her hair was against his face.

'You came for me. I shall never forget. I wanted you to know.'

It was more than enough for her and he could feel the drowsiness coming over her again as if it was his own.

He lowered her to the pillow and adjusted the sheets under her chin. In the adjoining cabin he heard the orderly humming loudly, a warning perhaps that the doctor was on his rounds.

Then he bent over and kissed her lightly on the mouth.

A telephone buzzed in the other cabin and he turned to face the door as the white-coated orderly peered in at him.

'The Admiral, sir.'

Hechler nodded and glanced down again at her face. She was asleep, a small smile still hovering at the corners of her mouth.

Hold on to what we have.

He found he could accept it, when moments earlier he had believed that he had nothing left to hold on to.

13

Revelations

Acting Commodore James Cook Hemrose trained his binoculars towards the oncoming cruiser and watched as she started to swing round in a wide arc, in readiness to take station astern of the *Pallas*.

It should have been a proud, satisfying moment. The newcomer was the third ship in his squadron, the *Rhodesia*, a graceful vessel armed with twelve six-inch guns. Fast, and fairly new by wartime standards, she was commanded by Captain Eric Duffield, a contemporary of Hemrose; they had even been classmates at Dartmouth. Hemrose grimaced angrily. That felt like a million years ago.

He saw the diamond-bright blink of her signal lamp, heard his chief yeoman call, 'From *Rhodesia*, sir. Honoured to join you.'

Hemrose would have liked to send a witty reply, but the moment had soured him. Duffield would hate being ordered here, to serve under his command. They had always been rivals. Even with women.

He snapped, 'Acknowledge.' It was strange, these *Mauritius* Class cruisers were in fact slightly smaller than his own ship, but they appeared larger, more rakish.

The destruction of the convoy by the German raider had been hard to take, when so many warships were out searching for her. But it had put an edge to their purpose; he had felt it too when he had visited the New Zealander, the *Pallas*. A spirit of determination, a need for revenge.

Now there would be a sense of disbelief, anti-climax even, with the obvious prospect of being returned to general duties. He tried not to face the other important fact. It would also mean dipping his temporary promotion. He ground his teeth. *For all time.*

He lowered his glasses and watched the new cruiser continuing to turn in a great display of creaming wash. The weather was quite faultless. Clear blue sky, sunshine to display *Rhodesia*'s square bridge and raked funnels, her four triple turrets. When Duffield had finished buggering about, getting his ship perfectly on station, he would doubtless make another signal. To say he was sorry that the hunt was over. Meaning exactly the opposite.

Hemrose saw the commander hovering nearby and said, 'What time is our ETA at Simonstown?'

The commander watched him doubtfully. Hemrose had been even more difficult since The News, as it was termed in the wardroom. He could sympathise with Hemrose, although in secret Commander Godson was not sorry to be spared from crossing guns with a ship like *Prinz Luitpold*.

'We go alongside at sixteen hundred tomorrow.'

Hemrose had thought about it until his brain throbbed.

They had received a lengthy signal from the Admiralty, and an even longer top-secret intelligence report. It was quite plain. He should swallow his disappointment, even his pride, and accept it. A United States submarine had made a brief emergency signal to announce that she was in contact with the raider. There had been a shorter one, too garbled to decode properly. It was her last word.

When US warships had finally reached the search area, they had found nothing for a full day, except for a two-mile oil slick, and some cork chippings of the kind used in a submarine's internal paintwork to diminish condensation. Then later, as another darkness had closed in, one of the ships had picked up some human remains. To all accounts there had been little enough to discover in the grisly fragments, except that they were German.

The American submarine was known to have collided with a freighter which had failed to stop after their brief contact. The US commander had signalled that he was returning to base only partly submerged because of the damage to hull and hydroplanes.

Hemrose had considered the signals with great care, and had called the New Zealand captain, Chantril, across for a conference.

The Kiwi had accepted it philosophically.

'So the Yank got in a lucky salvo. Beat us to the punch. But it cost him dearly for doing it.'

Hemrose slumped in the bridge chair and said, 'Get a signal off to Simonstown, Toby. The squadron will refuel on arrival. But *lighters*, not alongside.' He slammed his hands together. 'I want to be ready for sea at the first hint of news.'

The commander opened his mouth and closed it promptly. It was obviously going to drag on until the boss accepted the inevitable. He ventured, 'They won't like it, sir.'

Hemrose slid from the chair and snapped, 'Plotting team in the chart-room, chop chop. I've got a *feeling* about that bloody German.'

In the cool shadows of the spacious chart-room Hemrose glared at his team. A mixed collection, he thought. But he had to admit that they had done well in their new role. Even the chaplain, who had devised a special file of sighting reports and information from neutral sources. It had all come together far better than he had dared to hope. Until the news about the submarine.

He knew they were watching him, gauging his temper. That suited him. He had always found that fear was the best prop to naval leadership.

The navigating officer had updated the charts daily, adding known convoys, escort groups, and isolated strangers in the vast sea area which touched two continents.

Even the progress of a solitary hospital ship was noted. They were always at risk. A U-boat commander might put one down because he had not taken the time to identify the markings, or the brightly lit hull at night-time. Or another, who was on

184

his way back to base, might do it because his search for victims had been ill rewarded.

Hemrose pictured his German captain. No, he was not the sort to sink a hospital ship with its cargo of sick and wounded survivors. Hemrose held no admiration for Hechler whatever. He did not even know much about him, other than the intelligence reports and some newspaper articles, but he knew his worth as a fighting sailor. He could still remember the ship reeling over to the aggressive mauling of those eight-inch guns. Hechler was a man who took risks, who would not damage that reputation by killing wounded men.

He said, 'What do we know, gentlemen, *really* know?' They remained silent and he added, 'Some Jerry remains were picked up but we cannot be certain they were from *Prinz Luitpold*. Or if they were, she might be damaged, steaming away to put it right, preparing to come back into the fight when she's good and ready.'

The navigating officer, a fresh-faced lieutenant who had proved his ability even to Hemrose's satisfaction, said, 'My guess is the latter, sir. She was damaged, and is making for home base again.' He looked at the others as if for support. 'And why not? She's wiped out a convoy and other ships besides – she'll likely get a hero's welcome if she makes it back to Norway or wherever.'

Hemrose nodded, his heavy features giving nothing away. 'Good thinking, Pilot. In which case the Home Fleet will catch the bugger this time.' He looked round. 'Ideas?'

The chaplain cleared his throat. 'But suppose the raider is still at large, sir. Where will she go next? How does she find fuel?'

'Fucking good question.' He saw the chaplain wince at his crude comment, as he had known he would. 'She'll likely go for the big troop convoy, although my guess is that she's left it too late. The escort has already put down two U-boats, and they've not lost a single ship as yet.'

The navigating officer tapped the chart. 'There's the iron-ore convoy, sir. It should be near the Falklands about now.' He lifted the chart to peer underneath. 'Two more off Durban, both

185

destined for the UK, and of course the fast oil convoy from the Gulf.'

Hemrose pictured the network of convoy routes in and out of Britain. In two great wars those same lifelines had almost been cut. Had that happened, the country, and therefore her dwindling allies would have been brought down. So many times, the convoy losses in the Atlantic had outpaced their ability to build replacements. It had been a raging battle from the first day, and the casualties had been awesome. Yet still men went back to sea, again and again, with only a handful of clapped-out escorts to protect them or die too.

He tried to picture himself in *Wiltshire*, a lone raider like Hechler's ship. *At large*, as the chaplain had described it. He would. But the man of God had a point about fuel supplies. It had to be something big before *Prinz Luitpold* could run for home. Iron-ore? He peered at the chart, his shadow across it like a cloud. Once it could have been vital, but not now. Not unless Mister Hitler pulled another rabbit from his hat. The Russians were still advancing, and the Allies were about to burst across the Rhine. It was still almost too hard to believe after all the retreats and stupid mistakes.

The Durban convoys then? He examined the navigator's typed notes. Times, dates, weather, and already some hint of the escort. He said bluntly, 'I'd go for the big prize.' He thrust the upper charts aside. 'The oilers. Still the most valuable convoy, no matter what the newspapers blather about.'

The commander said, 'It would be a terrible risk, sir.' He flinched under Hemrose's red-rimmed stare. 'For the krauts, I mean.'

"Of course it would.' He stood back and decided he would have a Horse's Neck in a few moments to settle his thoughts. 'He could get cut off on the wrong side of the Cape of Good Hope if he decides to go looking for the convoy too soon.'

The commander said, 'But if their lordships and the C-in-C have already considered this, then surely—'

Hemrose beamed at him. Godson's stupidity was somehow reassuring. He had not missed the fact that none of them had further suggested that the *Prinz Luitpold* had been destroyed, or that they were all wasting their time.

He nodded, his mind made up. 'Did you signal Simonstown?'

The commander sighed. 'All agreed, sir.'

Hemrose rubbed his hands. 'Captains' conference immediately we anchor.'

The navigator looked up from the chart and asked simply, 'But if we're wrong, sir?'

Hemrose did not reply at once. 'You mean if *I'm* wrong, Pilot?' They all laughed politely.

Hemrose picked up his cap and studied it. It would look good with another row of oak leaves around the peak, he thought.

He said, 'My wife won't like it a bit.'

Not one of them realised that he actually meant it.

Korvettenkapitän Josef Gudegast stood with his hands on his hips and waited for the two Arado pilots to scribble a few more notes on their pads. It might be another warm day, but the dawn air in the conning tower was cold and dank. The massive steel door purred open on its slide and Gudegast saw the captain framed against a dull grey sky.

'Nearly ready, sir.'

Hechler glanced at the two pilots who had sprung to attention. 'At ease.' He knew Gudegast would take care of everything. He had done it often enough, but the pilots had to be certain of their orders. Both float-planes had been stripped of unnecessary weight, and would carry no bombs.

As Leitner had replied testily when this had been mentioned, 'We want to use the radio station, not blow its bloody mast down.'

He was up there now on his bridge, impatient, eager to get moving.

Hechler went over it again. Both aircraft would land in a tiny sheltered strip of water, and the landing party would go ashore without delay in rubber dinghies. The planes would be packed like cans of sardines, he thought. He lingered over the officer in charge, Oberleutnant Bauer. An obvious choice as he was a communications specialist. But he had done very little field training, so a good petty officer had been selected as second-

187

in-command. Eight men in all, excluding the pilots. The intelligence reports were definite about the radio station. It was never fully operational and reliable reports stated that it was about to be adapted as a giant radar beacon. The invasion of Europe had made that an unwanted luxury. There were only three men on that lonely pinnacle of rock. Gudegast had said, 'What a way to fight a war. The poor bastards might never be told if it's over, or who's won!'

Theil had snapped at him, 'The war will end for *them* if they try to sabotage the station!'

Poor Theil, he was looking more strained, with deep lines around his mouth.

Hechler said, 'Met reports are good.' He looked at each of the fliers and recalled Leitner's angry outburst when he had suggested that the new Arado should be sent, and so keep a fully operational one on board, just in case.

Leitner had shouted, 'That is defeatist talk, Captain! For a man of action you seem beset by caution! The new plane will be employed *when I say so!*'

He too seemed more on edge. The prospect of action, the apparent lack of enemy signals. It was like steaming into an impenetrable fog.

Hechler glanced at the bulkhead clock. 'Five minutes.' He nodded to the pilots. 'Good luck.' He recalled his letters to the parents of the men lost in the Baltic. Their faces already wiped from his memory. He resisted the urge to shiver.

He made his way to the forebridge, and noted the lookouts and gun crews huddled together at their defence stations.

There goes the captain. He could almost hear the whispers. *Does he look worried?*

He waited for a seaman to wipe the moisture from his chair and then climbed into it.

Korvettenkapitän Werner Froebe had the morning watch, his face red in the chilled air, his huge hands wrapped around the gyro-repeater so that it looked no larger than a coffee cup. Young Jaeger was nearby, ready to relay orders, watching and learning. He seemed to have become suddenly mature after the lifeboat, and the convoy.

Hechler thought of their two survivors. The aged boatswain was still in a kind of daze, and Stroheim said that he rarely paid attention to anything that was happening. The other one, the young mate called Ames, had made a complete recovery. Hechler pictured the drifting corpses. If anyone ever got over that sort of experience.

Theil joined him on the gratings, his fingers busily adjusting his powerful binoculars.

Hechler glanced at him. 'After we find the convoy, Viktor, we can turn for home. Fight our way right through the British Fleet if need be.'

The first Arado coughed into life and he tasted the sharp tang of high-octane fuel. Surprise was everything. It was unlikely that the crew of the radio station would even guess what had hit them. After all, it had never happened before.

A phone buzzed and the seaman who picked it up yelled, 'Ready, sir!'

Hechler could imagine Leitner peering down from his armoured nest. But he did not turn to look. 'Go!'

The plane roared along the short catapult, dived clumsily towards the water, rallied and then climbed away from the slow-moving ship.

Voices muttered by the starboard ladder and Jaeger said, 'Visitor, sir.'

Hechler glanced across in time to see Theil's frowning disapproval and a signalman's quick grin.

She crossed the bridge very carefully, her hair rippling over her coat collar while she rested on a stanchion for support. Hechler took her hand and guided her to the chair. Once, he glanced up to Leitner's bridge and thought he saw the admiral's cap move back quickly out of sight.

He asked, 'How are you?' He noticed the way she was holding her side and wondered why she had come. All those ladders, and she was still weak from losing so much blood.

She settled down on the chair and tucked her chin into a scarf. 'The doctor said it was safe.' She watched the second Arado as it roared away from the side, the camouflage dull against the dark, heaving water. 'I feel better already.'

189

Hechler heard Froebe say, 'The camera is cranking away, I see! God, we'll all be film stars yet!'

Hechler looked at her and found he was able to shelve his immediate problems. The next fuelling rendezvous. The convoy. The cost in ships and men. Perhaps after that, Leitner would be content. He ought to be.

He offered, 'You look fine. You've got your colour back.'

She looked at him, and for a few moments it was like a bond, a physical embrace although neither of them had moved.

A seaman called, 'From W/T office, sir. They are monitoring a broadcast and request instructions.'

Hechler nodded. 'You go down, Viktor. It may be nothing, but we need all the news we can get.'

He thought of Froebe's sarcastic comment, and then of the supply submarine's hideous end. Leitner had said originally that the women of the camera crew would be transferred to the supply boat with their cans of film. The milch-cow had been due to return to base to replenish stocks of fuel. He did not imagine that the two women would be very pleased at being made to wait for another rendezvous, with the prospect of a battle beforehand. With luck, the risk of damage should be minimal. All the enemy's heavy escorts were with the big troop convoy, and other units were still sweeping to the North for some reason. It was likely that valuable though it was, the convoy of oil tankers would rely on speed and a small, local escort until the last long haul to Biscay and beyond.

She was still watching him, her tawny eyes very bright in spite of the misty dawn reflections.

She said, 'It is like going on and on for ever.' She placed her hand on the rail below the screen so that it was just inches from his.

Another voice called, 'Lost contact with aircraft, sir.'

'Very well.' Hechler looked at her hand. It was almost a physical pain. But it was no longer ridiculous, even though any kind of future was nothing more than an idle dream.

She dropped her voice. 'Do you still miss her?'

Hechler stared. 'No. I – I'm not sure. To say I have wasted my other life beyond this ship, is like a betrayal – a deep hurt.'

The words seemed to burst out of him, yet he could not recall ever being so open with anyone. Like being stripped naked, left without any defences.

She said, 'I know what you're thinking, Dieter. You are wrong. I think all the more of you because of your frankness, your sense of honour.' •

Hechler was only half aware that she had called him by name, that for just a few seconds her fingers had rested on his wrist.

She added, 'I have never met anybody like you.' She withdrew her hand and shrugged. 'Will you make me say it? Would you despise me if I told you?'

He looked at her. The figures around the bridge seeming to mist over like moisture on metal fittings.

He heard himself say, 'I will not make you. Let me say it, no matter what the rights and wrongs are.'

She said, 'We can decide.'

'Yes.' He looked away, afraid she would change her mind because of his inability to find the words. 'I want you.' It sounded so flat, so crude that he looked at her, expecting to see anger, or contempt. He was shocked by the happiness in her eyes, a new brightness there like the moment in his quarters.

She whispered, 'It's all I needed to hear. I've known there was something, I think from the beginning.' She shook her head as if she barely believed it. 'We must talk.'

Jaeger said, 'W/T office, sir.' He held out the telephone, his eyes on the girl.

'Captain?'

It was Theil. 'It was just some Brazilian radio station, sir.' He sounded petulant, as if he thought a junior officer could have been sent to deal with it.

Hechler looked at the horizon. The light was strengthening all the time. He tried to picture it in his mind. One hundred miles to the Cable and Wireless outpost. They should have arrived by now. Give them another five minutes, then full speed ahead. The *Prinz* would be there in three hours. By that time – he glanced at the chair but it was empty. He looked at Jaeger who said, 'She went below, sir.' He sounded very calm, but his young face asked a million questions. Something to tell his hero father about, if they ever got home again.

He heard Theil, humming quietly in his ear. A nervous sound. Hechler said, 'Never mind, Viktor. Check it through. You might glean something, eh?' He put the telephone in Jaeger's hand. 'Ask the navigating officer to come here.' He smiled, glad of something to distract him as he saw Gudegast already present, stripping off the canvas cover from the ready-use chart-table after a quick glance at the clear sky.

'What do you think?'

Gudegast stuck out his lower lip so that his untidy beard sprouted over his uniform, mottled with grey like frost on a bush.

'Now, sir.'

Hechler nodded. The W/T office would have picked up any alarm call from the island if the mission had gone rotten on them. There was always the chance of course that the two pilots had lost their way. He saw Gudegast's expression and knew it was less than likely.

'Take over. Full speed. Warn radar, and tell the Gunnery Officer to muster his landing party.'

Hechler would not be able to step ashore. Nothing was safe any more. But it would have been like a release to tread on firm ground again. With her. Her fingers inside his. Just a few moments of make-believe. He had said it to her. *I want you.* He examined his feelings, and the words seemed stronger than ever. It was true. He climbed into the chair. She had been loved, perhaps even married. He took another glance at his thoughts. Nothing changed. It was not a dream after all.

Theil watched the stooped shoulders of the radio operators, and listened to the endless murmur of morse and static over the speakers. The junior officer in charge, Leutnant zur See Ziegler, stared at him anxiously and said, 'I am not certain, sir. My superior has left no instructions –'

Theil glared. 'I'll deal with it!' He gripped the handle of Leutnant Bauer's private office and then rattled it angrily.

Ziegler stammered, 'It's locked, sir.'

'I can see that, you dolt!' He knew he was being unreasonable, but somehow he could not contain it. Perhaps seeing Hechler with that girl had done it. He was married. What was he thinking of?

'Give me the key!'

The young one-striper wrenched open a desk and handed it to him. Theil saw that it had a red tag on it. To be used only in a final emergency. He ground his teeth. It was unlikely that anyone would bother about coloured tags with a ship on her last nose-dive to the bottom.

He slammed the door behind him and slumped down in Bauer's chair. It was curious that he had never set foot in here since the ship had been handed over by the builders. A secret place. A nerve centre.

He was growing calmer again and took several deep breaths.

There was a framed photograph of a young naval officer on the desk. Theil picked it up and grunted. It was Bauer himself. Typical of the man. He thought of Stroheim's outburst in the wardroom, the stares of the other officers while he shot his mouth off about some enemy propaganda. Naturally the British would claim all sorts of victories for themselves and their allies. They would hope for fools like Stroheim to listen in and spread the poison.

There was another key on the tag, a much smaller one.

Theil listened to the busy radio-room beyond the door. Back to normal, each man thinking of the one-striper's embarrassment when he had been told off. Serve him right, he thought savagely. We all went through it — he pushed the key into a steel drawer and held his breath as it clicked open.

He was the second-in-command. In battle he stayed with damage-control, whereas Hechler usually stood firm on the open bridge and disdained the massive armour plate of the conning-tower. Theil had thought about it often. He guessed that many officers in his position would consider the very real possibility of stepping into a dead man's shoes.

Even Leitner might fall in battle. Theil suddenly saw himself returning to his home in Schleswig-Holstein, to be decorated by the Leader.

His hand faltered on a pale pink folder with the eagle crest

193

and stamp of naval intelligence emblazoned on the cover. He flicked it open and felt his heart stop. His own name was at the top. Serial number, rank, date of commission, everything. There was his original photograph when he had joined this ship. His fingers felt numb, unable to turn the page. He wanted to lock the drawer, leave now, and to hell with the Brazilian broadcast. There was a freshly typed signal flimsy under the first page. His eyes blurred as he scanned the bottom first where Leitner's signature had been counter-signed by Bauer.

The name at the top was Britta's. Apart from a file reference there was little else except for the line which stood out like fire. *No further action by naval intelligence. Subject arrested by Gestapo.*

Theil did not remember locking the desk drawer, or even groping his way from the office.

The young officer snapped to attention and said, 'Nothing more from that station, sir. I—' He stared after Theil as he blundered past him and out of the W/T room.

Theil fought his way to the upper deck and clung to the safety rail by a watertight door for several minutes.

Britta arrested? It could not be. For an instant he was tempted to rush back there and read the file again. But it was true. It had to be.

Britta arrested. He squeezed his eyes tightly shut to find her face as he had last seen her. But all he could see was the empty house and dead flowers, the neighbours watching behind their curtains, the doctor's calculated advice.

He wanted to scream it out aloud. They all knew, must have done. Leitner, and that crawling Bauer. He thought of Hechler, his mind reeling like a trapped animal. He would know too, had probably been told weeks ago.

He allowed his mind to rest on the Gestapo. He had always avoided contact with them like most people. Secrecy had not always worked, and he had ignored that too.

But he had heard things. Torture, brutality for the sake of it. He thought of her face, her pleading eyes, the bruise on her body after she had tried to find out about her parents.

Gestapo. It was not just a word any more. It was death.

The ship began to shake and quiver around him and he knew they were increasing speed towards the tiny islet.

What should he do or say?

He turned his face this way and that, clinging to the rail as if he might otherwise fall.

Britta was dead, or was she even now screaming out her pleas to her torturers?

'No!' His one cry was torn from him, but rebounded against the iron plate as if it too was trapped and in agony.

14

'Auf Wiedersehen . . .'

Oberleutnant Hans Bauer strode down the steep, rocky slope and stared at the two float-planes as they lifted and swayed in the swell. They were safe enough, moored with their small anchors, and each with its pilot still aboard in case the sea should get up.

Bauer stood with his feet planted apart, his fine black boots setting off his uniform to perfection. The heavy pistol at his waist, like the silk scarf thrown casually around his throat, gave him a dramatic appearance, or so he believed. He had enjoyed every moment of it, the culmination of surprise and excitement when the two rubber dinghies had been paddled furiously ashore and his men rounded up their prisoners.

It had gone almost perfectly, but for one unexpected development. There had been two extra people at the radio station. He now knew they were mechanics who had been left here for some maintenance work.

Bauer considered what he would say to the rear-admiral. Leitner would give him the praise he was due for his quick thinking. He shaded his eyes to watch the cruiser's shortened silhouette as she headed towards the small islet, only her bow-wave revealing the speed she was making through the water. After she had topped the hard horizon line in the early light she had seemed to take an age to gather size and familiarity, he thought. He went over the landing, the exhilaration giving way to sudden alarm as the two additional men had appeared. Yes, Leitner would be pleased. He frowned. He was not so sure about the captain.

He turned, his boots squeaking on the rough ground, and surveyed the desolated station. A long, curved corrugated building which the British called a Nissen hut, and two radio masts, one small, the other very high and delicate. It was a wonder it could withstand the gales.

He saw two of his men, their Schmeissers crooked in their arms, and congratulated himself on his choice. Hand-picked, and all good Party members. It was right that they should profit by this small but obviously vital operation.

Closer to the building lay a corpse, covered by a sheet which was pinned down by heavy rocks.

One of the visiting mechanics. He had seen the landing party, and had turned, blundering through his astonished companions, and run towards the building. To send a message, a warning, or to sabotage the equipment, Bauer did not know even now.

He remembered his own feeling as the heavy Luger had leaped in his grip, the man spinning round, his eyes wide with horror as he had rolled down the slope kicking and choking. The second bullet had finished all movement. After that, the others had crowded together, shocked and frightened, seeing only the levelled guns, the sprawled body of the dead man.

Bauer had told them to obey each order without hesitation, and after the building had been thoroughly searched, the radio transmitter checked for demolition charges, they had been locked in a storeroom and left under guard.

Bauer adjusted his cap at a more rakish angle, rather as the rear-admiral wore his. Such a fine officer, an example to them all.

He saw the petty officer, a grim-faced man called Maleg, coming down the slope, two grenades bouncing on his hip. He was not one of Bauer's choice for the raid. He thought of Theil who had detailed the man for the operation. Bauer was suddenly grateful he had never cultivated Theil as anything more than a superior officer. He had had everything within his grasp, and had been stupid, instead of taking full advantage of his position. He owed everything to the Fatherland, everything. How could such a man become involved with a subversive, a traitor? He should have known his own wife better than anyone. He sighed. Instead—

The petty officer saluted. 'About the burial, sir?'

Bauer eyed him coldly. 'The prisoners will do it. It should dampen anyone else's foolishness!'

Maleg stared past him at the distant cruiser. They had found no weapons, no demolition charges either. Even the prisoners were harmless civilians. It was all the lieutenant's fault, but any aftermath would be shared amongst them. Bauer had enjoyed killing the man, he decided. Given half a chance he would have gunned down all the rest. Maleg knew about officers like Bauer. Why had he been the one to get saddled with him?

Later as the prisoners stabbed at the rocky ground with picks and spades, Bauer entered the makeshift radio station and looked with disdain at the garish pictures on the walls, the nudes and the big-breasted girls in next to nothing. Decadent. How could they have hoped to win the war, even with the Yanks as allies?

He pictured his family home in Dresden, the paintings of his ancestors, proud, decorated officers. A heritage which was a constant reminder of his own role and his promising future. Leitner had promised him an immediate promotion with an appointment to the naval staff as soon as they returned to a safe harbour. Bauer was not so blind that he did not know about the rear-admiral's relationship with Theissen, his flag-lieutenant, but nothing could mar his qualities as a leader and an inspiration.

Maleg watched him and was glad that the ship was getting nearer. The *Prinz* was something he could understand and work in. He had good comrades in the petty officers' mess. He sniffed at the aroma of fresh coffee from the hut's spindly chimney. It was quite amazing. They had proper coffee and piles of tinned food which he had almost forgotten. He would take some back with him to the mess, he thought. He tried not to dwell on an old newspaper called *Daily Mail* he had found in the sleeping quarters. He could read English fairly well, but even if he had not been able to, the war maps and photographs with their screaming headlines would have told him anyway. The Allies were said to be through France and Belgium, and the only German resistance was in isolated pockets in Brittany and the Pas de Calais. The sites of the rockets and flying-bombs, the much-vaunted secret weapons, were said to be overrun, their menace removed for all time. It could not all be true. There was mention of some 400,000 German troops being taken prisoner. That could not be accurate, surely?

And the newspaper was not new. What had happened while they had been attacking the convoy? He considered himself to be a good petty officer, and he had destroyed the newspaper before the others could see it.

He looked round as he heard Bauer reading crisply from a small prayer book while the others stood leaning on their spades. Maleg wanted to spit. Kill a man, then send him off with full respects. He watched as Bauer threw up a stiff Nazi salute, then pocketed the prayer book with the same detachment he had shown when he had reholstered his Luger.

The spades moved again and Bauer marched towards the hut.

He said, 'Duty is duty, Maleg, no matter what.'

The petty officer sat down on a rock and waited for one of the men to bring him his coffee.

Suppose. The word hung in his mind. Just suppose they lost the war. It was unthinkable of course, but if the *Prinz* was down here in the South Atlantic, what then?

He turned and peered out at the ship, which in the last minutes seemed to have doubled in size.

Hechler would get them home somehow.

The first Arado was being hoisted up from alongside, many hands reaching out to boom it away from the hull as the ship dipped heavily in the surrounding current.

Leitner had come down to the forebridge, and his cigar smoke drifted over the screen like perfume.

Leitner said, 'Like clockwork. What did I tell you, eh?' He was almost jocular. 'God, what a coup it will be.'

Hechler trained his binoculars on the lonely station. They would land a small party with two of the ship's wireless telegraphists. They would have all the right codes, and even if they had been changed by the enemy, no one would question their one frantic call for help. Several things could go wrong, of course. A vessel might unexpectedly arrive on a visit to the islet. If that happened, a prearranged alarm signal would be made, and the *Prinz* would be on her own again. Or the fuel convoy might be delayed or rerouted. That was so unlikely it could almost be discounted.

What else then? They might meet with enemy warships, be held down to an engagement until heavier forces arrived to join the battle. He had gone over the rendezvous points with Gudegast; there were three possible choices, and the supply submarines would be on station whatever happened.

He glanced at Leitner. The admiral was nobody's fool, and would want to return to Germany as soon as the next convoy was destroyed. They might fall upon other ships on the return passage, small convoys, single fast-moving troopers too.

There was a blackout on Allied radio communications, or so it seemed. The enemy must be puzzled about their sources of fuel supply, and it was likely that all other convoys in the Atlantic had been held up in their ports until the raider's position was verified.

Hechler was a practical sailor but had never ruled out the value of luck. Theirs simply could not last, and he had often imagined some special task force fanning out from Biscay for a sweep south in pursuit. They would have carriers, or at least one. Just a single sighting report was all the enemy admiral needed.

Feet clattered on the ladder and Theil entered the bridge, his eyes concealed by dark glasses.

He said, 'I've sent a double anchor party up forward, sir, and given orders to break the cable if need be.'

Leitner's shoulders shook in a small chuckle. 'More caution, eh?'

Theil ignored him. 'Have you selected the men to remain on the islet, sir?'

Hechler looked at him. 'I have spoken to the doctor, Viktor. Three are still in sick-bay after being thrown from their feet.'

Theil replied, 'I have their names, sir. I did think they were malingering.' His voice was quite flat and toneless.

Hechler turned so that Leitner should not hear. 'Are you all right?'

Theil straightened his shoulders. 'I am.'

Hechler nodded. 'Good. We can land the two survivors also.'

Leitner turned. 'When they are picked up eventually, nobody can say we were not humane!' It seemed to amuse him.

Theil stared past him. 'A man was killed over at the radio station.'

Hechler exclaimed angrily, 'When? Why was I not told immediately?'

Leitner said, '*I* was informed. You were busy anchoring the ship, remember?'

Hechler recalled Bauer reporting aboard when a landing party had been sent to relieve him. An hour ago? It seemed like minutes.

Theil had a hand to his chest as if he was in pain but dropped it as he explained, 'Bauer shot one of the mechanics.' He waited and added harshly, 'A civilian.'

Leitner swung round again. 'In God's name, man, what do you expect? I will not have our people put at risk for any reason! Bauer acted as he thought fit. I will uphold his decision. Millions have died in this war, and millions more will follow, I have no doubt!' He was shouting, ignoring the men on watch nearby. 'One bloody shooting is not my paramount concern, thank you, *sir*!'

Theil eyed him blankly from behind the dark glasses.

'Evidently, sir.' He turned and hurried from the bridge.

'Now what the *hell* was that all about?' Leitner grinned, but his eyes remained like cold glass.

Hechler thought he knew Theil. Now he was not sure of anything. He said, 'Nobody wants to see non-combatants killed, sir. I'll grant that it may have been necessary in this case. However—'

Leitner sniffed. '*However* sums it up, I think!'

Hechler was suddenly sick of him, even of Theil. When the latter discovered— he raised his binoculars to watch the party on the beach to hide his sudden apprehension. Suppose Theil already knew? How could he? As captain he had been told nothing until Leitner's anger had let the news spill out about Theil's poor wife.

Strain, combat fatigue, the yearning for a command of his own, of this ship most of all – moulded together they could have this effect on him.

Leitner said, 'You can speak to the men you have detailed. It will come better from you.' He was calm again, but as their eyes met Hechler could sense the spite in his casual remark.

Tell them you are leaving them behind. Why? For Germany? Would it be enough this time? He gritted his teeth. It was all they had.

He said, 'Tell the sick-bay I am coming down.'

Jaeger picked up a handset and watched him walk past.

Command – was this what it meant? Was this what it might do to the man who held it?

Leitner snapped, 'Don't gape! Do as you're told! By God, I intend to produce a full report on all this when we get back to Germany!'

A messenger called nervously, 'Camera team request permission to come to the bridge, sir.'

Leitner moved away from the side and loosened the collar of his white tunic.

'Of course.' He glanced at the others, Gudegast brooding by the chart-table, the petty officer of the watch, young Jaeger, and the rest of those subservient faces.

'All honour will be shown to this ship, gentlemen. A film which our children will remember!'

Gudegast watched him march to the rear of the bridge. Children? The admiral would have no problems there, he thought.

The ship was still in a state of immediate readiness, if not at action stations. On the petty officers' mess-deck, the air was hissing out of the shafts, compressed and smelling faintly of oil. The deadlights were screwed shut, and most of the watertight doors clipped home. The ship was stopped but only resting, and even the fans and muffled generators sounded wary and ready to switch to full power.

The small cluster of men at the end of one of the tables appeared to be engrossed in the one who was seated, his fingers busily arranging a pattern of coloured glass under an overhead light. Acting Petty Officer Hans Stoecker watched the man's hands working nimbly with the newly cut pieces of glass. Rudi Hammer was putting the finishing touches to yet another small box, a present perhaps for a wife or girlfriend. It was nerve-racking, unbearable, and yet Stoecker knew he must not break the silence. Opposite him, his grey head bowed with no outward show of impatience, Oskar Tripz also watched the box taking shape.

The fingers eased a fragment over and snipped a rough edge away. The man nicknamed Mad Rudi was pale in every respect, hair and lashes, even his skin; he was not far removed from an albino.

Stoecker tried not to think of that day when an unknown hand had given him the letter. The rest was a nightmare.

He glanced at the other petty officer named Elmke, a dour, humourless man whose only friend in the ship, it seemed, was Tripz.

Stoecker wanted to wipe his face. It felt wet with sweat. The sealed air perhaps? He knew otherwise. It was uncontrollable fear and disgust at what he had begun.

It had all seemed like a daring exploit when he had shared the letter with Tripz. He was friend and mentor all in one. But it had got out of hand. Even the boatswain Brezinka was impli-cated, and now Mad Rudi and Elmke.

He concentrated on the pattern of glass. What would his mother say, and his father when he found out? It had all been so simple, so right. As if it was a kind of destiny. Even meeting with Sophie. He turned the thought aside. She had been with Jaeger. An officer.

Tripz said, 'Well, come along, old fellow, spit it out!' He was grinning, but the tension was clear in his voice. 'We have to know, God damn it!'

Hammer put down the flat-jawed pliers he used for snapping off excess glass. 'I nearly broke that piece!' He shook his head. 'After the war they will need all the glaziers in the world to put the cities together again, you'll see!'

Tripz patted his shoulder. 'God, man, if it's true what we think, you can buy your own glass factory!'

Hammer smiled. He was always such a gentle, reserved man. In his petty officer's uniform he looked like an imposter.

He said severely, 'Well, it wasn't easy, I can tell you.'

Elmke said roughly, 'Come *on*, man!'

Tripz shot him a warning glance. 'Easy, Ludwig! Give him time!'

Hammer smiled. 'It is true. I opened just two of the boxes.' He spread his hands. 'Jewels by the thousand, gems of every kind. Gold too. A factory, Oskar? I could buy a whole town with my share.'

The others stared at each other but Stoecker felt as if his guts were being crushed.

They were speaking of a *share*. It was all accepted, decided even.

He heard himself say in little more than a whisper, 'But if we're found out?'

Surprisingly it was Hammer who spoke up. 'In this ship we can die in a hundred different ways, Hans. I do not believe in miracles. We have fought a just war, but we are losing.' He seemed surprised at their expressions. 'Face it, comrades, it is not so bad when we have discovered an alternative to oblivion, yes?'

Tripz produced a bottle of schnapps. Drinking on duty would cost him his rank, all of them for that matter.

Very solemnly he filled four mugs and they clinked with equal gravity together.

'To us.'

Only Stoecker felt that he wanted to vomit. But the nightmare had already grown in size and power. It had been too late when he had taken that letter.

Hechler walked along the port side beneath the elevated barrels of the anti-aircraft weapons, nodding occasionally to familiar faces, pausing to speak briefly with the petty officer in charge of a working party.

There was no difference from being here at this rock and

out on the high seas. The great ocean was the enemy, and yet being anchored made him feel vulnerable, unprepared.

A rising plume of smoke from the funnel showed that Stück and his engineers were equally impatient to move. Men off duty hung about in groups, nervous and not far from their action stations.

A lieutenant crossed the deck and saluted. 'The boat is ready, sir.'

Hechler stared past him at the small landing party, three of whom were still showing signs of their injuries.

It had been a difficult thing to tell them what was required. Hechler knew better than to make a speech. About Germany, the great sacrifice that others had made already.

He had explained simply, 'It is for us, comrades. The ship.'

A senior wireless telegraphist was in charge, with one other assistant, while the remainder were from the sick-bay.

'I shall come back for you if I can.'

He had sensed their efforts to be brave, not to let him down. It was, he thought, one of the hardest things he had ever asked anyone to do.

He walked with the lieutenant to the side, where a motorboat was waiting to transfer the small party to the radio station and bring back the others. After that— he sighed. It was best not to think of how they would feel when they watched their ship speeding away to disappear eventually below the horizon.

They were assembled by the accommodation ladder. Hechler shook hands with each one. He had entrusted a letter to the senior telegraphist to hand to the British or whoever arrived. Under normal circumstances he knew they would be well treated. But with a civilian lying buried on the islet, the letter might ease the situation.

He saw the two prisoners already in the tossing motorboat. The old boatswain had stared at him blankly when he had told him he would soon be released. The other one named Ames had met his gaze, not exactly hostile, but strangely defiant. He had warned the senior telegraphist about him. He was probably safer off the ship, he thought. As a mate, he knew about navigation and would have the *feel* of the sea like Gudegast. You

205

could not watch a man all the time unless he was in irons. He might have been able to escape and sabotage the steering gear or something else vital, even at the cost of his life.

He said, 'I shall send aircraft for you if I can. If not –' He had almost shrugged but had seen the pain on their faces. 'It is the war. Our success rests in your hands.'

He looked round and saw the sunlight flash on binoculars from the upper bridge, and guessed that Leitner was watching each magnified face and reaction.

He thought of Theil. He should be here too. Something would have to be done before they met the enemy again. When their luck ran out.

Hechler saluted as they climbed down the side, one with a plaster cast on his arm swinging round to stare up at his messmates who waved to him. Suddenly, as if at a sign, one of the sailors at the guardrails began to sing. He had a rich, mellow voice, and as Hechler watched he saw many of his men leaning over the rails, their voices joining and rising above the sea, and the splutter of the boat below the ladder.

'*Auf Wiedersehen – until better days!*'

Hechler watched the boat until it vanished around the high bows then walked slowly aft. He remembered his brother Lothar joining with his fellow cadets and singing that same, lilting song when he had gained his commission.

'That must have been dreadful for you.'

He saw her standing by a screen door, one foot on the raised coaming. How long she had been watching he did not know, and yet in some strange way he had been aware of her.

'It was.' He stood beside her, shielded from the rest of the ship by the heavy, steel door.

She said quietly, 'If the war is won they will be free very soon. If not –' She did not continue.

He took her hands in his. 'I have been thinking about you.' He felt her return the squeeze. 'Maybe too much. But I have not forgotten our words up there, in my eyrie.' He saw her smile.

She said, 'People, your men, think you are made of iron. An iron pirate, did you know that?'

He looked down at her, studying her mouth, imagining how

206

it would feel trapped in his.

She watched his face, his indecision. 'But I know the *real* man.'

He said, 'After we leave here –' He tried again. 'When we meet with the enemy – I want you safe. No matter what happens, I need to know you are spared the true danger. After the war –'

Her eyes left his face for the first time. 'I will not wait that long, Dieter.' She looked down and there was fresh colour in her cheeks. 'You think that is cheap, shameless?'

He touched her hair. 'No. I only feel shame for letting you say what I am thinking.'

The junior communications officer, Ziegler, appeared round the door and stared at them blankly.

Then he said, stumbling over the words, 'I have to report that the shore party has tested the signal, sir.' His eyes blinked quickly at the girl as he continued, 'No further enemy broadcasts intercepted.'

'Thank you.' They watched him march off and she said, 'We frightened him, poor boy.'

He knew he must go. 'Later on –'

She stepped back over the coaming, one hand to her side.

'I shall be there. Have no doubt of it.'

Hechler climbed to the bridge and walked to the fore-gratings. Voices hummed up and down the pipes, and messengers and boatswain's mates stood with handsets to their ears and watched the steam from forward as the cables clanked up and through the hawse-pipe.

'Stand by.'

Bells jangled and Gudegast said, 'Course to steer, one-three-five, sir.'

He heard someone murmur behind him, 'See the poor buggers on the beach, Max? I'd hate to be left –'

A petty officer snarled, 'I shall *personally* maroon you if I get the chance! *Stand to*, damn you!'

Hechler felt the sun warming his face through the toughened glass screen. The cable was coming in more quickly now. *Clank-clank-clank.* Would they ever drop anchor again? He smiled despite his anxieties. The Flying Dutchman. He smiled again and seemed to hear her voice. *Iron pirate*. The enemy probably had a less colourful name, he thought.

He craned forward and saw Theil with Leutnant Safer who was in charge of the forecastle, although in action he was quarters officer in Turret Anton. Theil had his arms folded, as if he was hugging himself. Perhaps when they got into open water again he would snap out of his mood.

How would I feel? It was strange that he did not compare Theil's wife's plight with Inger. He pictured Erika's face. Her defiance. And her defeat.

'Anchors aweigh, sir!'

Hechler glanced at the lieutenant of the watch. It was as if the man had had to repeat it before he had understood.

'Slow ahead together.' He felt the deck vibrate gently, the ugly hump of land begin to move past. 'Starboard ten.'

Gudegast crouched over the gyro to check a last fix on the tall aerial.

'Steady. Steer one-three-five.' He picked up the telephone and noticed it had been newly cleaned. 'Chief? This is the Captain. Revolutions for twenty-five knots in half an hour.'

Stück sounded surprisingly close. 'You told me.'

Hechler grinned. 'Getting old, Chief.' He put down the telephone and saw Jaeger talking with Stoecker, the youngster who should have taken his final exam for petty officer but for this raiding cruise. He was obviously worried about it, for his eyes looked quite red. Lack of sleep probably.

Theil came into the bridge. 'Anchor secured, sir. Hands dismissed.'

He stared round the bridge. 'I'm not sorry. Not in the least.'

'Is there something you want to tell me, Viktor?' He glanced past him. 'Now, while we're alone.'

'*I am worried about my wife.*' He seemed to be staring, although the dark glasses made it hard to gauge his expression.

'I can understand that.'

'Can you?' Theil watched two sea-birds rise above the screen, their raucous cries suddenly loud and intruding.

He added calmly, in an almost matter-of-fact tone, 'You didn't have to consult with the doctor about the landing party, sir.

I had it in hand, you know.'

Hechler tugged out his unlit pipe and jammed it in his mouth. 'It was my responsibility.'

Theil nodded very slowly, his dark glasses like two sockets in a skull.

'I see that, sir. A commanding officer must shoulder every burden where it concerns those who have to trust him.' He saluted. 'I must go to damage control and exercise the fire parties.' He added vaguely, 'Might help.'

Hechler made to climb into his chair but walked instead to the opposite side.

Theil was right. *I must tell him.* But Theil's words, his erratic behaviour, held him back, like a warning.

He turned and saw Gudegast watching him from the compass platform. The navigator dropped his gaze immediately, but not before Hechler had seen the concern there. Did he believe that Theil was falling apart? Even his bitter comment about asking the doctor. He was still angry about the scene in the wardroom, and Leitner's offhand indifference.

He raised his binoculars and trained them over the quarter towards the radio tower, but it was already blurred and indistinct. He thought of the unknown seaman's words. *I'd hate to be left.*

Korvettenkapitän Froebe, the executive officer, stamped on to the gratings and saluted.

'Well?' Hechler felt the warning again but could not recognise it.

Froebe shifted his long, ungainly legs.

'I hate to bother you, sir, but one of my divisional officers has made a complaint. He has threatened—'

Hechler stopped him. 'Nobody threatens you, Werner. You are part of my authority, a most important one.' He saw the words go home, some relief on the tall officer's features.

'The communications officer—'

Hechler kept his face impassive. It would be Bauer. A man of great conceit. He had certainly displayed no remorse over killing the civilian.

Leitner had given him his blessing. Was that all it took, after all? *I did my duty, nothing more.*

Froebe continued, 'He claims that the second-in-command entered his private office after forcing the watch-officer to give him the key.'

It hit Hechler like a steel bar.

So that was it. It was so obvious he could not understand how he had missed it. He had even ordered Theil to go there himself.

'You have told me, Werner. Leave it with me, eh?' He smiled, but his mouth felt like stiff leather.

Froebe bobbed his head, satisfied and relieved.

'And tell Bauer to mind his manners. Tell him from me.'

He heard Froebe clattering down a ladder and then bit hard on the pipe-stem.

Theil knew. Who would blame him? What might he do?

When the sun dipped towards the empty horizon he was still sitting in the chair, and his questions remained unanswered.

15

Middle Watch

Gudegast crouched over the chart-table and rubbed his eyes to clear away the weariness. It was two in the morning, but he could not sleep, and wanted to make sure he had forgotten nothing. He read slowly through his neatly written notes and paused again and again to check the calculations against his two charts. The ship was quivering violently beneath him, but he had grown used to that. She was steaming at twenty-eight knots, south-east, over an unbroken sea.

On deck it was easier to understand with a ceiling of bright stars from horizon to horizon. Here in the chart-room, it was all on paper. Noon sights, and careful estimations of tide, speed and weather. It was vaguely unnerving, with only the chart lights for company, but for a while longer he needed to be alone.

He tried not to think of a hot bath, scented with some of that Danish stuff he had picked up in Vejle. So long ago, he thought wistfully. He scratched himself beneath his arm as he pictured the voluptuous Gerda in her little house above the fjord. There would not be many baths from now on. Water was strictly rationed, and it would get worse unless they turned for home. Home? Where was that?

He heard feet scrape against steel and guessed that the watch was changing its lookouts yet again. An empty ocean outside, and yet in here you could see the inevitability of the embrace, the savagery of the approaching battle.

It would have to be a salt-water shower. He grinned into

his beard. He must be getting soft as well as old. In the merchant service, where the owners counted and begrudged every mark spent, you got used to faulty fans, bad food, and machinery which went wrong at the worst moment. It had taken him a long while to get used to the navy, its extravagance at the tax-payers' expense.

The door slid open and he turned with an angry challenge on his lips. Instead he said, 'I've been over it all again, sir.' He watched Hechler by the table, his body shining in an oilskin. So he could not sleep either. *If I were captain* – he stopped it there. Gudegast would not have taken command of a warship if she were ballasted with gold bricks.

Hechler compared the charts. 'At this rate, fifty-seven hours.' He pictured the desert of ocean, their solitary ship heading swiftly on a converging course. There had been no signals from Operations Division, and silence in this case meant that the convoy was on course, and should now be around the Cape and steering north-west. Fifty-seven hours was too long. He peered closer at the pencilled lines and crosses. To increase speed would dig deeply into their fuel supply. To risk a late confrontation might invite disaster. He said, 'Thirty knots.'

Gudegast regarded him gravely. The cruiser could go faster, but she was not on sea trials, nor was she within reach of help if something failed.

Hechler smiled. 'I have just spoken with the Chief.' He saw him in his mind, cautious as ever, but quite confident. 'He agrees.'

Gudegast watched him, feeling his disquiet. 'After this, we can refuel at one of the rendezvous.'

Hechler glanced at him and smiled. It had sounded like a question, a challenge.

'My admiral favours the second rendezvous, 2,500 miles to the west.'

Gudegast dragged the second chart closer. The bright cross marked the exact grid position only; dates and times were safely locked in Hechler's safe.

Gudegast pursed his lips. 'The last thing the enemy would expect.'

212

'What you really mean is, we could be heading further north to the other rendezvous, and cutting off some 900 miles, right?'

Gudegast showed his teeth. 'Something like that, sir.'

'Fuel economy is not always the answer.'

Gudegast picked up his parallel rulers. 'I'll work on it for a while. An alternative might come in handy.'

Hechler nodded. 'I shall be increasing speed in two hours when the watch changes. Let me know what you find in your search.' He paused, one hand on the door clip. 'But get some sleep. I depend on you. You know that.'

The door slid shut and Gudegast stared at it with quiet astonishment. He both liked and respected the captain, but he had never thought that his feelings had been returned.

He grinned and turned back to his charts. He would do a sketch of the captain at the first opportunity. Just him with the ocean behind his back. It was something to look forward to.

Hechler did not remember much about leaving the chart-room, nor did he feel the usual guilt at not being on the bridge or in his little sea-cabin.

The charts, Gudegast's finality over the converging ships, had cast a cloak over all else. There was nothing, could be nothing beyond this ship, he told himself. Even if his suspicions about Theil were correct, he could not reveal it now or Leitner would have him arrested, humiliated and disgraced before everyone. God, it was bad enough as it was. Theil loved the *Prinz* as much if not more than all of them. He would not do anything to destroy that loyalty. But if the shock of his wife's arrest had acted as a twist of guilt, he might not even be the man he had once known.

He almost smiled. He was the one who had told Theil about a captain's responsibility.

An armed sentry stiffened at attention as he clipped a water-tight door behind him. He stared at the passageway with its shaded emergency lights, the blank-faced doors, the racks of fire-fighting gear laid out like an omen.

Hechler walked past the sentry and knew the man was staring after him. It was strange but he did not care. Not about that

213

anyway. The whole ship had probably made up its mind long ago. Then he paused and listened to the movements about him, the gentle rattle of equipment, the shiver of metal as the great ship sliced through the water. Nearly a thousand souls were contained within her graceful hull. Men as varied as Theil and Gudegast, young Jaeger and the acid-tongued Kröll. On and on forever, she had said. With a start he realised he was standing outside the door of his own quarters. Perhaps he had known what he was doing, or had he allowed his heart to steer him?

He felt it pounding against his ribs, a terrible uncertainty which made him hesitate and stare at himself like a stranger. Tomorrow was the day which would tell. After that, their future could only be measured by hours and by luck.

But that was tomorrow.

He tapped the door and opened it.

The day-cabin was in total darkness and he saw her sitting beside the bunk in the adjoining one, staring towards him so that the door's rectangle stood out like an intimate photograph.

She wore his dressing gown, the one with his initial on the pocket, which his brother had given him on that last birthday together. It was shabby, but he would never part with it.

He walked towards her as she said, 'I have worn it several times.' She moved her arms beneath it. 'It helped.'

He rested his hands on her shoulders and drew her to her feet. They stood together for a long while until he pulled her against him. She did not resist, nor did she respond as he stroked her hair, and pressed his hand against her spine.

He murmured, 'I had to come, Erika.'

She lowered her face against his chest. 'I *willed* you to be here, with me.' She leaned back in his arms and studied his face. 'Welcome to our new home.'

She smiled, but he could feel the tension like a living thing, the nervousness which stripped away her outer confidence. Hechler sat her down on the bunk and knelt against her, his head pressed into her body. He felt her hand in his hair, moving back and forth, gentle and yet demanding, speaking for both of them.

She said softly, 'You won't stay, Dieter. I know you can't.'

214

When he tried to look up at her she gripped his neck and held him more tightly.

'No. Hear me. You said you wanted me. We cannot wait.' He tried to free himself but her arm was like a band around his head. 'I – I feel so shy now that I have said it. But it means so much –' He took her wrist and lifted his face to watch her, to share the emotion her eyes revealed.

Hechler said, 'I love the way you are.' He felt her shiver as he untied the dressing gown and pulled it open. He kissed the warm skin and then dragged the dressing gown down until her shoulders, then her breasts were naked. He kissed her hard on each breast, felt her gasp as he pressed each nipple in turn with his lips, until neither of them could stand it.

He laid her on the bunk and undressed her. It was without gentleness, but she reached out to help him, until she lay watching him, her naked body shining in the solitary light above the bunk.

Hechler did not even glance at the telephone above them – it could shatter their moment with the ruthless power of a torpedo. He saw the livid scar on her side, as if some beast had sunk its jaws into her body. She seized his head as he placed his mouth over the wound.

It seemed as if life was compressed into a single moment. There had been nothing before, and ahead was only uncertainty like an empty horizon.

He wanted her so much that it hurt, and yet he needed this moment to last forever. Even when he took her limbs, stroked and kissed them, or ran his fingers around and deep into the dark triangle of hair, he clung to each precious second as if it was the last. She was no longer passive, she was dragging at his clothing, pulling him over and against her until she could find and hold him.

For just a fraction of time more they looked at each other, their faces almost touching, and then, with her hand urging and guiding him into her, they were joined. Then, as they fell together, with love and in passion, Hechler knew that no matter what lay ahead, life without her would be pointless.

Hechler slumped in the tall chair, his face stinging with salt and spray, his ribs seemingly bruised by the pressure as his ship crashed through the long Atlantic swell. Was it lighter? Were those millions of stars smaller? It was said that only at sea, on an open bridge, could a man truly understand the reality and the power of God.

He rubbed his eyes with the back of his glove and heard a man move with alarm. It could be no fun to stand the middle watch with your captain always present. He thought of the friendly glow of the reading light above the untidy bunk in his sea-cabin. At any other time he would have dived into it, fully dressed, needing a shave as he did now, not caring for anything but escape. Not this time. He had wanted to stay awake, had needed to, in case he lost something of those precious moments.

It was so clear in his mind, her body thrusting against his, her cry of pain, the instant pressure of hands on his shoulders when he had made to draw away. He had hurt her. It had been a long time. How right. The same for them both.

He touched his face and decided he would have a shave. He looked into the black shadows below the chair, both happy and shamed. His face must have been as rough as the clothes which he had worn, when he had felt her beneath him, sensed her legs spread out and over the side of the bunk. He could not recall anything like it, so complete, like a frankness which had pitched all barriers aside. And afterwards it had remained between them. More than just a bond, far more than a momentary passion for sex.

He glanced at the lieutenant of the watch; it was Ahlmann again.

Hechler wanted to touch himself beneath the oilskin, as if he was still sharing it. For he could still feel her. As if it had just happened.

Figures moved behind him and he heard the boatswain's mate of the watch ask politely, 'Some coffee, Captain?'

Hechler glanced down at him and nodded. Whatever it was, it would taste like champagne.

He said, 'I shall go to my sea-cabin for a shave afterwards.'

He peered at his luminous watch. When the time came to

increase speed and alter course perhaps for the last time before—he did not dwell on the possibilities. They were all behind. Only this moment was real and important.

He thought of the small landing party he had left at the Cable and Wireless station. What would they be doing? Playing cards, writing letters, something sailors usually did without the slightest knowledge of when they would be sent on their way, let alone read by their loved ones.

His mind strayed to the convoy. It would make a big hole in the enemy's fuel supplies. For how long? Two weeks—ten? Even a few days could make all the difference to the embattled armies while they waited for winter, their most needed ally.

He thought of the meeting in Kiel with von Hanke, the way he had looked at him when he had disputed the German army strength on the Russian Front. An oversight? It seemed hardly likely. In his great command bunker was the Führer also deluded by the maps and victorious arrows and flags? Could it be that *nobody* dared to tell their leader the terrible truth? That half of his finest divisions were buried by their thousands in the mud and snow of Russia? It was stupid to think of such things. The ship was only a part of the whole; nobody, not the General Staff, Donitz, not even the Führer could see the complete picture.

Someone coughed behind him and several voices whispered pleased or sarcastic greetings to the morning watch as they changed places with those who had stood the past four hours.

Froebe stooped beneath the chart-table's protective hood and spoke briefly with Ahlmann and his junior assistant. Then he stood up, glanced at the captain as if to ascertain whether he was awake or dozing and said, 'The watch is relieved.'

Feet shuffled on wet steel, and the smell of coffee drifted amongst the newly awakened officers and seamen like a welcome drug. Between decks the watchkeepers threw themselves into their blankets, some in hope of sleep, others merely to find solitude when surrounded by so many.

Thoughts of home, worries about shortages there, bombing, the next leave and the last one. It was all part of a sailor's life.

In the great engine-room and adjoining boiler-rooms the men

217

on watch in their blue or white overalls shouted to each other or sang their bawdy songs, all unheard in the roar of machinery, but to one another. The duty engineer officer stood on his shining catwalk beside the little desk with its telephone and log book. Old Stück would be down again soon. He had led all of them from the moment the first machine parts had been installed in this great hull. And yet he trusted nobody completely when important orders had to be executed.

The engineer officer, whose name was Kessler, could feel his shoulders ache as he gripped the rail with his gloved fingers. He felt the ship, too, thundering around and beneath his feet. She was the finest he had known. He grimaced. Down here anyway. What he had heard about their gallant admiral hardly inspired anyone. Kessler stared at the quivering bilge water far below the catwalk, blue-green in the harsh lights; it reminded him of the Christmas tree at his home as a boy. The first glimpse of it on that special morning, the presents, his father's huge grin. He had made himself go there on that last leave. The house had gone completely. He had known about it of course, just as he had sensed Hechler's compassion when he had seen him after the town had been bombed; he had asked for leave when the RAF had gone after the ball-bearing plant there. But as Hechler had explained, had there been a dependant, a wife, children, then perhaps—

The captain had been right, of course. But Kessler had gone home all the same when his time for normal leave had come up.

He still did not know what he had expected, a gap in the houses, all that was left of his boyhood and his family memories. It had not been like that at all. The whole street had gone, and several on either side of it too.

He squeezed the rail until his fingers ached. Would he *never* get over it?

The telephone made a puny rattle above the chorus of engines and fans.

He pictured Hechler up there in the open bridge, the air and the ocean which seemed endless.

He said, 'Ready, sir.'

Over his shoulder he heard Stück's voice and turned to see his figure framed against the bright pipes and dials, almost shining in a fresh suit of overalls.

'The Old Man?'

Kessler glanced at the shivering clock. 'Yes, Chief.' Stück was even earlier than usual. But Kessler was glad without knowing why.

Stück leaned his buttocks against a rail and folded his arms. He could see through the haze of steam and moisture, and his keen ears told him more than any log book.

He looked at the lieutenant and guessed what his assistant had been brooding about. He toyed with the idea of mentioning it, but sentiment found little comfort in lip-reading, in competition with their sealed, roaring world.

His eyes came up to the dials above the deck as a bell rattled again, and the three speed and revolution counters swung round with expected urgency.

Stück grinned and pretended to spit on his hands. His lips said, 'Come on, Heinz, feed the beast, eh?' Seconds later, the three great shafts gathered speed, so that even the men on watch had to make certain of a ready handhold.

Stück watched the mounting revolutions. A thoroughbred.

Here we go again.

Theil lay on his back and felt the increase of speed creating a new rhythm as it pulsated through the bunk and into his body. He had tried to sleep, but had been wide awake since he had left the bridge. His eyes felt raw, and despair dragged at his mind and insides like some creeping disease.

If he went to the admiral and pleaded for him to make a signal through the next refuelling submarine, would it make any difference? He knew immediately that it would not. Leitner could have told him about the arrest before the ship had weighed anchor, might even have intervened on his behalf. He did not want to, did not care; it was that simple.

Theil rolled on to his side and stared desperately at his clock. He would be called by a messenger very soon, then he would have to put on an act again, or go mad under this terrible weight.

The ship was beginning to shake more insistently, so that objects in his cabin clattered together, as if to drive him out. Very soon now the ship would need him more than ever before. But for that sure knowledge he knew he would kill himself. Over the side in the night watches, lost in seconds in their ruler-straight wake. Or a pistol to the temple, a moment's fearful uncertainty – then nothing. The thought of the pistol which hung from his bunk made him violently angry, sick with it, until every limb trembled like the ship.

He saw himself in that cabin again, Bauer's stupid, handsome face exploding like a scarlet flower as the bullet smashed him down.

See if *he* could take it as well as he could shoot an unarmed civilian.

The thought brought no comfort. Unarmed civilian, like Britta. Perhaps she was released now, back at their house, putting right the damage to her beloved garden.

He buried his face in the pillow and found that he could not stop himself from sobbing aloud.

Two cabins away, Oberleutnant zur See Willi Meile, the stores and supply officer, lay on his side and stared at the naked girl who was clutching her breast and gasping with exhaustion.

Meile was no fighting sailor, his world was food and drink, paint and cordage, everything which fed and sustained his ship.

He had worked on one of the camera team ever since she had come aboard. She was certainly no beauty, but she was young and had a fine body. To Meile it was like being in heaven. Nothing like it had happened before, nor could occur again.

The executive officers and U-boat commanders had all the glamour. They were more than welcome to it, he decided. It was said that half of Hamburg was owned by ex-pursers of the Hamburg–Amerika Line, just as naval bases like Wilhelmshaven were profitable investments for retired supply officers like Meile.

No, after the war, those who controlled the food and drink would be the new heroes.

He leaned on one elbow and felt her breast. He had left lights switched on as he did not want to miss anything. Her bare

220

shoulders were quite red in places where he had squeezed, even bitten them. She gasped out that she could take no more. 'You are more than a man—' The rest was silenced as he kissed her hard on the mouth, his hand reaching for her, exciting her despite all exhaustion. Neither of them noticed the sudden increase of engine noise, nor considered what it might mean.

Meile dragged her wrists over her head and held them tightly. He said, 'Don't fight me. I'm going to take you. *Now!*'

In the next cabin, young Jaeger switched on his light and squinted at his wristwatch. He would not wait to be roused, but would have a shave before they tested action stations to start another day. He thought he heard the girl's stifled cry through the thick steel and shook his head. That Meile was like an animal where women were concerned. He tried not to think of the gentle Sophie; it was wrong even to picture her in his mind with all that was going on in the next cabin. The sooner they dropped the three women off in the next rendezvous supply-boat, the better. He thought of Hechler's face when he had been speaking with the girl pilot. No, perhaps not her.

He stood up and felt the carpet tremble beneath his bare feet. Then he looked at the disordered bunk. It was not so difficult to see Sophie here after all.

On the opposite side of the ship the girl gathered up her things and pushed them unseeingly into a small grip. She would return to her allotted cabin, which she shared with one of the camera girls. Like Jaeger, she switched on some lights and stood, swaying to the heavy motion in front of a bulkhead mirror. Where he adjusted his uniform before going to speak with his sailors. She pouted at herself. Or, in the past, leave to see his unfaithful wife.

She opened her shirt and watched herself touch the scar on her side. It still hurt. Her hand drifted slowly across her skin as his had done. She could still feel him; her body was both elated and sore from their need for each other.

She had not realised how it was possible to be both loved and possessed, to feel victor and conquered at the same time. She buttoned her shirt and looked very slowly around the empty cabin. She would not come back again. Not ever, unless they were together.

She heard quiet movements from the captain's pantry. Poor Pirk, his servant and guardian angel. In some strange way, his acceptance of her here had seemed like a blessing.

She supported herself in the doorway and listened to the mounting rumble of power. Like something unleashed, which would never be cowed until satisfied, or destroyed.

Her fingers rested hesitantly on the last light switch. She would remember everything. The rasp of his clothes against her nakedness, the thrust of his body which was like love and madness together.

The cabin retreated into darkness and she closed the door.

As she walked past the dozing sentry at the end of the passageway she knew she would regret nothing.

16

The Signal

Peter Younger, one-time radio officer of the SS *Radnor Star*, drew his knees up to his chin and shaded his eyes with one hand. He was still unused to being on dry land again, and for hours after his arrival with the small party of German sailors he had been light-headed, unsteady on his feet like some dockside drunk. When the raider had weighed anchor and had headed away from the tiny islet Younger had almost expected that each minute was to be his last. He had seen the rough grave, and had heard what had happened from one of the station's crew. It was curious, but the resident crew had been as withdrawn as the Germans from him, and of course Old Shiner. He glanced at the white-bearded boatswain who was sitting with his back to a rock, facing the sun, eyes closed. He could be dead, he thought.

He idly watched one German who was strolling up and down the slope, a machine-pistol dangling from his shoulder. Younger had heard the senior rating telling him off for not wearing his cap; it was absurd, when you knew you would soon be changing places with your prisoners.

Mason, the man in charge of the small station, had whispered to him that the place was no longer properly operational. So no regular monitoring or signals would be missed or expected. The enemy had worked it out very well. The man had said that when the German operator made his false signal, someone on the receiving end might realise it was not the usual telegraphist.

He had added somewhat condescendingly that only a radio man would understand that. Younger had contained his impatience and irritation. *You can say that again*, his inner voice had answered.

Younger had decided not to share his plan with anyone just yet. The station crew seemed too dazed and shocked by what had happened to their companion. Cowed was putting it mildly, he thought angrily. The Germans would not want to kill anyone for no purpose. If the British or American warships arrived to find more graves, they might forget the Geneva Convention, so far from home, and take their own revenge. The krauts would think that anyway.

It would have to be after the false signal and without giving them time to destroy the transmitter. Younger had measured up the distance he had to cover, had even selected the sailor he would overpower to reach the radio-room. The German sailor in question was often on guard duty; he was apparently useless as a cook or anything else with one arm in plaster. He could not therefore carry more than a pistol, and he usually kept that buttoned in his holster. And why not? They had no means of escape, nowhere to run to. They were all prisoners now. He tried to gauge their feelings, those of the senior operator in charge anyway. He could see him now, standing by the ladder to the radio-room, his cap dangling from one hand as he shared the frail sunlight.

He was young but prematurely bald, a fact made more obvious by the dark hair on either temple. He was a thoughtful-looking man, introspective, with the sensitive features of a priest. He was probably brooding on his own predicament, which had been thrust on him in the name of duty.

Younger licked his lips and tried to relax his body, muscle by muscle. When he considered what he intended to do he was surprised at his strength and conviction. There was no fear at all. He thought of the torpedo which had blasted the old ship apart, men screaming and on fire, others being carried away by the suction to the same Atlantic grave.

This would be for them. The Old Man, Colin Ames, all of them.

With a start he realised that the old boatswain had opened his eyes and was watching him without recognition. His eyes were washed-out blue, so pale in the glare that they were like a blind man's.

Younger smiled. 'Okay, Shiner?' He wondered if he knew where they were. How they had got here.

The boatswain opened and closed his hands. They lay on the rock beside him, as if they were independent of their owner.

He said huskily, 'Wot time we goin' to eat, Sparks?'

Younger shot a quick glance at the two Germans, but neither had noticed.

He hissed, 'Don't call me that, mate!'

The eyes did not blink. 'You're Peter Younger, that's who.' He nodded, satisfied. 'Sparks.'

Younger sighed. 'Ames is dead. I've taken his place.' He could feel his plan running out like sand. 'The krauts wouldn't let me within a mile of this lot if they knew.' He gripped his arm fiercely. Through the ragged jersey it felt like a stick. 'Help me. To even the score for the lads and the old *Star*, eh?'

He saw understanding cloud the pale eyes for the first time. He said shakily, 'All gone. The lot of 'em. Jim, Colin, and –' he stared round, suddenly desperate – 'where's –'

Younger gripped his arm and said quietly, 'It's all right, Shiner. The cat didn't feel anything. He's buried with the lads now.' He watched the sentry's shadow reaching across the rough slope. 'Because of these bastards.'

The old man closed his eyes. 'Dead, you say?'

Younger looked down. *Please help me. In God's name, help*.

He said aloud, 'It was a U-boat. But they're all the same. The crew here don't understand like we do. They seem to think a war's for someone else to fight.' He steadied himself, knowing he would break down otherwise. 'Will you give me a hand?'

'Just tell me what to do, Sparks.' He smiled but it made him look even sadder. 'Sorry, I mean *Mr Ames*.'

Younger sat back on his haunches. It was suddenly crystal-clear what he would do. As if he could see it happening in slow motion, something already past.

He considered what the man Mason had told him about one

operator being familiar to another. He had always known it, and the radio officer who had taught him had described how you could often recognise the sender before the actual ship was identified.

Did that mean Mason or one of the others would make the signal to keep in with their captors?

It made him sweat to think of it. The raider was off to attack the biggest prize yet. It must be really important to leave some of their own people behind. None of them seemed to know where the attack might be launched. In case they were captured and interrogated before the raider could make good her escape. The stark picture of the drifting lifeboat, the moments when he had been almost too terrified to open his eyes when he had drowsed over the tiller. They had all been waiting for him. The nightmare had never gone away. They had died one by one, mostly in silence with a kind of passive acceptance.

It would not be much, but his actions might help to save other helpless merchant seamen. He hoped his old mother would find out that he had died this way. His dry lips cracked into a smile. Might get the George Cross. Something for his Dad to brag about down at the Shipwright's Arms.

Another shadow fell across them. 'We eat soon.' It was the senior operator, apparently the only one who spoke English. He would, of course.

'Thanks.'

The German glanced down at the old boatswain. 'He okay?'

Old Shiner did not open his eyes. 'Right as bloody ninepence, ta.'

The German turned away. That last sentence had thrown him.

He walked down to the water's edge and stared at the dark water. It shelved away steeply after that. Just a pile of rock in the middle of nowhere, he thought.

His name was Ernst Genscher and his home was in Leipzig. It would be cold there now. Winter always came early to that city. He tried to see it as in his boyhood, the spires and fine buildings. Not as on his last leave. The bomb debris, Russian prisoners working to clear the streets of corpses and rubble. The prisoners had looked like human scarecrows, and had been guarded by units of the SS. He thought of his divisional officer, Leutnant Bauer. They had never got on together. He smiled bitterly. That was why he had been detailed for this final job. Bauer would have been right at home in the SS.

How much longer would the war last, he wondered? He and the others would end up in some prisoner-of-war camp in England or Canada. It might not be too bad. It was like their situation here in this damnable place, he thought. Neither side wanted to antagonise the other in case the wrong one came out victorious.

He thought of his companions. They were more worried than they admitted. Some even expected the *Prinz* to come back for them. A tiger had never been known to come back to release a tethered goat.

Genscher replaced his cap and smiled at his earlier show of discipline with the sentry.

He looked at his watch. He would send the signal in a few hours' time, just before sunset. His priest's face brightened into a smile.

It was somehow appropriate.

The three captains sat in Hemrose's deep armchairs and held out their glasses to be refilled.

Hemrose crossed one leg over the other and plucked his shirt away from his body. The air was hot and lifeless, and even with the scuttles open it was hard to ease the discomfort. The glass seemed steady enough, Hemrose thought, but it smelled like a storm. It was all they needed.

He watched his steward pause to take Captain Eric Duffield's glass to be topped up. *Rhodesia*'s captain was a big, powerful man, whose face had once been very handsome. A bit too smarmy for Hemrose's taste. Always excelled at sport and athletics. Not any more, Hemrose thought with small satisfaction.

He had forgotten how many Horse's Necks he had downed, nor did he care much. It was getting more like a wake than a relaxed drink in harbour with his captains, with a good dinner to follow. They would not be *his* captains much longer. He shied away from the thought.

With an effort he stood up and crossed to the nearest scuttle. The lights of Simonstown glittered on the water like a swarm of fireflies, while here and there small boats moved through the dusk between the anchored warships. It could be peacetime, he thought. Well, almost.

He heard Duffield say, 'Good place to settle down, South Africa. I'd think about it myself after this lot's over, but you never know.' Hemrose gritted his teeth together. He meant that he would be staying on in the service, promoted probably to end his time in command of a base, or with a nice staff job in Whitehall.

The New Zealand captain, Chantril, replied, 'We've not won the bloody war yet.' His accent took the edge from his words. He was feeling it too. The chance to meet and destroy the raider. Become a part of the navy's heritage.

Hemrose turned and signalled to his steward. 'I still can't believe it, you know.'

Duffield smiled. 'Believe or accept? There's a difference.' Hemrose ignored him. 'A whole ship gone west, not even a scrap of wreckage discovered?'

Chantril said, 'It happened to HMAS *Sydney*. Her loss is still a mystery.'

Duffield glanced at his watch. He could not wait to eat up and go. Get back to his own ship and tell them all how Hemrose was taking his unfought defeat.

He said, 'The backroom boys at the Admiralty know more than they let on.'

Hemrose glared. 'Bloody useless, most of them!'

Duffield coughed. 'We'll probably never know.'

Hemrose pushed a strand of hair from his eyes. He was getting drunk. 'That Jerry is still around. I'll stake my reputation on it.'

The others remained silent. They probably considered his reputation had already slipped away.

'I've had my team working round the clock.' Hemrose pictured the charts, the layers of signal pads and folios. All for nothing. 'We had a damn good try anyway.'

They both stared at him. It was the nearest he had ever come to an admission of failure.

The thought of sitting through dinner with them made Hemrose feel slightly sick. Chantril was all right, a real professional, but tonight was not the time. He had a letter to write to Beryl, and a report to complete for the Admiralty. After that, he could almost feel the carpet being dragged from under him. Perhaps they would both accept an excuse, go back to their ships instead –

He looked up, angry and startled, as if he had spoken aloud.

'Well, what is it now?'

The commander nodded to the seated officers and then handed a signal pad to his superior.

Hemrose had to read it twice, his face shining with sweat, as if he had been running.

He said slowly, 'From Admiralty, gentlemen. Thirty minutes ago a signal was received from the Cable and Wireless station on St Jorge.' He could tell from Duffield's expression he hadn't a clue where that was. 'It reads *Am under attack by German cruiser.*' He lowered the pad and eyed them grimly. 'There was no further transmission. We may draw our own conclusions.'

Chantril exclaimed, 'I know the place! Christ, it's nor'-east of Ascension. What the hell is he –'

Duffield said, 'And all the time –'

Hemrose remained grave and under control even though he wanted to yell out loud. It was like having a great orchestra or band pounding into your ears, shutting out all else but those vital words.

He said, 'Yes, all the time we thought the German was destroyed.' He could not resist it. 'Some of us, anyway.'

Chantril stood up and knocked over a glass without even seeing it.

'What is he trying to do?'

Hemrose smiled gently. '*Do?* Who really cares? He probably intended to carry out a last attack before running to some friendly South American bolthole, *Graf Spee* all over again. *Kapitän Hechler –*' he spat out the name '– will know that heavy forces are to the north of him.' He nodded. 'He will head south after this, then scuttle, whether *he* likes it or not.'

'Can we rely on that signal, sir?'

Hemrose looked at him and beamed. 'What? Can you doubt your *backroom boys* at the Admiralty? Tch, tch!' It was like a tonic.

Commander Godson shifted from one foot to the other. The signal had knocked the breath out of him. It was like opening a door and expecting to meet an old friend, only to be confronted by a maniac.

Hemrose looked at him, but saw his own expression as it would be remembered after this day. Grave and confident.

'Make a signal to Admiralty, Toby. *The squadron is leaving without delay.*' Thank God he had insisted on fuelling from lighters; it would have taken another hour to clear the port otherwise. He took his time to look at the gold wristwatch which Beryl had given him.

'Pipe special sea dutymen to their stations in one hour.' He looked at the others as poor Godson fled from the cabin. 'Another drink, eh?' He grinned. '*Afore ye go*, as the man said.'

He watched their faces, each man thinking of his own ship's readiness for sea. Hemrose added gently, 'Call up your ships from here.' He recalled the *Rhodesia*'s great display of speed and swank when she had joined the squadron. 'I don't want to leave here alone!'

Later he said, 'It must be fate. I knew we were destined to meet. Right from the beginning, I always knew.' He glanced round the cabin affectionately. 'Settle the score.'

At the prescribed time, as watertight doors were slammed shut and men bustled to their stations for leaving harbour, Hemrose mounted the *Wiltshire*'s bridge and looked towards the lights of the shore. The raider had not allowed for anyone making a last desperate signal, any more than they would expect three British cruisers to be ready, and in the right place.

In his mind he could see the chart, south-west. Close the trap which the German had sprung on himself.

He touched his cap to Godson as he reported the ship ready to proceed.

It was no longer just a remote possibility. There soon would be two lines of oak leaves around his peak.

It was a proud moment. There should be a band playing.

He turned and looked at the chief yeoman of signals.

He said, 'Make to squadron, Yeo. *Weigh anchor and follow father.*'

The sort of signal they always remembered. He could not stop grinning. The fact that Duffield would hate it, was a bonus.

Hechler came out of his dream like a drowning man fighting up for a gasp of air.

Even as he propped himself on one elbow and jammed the telephone to his ear he knew what it was. The only surprise was that he had been able to sleep at all.

It was Froebe. 'W/T office has reported the signal, sir.' He sounded cheerful. 'Right on time.'

Hechler stared around the tiny sea-cabin, his things ready to snatch up, the place in total disorder.

'Thank you. You know what to do.' He thought of the wild dream which had been driven away by the telephone's shrill call. Her nakedness, her desire, the way she had writhed beneath him as if to postpone the conquest.

He said, 'I'll be up shortly.' He hung the phone on its cradle above the bunk and wondered what she was doing now. Thinking, but not regretting? Hoping, but not allowing it to reach out too far. He slid from the bunk and suddenly craved a shower. Even that was already too late.

He thought of the senior operator, Genscher, he had left on the islet. He had obeyed orders, no matter what he thought about the need or the futility of it.

Even now the signal would be flashing around the world. The raider had been verified and slotted into one section of this great ocean. Brains would be working overtime as staff officers rearranged their thinking and defences, like drawing the strings of a huge bag. Except that the *Prinz* was nowhere near the small islet, and was speeding in the opposite direction.

Hechler deliberately stripped himself to the waist. The narrow door opened slightly and he saw the faithful Pirk peering in at him with a steaming bowl of water for his shave. He had understood. But Pirk always had. Ice, sunshine, bombardments or dodging enemy aircraft, Pirk's world ran on quite different

231

lines.

The telephone rang again and Pirk handed it to him.

Hechler said, 'Captain?'

This time it was Theil. 'Exercise action stations, sir?'

'Not yet.' He thought surprisingly of Nelson. 'Let them have one more good meal. It may be the last for some time.'

Theil grunted. 'Dawn attack, sir?'

'Yes. As planned, Viktor. Let me know when the admiral is on his bridge.'

He turned to the mirror and touched his face. As she had done. 'It's going to be a very long night, old friend.' But Pirk had left. He lathered his cheeks with care and though of each last detail. The Arados would have to be prepared well before dawn. Every station and gun-mounting checked and visited by a senior officer. The last meal for some time. Forever, if things went badly wrong. He searched through his mind for flaws. His landing party had played their part. Now it was up to them. He grimaced at his image in the mirror. At one time he had nursed doubts. He had imagined then that the enemy had some secret strategy which neither he nor Operations had recognised.

Now he knew differently. There was no secret plan. Once again, the *Prinz Luitpold*'s luck had won through.

Shortly after midnight Hechler made his way into the bridge. That last cat-nap had driven the tiredness away. Or was it the prospect of action?

In the darkness figures moved towards him, or held motionless at their positions. As if they had never shifted. It was a beautiful night, bright stars, and a deep, unbroken swell again. Gudegast had already reported that there might be rain with a south-easterly wind. He never sounded as if he trusted the signalled broadcasts as much as his own intuition.

Leitner's pale outline glided through the watchkeepers, and Hechler could smell his cologne as he groped his way to the forward part of the bridge.

'A good beginning,' he said calmly. 'They'll not forget this day.'

Hechler was glad when the admiral had departed for his quarters. To prepare himself, or to share the last hours with his aide, he did not know or care.

As the time dragged on, the weather began to change. It grew much colder, and the steep swell became visible on either beam as a rising wind broke the crests into ragged, white lines. The *Prinz* was built for this kind of weather, and as she dipped her forecastle until spray burst over the stem or spouted through the hawsepipes she seemed almost contemptuous.

More signals came in a steady stream. It must be strange for those far-off operators, Hechler had thought many times, to send off their instructions and messages, while the recipient had no way of risking an acknowledgement.

Operations Division sent one signal about a small British cruiser squadron leaving Simonstown. Agents there must have started a chain of messages almost as soon as the Tommies had hoisted their anchors.

It was hardly surprising, he thought. Germany had many friends in South Africa. When the Kaiser had been forced to surrender in the Great War, it was said that black flags had been raised over Johannesburg to show where their true feelings had lain.

Hechler said, 'Action stations in ten minutes.' He felt his pockets in case he had forgotten anything. He remembered as he had left the sea-cabin how he had seen Inger's familiar picture in the drawer. He had looked at it for the first time without feeling, even bitterness.

'Tell the supply officer to keep the galley on stand-by. I want soup and coffee sent around every section until the last moment.'

A winch clattered loudly and he knew the aircraft handling party were at work with the first Arado preparing for launching. If the launch misfired, the plane would be left to fend for itself. He thought of the girl's own aircraft, dismantled and folded into its nest. A last display for the cameras? Or did Leitner have some other scheme in mind?

Gudegast stood beside his chair. 'Time to increase to full speed in twenty minutes, sir.' He sounded calm enough.

'Good.' Hechler peered at his Doxa watch. 'Sound off.'

The alarm bells clamoured throughout the ship, followed by a few thuds as the last of the heavy doors were clipped home.

Voice-pipes and handsets muttered around the bridge, an unseen army.

'Anton, Bruno, Caesar and Dora turrets closed up, sir!'

'Secondary and anti-aircraft armament closed up, sir!'

From every gun, torpedo and magazine the reports came in.

Hechler pictured his men within the armoured hull. Down in the sick-bay, Stroheim and his assistants would be waiting, their glittering instruments laid out, waiting for the pain and the pleading.

As it must have been at Coronel and Falklands, at Dogger Bank and Jutland. Hechler jammed his pipe between his teeth and smiled. Trafalgar too probably.

He heard himself ask, 'What about Damage Control?'

Froebe replied, 'Closed up, sir. Some delay over a lighting fault.'

Theil was there entrusted with saving the ship if the worst happened. Or taking command if the bridge was wiped out.

'The admiral, sir.'

Hechler took the handset. 'Sir?'

Leitner said, 'I want another flag hoisted today. See to it, eh?'

He meant another rear-admiral's flag.

Hechler said, 'Ship at action stations, sir.'

'I shall come up presently.' The line went dead.

Hechler said to the bridge at large, 'I'm going to the plot.' He walked to the ladder as Gudegast picked up a chart and followed him. He could visualise it clearly in his mind. Training, experience, skill. He heard Froebe telling a signalman to fetch another flag and take it aft. He wondered if the camera would record that too.

While their captain climbed to the conning tower, the men throughout the ship went grimly about their preparations. Ready-use ammunition in place, magazine lifts sliding smoothly up and down their shafts, gun crews testing training and elevation gear, the gleaming breeches open like hungry mouths.

Above them all, Kröll the gunnery officer sat in his small steel chair and adjusted his sights while he studied the radar repeater. His team, hung about with stop-watches, earphones and the tools of their trade, watched him, keyed up like athletes under the starter's gun.

The most junior member of the fire-control team, Acting Petty Officer Hans Stoecker, stared at his empty log, one hand wrapped around his telephone.

They had all worked together so long that there were no hitches, nothing to bring Kröll's wrath down on them.

It was like a small self-contained world. Essential to the ship's firepower, but entirely separate, so that when the heavy guns roared out, they too seemed like something apart.

He tried not to think of Rudi Hammer's mild features just as the bells had sent them all racing to their action stations.

He had smiled almost shyly and said, 'A very good time for our little plan, yes? Everybody minding his own business!'

They would be found out. Stoecker gripped the telephone with both hands, his eyes misty as he stared at the log book. It was madness, a lunacy which would cost them their lives.

The speaker intoned, 'Main armament, semi-armour piercing shell, *load*!'

Stoecker felt his seat tilt under him as the helm went over. The ship was increasing speed. Sometimes it felt as if their steel pod would tear itself away from the bridge superstructure as every strut and rivet shook violently in protest.

Kröll twisted round in his chair and glanced at the intent figures below him, lastly to Kapitänleutnant Georg Emmler, the assistant gunnery officer. Together they held the reins. Beyond here, quarters officers, gun captains, and even individual sailors strapped in their rapid-fire automatic weapons, waited for the word. *Bearing, range, target.*

Kröll bit his lip. Another convoy. One day he would get his chance to pit his skills against a powerful enemy warship.

'Loaded, sir.'

Kröll scowled. Ten seconds too long. He thrust the watch into his pocket. He would soon put that right.

On the bridge once more Hechler looked at the stars. Fainter now. He felt spray cutting his face, heard it pattering over the chart-table's canvas cover to make puddles in the scuppers.

A voice said, 'First-degree readiness, sir.'

The galley was shut; the cook and his assistants would be sent to help damage-control and the stretcher parties.

Hechler gripped the rail below the screen and stared into the darkness.

They should hold the advantage with the convoy framed against the dawn. The escort had not been identified, which meant that it was nothing important. They were holding that for the next leg. He looked at the stars. But that would be denied them.

'Port fifteen!' Hechler heard his order repeated, almost a whisper, lost in the clamour of fans, the great writhing bank of foam which surged down either side.

'Steady! Steer zero-four-zero!'

The bows plunged into a deeper trough than usual and the sea boiled up and over the forecastle as if a broadside had fallen silently alongside.

As the ship turned, the two big turrets below the bridge trained across the starboard bow. Without turning Hechler knew that the two after ones, Caesar and Dora, were also swinging round in unison, until all four guns were pointing on the same bearing, the long muzzles like wet glass as they steadied over the side and the great surge of spray.

The sea was still in darkness, so that the leaping crests looked like birds, swooping and falling to appear elsewhere in another guise.

'Admiral's on his bridge, sir.'

'Very well.' Hechler tightened the towel around his neck as more heavy spray burst over the screen and pattered against their oilskins.

Leitner had made a suitably timed entrance. Hechler thought of the girl. She had shown no fear, but being sealed below behind massive watertight doors would test anybody.

Somebody whispered and was instantly rebuked by a petty officer.

Hechler kept his binoculars sheltered beneath the oilskin until the last moment to keep them dry. But he had seen what the lookout had whispered to a companion.

A thin pale line, like polished pewter, cold and without colour

Dawn, or nearly so. Hechler thought suddenly of his father. How he had described his horizon of that other war. It had been first light on the parapet of his trench. That had been the full extent of his world in that horrifying arena in Flanders.

'*Radar – bridge!*'

They all tensed.

Then the speaker continued, 'Target in sight. Bearing Green four-five. Range twelve thousand!'

Hechler tugged his cap more firmly across his forehead. The peak was wet and like ice.

He stood up and let the spray dash over him as he peered towards the starboard bow.

They had found them. Now it was up to Kröll.

'*Open fire!*'

17

Blood for Blood

The paired explosions from the after-turrets were deafening, and with the wind thrusting across the starboard quarter, the down-draft of acrid smoke made several of the men duck their heads to contain their coughing fits.

Hechler held the binoculars on the bearing and watched the tiny pale feathers of spray as the shells fell on the horizon. Harmless, without menace, although he knew that each waterspout would rise to masthead level. The explosions sighed through the water and faded again.

The speaker said, 'Twelve ships in convoy, estimate three escorts.'

Froebe called from his bank of handsets, 'W/T office reports signals from enemy, sir.'

'*Shoot!*' Kröll sounded quite different over the speaker, his words drowned by the immediate response from all four turrets.

Hechler watched the sky. After the previous days it looked threatening. There was cloud there too. He imagined signals beaming away to the enemy's supporting squadrons and to London.

He tensed; a bright flash lit up the horizon and several of the ships for the first time. They looked low and black, but in the spreading glow of fire he could just determine their course and speed.

The speaker again. 'One escort hit. Sinking.'

Hechler could picture the gunnery team's concentration on

the radar screens. One tiny droplet of light falling out of station, dropping further and further astern of the fast tankers. It would vanish from the screens altogether.

The guns roared out again. Surely the tankers would scatter soon? He held his breath as a straddle of shells fell across one of the ships below the horizon. She was instantly ablaze, but it was made more terrible by distance as the fire seemed to spread down from the horizon, like blood brimming over a dam.

'*Shoot!*'

Hechler waited and winced as the eight big guns thundered out.

'Slow ahead!' He crossed the bridge and saw a signalman watching him, a handlamp at the ready.

'*Now!*' The first Arado lifted from the shadows and circled quickly round and above the mastheads.

'*Shoot!*'

The whole bridge structure shook violently and Hechler had to repeat his order to the engine-room to resume full speed. He would launch the second plane if there was time.

Someone was yelling, 'Another hit! God, two of them are on fire!'

Hechler glanced round to silence the man, but all he saw was Leitner's second flag breaking out from the mainmast truck, the only patch of colour against the sky. It was raining more persistently now, but even that tasted of cordite. It was hard to believe this same sky had been full of stars.

Hechler moved across the bridge, half-listening to crackling static as the Arado pilot reported back to the ship.

It was a sea of fire. The great shells must have come ripping down out of the darkness without the slightest warning. He saw lazy balls of bright tracer rising from the sea and guessed that the Arado was already near the convoy. How slow it looked. How deceptive. He hoped the pilot had his wits about him.

'Convoy breaking up, sir!' Kröll's voice cut through the murmur of orders and instructions behind him. It was as if the fire-control position, the pod, was alive and speaking of its own free will.

Kröll added, 'Two lines diverging, sir.'

Hechler lowered his glasses and wiped them with fresh tissue.

'Acknowledge.' He pictured the convoy; they would need no encouragement to break away. *We must close the range.*

'*Shoot!*'

'*Cease firing!*' It was Kröll but he sounded momentarily confused.

Hechler picked up the fire-control handset. 'Captain. What is it?'

Kröll must have been leaning away to study his radar; when he spoke he seemed angry, as if he no longer trusted what he saw.

'A ship turned end-on, sir. Rear of second line.'

'Wait!' Hechler pushed his way aft and into the tiny steel shack which had been added to the bridge to house a radar repeater alongside that of the sonar. He bent over the screen and as his eyes accustomed themselves to the flickering symbols he saw the complete picture as seen by *Prinz Luitpold*'s invisible eye. The diverging ranks of ships, and then as the scanner swept over them, the motionless blobs of light, ships burning and dying in the spreading flames. Then he saw the isolated echo. A large one which had until now been mistaken for one of the tankers. But it was much bigger and was not standing away, but coming straight for the *Prinz*. Hechler had to force himself to walk back to the bridge.

'Can you identify it?'

Kröll sounded very wary. 'There are no major warships listed with the convoy.'

Hechler turned away. 'Carry on. Tell the conning-tower to alter course. Steer zero-six-zero!'

The bridge quaked again as the after guns bellowed out, their bright tongues lighting up the rain-soaked superstructure and funnel. A figure stood out in the flashes and Hechler heard Jaeger call, 'Captain, sir! Message from Arado pilot! The ship is a merchantman!' He hesitated, baffled. 'A liner!'

For an instant longer Hechler thought she might be a hospital ship, one which was trying to keep clear of the convoy, or which had been damaged and was out of control.

A figure in shining oilskins brushed Jaeger aside and Gudegast exclaimed, 'Steady on new course, sir. Zero-six-zero.' He clung to the safety rail, his body heaving from exertion.

Hechler said, 'Do you know what it is?'

Gudegast nodded jerkily. 'It was in the recognition despatches, sir. Oh, yes, I know her all right! He ducked as the guns fired again. Flashes rippled along the horizon. Kröll was ignoring the solitary ship in case the heavy tankers might escape.

Gudegast stared at him, his eyes wild in the reflections. 'She's the old *Tasmania*. Used to come up against her when she did the Scandinavian cruises in the thirties.' He pounded his fist on the rail and shouted, 'They've made her an Armed Merchant Cruiser, for Christ's sake!'

Hechler snatched up the handset. 'Gunnery Officer! Shift target to the big liner – she's the *Tasmania*, armed merchant cruiser!'

'Immediately, sir.'

Gudegast was staring at him. 'She won't stand a chance! You know what they're like! No plating at all and just a few guns from the Great War!'

Hechler called, 'Warn the secondary armament, then call up the Arado.'

He swung on Gudegast and said, 'Have you forgotten the other AMCs, man? *Jervis Bay*, an old cargo liner, but she held off *Admiral Scheer* nonetheless! An old merchantman too, set against a battleship! She was sunk, she knew it was hopeless when she turned to face the *Scheer*, but by God, her sacrifice saved her convoy, and *don't you ever forget it!*'

He turned back to the screen as the four forward guns edged round, paused and then fired in unison.

The sky was brightening, although with all the smoky rain it seemed to have taken them by surprise. Hechler watched the exploding shells, the ice-bright columns of water. Then he saw the oncoming ship. In her dull paint she still looked huge, with her three tall funnels overlapping as she turned still more to steer towards the heavy cruiser. The next salvo fell right across her path, and for an instant, Hechler thought she had been hit.

Jaeger called thickly, 'She mounts eight-inch guns, sir!'

It was ironic. The same armament as the *Prinz*, in size and numbers only.

'Speed?'

Jaeger replied, 'Twenty-eight knots maximum, sir.' He faltered as the after turrets fired, paint flaking down from the upper bridge fittings because of the blast. 'In peacetime.'

Hechler stared at her dull shadow while he wiped his glasses again. They were on a converging course, approaching each other at the combined speed of some sixty miles an hour. Old she might be, and to all intents she could not survive, but just one lucky shot was all it took to delay them, while the convoy clapped on speed to escape. Spectators would remember this day if they were fortunate enough to survive.

'Shoot!'

A straddle. The liner was hidden by falling spray, and at least one shell had smashed into her unarmoured side and exploded deep inside the hull. It was like a glowing red eye.

Hechler heard Jaeger shout, 'That should stop her!'

Gudegast seized his arm. 'Take a good look, boy!'

Jaeger stared with disbelief. 'She's hoisting flags to each mast!'

Gudegast stared past him at Hechler's shoulders, shining in the grey light as the rain bounced down on them.

'They're battle ensigns! They sent the poor old girl to fight, and by God she's about to!'

'Shoot!'

It was a controlled broadside from all four turrets, the heavy shells straddling the tall hull, and blasting one of the outmoded, stately funnels overboard, like paper in a wind.

Jaeger gripped the chart-table as it tried to shake itself from his fingers. He wanted to screw up his eyes as a great scream of shellfire shrieked over the bridge and exploded in the sea, far abeam.

He wrote in the log, 'The enemy opened fire at –' The rest was a blur.

Hechler turned to watch the falling spray. 'Tell our pilot to take a fly over that ship. He might get a lucky hit.'

He did not let himself blink as two flashes lit up the liner's side. Her armament was divided out of necessity. At most she could train only three or four guns at a time.

242

He bit his lip as Kröll's next salvo erupted on her waterline. Smoke and fire seemed to roll across the waves, and he guessed that one shell had burst deep inside her.

But she was firing back, the old guns sounding strangely hollow when compared with the *Prinz*'s.

A messenger handed him a telephone, his face ashen as a shell screamed past the bridge.

It was Leitner. 'What is the matter with your gun crews!' He was almost screaming. '*Kill them! Stop that ship!*'

Hechler handed the phone to the seaman and watched a livid flash fan out from beneath the liner's bridge. A mast was falling, but the white battle ensigns still seemed to shine through the rain, and her bow-wave was as before.

Froebe shouted, 'She's on fire aft, sir! What's holding her together?'

Hechler let his glasses fall to his chest. The range was dropping rapidly so that she seemed to tower over the sea like a leviathan.

He said, 'I shall have to turn to port. It will give our spotters a chance.' It would also expose the whole broadside to the enemy, but speed was essential now. It was all they had.

'She's slowing down!' A man's cheer was cut short as the liner's two most forward guns fired together. It was all confused, and even the thundering crash of the explosion was muffled.

Half-deafened by the shell-burst Hechler dragged himself along the rail to the starboard side. A man was screaming, his face cut to ribbons, and Hechler saw that most of the glass screen had been fragmented by the burst. There was a lot of smoke, and he could smell the stench of burning paintwork and cordite.

'Steady on zero-six-zero, sir!' The voice-pipe from the wheelhouse was unattended and Hechler saw a petty officer lying dead against the flag lockers. There was not a mark on him, but his contorted face told its own story. Hechler thrust a man into his place.

'Tell the wheelhouse to remain on course.' He slipped on blood and trained his binoculars on the other ship. She was listing badly, flames bursting through her side as if from jets. The last internal explosion had found her heart.

'Engine-room request permission to reduce speed, Captain!'

'What is it, Chief?' Hechler pressed the phone under his cap.

Stück's voice was very steady. 'Pump trouble. Nothing we can't fix. I'm still waiting for reports. That last shell –'

. Hechler did not wait. 'Half speed, all engines.' A massive explosion rolled across the water, and fragments of steel and timber rained down until every trough seemed full of charred flotsam.

A man cried, 'She's going!'

Some smaller shells exploded close to the capsizing ship, and Hechler snatched up the gunnery handset, suddenly remembering Gudegast's despair. 'Shift target to the convoy!' It was not a rebuke for the gunnery officer, but it sounded like one.

The two forward turrets were already training round, seeking their targets. But the ships were scattering in several directions; each one was a separate attack.

In the armoured conning tower Gudegast had his face pressed against an observation slit. The *Prinz* had been hit, how badly he did not know. He could hear the intercom chattering, the stream of demands and orders as the damage-control parties swung into action. Gudegast had felt the explosion come right through the deck plates. As if they had hit a reef. Now all he could see was smoke, some small running figures by a dangling motorboat, cut in halves as it hung from its davits.

All he could think of was the sinking liner. The old *Tasmania*, of the Cunard White Star Line. He had seen her many times when she had been taken off her Atlantic runs to do some cruising in and around the lovely fjords of Norway. He had even been on board her once for an officer's birthday.

He could see her clearly, so different from his own timber ship. Spotless, well-laid decks, passengers drifting about with cameras, the elegance, the style of the liner and what she represented. He watched, sickened, as she rolled heavily on to her side, another funnel tearing adrift. There were more explosions, and Gudegast thought for a moment that Kröll was still directing guns on her.

He shouted wildly, 'Leave her! She can't hurt you now! Leave her alone, you bloody bastard!'

His assistants watched anxiously from the rear, their eyes glowing in the reflected explosions through the narrow slits.

Gudegast pressed a button and felt icy rain on his face as the massive steel door slid to one side.

He clambered out on to the little catwalk and then without realising what he was doing, removed his cap.

A ship had just been destroyed because fools had sent her to war.

He wiped his face with his sleeve. And she died with that same old dignity he had always admired so much.

Peter Younger knelt on the floor of the storeroom where the prisoners had been locked up for the night, and pressed his eye to a hole in the wall where a bolt had rusted away.

It was early morning and he heard some of the German sailors calling to each other. He found it hard to tell if they were angry exchanges or not.

Old Shiner sat with his narrow shoulders against the wall, idly watching the young radio officer's eyes in the filtered sunlight. 'They'm makin' a bloody row,' he said irritably. 'Couldn't sleep 'cause of it.'

Younger ground his jaws together as he concentrated on his tiny view of the station.

He said, 'They broke open a stock of booze, that's what all the racket's about.'

He should have guessed that something of the sort might happen. As soon as the false signal had been made, the prisoners had been herded together. It was as if the Germans had to let off steam, now the reality of their position was out in the open. Celebrating their part in the plot, or commiserating together at the prospect of early captivity he did not know, but he cursed himself for not taking precautions.

Mason, the man in charge of the station, dropped down beside him.

'It's too late then?' He sounded wary after Younger's outburst during the night, when he had told them what he was going to do. Mason had asked then, 'How do you know all this anyway?' Younger had exploded. 'We were bloody prisoners aboard the raider, that's how!'

He said, 'I must try. There's still a chance we might save a few lives, or call our blokes down on the krauts.'

Old Shiner said, 'If they don't open the bloody door I'm goin' to drop me trousers right now!'

Younger closed his eyes and thrust his forehead against the warm metal until he could think properly again. Poor old Shiner was halfway round the bend. He looked at Mason. 'When the guard unlocks the door we'll grab him and get his gun.'

Old Shiner remarked, 'Accordin' to the Geneva Convention we should 'ave proper toilet arrangements. I seen it in a book somewhere.'

Mason stared at him. 'God Almighty!'

Younger persisted, 'Are you with me?' He nearly said, *or are you like your chum over there who sent the signal under the German's supervision?* But he needed Mason. He was the only one now.

Mason nodded unhappily. 'It'll be the end of us, you know that?'

Younger shrugged. 'I'm not going to think about it.'

He stood up and walked to the corrugated door. The others would probably let him get on with it, watch him gunned down to join the dead mechanic.

Like the shutter in a camera he saw the drifting lifeboat for a split second. The patient, eyeless faces. The very horror of it. He glanced at Old Shiner. Poor bastard. He had been torpedoed and sunk so many times it was a wonder he was still breathing.

Mason said quietly, 'I'll *try*.' He sounded terrified, as if he could barely get the words out.

Younger touched his arm. 'Once inside the transmitting-room I'll have a signal off before you can blink.' He was amazed he could speak so confidently, when he had not even seen inside the place. It might already be out of action, smashed by the Germans after raising the trick alarm. He decided against that. Germans or not, they were all sailors. No sailor was ever keen to sever a possible lifeline.

Mason exclaimed, '*He's coming!*' He pressed himself to the

246

wall and whispered, 'Jesus!'

Younger tested the weight of the makeshift club in his hand. It was a length of firewood, probably left at the station for the winter months. It was not much, but the guard might be half-cut from the night's drinking. He thought of the balding senior operator. Obviously his sense of discipline was no longer shared by his companions. He held his breath until his temples throbbed as the man fumbled with the padlock and tried several times to insert a key. Younger heard him curse, and the clatter of the padlock as it fell on the rock floor.

Please God, let it work! He flung his weight against the door, it flew back and thudded heavily against the guard's skull as he stooped down to recover the padlock.

It all happened in seconds, and yet it lasted forever. The man's face squinting up in the sunlight, blood seeping down his face from the blow, then jerking back as Younger slammed his sea-boot into his gaping jaw. He did not recall how many times he brought the heavy piece of wood down on his head, but it was running with blood and torn skin as he threw it aside and wrenched the sub-machine gun from the man's shoulder.

Then he was running towards the rough ladder, expecting at any second to hear a challenge, feel the agony of a bullet between his shoulders. He heard Mason panting behind him, sobbing and muttering to himself as he followed.

At the top of the short ladder Younger turned for a quick glance. The shutter again. The sprawled sailor, and some terrified faces peering from the storeroom. Younger felt his heart breaking as he looked at the sea. So vast and impersonal, and suddenly without hostility.

It was all over. His ship, his friends, everything.

With a cry he kicked open the door and saw the German with the plastered arm staring at him, a mug of something in his free hand. Several things happened at once. The German lunged for his holster, which was dangling from a chair; Younger squeezed the trigger, but stared aghast as the gun remained silent. *Safety catch.* He fumbled for it, dimly aware that the German had dragged out his pistol, and that Mason was on his knees behind a packing case, burbling incoherently and in tears of terror. Something blurred across Younger's vision and he saw a heavy iron bar smash down on the man's plastered arm to crack it like a carrot. The German dropped his pistol and fell to the floor, his lip bitten through as the pain exploded in his shattered arm.

Old Shiner, his washed-out eyes blazing wildly, stepped further into the room and swung the long bar once more. It must have taken all his strength, but the German lay quite still, probably dead. Old Shiner tossed the bar aside and snatched the sub-machine gun from Younger and snorted, 'Yew'm never took a DEMS course like me. 'Ere, I'll keep them buggers off!'

With a gasp Younger sat down before the transmitter, his heart pumping as with a purr of power he switched it on. It was not so different from the one he had trained on. He dashed the sweat, or were they tears, from his eyes, and concentrated every fibre on the key. He knew most of the abbreviated codes issued by the navy. They needed to in Atlantic convoys, with ship after ship falling out of line, falling astern for the wolves. He blinked hard. Like *Radnor Star*.

He pressed the headphones over his ears and managed to hold the new sounds at bay. Sudden shouts, the blast on a whistle.

He came out in a rush of sweat. *The signal was already being acknowledged*. He grinned uncontrollably at the key. *You're the one who's too late, Baldy!* He was thinking of the senior operator, who probably wondered what the hell was happening.

There was a rattle of machine-gun fire and a line of holes punched through the wall, so that dusty sunlight cut across the room like thin bars.

Old Shiner had the door open just an inch and the room filled with smoke as he fired a long burst down the slope.

'Got one o' the buggers!' He was laughing as he crossed to the opposite side. Neither of them even noticed that Mason, the unwilling volunteer, had already been killed by the first shots.

Younger heard Old Shiner cursing as he snatched up the other German's pistol. He must have emptied a whole magazine in one go.

Younger winced as more shots crashed through the room and

248

some exploded the dials and fuses at the top of the transmitter.

Too late. Too late. The words seemed to deafen the clatter of small arms fire, the occasional heavy bang as Old Shiner took a potshot at someone below the building.

More crashes, and the transmitter went dead. Younger threw the earphones on the bench and swung round. '*We did it!*' But the old boatswain did not hear him. He sat lopsided against the wall, blood seeping through his tattered jersey. His eyes were tightly closed, like those last moments in the lifeboat.

A window shattered and he stared without comprehension at a heavy cudgel-shaped object as it fell at his feet. He had not, of course, ever seen a German hand-grenade before.

His mind had just time to record that Old Shiner even had his arms cradled, as he had been when he had nursed his cat, when the grenade exploded and there was only darkness.

There was less smoke now and Hechler guessed that the fire-fighting parties had doused most of the flames between decks.

Voice-pipes chattered incessantly until Froebe shouted, 'Damage-control, sir!'

Hechler jammed the telephone to his ear while he watched the dead petty officer being dragged away. The man with the glass-flayed face had already gone; only his blood remained, spreading and thinning in the steady rain.

Theil said, 'A fluke shell, sir.' Someone was screaming in the background. 'A shot in a million.'

Hechler watched the smoke spiralling above the broken screen.

'Tell me.'

Theil explained in his flat, impersonal tone. One of the armed merchant cruiser's last eight-inch shells had plummeted down to pierce the battery deck between the bridge and Turret Bruno. As Theil had said, it was a chance in a million. It had struck the air shaft of a mushroom ventilator and been deflected through the armoured deck before exploding against a magazine shaft. Sixteen men of the damage-control party there had been killed. In such a confined space it was not surprising. But it was a double disaster. The explosion had severely damaged the

249

training mechanism of Turret Bruno. Until the damage could be put right, the whole turret was immobile. It could not even be trained by manual power.

Hechler considered the facts as Theil described them. The engine-room was confident that all pumps would be working again at full power within the hour. Casualties elsewhere were confined to the bridge, and two seamen who had been putting out a small fire below the funnel. They must have been blasted over the side without anyone seeing them go.

'Report to me when you have completed your inspection.'

Froebe whispered, 'The admiral, sir.'

Leitner seemed to materialise on the bridge like a white spectre.

'What the *hell* is happening?' He glared through the trapped smoke, his shoulders dark with rain. 'I am not a bloody mind-reader!'

Hechler looked at him coldly. 'B Turret is out of commission, sir. We've lost nineteen men killed, and three injured.' He glanced at the blood. It had almost been washed away now. 'One man was blinded.'

'*I do not hear you!* What are you saying?' Leitner strode from one side to the other, his shoes crunching over broken glass. 'We have lost the convoy – don't you understand anything?'

Hechler looked up as Froebe called, 'New course is two-three-zero, sir.'

Hechler said, 'We have to turn, sir. Radar reports three tankers sunk and two, possibly three escorts as well.'

'*I don't care!*' Leitner was beside himself with rage, and did not even notice the astonished watchkeepers around him. 'Three tankers! A pinprick! We should have taken the whole convoy.'

Jaeger waited for Leitner to rush to the opposite side and stammered, 'W/T office has picked up a signal from the radio station, sir.'

Hechler eyed him calmly, although his nerves were screaming. 'Well?'

'They are not sure, sir. But it seems as if another operator has disclaimed the first signal. Now there is only silence.'

'Steady on two-three-zero, sir. All engines half-speed ahead.'

Leitner was suddenly facing him, his face streaming with rain. 'What was that? Am I to be told nothing by these idiots?'

Hechler replied, 'The information will doubtless have been sent to your bridge, sir.' He tried to contain his patience, when all he wanted to do was discover how badly the *Prinz* was damaged.

'It means that somebody on St Jorge took over the transmitter. Had it been any earlier we would have had to abandon the whole convoy. I —'

Leitner thrust his face so close he could smell the brandy. 'I don't want your snivelling excuses! I'll have those men court-martialled and shot, and I'll personally break the officer responsible for the landing party!'

Hechler stood back, sickened. 'It was a risk. We knew it. It might have been worse.'

'Worse? *Worse?*' Leitner waved his arms at the bridge. 'I don't see that! A relic of a merchant ship stood against *Prinz Luitpold*, and because of someone's incompetence we had to withdraw! By God, Hechler, I'll not be a laughing-stock because of it! Do you know what I call it?'

Hechler pressed his hands to his sides. He wanted to hit Leitner, to keep on hitting him. A laughing-stock, was that all he saw in it? Men killed, and this fine ship isolated and at bay because of his haphazard orders.

'I call it cowardice! In the face of the enemy — what do you think of *that*?'

'I can only disagree, sir.'

'Can you indeed.' He stared around the bridge. 'There are some who will live long enough to regret this day!' He stormed off the bridge and Froebe hissed, 'I'm no coward, damn him!'

Hechler ignored him. 'Recall the Arado. Tell W/T to monitor every signal. We have roused a hornets' nest.'

He looked round, surprised, as sunlight broke through the dull clouds. 'And I want the navigating officer here at once.'

There was no point in wondering about the hand on the transmitter. It was probably as dead as the men trapped below when the shell had exploded amongst them.

A messenger handed him a telephone. Leitner's voice was quite controlled again. It could have been someone else entirely.

'We will rendezvous at the *second* grid-point. It will be safer than heading north right away.'

'Very well, sir.' *Why don't I argue with him? Tell him that we are wasting sea miles and precious time. Steer north and take the risk.* It would be 900 miles closer to home. But even as he thought it, Hechler knew it was fruitless. Leitner was unstable in his present mood. All he could think of was their failure to destroy the whole convoy, the effect it might have on his own reputation. He had made it quite clear that he would see that all blame would rest elsewhere. On the captain's shoulders, no doubt. Hechler was quietly surprised that the realisation did not touch him.

What they had achieved this far, they had done well. The courage and sacrifice of that one old liner had shifted the balance, from offensive to the need for survival. That was war. It was also luck.

He heard Gudegast's seaboots crunching over the glass and turned to face him.

'You've heard about St Jorge?'

Gudegast met his gaze, troubled and wary. 'Yes, sir. The whole ship has.' He seemed to expect anger, even dismissal.

Hechler said quietly, 'You were right, Josef. She *was* a fine old lady.'

Gudegast's bearded features softened. 'No, I was a fool to question your actions. It was not my place to speak as I did.'

Hechler looked up at the rain. A man had died here, another had been blinded, just feet away. *It could have been me.*

He said, 'My guess is that the Tommies are on their way to St Jorge, or were until that last signal was sent. It will give us some sea-room, I think. Maybe our admiral is right to head for the second rendezvous. It will keep us out of the air patrols, and I think that the hunters will be expecting us to head for the North Atlantic without further delay.'

Gudegast shrugged. 'Home then, sir.'

'Yes. But we'll not reach Germany again without a fight.'

Theil entered the bridge and eyed them grimly. 'I have done my rounds, sir.'

Hechler nodded. 'Tell me the worst, Viktor.'

Theil looked at the broken screen. He had heard the blinded man screaming before he had been silenced by Stroheim's staff.

'One of my petty officers, Hammer, is trapped in the empty, ready-use room, sir. The mechanism was broken in the explosion.'

Gudegast said, 'But he should not have been in there surely?'

He saw the petty officer in his mind, a mild man, yet one who always seemed to be against authority in his mad desire to keep stocks of glass in any vacant space.

Hechler said, 'I have the key in my safe, Viktor.'

Theil faced him. 'Yes. And the admiral had the other. I am fully aware of the security arrangements in this ship. I —' He seemed to check himself with a real effort.

'Well, he's trapped inside. With the admiral's boxes.'

It would have to be solved, but against what had happened it seemed trivial.

He would go round the ship as soon as the Arado had been hoisted inboard. With more and more enemy ships being homed either towards the broken convoy or the silent radio station, they would need all their eyes to avoid discovery.

'See what you can do.' Hechler looked at each of them in turn. 'And thank you.'

He felt utterly drained. Yet he must inspect the immobilised turret, see his heads of department, and bury their dead.

He thought of the girl's face so close to his own, the need to see her. It might be the last time.

He thought too of the unknown hand on the transmitter key, and the captain of the old ocean liner as she had charged to the attack. His men could and would fight like that. He pictured Leitner's insane fury and felt a sudden anxiety.

The legend and the luck were no longer enough.

18

No Hiding Place

Acting Commodore Hemrose moved restlessly to the starboard side of the *Wiltshire*'s bridge and fastened his duffle coat more tightly. The rain was getting heavier, he thought irritably. They could do without it.

He peered through a clearview screen and watched the long arrowhead of the cruiser's forecastle begin to shine through the darkness. Dawn soon. He felt like rubbing his hands but it was too wet for that. Since leaving Simonstown the three ships had maintained almost their full speed, and each had been closed up at action stations since midnight. Exciting, exhilarating, it was much more than either, Hemrose thought. Gone was the boredom and the nagging suspicion that the German raider was cocking a snook at them. For two days they had pounded through the heavy ocean swell, gun crews exercising without all the usual moans. This time it was in earnest.

Hemrose could picture his ships clearly despite the darkness. The *Rhodesia* was half a mile astern, while the light cruiser *Pallas* was way ahead in the van. If the German's radar was as good as the experts had implied, it was better to have the smallest ship in the lead. The *Prinz Luitpold* was a powerful and formidable opponent, but they would dart in to close the range, singly, while the others maintained covering fire to halve the enemy's resources. Hemrose thought of their old Walrus flying boat, the Shagbat as it was affectionately known in the navy. One engine, a *pusher* at that, with a ridiculous maximum speed of 130 odd miles per hour. But it only needed one sighting report, and the ancient Walrus could do that just as efficiently as any first-rate bomber.

Hemrose glanced at his bridge staff. The first lieutenant and officer-of-the-watch, the navigating officer, two junior subbies, and the usual handful of experts, signalmen and the like. As good a ship's company as you could find anywhere, he decided.

He licked his lips and tasted that last mug of cocoa, *pusser's kye*. It had been laced with rum, his chief steward had seen to that. Just the thing to meet the dawn.

He heard the OOW answering one of the voice-pipes, then turned as he said, 'W/T office. Chief telegraphist requests permission to come up, sir.'

'*What?*' Hemrose dug his hands into his damp pockets. 'Oh, very well.'

The chief telegraphist was a proper old sweat. Not the kind to make fruitless requests when at any moment they might make contact with the enemy.

The man arrived on the bridge and paused only to nod to his messmate, the Chief Yeoman of Signals.

'What is it?'

The man had a signal pad in his hand but did not seem to need it.

He said, 'From Admiralty, sir, repeated Rear-Admiral commanding Force M.' He swallowed hard. 'The signal from St Jorge was a fake, sir. The northbound tanker convoy is under attack by the raider. HMS *Tasmania* is engaging.'

Some of the others had heard what the chief petty officer had said and were watching Hemrose, waiting for him to explode. Hemrose was surprised that he should feel so calm. And yet he had never expected this to happen. Not in a thousand years.

The chief telegraphist added, 'Also, there was one further transmission from that radio station, sir. Someone there was apparently trying to warn us.'

Hemrose looked up sharply as the first lieutenant murmured, 'Brave bastard!'

'Get the commander up here.' He had to think, but all he

could see was the convoy, the shells ploughing amongst those heavily laden oil tankers. 'Call up the squadron. Remain on course. Reduce to cruising speed.' He hated to add, 'Fall out action stations. I'll speak to our people presently.'

'More kye, sir.' His chief steward had appeared by his side.

'Thanks.' He tried to grin, but his face felt rigid. 'I bloody need it.'

Godson clattered up the ladder and exclaimed, 'I just heard, sir. Bad show.'

Is that what you really think? Aloud Hemrose said, 'We'll be getting our marching orders soon, hence the signal repeated to Force M.'

Godson remained silent. Force M was one of the fleet's powerful independent groups, a battle-cruiser, a big carrier, with all the support and escorts they needed. It would be the end of Hemrose's little squadron. He would become a small fish in a much grander pool. Godson hated himself for being pleased about it. But it would be a whole lot safer.

The navigating officer murmured, 'When it's convenient, sir –' He hesitated as Hemrose turned towards him.

Hemrose said, 'We shall maintain this course for the moment, Pilot.'

Godson offered, 'Someone will have to lie off St Jorge and pick up the Germans if there are any.'

Hemrose said harshly, 'Well, not me. Leave that to some errand-boy!'

His sudden anger seemed to tire him. He said, 'I shall be in my sea-cabin. Call me if –' He did not finish it.

Alone in his cabin abaft the bridge he lay fully clothed, staring into the darkness.

When the telephone rang he snatched it up and snapped, 'Well?'

It was Godson. 'Signal from Admiralty, sir.' He cleared his throat as he always did when he was about to face something bad. 'The Armed Merchant Cruiser *Tasmania* has been sunk. One escort reported seeing a shell-burst on the raider. Most of the convoy has survived. We are to await further instructions.'

Hemrose slumped down again. Poor old *Tasmania*. It must

have been the last thing her captain had expected too. He clenched his fists with sudden despair and anger. What was it he had learned when he had been a cadet at Dartmouth? *God and the Navy we adore, when danger threatens but not before.* How bloody true it had been proved over and over again in this war. Pleasure boats and paddle steamers used for minesweeping, Great War destroyers fighting the Atlantic and anything the krauts could fling their way. And it would be the same in any future conflict. Spend nothing, but expect a bloody miracle, that was John Citizen's battle cry.

He heaved himself up and stared at the luminous clock. What was the matter with him? Was he so overwhelmed by the German's trick that he had missed something so obvious? No ship as good as *Prinz Luitpold* would be deterred by the second signal from St Jorge. Not at that stage, with helpless tankers falling to her broadsides. The old AMC had scored one hit, they said. Well, it might only take one. It must have been bad enough to make Hechler break off the action.

He seized the telephone and heard the OOW reply, 'Bridge, sir?'

'Get me the commander.'

Godson sounded alarmed. 'Something wrong, sir?'

'*Tasmania* hit the raider, Toby. The *Prinz Luitpold* must be in trouble.'

Godson stammered, 'One shell, sir – well, that is, we don't know –'

'Shut up and listen. I want the attack team mustered in the chart room in ten minutes.'

There was no comment and he snapped, 'Are you still there?'

Godson replied weakly, 'Are you going after the raider again, sir?'

Hemrose touched his face. He would shave, and meet his little team looking refreshed and confident.

He said, 'We needed a bit of luck, Toby. That poor, clapped-out AMC may have given us just that.'

Godson persisted, 'The Admiralty will probably decline to –'

'Don't be such a bloody old woman.' He slammed down the phone.

It was so obvious he wanted to shout it at the top of his voice. The US submarine had been damaged, but had fired at the raider because her skipper had never seen such a target. But his torpedoes must have hit something else, hence the remains of German corpses and a massive oil-slick. The so-called experts had acted like a ship's lookout who saw only what he expected to see. It must have been another submarine. He wanted to laugh, when he recalled it was the poor chaplain who had first put the doubts about the raider's fuel supply in his mind.

It had to be that. But just because it had never been done before, nobody, not even Duffield's back-room boys had even suspected it.

God, the enemy must have been planning all this for months, and everything, even the RAF's recce reports over the Norwegian fjords, had been fooled by one ruse after another.

The door opened. 'I've brought you your shavin' gear, sir.' The steward showed his teeth. ''Ad a feelin' you might be askin' for it.'

Hemrose stared at himself in the mirror. He could still be wrong. There was nothing really solid to go on. But it was all he had. They would go right through every report and signal. If they found nothing they would do it all over again until they did.

Nobody had really considered submarines before. The Admiralty and intelligence sources had concentrated on checking lists of so-called neutrals, especially those in South American ports, where a supply ship might have been waiting for a rendezvous.

Later in the chart-room Hemrose explained his thoughts on the raider's performance.

'Hechler had that convoy on a plate. He'd knocked out the escort, and picked off the first tankers like fish in a barrel. But for the old AMC he would have polished off the whole boiling lot.'

The young navigating officer said, 'If he's damaged, he'll also need fuel.'

Hemrose nodded. 'Good thinking. When his bunkers are topped up he'll make for safe waters again – my guess is Norway.' He added grudgingly, 'Even with the Home Fleet and Force M on the alert he's the sort of captain who might just pull it off. If he sails safely into port after cutting our blockade in both directions he would do far more good for German morale at home than by wiping out that convoy.'

Godson said, 'The Germans have been using the big supply submarines in the South Atlantic for two years, I believe.'

Hemrose waited silently, seeing his hazy ideas forming into a possibility on their faces.

The first lieutenant said, 'They work to a grid system, don't they?'

Hemrose smiled. 'Check all the U-boat reports in that area, ours and the Yanks.'

Hemrose rocked back on his heels. He was already heading into disaster, so where might this additional risk take him?

'Then make a signal to *Pallas* and *Rhodesia*. I'd like to see the captains before we begin.'

Godson wilted under his stare but asked, 'And Admiralty, sir?'

'Balls to their lordships, Toby! I was given this job and I intend to see it through!' He glanced at the chaplain. 'And thanks to our warlike padre here, I think we may be on the home stretch!'

Hemrose walked out into the daylight and lifted his face to the rain.

It was hard to accept that within two hours he had risen from despair to optimism.

As he passed the forward funnel he saw the ship's crest bolted to a catwalk. Beneath it was her motto in Latin. Hemrose's red face split into a grin so that two Oerlikon gunners peered down with astonishment to watch him.

Translated, their motto was *Count your blessings*.

It was not much, but it was a start.

Leitner looked up from his littered desk and eyed Hechler for several seconds.

'You wish to see me?'

Hechler nodded. He wondered how Leitner could leave the

upper bridge to spend time in his spacious quarters. The cabin was unusually chaotic, with clothes strewn about, and a life-jacket hanging on the door.

Hechler said, 'We have just buried the men who were killed, sir.'

Leitner pouted. 'Yes. I felt the ship slow down.' Some of the old edge returned to his tone. 'Not that she's exactly a greyhound of the ocean at the moment!'

'The engine-room expects the pumps will all be working at full pressure soon.' They had said that yesterday, but this time Stück seemed quite confident. 'It's B turret that worries me.'

'You? *Worry?*' Leitner put down his pen and regarded him calmly. 'After their performance with the convoy I'd have thought the whole gunnery team should be *worried*!'

It was pointless to argue, to explain that the single shell from the *Tasmania* had been a fluke shot. Anyway, Leitner seemed so preoccupied he would only have challenged that too.

Hechler said, 'The rendezvous with the supply-boat, sir. I am having second thoughts. At this reduced speed we will meet the milch-cow on her final day in the prescribed grid. After that we may not find the time to refuel before we turn for home.'

'I had considered that, Dieter.' The sudden use of his name was also unexpected. 'But we still stick to our plans. I intend to transfer the camera team to the submarine. They can make their own arrangements when she reaches Germany.' He sounded vague, almost disinterested.

'And the woman pilot?'

Leitner gave a small smile. 'Ah, yes. The lovely Erika. I am afraid she has not earned *her* release just yet.' He dragged a chart from beneath a pile of papers. 'The rendezvous is here, right?'

Hechler bent over the desk. Why go over it again? All he could see were the lines of flag-covered bodies, the rain sheeting down while he had read the burial service. Then the signal to the bridge to reduce speed, the last volley of shots, and the seamen rolling up the empty flags for the next time. Faces and groups lingered in his mind, like little cameos of war itself. A young seaman wiping his eyes with his sleeve and trying not

260

to show his grief at the loss of a friend. The camera crew filming the funeral, a petty officer staring at them, his eyes filled with hatred and disgust. Leitner should have been there. It was the least he could do. And he had seen the girl too, her coat collar turned up as she had gripped a stanchion below two manned anti-aircraft guns and watched him, listening to his words as he had saluted, and the pathetic bundles had splashed over the side.

Hechler had been kept busy with hardly a break. Now, in the sealed cabin it closed in like a blanket. He was dog-tired at a time when he needed to be at full alert.

Somewhere overhead one of the Arados was testing its engine.

They were off the shipping lanes, and as far as Bauer's telegraphists had been able to determine, all enemy forces had been directed either to the convoy or further north. OKM Operations Division had been silent. It was as if the *Prinz Luitpold* had already been written off as a casualty, left to her own resources.

Hechler closed his fingers. One more cargo of fuel and he would be able to assess their immediate future. If they avoided the enemy Kröll and his artificers would repair the turret's training mechanism. Otherwise all their main defences would be down aft.

Leitner did not look up from the chart, and some of his sleek hair fell forward like a loose quill. It was so unlike him that Hechler wondered if the last engagement had broken his faith.

Leitner was saying, 'Now about my boxes, hmm?'

Hechler thought of the petty officer who was still trapped. The damage control section had told him that the door was buckled, and it would have to be cut away with torches. There was an air vent, so the luckless Hammer was in no danger. Yet.

'They are working on the door, sir.'

Leitner did not seem to hear. 'That man had a key. He must have stolen it or made it. He is a thief, a menace to this ship, a traitor. I intend that he shall stand trial as soon as he is freed.' He raised his eyes suddenly. '*I want that door open.*' His eyes hardened. 'It can be done, *yes* or *no*?' He swung round. 'What now?'

Theil stood in the entrance, his cap dripping with rain.

'The door won't move, sir. The engine-room is supplying some heavier cutting gear –'

Leitner screamed at him, 'Don't come here with your snivelling excuses! I want the door forced open immediately! Blow it down with a limited explosion!'

Hechler stepped between them. 'It could kill Hammer, sir. In such a confined space –'

Leitner glared at him wildly. 'It will save him from the firing squad! He was spying on me, and he's not the only one! Must I repeat everything? Blow it open!'

Theil looked at Hechler, his face pleading. 'He's one of my men!'

Leitner was breathing hard. 'I have no doubt of that!'

Theil faced him. 'What exactly do you mean, sir?'

Leitner stared at him, astonished. 'Are you questioning me or my orders?'

Hechler snapped, 'I would like to remind both of you that we are in some danger.' To Theil he added, 'Wait outside. I'll deal with this matter.' As the door closed he said, 'How dare you accuse my officers of plotting against you?' He could not stop himself. 'You are supposed to offer leadership to this ship's company, not act like some sort of god!'

Leitner's jaw hung open. It was as if Hechler had struck him, or screamed some terrible curse.

Hechler continued flatly, 'I intend to fight this ship back to Germany, and to do that I need the trust of every man aboard. Respect, not fear, *sir*, is what we survive on.' He watched him coldly. 'Or we go under.'

Leitner dragged out a spotless handkerchief and slowly dabbed his lips.

'So that is your attitude?'

'It is.'

He waited, half expecting Leitner to call to the sentry and put him under arrest. A Luger lay on the table nearby. He might even drag that out and shoot him in his present unstable mood.

Leitner nodded jerkily. 'I shall remember this. Now get that door open and have that man arrested.'

Hechler stepped away from the table. Leitner had again become very calm. It was unnerving.

Leitner continued, 'Let me know when you are increasing speed to this rendezvous.' He was pointing at the chart, but his fingers were nowhere near the pencilled position. 'I shall be receiving the final instructions shortly. When I do –' He looked away. '*Leave me!*'

Hechler stepped out of the cabin and found Theil waiting.

'You think I knew, don't you?'

Theil gaped at him. 'I – I don't understand.'

'You love this ship, Viktor. I know that. In a matter of days, maybe hours, we shall be called on to fight, against odds. I shall need your loyalty then, and so will the *Prinz*.'

He looked away, unable to watch Theil's despair as he said brokenly, 'She was arrested by the Gestapo. I was not told. The house was empty.' The words were spilling from him in a torrent. 'If I hadn't read that file –'

Hechler said gently, 'It was too late to do anything when I found out about it. We were under enforced radio silence, you know that. It may not be as bad as you think –' Their eyes met and he knew it was pointless to go on. Even if the Gestapo had made a mistake, it was unlikely they would admit it. What was one more life to them?

Millions had perished. He thought of the unknown hand on the morse key at St Jorge, the men he had buried, the petty officer who had died without a mark on him. He looked around at the grey steel. They could still break through. He touched Theil's arm and this time he did not drag away. It was already too late for him.

'I am the captain of this ship, Viktor, and many people probably think I am too remote, too secure to watch minor events under my command. But I have seen and heard things. I will not allow this ship's reputation to be smeared.' His eyes were hard. 'By anyone.'

Theil touched his cap. 'I'll do what I can.' He swallowed hard. 'I wasn't certain – I –'

Hechler walked out to the open deck; it was like sharing a terrible secret to see the tears running down Theil's cheeks. He felt suddenly sickened by it. By Leitner's inconsistent behaviour, his malice and his instability. But more by his own uncertainty. Like a man who has been given a weapon he suspects is faulty.

'You walk alone, Dieter?'

She stepped from beneath the same gun-mounting, her cheeks glowing from wind and rain.

He faced her and wanted to fold her in his arms, forget everything but this moment.

'I need to talk, Erika.' He knew some of the seamen were watching him. It was like a farewell at a railway station. Alone within a crowd. No words until it was too late to utter them.

'I know.' She gripped his arm. 'I was afraid.' She shook her head so that her damp hair bounced on the fur collar. 'No, not of war, of the fighting and the dying. But afterwards. I thought you might think it was a momentary lapse, a need which we both shared, but only for a moment.' She gripped him more tightly. 'I want you for myself.'

He smiled down at her, the other faces and figures fading into distance. 'I shall never give you up.' He turned as a messenger bustled up to them and saluted. 'From the bridge, sir. The engine-room can give full speed now.' His eyes flickered between them.

'Tell the bridge to wait. I am coming up.' He looked at the girl's eyes, hung on to what he saw, needing her to believe him, to trust him, no matter what happened.

He said, 'I love you, Erika.' Then he stepped back and saw the way she lifted her chin. It was as if they had both found a strength they had not previously recognised.

As he vanished up the ladder to the forebridge she whispered aloud, 'And I you, dearest of men.'

The deck began to tremble and she watched the wash rise up alongside as once again the bows smashed into the sea as if they despised it. She walked slowly below the high bridge structure and saw the black hole where the shell had plunged through to explode between decks. It was all so unreal to see and feel the enemy right here amongst them. She thought of Hechler's features as he had read the burial service, his strong voice raised above the laboured roar of fans, and the hiss of rain across the armour plating. She smiled sadly. *The iron pirate.* She could not see more than a day ahead, and she guessed that most of her companions felt much the same. But after this precious moment she knew she would find him again, that she could love nobody else.

The following morning, with less than an hour left of the pre-arranged rendezvous time, they made contact with the giant submarine. Men lined the guardrails as it surfaced, the water streaming from the casing and squat conning-tower, many of the onlookers remembering the other submarine's savage end, and wondering if this one's commander even knew about it.

Theil, megaphone in hand, watched the lines being fired across, the engineering party ready and waiting to sway the huge fuel hoses inboard and connect them to the bunkers.

He kept seeing Hechler's face, the sadness he had shown when he had confronted him about Britta.

Nothing seemed to matter any more. If they reached home there was nobody waiting for him. Anyway, Leitner would make certain he would climb no further in the navy. If they met with the enemy, he might at least save the ship.

He waved his megaphone to the boatswain's party at the guy-ropes and tackles. Either way, only Leitner could win. He stared so hard at the swaying wires and ropes between the two ill-matched hulls that his vision became blurred. Leitner had known all about Britta. He could have made a signal when they were still in safe waters, if he had wanted to help.

Theil was suddenly quite calm. He knew what he was going to do.

The pilot of the *Wiltshire*'s twin-winged Walrus was a young Wavy Navy lieutenant. Despite what other Fleet Air Arm officers said about his antiquated flying-boat he had grown extremely fond of it.

He was singing silently, his voice lost in the throaty roar of the Pegasus radial engine which hung above the cockpit like some ungainly cradle, and watching patches of blue cutting through the cloud layer, like a sea on a beach.

The three other members of his crew were peering down at the ocean, where occasionally their inelegant shadow preceded them as they tacked back and forth over a forty mile line.

Rumours had spawned in the cruiser's wardroom at a mounting rate. Ever since it had been announced that the German's presence at St Jorge had been a clever ruse, and then that the Admiralty was ordering Hemrose to withdraw and join up with Force M. A new buzz had spread through the ship before the old one had been found true or false.

How vast the ocean looked from here, he thought. Nothing, not even a hint of land. It was a vast grey-blue desert, broken here and there by tiny white ridges, and dark troughs which from the sky seemed quite motionless.

A great ocean, with nothing ahead but the winding coastline of South America. He chuckled. And that was 500 miles away. Hemrose would have to give in soon, he thought. He had pushed his luck too far with the Admiralty this time. Old Godson would be pleased. He was scared of his own shadow.

His observer and navigator climbed up beside him and switched on his intercom.

'Time to turn in five minutes, Bob. Then one more sweep to the south and back to Father.' He peered at the endless terrain of water.

'The Old Man's not going to like it.'

The pilot eased the controls and glanced quickly at the compass. The news from Europe was amazing, advances everywhere. Only the coming of winter would slow things down now. He had been at school when the war had started, and the navy, temporary or not, was all he knew. It would probably carry on in Japan afterwards, he thought.

It was strange, but he had never dropped a bomb or fired one of their elderly Vickers machine-guns in anger. Just up and down lines of convoyed ships, or scouting like this ahead of the cruiser.

It would have been a nice thing to remember. 'What d'you reckon, Tim?'

His companion grinned. 'No chance. The Old Man's dropped a right clanger this time!'

They both laughed into their mouthpieces and then the pilot looked again and gasped, 'Christ, Tim! *It's her!*'

The old Walrus leaned over, the engine protesting shakily as he thrust the stick hard against his knee.

It was not a silhouette like the ones in their charts and manuals. It was a flaw in the sea's face, a hint of shadow, solid and somehow frightening.

'Quick! Back to Father!' They clung on as the Walrus tacked into a low bank of cloud with as much dignity as it could manage.

There was so much the pilot wanted to know and to recognise. He could have risked flak and worse by going nearer, but he knew what Hemrose would say if he disobeyed orders.

He felt his friend punching his shoulder and stared at him, his eyes suddenly bright with understanding pride as he shouted, 'Never mind the bloody fleet, Bob! Just remember this day! *We found the bastard!*'

Had the Germans seen them? It no longer mattered. They had indeed done what everyone else had failed to do. In all this ocean, it was a bloody miracle!

They both fell about laughing when they realised that neither of the other crew members as yet knew what had happened.

Aboard their ship Hemrose sat nodding in the noon sunlight, his cap tilted over his reddened face.

The Chief Yeoman of signals steadied his telescope and said, 'Signal from *Pallas*, sir. *In contact with your Walrus*. Message reads.' The yeoman licked his dried lips. '*Enemy in sight!*'

Hemrose slid from the chair, feeling their eyes on him. As if he had just parted the Red Sea.

'Make to squadron, Yeo. *Increase to full speed*.' He saw the yeoman watching him too, his eyes asking a question. They had been together a long time and Hemrose did not disappoint him.

'Hoist battle ensigns!'

19

Last Command

Hechler stood on the bridge wing and watched the huge submarine manoeuvring abeam. The sea seemed to flood between them, as if both vessels were stationary. Hechler knew differently, could sense the group of junior officers who had been summoned by Froebe to the bridge to study the formidable art of ship-handling. The supply-submarine had all her work cut out to maintain proper buoyancy and trim as the big hoses began to quiver like oily snakes, and the first of the precious fuel was pumped across.

Theil was with the boatswain on the maindeck, his megaphone or one hand slicing the air to control the seamen at the guy-ropes and wires.

'Revolutions seven-zero.' Hechler heard the order repeated behind him and pictured the intent group far below his feet in the armour-plated wheelhouse.

'*Stop starboard!*' He watched narrowly as the bows straightened up again, and the channel between the hulls became even.

'Slow ahead all engines.' He gripped the safety rail and leaned right over, the rain slashing across his oilskin, although he barely noticed it.

He loved to feel the might and power of the ship beneath him, as if he was holding her, as a rider will control a wilful mount. He saw a lamp blink from the conning tower and resisted the urge to smile. He knew already what the brief signal would ask.

'Signal, sir. *Request send boat with passengers.*'

'Negative. Tell the commander to break out a rubber dinghy.'
It would be a lively crossing between the cruiser and the submarine even when controlled by hand-lines and tackles. He knew
the camera team was already mustered by the guardrail, their
cans of film safely protected in heavy bags. If he had one of
their own boats lowered, the submarine might be tempted to
break away and dive at the first suggestion of danger. Her commander would know this of course, but it was always worth
a try.

He craned still further across the rail and saw one of the
camera girls clinging to Meile, the supply officer, in a tearful
embrace. Some of the sailors were grinning at them, and one
hidden soul gave an ironic cheer.

Whatever happened from now on, it would be done without
the benefit of a filmed record, he thought.

He said, 'Tell the wheelhouse to allow for the drag. Ease to
port. Hold her there!'

The big submarine would not have a smooth passage home,
he thought. All the long haul up to Iceland and around through
the Denmark Strait before the ice came down. Then over to
Norway, following the coastline to the narrows which guarded
the way into the Baltic. What would they find when they finally
reached Kiel, he wondered? It would be a prime target for the
Allied air forces, and all the flak in the world could not hold
out against such odds. He could picture his last visit there without effort .... He called sharply, '*Half astern starboard!*' He
counted the seconds as the drag of one screw took effect. 'Slow
ahead starboard!' He wondered if the fledgling one-stripers had
noticed that his attention had drifted for those few vital seconds.
He saw Theil peer up at the bridge; he of all people would
know how simple it was to veer too close and grind into the
supply-boat. Or to drag away, snapping lines and hoses and
covering the sea with fuel.

He heard Froebe lecturing to the young officers. Hechler took
a deep breath. Close thing.

A messenger called, 'Half completed, sir.' He had the engine-
room handset pressed to one ear. 'Another thirty minutes.'

Hechler waved his hand without turning. There were no hoses immediately below the bridge, and he pictured the luckless petty officer, the one they called Mad Rudi, locked in his steel prison. It was still not clear how he had got there, or why, and communication between him and the working party outside was limited to a series of frustrating exchanges with hammer-taps on the heavy door.

Leitner's order to blow it open was absurd. The compartment was next to the forward flak switch-room, while beyond that was one of the great bunkers, still full and untapped.

The right gun, then the left in Turret Bruno lifted a few degrees, and the whole structure gave a drawn-out groan, as if steel were grating on steel. The turret remained motionless. Only one shell had found its mark, but the effects showed no sign of improving. Kröll was fuming with anxiety and impatience and had every artificer from his department hard at work to clear the training mechanism. No, even a controlled charge to open Hammer's prison would be courting disaster. Like a man tossing a lighted cigarette into a barrel of gunpowder.

Leitner had not thought fit to discuss this further setback, but had sent Theissen, his aide, to enquire about progress.

The man obviously knew nothing of his admiral's original intention. To offload his mysterious boxes into the submarine, perhaps? If so, why bring them this far?

He heard Gudegast rumbling away in the background, pointing out the behaviour of wind and sea and their effect on two tethered hulls.

He recalled Gudegast's outburst over the old AMC. It added to the man in some way, as if he had always managed to keep his real self hidden in the past.

The boatswain walked towards the forecastle, his arm gesturing to some men with heaving lines. Brezinka knew just about everything that happened in the ship. He would certainly know the truth about Hammer.

Hechler tried not to think of the girl, how she had looked when he had blurted out his true feelings for her. He knew he would never forget. He screwed up his eyes and concentrated on the taut or slackening wires, the way that the sea was breaking

270

over the submarine's nearest saddle-tank.

He had to see her again. Was it so hopeless that it must remain just an incident, like so many thousands in wartime?

And what of Theil? Fretting, hating, nursing his despair, which was as deep as any wound. Which would last? His love for the ship, or the inner madness that would in time destroy him?

'Radar – bridge!' The speaker made the young officers peer up with alarm.

Hechler seized the handset. 'Captain speaking.'

'Aircraft at Green one-five-oh! Moving left to right, extreme range.'

A dozen pairs of powerful glasses swivelled round and a man exclaimed, 'I saw a flash, sir!'

Hechler kept his eyes on the submarine. 'Keep watching!' He dared not hand the con to one of the others.

Froebe said, 'It's gone into some clouds, sir.' He sounded interested but nothing more. 'Dead astern now. Target moving very slowly.' He swore silently. 'Lost it again.'

The speaker intoned, 'Secondary armament stand by!'

Hechler wanted to turn, but snapped, 'Cancel that order!'

Gudegast joined him and together they stared down at the supply-boat's great whale back. The dinghy had been warped alongside and he saw one of the women being guided or dragged to the open forehatch. The sooner the passengers were safely below and the hatch slammed shut, the happier the commander would be.

Gudegast said, 'Maybe it didn't see us, sir?' He sounded doubtful.

Hechler considered it. A small aircraft, over 500 miles from land – it had to be hostile. Everyone had reported it as being very slow. He felt the dampness of sweat beneath his cap. Had it been from a carrier, it would have been swift, and soon to be joined by others.

He replied, 'It saw us all right. Might be a neutral.' He shook his head, dismissing his own assessment. 'My guess is that it's a float-plane of some kind.' He felt Gudegast sigh and added, 'I intend to assume it's from a warship, but not a carrier.'

Gudegast gave a chuckle. 'That's something, I suppose.'

Theissen appeared on the bridge companion ladder. 'I have been sent to enquire about –'

Hechler said bluntly, 'An aircraft, presumed hostile. If the Admiral wishes to know why I ordered the gun crews to stand down, please tell him that I would prefer that the enemy thinks we did *not* see him.' He watched the hoses throbbing across the lively wash of trapped water. 'I intend to complete oiling.'

As the man hurried away Gudegast asked quietly, 'What then, sir?'

Hechler was picturing the immediate chart in his mind. Soon the submarine would vanish. The ocean would be a desert again.

'Warn the first Arado to prepare for launching.' He waited for the big navigator to pass the order. 'My guess is that an enemy ship,' he hesitated, 'or *ships*, are close by. I'd say one hundred miles maximum. That plane will be going to its superior officer with the haste of hell. No radio, in case we pick him up – he'll be depending on surprise.'

Gudegast murmured, 'You saw all this in a few seconds, sir. I admire that very much. Gunnery patrol would have had every weapon with that range banging away in one more moment!'

Hechler smiled. 'You used to carry timber as you have often told me. I have always done this, since I was a boy. It is my life.'

'Arado ready, sir.'

Hechler said, 'See the pilot and give him a course. I want him to find the enemy and report back to me.'

Gudegast watched his profile. It would be a suicide mission. He was glad he did not have to make such decisions.

Hechler turned his attention to the other vessel. At best, the other ship would be in sight before sunset. If the enemy stood off to await reinforcements to ensure their kill, it might offer time enough to alter course, lose them in the darkness. With their far-reaching radar they had an edge on the enemy. But for it, he would never have known about that speck in the clouds, the slow-moving aircraft.

One thing was certain, no battleship or battle-cruiser had been reported in this area as yet. They were all to the north, employed with the convoys or protecting the supply lines as more and more of their troops flooded across the English Channel and into France. He bit his lip. Into Germany.

So it had to be a cruiser. He viewed his unknown adversary from every angle. If they could hold him off, or cripple him without sustaining more damage to the *Prinz*, they could still break through. Once their intentions were known, the British in particular would pull out all the stops. He remembered when the battleship *Bismarck*, the greatest warship ever built except for the trapped *Tirpitz*, had gone down with all guns firing. But it had taken the whole of the Home Fleet to find and destroy her. Revenge gave an edge to every commander, he thought. Their own sister-ship *Prinz Eugen* had slipped through the blockade then; so could they!

He heard men stand to attention and Froebe's whispered warning. Leitner moved through the bridge, his uniform soaked with rain. He stared at the submarine, his eyes listless. 'How much longer?'

'Ten minutes, sir.'

Some of the visiting one-stripers ducked as the Arado roared from the catapult and lifted above the bridge like a huge eagle on floats.

Hechler glanced quickly at the admiral. He had expected another outburst as to why the plane had been launched without his first being told.

Leitner merely grunted. 'Taking a look, eh?'

'It seems likely we'll have to increase to full speed, sir.' Hechler watched him in brief snatches while he never lost his hold over the ship. 'As soon as it's dark I shall –'

Leitner shrugged. 'The Führer will be watching us. We must not break that faith.'

He moved away and moments later, left the bridge.

Gudegast passed him on the ladder, but knew the admiral had not even seen him. He whispered to Froebe, 'What did you make of that?'

Froebe spread his big hands. 'He knows we shall fight, Josef. He feels sick about it, and so would I in his shoes.'

Gudegast eyed the captain's intent shoulders. Thank God he was in command, he thought fervently. There had to be a way out. They had done the impossible, sunk, burned and destroyed to the letter of their orders. What was there left?

He clenched and unclenched his fists. In a few moments now the submarine would slide beneath the waves and they would stand alone. He found himself hating it and all its kind. They, more than any other weapon, had brought horror and brutality to the sea. In a few months they had trodden down all the time-won lessons and the code of the brotherhood of sailors, which had once meant more than anything. It was never a perfect world, and some wars were inevitable. But that kind of cruelty would never be forgotten. He glanced up at their flag, like blood against the jagged clouds. Because of them, they were all branded the same.

'Ready to cast off, sir. Engine-room reports fuelling completed.'

Hechler straightened his back. 'Pass the word. Stand by, all lines. Warn the wheelhouse.'

He turned and glanced beyond the bridge, past the raked funnel and Leitner's command flag.

Come what may. He was ready.

'New course, zero-one-zero, sir.'

Hechler loosened his collar. The rain, thank God, was moving away.

'Full revolutions.' He stared astern, his hand to the peak of his cap as if at a salute. But there was no sign of the big supply-submarine. It was as if she had never been.

The clouds were much thinner too. Fine for the flak crews, not so good for their Arado, wherever it was.

He felt the ship trembling more urgently and pictured the engine-room dials misting over to the thrust of the three great screws. The wake was rolling away on either quarter, stiff and almost silver against the shark-coloured sea. If only –

He took a telephone from one of the boatswain's mates.

'Captain.'

It was a lieutenant with the damage-control party.

'The compartment is almost open, sir!' He sounded jubilant, as if nothing else mattered. 'Hammer is still all right.'

Hechler smiled grimly. 'Thank you. Stay with him.'

He shaded his eyes again to watch the sea which seemed to be rushing to meet them, as if he should feel some kind of impact before it parted and sliced away on either beam.

He said, 'Check Turret Bruno. I want a full report.'

As if to mock him, the left gun in that turret lifted like a tusk and then depressed again.

He heard someone say, 'There goes the admiral's crawler.' He did not have to look to know it was Bauer, the communications officer. No one seemed to like him, even less so since the incident on the island.

Hechler beckoned to Gudegast. 'Call communications and try to discover what has happened to our aircraft.' He saw Froebe watching him, gauging his own fate perhaps.

Hechler moved restlessly around the bridge. Horizon to horizon, shining and empty. It made him feel vulnerable, as if he was suddenly stripped naked.

'The admiral, sir.'

He took the handset. 'Sir?'

'I have had an important signal, Dieter.' He sounded emotional. 'Direct from our Führer. Germany is expecting great things from us—' He broke off with a curse as the intercom cut through.

'Aircraft, bearing Green four-five!' A pause, then, 'Disregard, friendly!'

Someone muttered hoarsely, 'About time too!'

Hechler held up his hand. '*Silence on the bridge!*' Apart from the wind through the halliards and superstructure it was suddenly still.

Gudegast whispered, 'Gunfire.'

Every glass was raised yet again, and even men on the gun sponsons crowded to the rails to stare at the empty sky.

Then they saw the long trail of smoke before they could identify the Arado. The smoke lifted and dipped behind the plane like a brown tail, and Hechler saw the drifting tracks of shellfire which told their own story. The pilot must have dared too much and had gone too close to the other ship, or had been trapped by her main armament.

275

'Stand by on deck to retrieve aircraft!'

Hechler tried not to lick his lips as he watched the Arado's desperate progress. Lower and lower, until he imagined he could see its blurred reflection on the sea's face.

He said, 'Tell damage-control what is happening. I want a side-party with scrambling nets immediately!'

It would mean reducing speed, stopping even, but he could not just leave these men to drown after what they had done.

Someone was using a hand-lamp. So they had been badly mauled, hit with flak enough to knock out their radio.

The senior signalman opened his mouth but Gudegast said, 'Signal reads, *enemy in sight to north-east.*' They were all watching him. '*One destroyer.*' He winced as the plane dived and almost hit the the water before rising again like a dying bird. '*Two, repeat two enemy cruisers!*'

Froebe said tersely, 'Damage-control, sir.'

Hechler dropped his binoculars to his chest as the Arado lifted towards the sky, staggered and then exploded in a livid, orange ball of fire.

'Tell them to dismiss the side-party.'

Jaeger offered him the telephone, his face ashen.

Hechler watched the smoke as it clung to the heaving water, and pictured the fragments drifting to the ocean's floor like ashes.

'Sir?'

He had to hold the telephone away from his ear as Leitner yelled, '*Two* cruisers and a *destroyer*! So much for your reckoning, damn you!'

Hechler said sharply, 'There are people here, sir. We just lost some brave men!'

'Don't you dare to interrupt me! The Führer entrusted me with a mission!' He slammed down the handset, and Hechler looked at Gudegast with a wry smile. 'Not pleased.'

Minutes later Theil appeared on the bridge and stared wild-eyed, as if he could barely speak.

Hechler faced him, his patience almost gone. 'This had better be urgent!'

Theil swallowed hard. 'Is it true, sir? I have just been ordered to load those boxes aboard the spare Arado!'

Hechler grappled with the words, his mind still lingering on that last hopeless message. Three ships, but one only a destroyer. There was still a chance.

He said, 'Tell *me!*'

Theil recovered with considerable effort. 'The admiral's aide told me personally. I had just reported that we have forced open the compartment. The boatswain and his men did it. I sent Hammer to the sick-bay. Then I got this order!'

It was all suddenly so clear and simple that Hechler was surprised he could accept it so calmly.

'Then do it, Viktor.' He lifted the telephone from its special rack, half-expecting there would be no reply.

Leitner said, 'Under these circumstances I have no choice. Neither have you. My instructions are to fly immediately to the mainland. The fight goes on.'

Hechler saw the others staring at him, officers, seamen, young and not so young. All seemed to have the same stunned expression. Disbelief. Astonishment. Shame.

'And my orders, sir?'

Leitner shouted, 'You will take immediate steps to prevent this ship from falling into enemy hands! Close the shore and *scuttle her!*'

Gudegast murmured, 'Dear Christ!'

Hechler put down the telephone and looked at Theil. 'Load the aircraft and prepare for launching.' His voice was toneless. 'Then report to me.'

Theil stared at him despairingly. 'Not you too? You of all people!'

Hechler regarded him gravely. 'We do not have much time left.'

As Theil turned in a daze he added softly, 'No, Viktor. *Not me!*'

He was not sure if Theil heard him. He was not certain of anything any more. He crossed to the bridge wing and watched the crane dipping over the catapult, the brightly painted Arado suddenly perched there, as if this moment was a part of destiny.

He heard her voice on the bridge ladder and said, 'No visitors!' But she knocked Jaeger's arm aside and ran towards him. '*I won't go!* Do you hear? I won't run away because of that coward!'

He caught her and held her, his eyes looking beyond her as he said, 'Slow ahead all engines.'

Then he said, 'I am ordering you to leave.' His voice was hoarse. He tried again. 'I should have guessed, Erika. A hero's return, or a hiding-place in Argentina. You will take him.' He pressed her against his body. 'I have to know that you at least are safe.'

She sobbed into his coat, her face hidden. '*No!* Don't force me!'

Hechler said, 'I need my remaining Arado. Please go now, my dearest Erika. *Please*, my men are looking to me.'

She stood back, her face very controlled despite the unheeded tears on her cheeks.

Then she said quietly, 'You'll not scuttle, Dieter? That's what you're saying?'

He did not reply directly. 'I shall never forget.'

Then he turned away. 'Escort her to the plane.'

He did not look again until she had left the bridge. He heard the Arado's engine roar into life, saw Theissen holding his cap in place, his face creased with dismay as he realised for the first time he was being left to fend for himself by the man he admired, perhaps even loved.

'*Radar—bridge!*' The merest pause. '*Enemy in sight!*'

Hechler barely heard the babble of instructions to the main armament. He strode to the wing and saw Theil by the catapult, then watched with surprise as Theissen was pushed up into the cockpit behind the girl.

'What the *hell*—!'

Froebe called, 'From damage-control, sir! The door to the admiral's bridge has jammed! A power failure!'

Hechler stared at the brightly painted plane, then very slowly lifted his cap high above his head.

With a coughing growl the Arado bounced from the catapult and lifted away from the ship, its wings glinting in the glare.

'Full ahead, all engines!' Hechler watched the Arado until it turned away and headed towards the western horizon.

278

Froebe said huskily, 'The admiral demands to speak with you, sir.'

Hechler recalled Theil's face. He alone must have cut the power from damage control to seal Leitner in his own bridge.

'Starboard twenty!' Hechler removed his oilskin and tossed it behind a flag locker.

'My respects to the admiral, but I have to fight a battle.'

When he looked again the tiny plane had vanished. And yet he could still feel her pressed against him, feel her anguish like his own when they had parted.

He said, 'We shall share our victory, but I'll never share his dishonour!'

Gudegast regarded him soberly. His one regret was that he had not yet begun the painting. Now he never would.

Hechler levelled his glasses with difficulty as the bridge shook to the vibration.

'Steady on zero-five-zero, sir.'

Hechler took the engine-room handset. 'Chief? Captain here. I need everything you can give me.'

'Can I ask?' Stück sounded faraway as if he was studying his dials.

'We are about to engage. Three ships. Do your best.' He hesitated, knowing that Stück wanted to go to his men. 'If I give the word –'

Stück's voice was near again. 'I know, sir. I'll get my boys on deck, double-quick.'

Hechler turned away and plucked at the grey fisherman's jersey. It was quite absurd but he wished he had changed into a clean shirt and his best uniform. The others nearby saw him grin and were reassured. But Hechler was thinking of the little admiral. What Nelson would have done.

The speaker intoned, 'Range fourteen thousand. Bearing steady.'

Two cruisers in line abreast to offer their maximum firepower. Hechler could see them as if they were right here. The destroyer was slightly ahead; they would sight her first.

He heard Kröll's clipped tone, caught in the intercom to give another small picture of their world high above the bridge.

'Anton, Caesar and Dora will concentrate on the cruisers. Warn flak control to expect enemy aircraft, spotters, anything.'

Hechler glanced around the open bridge. He might be forced to go up to the armoured conning-tower, but he would hold out as long as possible. He had been brought up on open bridges, where he could see everything. When their lives were in the balance it was even more important that his men should see him.

Kröll again. 'Large cruiser at Green one-oh.' A brief pause. 'She's opened fire.'

Hechler found that he could watch like any spectator as the enemy salvo exploded in the sea far off the starboard bow. A leaping wall of water which seemed so slow to fall. The wind was whipping it towards them, and he could imagine that he tasted cordite. Death.

'Second ship's fired.'

Someone laughed in the background, a nervous, unstable sound, and Kröll's deputy silenced the man with a sharp obscenity.

'Main armament ready, sir!'

Hechler watched the two forward guns swing across the side, at odds with the jammed barrels of Turret Bruno. Aft, the other turrets were already lining up on Kröll's directions and bearings. Hechler jabbed the button below the screen and seconds later the six big guns lurched back on their springs, the roar and earsplitting crashes punching at the bridge plating like giant battering rams.

More enemy salvoes fell and churned the sea into a maelstrom of leaping waterspouts and falling spray.

More seconds as the layers and trainers made their last adjustments.

'*Shoot!*'

The deck jumped beneath the bridge and a huge column of smoke burst over the side while patterns of falling debris were lost in seconds in their rising bow-wave.

The voice-pipes settled down into a staccato chorus, reporting, asking, pleading.

Hechler heard the taut replies from his bridge team. More like robots than men.

'Send stretcher bearers. Fire party to torpedo TS. Report damage and casualties.'

Froebe shouted, 'One hit, sir. Under control.' He ducked as another salvo screamed over the bridge and exploded far abeam.

'*Port fifteen!*' At this speed the ship seemed to tilt right over before Hechler's calm voice brought her on course again. The din continued without a break, giant waterspouts rising and fading astern as the *Prinz Luitpold* tore towards the enemy, her own guns firing more slowly than the enemy's. Hechler knew that Kröll was marking every fall of shot, making certain that his crews concentrated on their markers and did not allow them to fall into the trap of a pell-mell battle.

'Direct hit on left ship!' Someone cheered. 'Still firing!'

A great explosion thundered alongside so that for a few moments Hechler did not know if they had received a direct hit in return. As the smoke filtered downwind he felt rain on his face, and was grateful that the clouds had returned. If they could keep up a running fight until dusk ... He winced as two shells exploded inboard and a huge fragment of steel whirled over the bridge to plough down amongst some men at a Vierling gun. He stood back from the screen, tasting bile in his throat as he saw a seaman hacked neatly into halves before pitching down amongst the bloody remnants of his companions.

'*Another hit!*' The speaker sounded excited. 'Left ship is losing steerage way!'

Hechler wiped his face. 'Tell them to concentrate on the heavy cruiser to the right!' Kröll needed no telling, and as if to show its revived determination, Turret Bruno began to swivel round until it was trained on the same bearing as its twin.

'*Shoot!*'

All four guns recoiled together while the after-turrets followed immediately.

'*Short!*'

Hechler swung round and saw Leitner, hatless and staring, as he groped his way across the bridge. Theil must have returned the power and released him.

Leitner seemed unaware of the danger, and barely flinched as Kröll's trigger released another shattering salvo from all four turrets.

'You treacherous bastard! *You trapped me!*'

He peered around and coughed in the billowing smoke.

'I'll see you praying for death! It will be denied you!'

Hechler ducked as steel splinters shrieked and clattered around the bridge. *Another hit.* He tried to listen to the garbled reports, picture his men at their action stations in magazines and turrets; tending the boilers or just clinging to life.

He shouted, 'Don't lecture me! This is my ship! You are the traitor, Andreas Leitner!' He seized him violently, all caution and reserve gone in the din and thunder of gunfire. 'You were going to run like a bloody rabbit when you found you weren't your own propaganda hero after all!'

'*Captain!*' Jaeger was holding out a telephone, his face white as a thin scarlet thread ran down from his hairline.

Hechler snatched the phone. It was Gudegast.

'We should alter course now, sir.'

'Very well.' Hechler slammed it down. 'Hard a-port. Steer—' He ran to the compass repeater and wiped dust and chippings away with his sleeve. 'Steer *zero-one-zero.*' It would leave the badly damaged ship where she could not interfere and allow Kröll to concentrate on the enemy's heavy cruiser. '*Steady as you go!*' He saw a great column of water shoot up by the port quarter and felt the bridge jerk savagely as another shell slammed down near the quarterdeck. As if by magic, black, jagged holes appeared in the funnel, while severed rigging and radio wires trailed above the bridge like creepers.

'Request permission to flood Section Seven, sir?'

Hechler could imagine Theil down there with his team, watching the control panel, the blinking pattern of lights as one section after another was hit or needed help.

The main armament was trained almost directly abeam, their target hidden in smoke and distance.

Hechler dragged himself to a safety rail and squinted to clear his vision.

Small, sharp thoughts jerked through him. She would be on

her way to safety. Five hundred miles was nothing to her. He wanted to shout her name. So that she would hear him. Like a last cry.

The hull shivered and flames seared out of the deck below the secondary armament. Men ran from their stations, some with extinguishers, others in panic, and one screaming with his body on fire.

'A straddle!' The voice almost broke. '*Two hits!*'

Hechler clambered above the rail and waited for the smoke to funnel past him. He had to hold his breath to stop himself from choking, but he must see, must know.

Then he caught a misty picture in the powerful binoculars, like a badly distorted film.

The big enemy cruiser, so high out of the water, was ablaze from stem to bridge, and both her forward turrets were knocked out, the guns either smashed or pointing impotently at the clouds.

A voice yelled, 'The pumps are holding the intake aft, sir!'

'Casualties removed and taken below!' He pictured Stroheim with bloodied fingers, his gold-rimmed glasses misting over in that crowded, pain-racked place. In his wildness he pictured the scene with music playing, Handel, from Stroheim's dusty stack of records.

A shell ploughed below the bridge and more splinters smashed through the thinner plating by the gate. Two signalmen were cut down without a sound, and Froebe clung to the gyro compass, his eyes bulging in agony as he gasped for air. There was a wound like a red star punched in his chest. Hechler reached for him, but he was dead before he hit the gratings.

Hechler yelled, 'Take his place, Jaeger!' He shook the youth's arm. 'Move yourself! We'll beat the Tommies yet!'

He saw the incredulous stare on Jaeger's face, and guessed that he must look more like a maniac than the stable captain. But it worked, and he heard Jaeger's voice as he passed another helm order, quite calm, like a complete stranger's.

Kröll's intercom croaked through the explosions. 'Both cruisers have lost way, sir. Shall I engage the destroyer? She now bears Red four-five!'

Hechler wiped his streaming face. Exertion or rain he neither knew nor cared. The destroyer would stand by her consorts; she was no longer any danger. By nightfall . . . he swung round as men ducked again and the air was torn apart by the banshee scream of falling shells.

For a split second Hechler imagined that another cruiser had got within range undetected. He knew that was impossible. Then the salvo fell across the ship in a tight straddle, the shells exploding between decks, while others brought down rangefinders and the mainmast in a web of steel and flailing stays.

Hechler expected to feel pain as he struggled to the opposite side. Even as he levelled his glasses again he knew the answer. The flaw in the picture, which even Kröll's instruments had overlooked.

The destroyer had zigzagged through a smoke-screen, although there was already smoke enough from gunfire and burning ships, and had fired a full broadside into the *Prinz*. Hechler coughed painfully. Except that she was no destroyer. She was a light cruiser, which nonetheless had the fire-power to do real damage if only she could get close enough. Her two heavier consorts had seen to that.

Another scream of falling shells and this time the full salvo struck them from funnel to quarterdeck.

Hechler gripped the rail, could feel the power going from his engines as Stück fought to hold the revolutions steady.

Gudegast had appeared on the bridge and was shouting, 'Engine-room wants to reduce speed, sir!'

'*Half ahead!*' Hechler watched the two forward turrets swing round, hesitate and then fire, the shockwave ripping overhead like an express train.

There was no response from the after-turrets. The last enemy salvo had crippled them.

'*One hit!*'

The light cruiser was zigzagging back into her own smoke-screen, one yellow tongue licking around her bridge like an evil spirit. 'Tell the gunnery officer –' Hechler wiped his eyes and stared up at the control position. It was crushed, like a beer can, riddled with holes despite the thick armour.

'Transfer fire control –' He watched, sickened, as dark stains ran down Kröll's armoured cupola, as if the whole control position was bleeding. Which indeed it was.

Throughout the ship, men groped in darkness as lights were extinguished or passageways filled with choking smoke. Others clung together behind watertight doors which would now remain closed for ever.

In his sick-bay Stroheim put down a telephone and shouted, 'Start getting these men on deck!' The smoke had even penetrated down here, and spurted through doors and frames like a terrible threat.

Deeper in the hull Stück clung to his catwalk and watched his men stooping and running through the oily steam, like figures in hell. The three massive shafts were still spinning but he would have to slow them still further. Was it to be now? Like this, he wondered? He felt the hull lurch as more shells exploded close by. His instinct told him they came from a different bearing, and he guessed that one of the damaged cruisers was rejoining the battle.

The two forward turrets were still firing, but more slowly under the local control of their quarters' officer.

There were fires everywhere, and not enough men to carry away the wounded, let alone the dead.

One man lay where he had fallen from a ladder, after Kröll had sent him to Turret Dora to discover the extent of the damage. Acting Petty Officer Hans Stoecker sprawled on his back, his face tightly pinched as if to protect himself from the unbroken roar of gunfire and internal explosions. Even the deck plating felt hot, and he wanted to call out for someone to help him. Each time he tried, the agony seared through him like a furnace bar, but when he attempted to move his legs he could feel nothing.

A bent-over figure slithered down beside him. It was the grey-headed petty officer, Tripz.

He made to cradle his arm under the young man's shoulder, but as a freak gust of wind drove the smoke aside he bent lower still. There was little left of Stoecker below the waist, and he tried to protect him from its horror.

285

He gasped, 'We did it, Hans! All that gold and jewellery! *We did it!* We'll all be rich!'

Stoecker sobbed as a single shell exploded against the bridge superstructure and sheets of steel drifted overhead like dry leaves. 'I – I – did – not – mean – to –' He clutched the other man in a pitiful embrace. His eyes blurred with agony, so that he did not see the cruel splinter which had just killed his comforter.

Stoecker lay back, the pain suddenly leaving him as he pictured his mother, and the girl called – he tried to speak her name but the effort was too much, so he died.

There were more corpses than living men on the forebridge and Hechler stared down at himself as if expecting to see blood. He was untouched, perhaps so that he should suffer the most.

Gudegast arose, shaking himself from a collapsed bank of voice-pipes, dust and paint flakes clinging to his beard as he stared around like a trapped bear.

Hechler heard Theil on the handset. 'Come up, Viktor. Tell your assistant to take over.'

He turned and saw Leitner standing in the centre of the bridge.

He screamed, '*Where is Theissen?*'

'He went in the plane with your boxes!'

Hechler wondered how he could find words even to speak with him.

Leitner held out a canvas pouch and shook it wildly.

'These are mine! All that's left! Someone broke into my boxes, damn you!' He flung the pouch down in a pool of blood which was quivering to the engines' beat as if it was trying to stay alive. '*See?*'

Hechler watched as jewelled rings and pieces of gold scattered amongst the blood and buckled plating. So that was it.

He heard himself answer, 'So it was all wasted?'

'Not quite, you *bastard!*' The Luger seemed to appear in his fist like magic and Hechler knew he could not move aside in time.

All around him men were dying, or waiting to be struck down. Because of men like Leitner. He felt suddenly sickened and cheated. No wonder Leitner could never understand his ideals, his love for a ship, her loyalty.

A voice shattered the sudden stillness. '*Torpedoes to port!*'

The explosions were merged into one gigantic eruption, so that it seemed to go on and on forever.

Hechler was vaguely aware of objects crashing past him, the sounds of heavy equipment tearing adrift and thundering through the hull between decks.

His mind was cringing but all his skill and training tried to hold on, just long enough.

The light cruiser must have darted in to launch her torpedoes while her battered consorts had kept up a ragged covering fire.

He knew without hearing a single report that it was a mortal blow. Corpses were moving again, returning to life perhaps as the deck tilted over.

Gudegast hopped and limped towards him, his eyes blazing as he exclaimed, 'Thought you were done for!'

Hechler hung on to his massive shoulder. How long had he been unconscious? He could recall nothing beyond the great gout of fire as the torpedoes had exploded alongside.

The admiral lay on his side, his tongue protruding in a crude grimace. One hand still held the Luger; the other was like a claw as it reached out for the scattered fragments of his fortune.

Gudegast aided the captain to the bridge chair. 'He's dead, sir.'

He watched the anguish on Hechler's profile. There was no point in adding to his pain by telling him that he had seen a bullet hole in the middle of Leitner's back. Someone must have gunned him down deliberately as he had aimed at the captain, when the torpedoes had abruptly ended all their hopes.

'The enemy's ceased fire, sir.' That was Jaeger, a bloody hand-kerchief pressed to his forehead.

Hechler heard the distant shouts of men on the deck below and Gudegast said, 'When I thought you were –'

Hechler held his arm. 'You ordered them to clear the lower deck?' He nodded painfully. 'Thank you, Josef. *So much.*'

Would I have done that, he wondered? Might more of my men have been made to die?

Now he would never know.

The deck gave a terrible lurch and the chart-table shattered into fragments.

Gudegast said, 'I'll pass the word, sir.'

Hechler shook his head. 'No. Let me. I must do it.'

He clung to the screen and saw the nearest enemy cruiser for the first time. Her fires were out, and her turrets were trained on the *Prinz* as she began to heel over very, very slowly.

Hechler raised his hand to the men nearest him. 'Abandon ship!' The words to wish them well choked in his emotion and he heard Gudegast mutter, 'Come on, sir. We'll still need you.'

Hechler tried to stand, but when he gripped the rail he found that he was staring not at the enemy but straight down at the littered water. Floats, broken boats, corpses, and swimmers, some of whom trod water to watch as the heavy cruiser began to roll over.

Hechler knew he had hit the sea, and that his lungs were on fire when hands seized him and dragged him into a crowded float. Someone cried, 'Here's the Captain!'

Hechler hooked his arm round Gudegast's shoulder and heard him murmur, 'Come *on*, old girl, get it over with, eh?'

It was like a great bellow of pain, an indescribable roar, as with sudden urgency the *Prinz Luitpold* lifted her motionless screws from the sea and dived.

Hechler struggled upright on the float and watched the maelstrom of flotsam, the tell-tale spread of oil.

They were still a long way from home.

But those who survived would speak for many years of the *Prinz*.

He stared up at the first, pale stars.

The Iron Pirate. The legend.

Epilogue

The train was moving very slowly as if weighed down by the packed humanity which crammed every seat and compartment. Hechler was glad he had been able to find a place by a window, although it was so gloomy beyond the misty glass he could see very little.

It was hard to believe that the journey was nearly over, that the long train was already clanking through the outskirts of Hamburg.

Prinz Luitpold had begun her life in this port. It all seemed so long ago. He glanced at his companions, mostly in army field-grey, like the rest of the train, creased, worn-out, huddled together for warmth and comfort.

It was about noon, but it could have been evening, he thought. Winter already had its grip on the countryside. He stirred uneasily as his mind explored the past like a raw wound. A year since that day in the South Atlantic when the *Prinz* had lifted her stern and had dived. So many familiar faces had gone down with her; too many.

The survivors had been gathered into the British ships, and Hechler had found himself aboard the light cruiser *Pallas*, the one which had fired the fatal salvo of torpedoes.

It was strange, but he had sensed no elation amongst the victors. It had been relief as much as anything. He had learned snatches of the final action, of the British commodore being killed by the *Prinz*'s first straddle, and the New Zealander's initiative in pressing home the attack despite an overwhelming adversary.

Hechler had been separated from his men, then from most of his officers. Some he knew had died in the cruiser's final moments. Kröll directing his guns, the taciturn Stück, dying as he had lived with his engines roaring around him when the torpedoes had burst in on him and his men.

Hechler had managed to stay with Gudegast, even after they were transferred to a fast troopship with an armed escort, to be landed eventually in the port of Liverpool.

He had seen young Jaeger for a while, but once in England Jaeger had been sent to an officers' prison camp somewhere in the south.

Gudegast had told him of Theil's last appearance, all that anyone had seen of him. As the ship had taken on her final list, with men pouring up from the smoke and fires between decks, several of the survivors had seen Theil returning below, as if going to his quarters. Hechler had asked if he had seemed to be in a great hurry? Perhaps he was trying to retrieve some small item of value from his cabin before he abandoned ship with all the others.

Gudegast had shaken his head. 'They said he was just walking. As if he had all the time in the world.'

A way out. Remain with the ship he loved, which was finally being taken from him. Now they would never know the truth.

Hechler thought of the months as a prisoner-of-war. He gave a faint, wry smile. *In the bag*, as his British captors termed it.

The camp had been in Scotland, a bleak, lonely place, shared mostly with embittered U-boat commanders.

Hechler had been interrogated several times, on arrival, and later by officers in civilian clothes who were described as being from Naval Intelligence.

They questioned him mostly about the incident at St Jorge, and whether he considered that as captain he was solely responsible for the shooting of the civilian mechanic. Bauer was probably the only one who knew the whole truth of that, but he had been blasted to fragments with the rest of his staff early in the engagement.

After that, nobody took much interest in him. Gudegast was

good company, and when they were not walking around the wire fences and looking at the varying colours of the heather, Gudegast would be busy with his paints and sketches. He obtained all the materials he needed by offering to do portraits of the guards. It was an amicable arrangement.

Then one day Gudegast was ordered to leave for another camp in the south.

It had been a sad if unemotional farewell. They had survived too much for anything more.

He had asked Gudegast what he would try to do after the war.

The big man had plucked at his beard. 'Back to the sea. It's all I know.'

Before he left he had handed Hechler a small roll of canvas.

'For her,' he had said awkwardly. 'You'll meet her again, don't you fret.'

Then he had marched away with some others, and Hechler had saluted without knowing why.

After that it had been a matter of waiting and enduring. Christmas, with local children gathering outside the wire to sing carols. One of the U-boat officers had killed himself shortly afterwards. Hechler had withdrawn even further from his companions. They seemed alien; their war was not one he had shared, and he wished that Gudegast was still with him.

He often thought of the others, men like Brezinka who had survived, and the doctor Stroheim who had last been seen tying his own life-jacket to a badly wounded seaman. The quiet hero.

Then the time when the guards had fired their weapons in the air, and all the lights had been switched on.

Hechler had accepted the end of Europe's war with mixed feelings. The time seemed to drag, and yet he almost dreaded his release. He had written to Erika Franke several times at the two addresses she had left for him, but had received no reply.

His head lolled to the monotonous clank-clank-clank of the wheels and he stared through the window at some great white lumps of land. He saw the khaki uniforms of British NCO's who were directing some tractors and a great army of German

291

workers. He realised with a chill that the humps were all that was left of buildings, whole streets, now mercifully covered with the first snow of this bitter winter.

Someone said, 'Nearly there! Home sweet home!' Nobody else spoke. One man, an infantry captain, was dabbing his eyes with a soiled handkerchief, another was trying to pull his threadbare coat into position. Home? There was not much of it left.

Hechler thrust his fingers into his pocket as if to reassure himself that his pipe was still there. In his other hand he held the parcel which contained Gudegast's gift. It was a small portrait of himself, not aboard ship, but with some Scottish heather as a background. So typical of Gudegast, he thought.

He felt his stomach contract as he realised that the train was suddenly running into the station. Again there seemed to be wreckage everywhere, the platform roof blasted open like bare ribs against the dull sky.

He sensed a new tension all around him. Most of the soldiers had only just been released; many had come from the Russian Front, gaunt, despairing figures who rarely even spoke to each other. The train stopped with a final jerk and slowly at first then with something like panic, the passengers spilled out on to the platform.

Here and there were signs of occupation. Station direction boards in English with regimental crests on them. The bright red caps of the military police, khaki and air force blue, voices and accents Hechler had taught himself to know while he had been *in the bag*.

He stared at the barrier beyond the mass of returning German troops. Police, service and military, a British provost marshal smoking a pipe and chatting with a friend. Further still, an unbroken wall of faces.

He came to a halt, his heart pounding. Was this freedom. Where was his courage now?

A solitary German sailor, the two ribbons whipping out from his cap in the chill breeze, dropped a package and Hechler picked it up.

'Here!'

The sailor spun round and snapped to attention.

Hechler handed him the parcel, and they both stared at one another like strangers. Then the man gave a slow grin, and reached out to shake his hand.

The saluting, like the war, was finally over for both of them.

The girl, Erika Franke, stood by one of the massive girders which supported the remains of the station roof and watched the train sigh to a halt.

It was the third one she had met this day, and her hands and feet were icy cold. Or was it the awful uncertainty? Not knowing? As each train had trundled into the station to offload its cargo of desperate, anxious servicemen she had seen the reactions of the crowd, mostly women, who waited there with her. Like her. She looked at the noticeboards which had once recorded the most punctual trains in the Reich. Now they were covered from top to bottom with photographs, some large, others no bigger than passport pictures. Addresses and names scrawled under each one. It was like a graveyard.

Now as the first hurrying figures approached the platform gates and the line of military policemen, she saw many of the same women surge forward, their pitiful pictures held out to each man in uniform.

'My son, have you seen him?' To another. 'He was in your regiment! You *must* have known my man!'

She wiped her eyes, afraid she might miss something.

A young British naval lieutenant with wavy stripes on his sleeve asked, 'You all right, Fräulein? I've got a car outside if—'

She shook her head and replied politely, 'No, thank you.'

A woman in a shabby coat with two photographs held up in front of her pushed past a red-capped policeman and asked that same question. The soldier brushed her away; he did not even look at her. He seemed embarrassed, afraid that he might recognise someone he had left in the mud with a million others.

The girl watched the other wave of figures coming through the gates. Not many sailors, this time. She would come back

293

tomorrow.

She remembered his letters, bundled together, when she had finally returned home. It was all like a dream now, and the last flight to Argentina, an impossibility.

She recalled the moment when she had climbed down from the Arado and into a waiting launch. She had felt nothing but a sense of loss. Even when German consulate officials had opened the boxes to find them full of broken fragments of coloured glass, she had thought only of Hechler, with every minute taking him further away, perhaps to his death.

Leitner's aide had had hysterics when he had seen the broken glass. She had heard him shout the name of a petty officer called Hammer. Whoever he was, he must be a very rich man if he was still alive.

The woman with the two photographs pressed forward. 'Please, sir! Tell me, *please*! Have you seen my boys?'

The man stopped and took the photographs.

The girl felt her heart stop beating. It was Hechler. For a long moment she stared at him without moving, taking in every precious detail. The lines were deeper on either side of his mouth, and there were touches of grey beneath his cap. He was wearing that same old fisherman's jersey under his jacket. He seemed oblivious to the cold.

Hechler said quietly, 'I am sorry, my dear, I have not seen them. But don't lose hope –' He looked up and saw her and the next instant she was wrapped in his arms. He did not even see the woman staring after him, as if he had just performed a miracle.

How long they clung together, neither of them knew.

She whispered, 'It had to be the right train!' She ran her hand over him as if to reassure herself he was real. She saw the loose threads on his right breast where the Nazi eagle had once been, and looked up to see a new brightness in his blue eyes.

He said, 'I knew I'd find you, my little bird. Somehow –'

Some British sailors were waving and cheering as some of their companions boarded another train.

Hechler put his arm around her shoulders and they walked out into the drifting snow.

Once he glanced back at the station and the jubilant British sailors.

Then he squeezed her shoulders and said softly, 'Like us, they're going home.'

THE BEST IN WAR BOOKS

__DEVIL BOATS: THE PT WAR AGAINST JAPAN
William Breuer 0-515-09367-X/$3.95
A dramatic true-life account of the daring PT
sailors who crewed the Devil Boats—outwitting
the Japanese.

__PORK CHOP HILL S.L.A. Marshall
0-515-08732-7/$3.95
A hard-hitting look at the Korean War and the
handful of U.S. riflemen who fought back the
Red Chinese troops.
"A distinguished contribution to the literature
of war."—New York Times

__THREE-WAR MARINE Colonel Francis Fox Parry
0-515-09872-8/$3.95
A rare and dramatic look at three decades
of war—World War II, the Korean War, and
Vietnam. Francis Fox Parry shares the
heroism, fears, and harrowing challenges of
his thirty action-packed years in an
astounding military career.

To My Family

ACKNOWLEDGEMENTS

I wish to thank the publishers of *Commonweal* and *Interpretation: A Journal of Political Philosophy* for allowing me to use passages from my previously published articles on Toynbee. I am also grateful to Houghton Mifflin Company for granting me permission to incorporate some material from chapters I wrote for *Western Civilization: A Concise History*.

TABLE OF CONTENTS

Foreward by Theodore H. Von Laue   ix

Preface   xiii

Chapter 1   Historian in an Age of Crisis   1

Chapter 2   Historian with a Mission   11

Chapter 3   Hellenism and Christianity   35

Chapter 4   Transition to the Modern West   49

Chapter 5   Problems of the Modern West:
Ideologies and Technology   57

Chapter 6   Prospects of the West   83

Chapter 7   The World-State   95

Chapter 8   Assessment   111

Bibliography   129

Index   135

FOREWORD

Arnold Toynbee's life (1889-1975) coincided with the most breath-taking knowledge explosion in human existence. The boundaries of human awareness expanded precipitously in all directions -- into every nook and cranny of inanimate and animate matter, into the structure of the atom and the living cell, into the origins of the universe and human life as well as into the recesses of the human psyche, into ever more sophisticated skills of saving life and destroying it, into the complexities of intense global interdependence. Yet only he among historians let his imagination be fired by that spectacular outburst. Only he can be called a historian truly representative of his time, truly in scale with its enormity. Even the best practitioners of the historical profession (which in these years produced many outstanding scholars) looked the other way, picking partial or even minute aspects of a past that bore little relation to the unprecedented events into which their lives were set. When they talked of historical studies devoted to phenomena of "long duration," they crawled perhaps a yard while Toynbee traversed seven leagues. Only he ventured an all-inclusive perspective covering human existence from the beginnings of recognized civilization down to the formation, during his own lifetime, of an irreversibly interdependent global civilization including all religions, all nations, all surviving previous civilizations despite their diversity or even incompatibility.

One may argue endlessly with Toynbee about detail -- historians have done so with their ant-like, fact-centered intensity. But one cannot deny the exceptional and monumental scope of his work. While his critics still labored on the ground-floor, he matched the astronauts' feat of viewing the earth from the moon, pressing the all-inclusive question: what of the fate of our own civilization? He did so largely on his own and with heroic industry, combining scholarship with analysis and synthesis, writing, as it were, with both hands simultaneously. All the while he kept his vision clear and keen.

Commentators on Toynbee's work have noted its poetic quality. The analogy with poetry is well chosen. The immensity of his subject required an immensely open and concentrated perception nurtured by an inward wholeness that, like poetic inspiration, knows no distinction between intellect, moral sensibility, and spiritual-aesthetic awareness. Concerned with the fate of civilizations -- specifically his own as it spread over the entire world -- he thought holistically and judgmentally like an Old Testament prophet, painfully conscious of the fragility of civilized life and of the unceasing self-denying spiritual effort necessary to maintain it. In the face of a mind-destroying profusion of data he stuck to the central issues, fully alert to the need for original abstraction and radical synthesis; he appreciated myth and symbol, and above all religion, as conceptually simplifying, civilizing, and community-building essences. In this respect too he was a far greater human being than all his critics who looked at the world through the narrow portholes of a "scientific method" corrupted by the prevailing spiritual shallowness.

Such praise need not deny that Toynbee too had his limitations. In pursuing his grand inquiry he moved into an intellectual *terra incognita* without guidelines or supporting consensus. He worked there with the resources of his cultural tradition and of his times, both of them less universal than he considered them to be yet, everything considered, also comparatively advanced for stretching out historical perspectives to the global scale. Future historians, no doubt, will restructure that inescapable globalism into a meaningful whole with the help of different abstractions and symbols. Yet they cannot do so without the far-sighted capaciousness of mind and perspective that Toynbee developed.

These brief reflections are merely one reader's response to Professor Perry's manuscript. As a guide to the "essential Toynbee" this book will inspire many other responses. It traces the origins

of Toynbee's thought in the aftermath of the first
World War and follows the unfolding of his convictions down to the final Olympian pronouncements on
the condition of contemporary world civilization.
Toynbee's views as they are here presented are perhaps more apt now than they were during his last
years. They certainly need to be read by all open-
minded young historians trying to make sense of
their world -- the whole world -- for themselves as
well as their students and readers. The book will
also assist general readers not only in assessing
one of the great minds of the twentieth century but
also in clarifying their own attitude toward the
world in which they are caught. What could be more
liberating than to rise to the commanding heights
of Toynbee's mind?

                              Theodore H. Von Laue

PREFACE

Arnold J. Toynbee's *A Study of History* was a deeply felt response to the world wars and totalitarianism that nearly wrecked Western Civilization in the first half of the twentieth century. It was a protest against the materialism and spiritual uneasiness that have pervaded our century; it was a cry of pain by a humane and sensitive thinker who saw the collapse of his Victorian optimism and struggled to comprehend why.

Toynbee made a comparative study of all the world's civilizations, living and dead, analyzing their rise, growth, breakdown, and disintegration. At the core of Toynbee's thought were the convictions that secularism has been a miserable failure, that reason, not guided by spiritual values, is an insufficient integrating principle to sustain civilization, and that tribal-mindedness, which manifests itself in warfare between states, is the principal reason for the breakdown of civilizations. Toynbee considered higher religions to be mankind's greatest achievement and religious prophets humanity's noblest figures. To deal with the ills afflicting the modern world, Toynbee advocated a renewed commitment to the spiritual values of higher religions and the creation of a world-state.

This work is neither a biography of Toynbee nor an analysis of his treatment of the world's civilizations. It is concerned principally with Toynbee's understanding of the nature, meaning, and destiny of Western Civilization.

I am grateful to George Bock for his valuable suggestions.

M.P.

HISTORIAN IN AN AGE OF CRISIS

World War I had a profound impact on the Western mind. Like other intellectuals, Arnold Toynbee, then a promising academic, was disillusioned and demoralized by the war. It left him with the gnawing feeling that Western Civilization had lost its vitality and was caught in the rhythm of breakdown and disintegration. It seemed that Western Civilization too was fragile and perishable, that Western man, despite his extraordinary accomplishments, was never more than a step or two away from barbarism. The orderly, peaceful, and rational world that he had known before the Great War had been shattered. How could one speak of the inviolability of the individual when Europe had become a vast graveyard? Or of the primacy of reason when the nations permitted the slaughter to endure for four years? Or of continuous progress and human perfectibility when civilized men had employed their organizational and technical talents to slaughter millions?

Overwhelmed by the senseless slaughter, Toynbee came to believe that the West was suffering from a profound spiritual crisis. He now felt that Gibbon was wrong in holding that the West could not suffer the same fate as Rome.

> I had continued to concur in Gibbon's judgment till, in the first days of August, 1914, the disaster, unforeseen by me, into which my own world was now rushing, suddenly opened my eyes to the truth. The illumination had caught me in a flash; my illusion that I was the privileged citizen of a stable world had been shattered by a thunderbolt. Since that moment I have seen the world with different eyes and have found that it is not the kind of world that, until then, I had naively imagined it to be.[1]

The shock of the Great War instilled in

Toynbee a profound need to comprehend and confront
the crisis that had afflicted the modern West.
Never had Thucydides seemed more alive and appropriate to him. The ancient Greeks had destroyed
themselves by an overzealous attachment to the
city-state; the modern West's devotion to the national state was producing a comparable tragedy.
The system of national states,which many people had
regarded as the source of Europe's greatness,became
for Toynbee the vehicle of the West's decline. The
war also gave Toynbee a sense of mission. Disqual-
ified for military service because of dysentary,
Toynbee would always regard himself as a fortunate
survivor of a conflict that took the lives of half
his classmates. Their deaths would always grieve
him; as a survivor he would always feel that his
declining years were a gift that must be used in
the service of humanity. "The longer I live, the
greater grows my grief and indignation at the wick-
ed cutting short of all those lives. ... The writing of [A Study of History] has been one of my responses to the challenge that has been presented
to me by the senseless criminality of human affairs."[2]

   Toynbee's thought was a deeply felt response
to the spiritual crisis that afflicted Western Civilization in the twentieth century. Many Europeans
believed that Western Civilization had lost its
vitality and had entered its decline; some, adhering to Spengler's determinism, insisted that the
decline was irreversible and the fall imminent. To
this day it is impossible to escape from the trem-
ors of anxiety that have swept across the West in
the twentieth century. In contrast to nineteenth-
century liberals who spoke glowingly of the future,
twentieth-century intellectuals have been preoccupied with the phenomenon of decay and dissolution.
The crisis is total, as Hans Kohn points out, for
it embraces the West's "intellectual foundations,
its spiritual outlook, its social order, its political forms, and its economic structure. ... This
crisis endangers the survival of that civilization
which seemed so secure in the nineteenth century."[3]

   What is the nature of this crisis that caused

many intellectuals, including Toynbee, to lose their Victorian optimism and to contemplate the demise of the West? The crisis may be defined as the Western mind's loss of confidence, and, in some instances, conscious repudiation of the Enlightenment tradition of reason and freedom. The Enlightenment was the intellectual culmination of the trend toward secularism, rationalism, and individualism that had emerged with the breakup of the medieval world-view. In a broad view of Western history, the Enlightenment also represented a harmonizing of a Greek legacy -- a method of perceiving truth, that is, reason -- a Stoic and Roman legacy -- the idea of natural law applicable to all men -- and a Judaeo-Christian legacy -- the belief in human dignity and brotherhood. In 1789 it appeared to both revolutionaries and foreign observers that a new era was dawning that promised to realize the ideals of the Enlightenment: the emancipation of the human personality from superstition and irrational traditions, the triumph of liberty over tyranny, the refashioning of institutions in accordance with reason and justice, the tearing down of barriers to equality. Freedom was man's birthright which would be reclaimed once tyranny and superstition were eliminated; the natural rights of man, hitherto a distant ideal, would now reign on earth, terminating centuries of oppression and misery. Never before had man displayed such confidence in the power of human intelligence to shape the conditions of his existence; never before had the future seemed so replete with hope. In the midst of the French Revolution, Condorcet expressed the hopes of a generation nurtured by the thought of the philosophes:

> The time will therefore come when the
> sun will shine only on free men who
> know no other master but their reason;
> when tyrants and slaves, priests and
> their stupid or hypocritical instru-
> ments will exist only in works of his-
> tory and on the stage; and when we
> shall think of them only to pity their
> victims and their dupes; to maintain
> ourselves in a state of vigilance by
> thinking on their excesses; and to

3

learn how to recognize and so to destroy,
by force of reason, the first seeds of
tyranny and superstition, should they
ever dare to reappear amongst us.[4]

Reason embodied in law, reality planned, shaped,
and governed by the human intellect -- this exalted
conception of human capacities, observed Hegel,
thrilled the world with a spiritual enthusiasm.

After the Great War, Paul Valéry summed up the
mood of a generation for whom Condorcet's vision
had lost its power to inspire.

The storm has died away, and still we
are restless, uneasy, as if the storm
were about to break. Almost all the
affairs of men remain in a terrible uncertainty. We think of what has disappeared, we are almost destroyed by
what has been destroyed; we do not know
what will be born, and we fear the
future, not without reason. We hope
vaguely, we dread precisely; our fears
are infinitely more precise than our
hopes; we confess that the charm of
life is behind us ... but doubt and
disorder are in us and with us. There
is no thinking man ... who can hope to
dominate this anxiety, to escape from
this impression of darkness, to measure the probable duration of this
period when the vital relations of
humanity are disturbed profoundly.
... all the fundamentals of our
world have been affected by the war.
... *But among all these injured
things is the Mind.* The Mind has indeed been cruelly wounded; its complaint is heard in the hearts of intellectual men; it passes a mournful
judgment on itself. It doubts itself
profoundly.[5]

Between Condorcet's paean to progress and our
century's testimony of pain, the consciousness of

Europe had been altered. The self-assured confidence in the future gave way to doubt and despair; the unswerving faith in reason was shattered. All of us, like Arthur Koestler, have been "born at the moment when the sun was setting on the Age of Reason."[6] Whereas the philosophes possessed beliefs whose certainty seemed self-evident, the twentieth century is devoid of a unity of outlook; it knows only incoherence, doubt, and confusion. The normative principles, which for the philosophes constituted a standard for political and social reform and a guarantee of human rights, are no longer linked to the natural order. "We certainly no longer believe," says Hannah Arendt, "as the great men of the French Revolution did, in a universal cosmos of which man was a part and whose natural laws he had to imitate and conform to."[7] Dispensing with the belief that there is a natural or rational order from which universal principles can be derived, we no longer hold as self-evident the natural rights of man.

Man's conception of himself has also become problematic. We can no longer define man exclusively in terms of his ability to reason as did Descartes in his famous dictum: "I think therefore I am." Our art, literature, psychology, political behavior all reveal a mysterious underworld of turbulent emotions. The intellect does not seem autonomous, self-regulating, a sovereign master; more often than not it is subject to the rebellious demands of unconscious drives and impulses. Now we cannot escape from the feeling that man's propensity for goodness, his capacity to improve society, his potential for happiness are severely limited by an inherent irrationality, that civilization itself is threatened by our instinctual needs as Freud noted:

> The element of truth behind all this,
> which people are so ready to disavow,
> is that men are not gentle creatures
> who want to be loved and who at the
> most can defend themselves if they are
> attacked; they are, on the contrary,
> creatures among whose instinctual

endowments is to be reckoned a powerful share of aggressiveness. As a result, their neighbor is for them not only a potential helper or sexual object, but, also someone who tempts them to satisfy their aggressiveness on him, to exploit his capacity for work without compensation, to use him sexually without his consent, to seize his possessions, to humiliate him, to cause him pain, to torture and to kill him. *Homo homini lupus.* ... In consequence of this primary mutual hostility of human beings, civilized society is perpetually threatened with disintegration.[8]

And yet to deny the instinctual, to thwart the non-rational side of our nature, may lead, as Freud tells us, to psychic distress, or to a stifling of our creative capacities, as Nietzsche proclaimed, or even to a blunting of our moral sentiments, as Rousseau warned. We cannot have society without reason and yet man cannot live by reason alone. Can man provide for intuition and feelings without undermining the rationality upon which modern civilization rests? Emphasizing the autonomy and uniformity of human beings and the sovereignty of reason, the philosophes were largely untroubled by this awesome problem.

This irrational side of human nature, to which the philosophes had paid scant attention, throws into confusion the blueprints of philosophers and social planners. As thinkers doubted, attacked, and renounced the basic assumptions of the Enlightenment, the West entered into an age of intellectual fragmentation and doubt.

Along with the diminishing confidence in reason, the twentieth century has seen a loss of faith in man's capacity to preserve freedom. Even more distressing, we wonder whether the average person desires freedom or knows what to do with it. The enfranchised masses have not been staunch defenders of political liberty. It seems that without much reluctance man will trade freedom for security or national grandeur. In 1939 John Dewey reflected on this dilemma.

> Does freedom in itself and in the things
> it brings with it seem as important as
> security of livelihood; as food, shelter,
> clothing, or even having a good time? ...
> How do the fruits of liberty compare with
> the enjoyments that spring from a feeling
> of union, of solidarity, with others?
> Will men surrender their liberties if
> they believe that in doing so they will
> obtain the satisfaction that comes from a
> sense of fusion with others and that re-
> spect by others which is the product of
> strength furnished by solidarity?[9]

The paradox of freedom, compellingly stated in Dostoyevski's fable, "The Grand Inquisitor," contin- ues to thwart the best laid plans of liberals. Does freedom of choice plunge the soul into an- guish? Is freedom a burden that man cannot toler- ate? Will frightened and isolated souls yearn to replace freedom with "miracle, mystery, and author- ity?" Are the masses far "more satisfied by a doc- trine tolerating no other beside itself, than by the granting of liberal freedom,"[10] as Hitler felt?

The crisis of our civilization then is the shattering of the unity of outlook of the Enlight- enment and the failure to replace it with another frame of reference. We have lost our spiritual center and are floundering in a sea of uncertainty unable to drop anchor. The crisis of the West is the distressing awareness that reason and freedom, the goals of the philosophes, are fragile and per- ishable, that the instruments of reason that have expanded man's knowledge of the universe and have given him mastery over nature operate only partial- ly in political and social life, that "the postu- late of objectivity has conquered its place in ... men's practice but not in their hearts."[11] It is the feeling that civilization is fighting an unend- ing and, at times, seemingly hopeless battle a- gainst the dark forces of the irrational. It is the comprehension that reason has not learned how to provide for the irrational. To crush it by total ratiocination is to deny a fundamental component of human nature to which man cannot submit; to give it full play is to regress into a world of myth in which our modern civilization cannot survive. It is the fear that reason is creating a Frankenstein technology and giant bureaucracies that can depersonalize man and estrange him from himself. It is the painful awareness that while men will fight for freedom, they will also seek to escape from it and will willingly surrender it. It is the recognition that the perfectibility of man and linear progress are only expressions of naive optimism and that our civilization too is mortal.

The crisis of the West is exemplified by the disarray of its intellectuals. Some intellectuals, recognizing the enormity of the crisis, asserted the need to recreate freedom constantly and to salvage respect for reason by enlarging our knowledge of the irrational so that it could be regulated in the interests of civilization. Others, regarding reason as a puny instrument incapable of satisfying man's emotional needs or resolving the problems of industrial society, exalted instincts, drives, feelings. Still others proclaimed that everything is absurd; there is no meaning, only nothingness. Finding a saving faith in fascism, some expressed a hatred for liberal institutions and attitudes, a fascination for violence, and a consuming reverence for the nation.

Overwhelmed by World War I, which took the lives of so many of his contemporaries, and the approach of a second world war, distressed by a ruinous nationalism, a pathological totalitarianism, a paralytic liberalism, and a destructive technology, Toynbee urged mankind to listen to its prophets who have taught the presence of God, the dignity of man, the unity of mankind, and the spiritual purpose of existence. Only by restoring its divine center can Western Civilization rescue itself from crisis. For Toynbee the crisis of Western Civilization was due to its breaking away from Christianity and its unreserved embracing of secularism.

He would agree with Jacques Maritain; "This world was born of Christendom and owes its deepest living strength to the Christian tradition. ... Its ultimate error lay in believing that man is saved by his own stength alone, and that human history is made without God."[12] To one steeped in classical civilization with its notion of overweening pride and retribution and in Christianity which inherited the Hebrew view of history as a conflict between God's law and sinful man, it seemed that world war and totalitarianism were punishments for the West's apostasy from Christianity. Toynbee came to see Western Civilization since the Renaissance moving in the direction of catastrophe.

NOTES

1. Arnold J. Toynbee, *Experiences* (New York: Oxford University Press, 1969), p. 202.

2. Arnold J. Toynbee, *A Study of History*, revised, abridged, illustrated one-volume edition (New York: Oxford University Press and American Heritage Press, 1972), p. 11. Hereafter referred to as *Study*, one-volume edition.

3. Hans Kohn, *Political Ideologies of the Twentieth Century*, 3d. ed., rev. (New York: Harper, 1966), p. 33.

4. Antoine Nicolas de Condorcet, *Sketch for a Historical Picture of the Human Mind*, trans. June Barraclough (London: Weidenfeld & Nicholson, 1955), p. 179.

5. Paul Valéry, *Variety*, trans. Malcolm Cowley (New York: Harcourt, Brace, 1927), pp. 27-28.

6. Cited in Franklin L. Baumer, *Religion and the Rise of Scepticism* (New York: Harcourt, Brace, 1960), p. 187.

7. Cited in Harry S. Kariel, *In Search of Authority* (Glencoe, Illinois: The Free Press, 1964), p. 246.

8. Sigmund Freud, *Civilization and Its Discontents*, trans. James Strachey (New York: W. W. Norton, 1962), pp. 58-59.

9. John Dewey, *Freedom and Culture* (New York: G. P. Putnam's

Sons, 1939), pp. 3-4.

10. Adolf Hitler, *Mein Kampf*, trans. Ralph Manheim (Boston: Houghton Mifflin Co., 1962), p. 42.

11. Jacques Monod, *Chance and Necessity* (New York: Alfred A. Knopf, 1971), p. 170.

12. Jacques Maritain, *Christianity and Democracy* (New York: Scribner's Sons, 1944), p. 21.

HISTORIAN WITH A MISSION

Arnold Toynbee was born in 1889, the son of Harry Toynbee, a social worker, and Sarah Marshall Toynbee, one of the first women in England to receive a college degree. His interest in history was prompted by his mother, who was an historian, and by his great-uncle, a sea captain, whose stories about voyages to the East excited the young Toynbee. Toynbee attended boarding school at Winchester where he cultivated "the classics with an almost demonic fervor,"[1] reading, composing, and translating beyond the requirements of the demanding curriculum. He won a classical scholarship and entered Oxford in 1907. After completing his studies, he received a fellowship to teach ancient history at his college, Balliol. Before assuming his duties at Balliol, Toynbee spent the academic year 1911-1912 hiking, primarily in the Greek countryside, an experience that intensified his feelings for the Graeco-Roman world which had become his spiritual home as a result of his classical education.

From Graeco-Roman civilization Toynbee acquired a model by which to measure the rise, growth, and decline of all the world's civilizations. From the Bible, which he also studied in great depth, Toynbee learned to look for a religious meaning behind the facts of history; history is the unfolding of a divine plan. Thus from youth Toynbee was steeped in the outlook and values of Hellenism and Christianity the two traditions that are the foundation of Western Civilization. Like Thomas Aquinas, Toynbee would seek a creative synthesis between the rationalism of Athens and the revelation of Jerusalem.

In 1915 Toynbee left Oxford to work for the Political Intelligence Department of the Foreign Office and in 1919 served as a member of the British delegation at the Paris Peace Conference. From 1919 to 1924 he held a chair in Byzantine and modern Greek studies in the University of London. In 1924 he was invited by Chatham House to launch the annual *Survey of International Affairs*.

Toynbee conceived *A Study of History* in 1921 and began writing in 1927. Volumes 1-3 were published in 1934, volumes 4-6 in 1939, volumes 7-10 in 1951, volume 11, an historical atlas and gazetteer, in 1959, and volume 12, a reconsideration of his theories and a discussion of the views of his critics, in 1961. Remarkably, from 1924 to 1956 Toynbee also wrote or edited the annual *Survey of International Affairs*. Toynbee confessed that he would have been conscience stricken and unhappy if he had slackened in his work. But it was more than a work ethic that drove him to devote himself to *A Study of History*. The impulse behind this monumental effort was a deeply felt need to be of service to humanity.

In *A Study of History* Toynbee listed 21 (later 26) civilizations, living and dead, and examined their rise, growth, breakdown, and disintegration, always, in the process, searching for valid patterns that apply to civilization in general. Toynbee demonstrated immense learning and research, ranging over the histories of ancient Mesopotamia and Egypt, Greece and Rome, Byzantium and Islam, China and India, the Americas and Polynesia.

The first six volumes were written with the memory of World War I still strong and when it appeared that the worn out Western democracies might well succumb to one of two dynamic totalitarian ideologies. That the modern West could give rise to World War I and totalitarianism convinced Toynbee that Western Civilization was now far into its Time of Troubles. In volumes 7-10, written in the aftermath of Hiroshima and in the early stages of the Cold War, Toynbee still had doubts about the vitality of the West and its ability to escape from the rhythm of breakdown and disintegration that had ruined other civilizations. However, in these later volumes, Toynbee emerged more and more as a prophet of world integration, a theme that was expanded in his writings of the 1960's and 1970's.

Toynbee's goal was a world-state dedicated to achieving peace and social justice.

SYNTHESIS AND UNIVERSALISM

Toynbee insisted that it was the duty of the historian to search for the larger meaning of history. History must be more than fact finding; the historian must be more than an antiquarian who collects data encyclopaedicaly and shapelessly; he must be more than a specialist who divides human affairs into numerous and minute morsels. From his classical education Toynbee derived the conviction that human affairs are intelligible only when viewed comprehensively. As a student of the classics, he learned to view the literature, art, philosophy, politics, and history of antiquity not as isolated subjects but as facets of a distinct world-view. To be understood properly, they must be seen as expressions of a humanist outlook that pervaded Greek civilization. Among the modern historians that inspired Toynbee were Gibbon, Freeman, Bury, and Mommsen, for each of them was motivated by a comprehensive-mindedness. This need for synthesis led Toynbee to reject national histories as too parochial. In order to comprehend English history, for example, it is necessary to examine it within the context of the broader field of Western Civilization. Toynbee would study nothing less than an entire civilization.

Toynbee's approach to history was also universal, for ultimately the boundaries of his investigation encompassed all the world's civilizations, surviving and extinct. To comprehend the historical forces that cause a civilization to grow and to decline, it is necessary, said Toynbee, to compare the histories of various civilizations. Such comparisons permit the historian to discern general principles and patterns that are common to all civilizations. To study all the world's civilizations and to give form to the great variety of human history -- could there be a more ambitious and demanding task?

13

By eschewing specialization in preference to comprehensiveness, Toynbee's *Study* is vulnerable to criticism by specialists who have mastered small segments of history and can detect errors which an enterprise of this scope must contain. Nevertheless, this does not negate Toynbee's achievement. The true importance of the *Study* is that it challenges historians to think critically about broad themes in history, about patterns in human affairs; it forces the analytic historian to transcend his special area of professional interest and to deal with the larger meaning of the human experience. From the vantage point of a Toynbee-like history, says William H. McNeill,

> New insights may arise with breadth of view; fallible and never completely provable perhaps, yet enormously stimulating to exact and careful study which may find new questions to ask of familiar data in the light of general ideas generated by men like Toynbee. No multiplication of specialisms or narrowing down of fields of history in the interest of more perfect accuracy can by itself hope to achieve such an enrichment of our understanding of man's past. Interaction between large views, bold hypothesis, fallible intuitions, and exact, detailed scholarship is what we need. If we concentrate upon the latter alone, by drawing ever closer to the facts and seeing details ever more completely, we may blind ourselves to other aspects of reality.[2]

Toynbee's decision to study world history showed his debt to Polybius from whom he acquired "a universal view of history which has interested me all my life."[3] Polybius sought to explain Rome's march to world empire by examining history on a grand scale. He said that it was impossible to understand the reduction of the Mediterranean world to Roman power by writing isolated narratives of Roman activities in Spain or Sicily; Roman history must be examined on a universal scale.

Polybius' history linked together the affairs of Italy, Greece, Africa, and Asia, giving expression to the universalism and cosmopolitanism of the Hellenistic Age.

But the principal source of Toynbee's universalism was religion. Adapting the thought of the prophets of higher religions, who have taught that as God is one so too should there be the unity of mankind, Toynbee, held that mankind is one family in the making. A universal history accorded with Toynbee's sense of mission. He hoped that such a history would contribute to the world-mindedness which he considered a precondition for man's self-preservation; mankind must become one family, he said, or it will destroy itself.

Toynbee's world-mindedness demonstrated a humanitarianism and tolerance which, said Hans Kohn, resembles that of Tolstoy, Schweitzer, and Lessing. Like Lessing, Toynbee held that actions and an ethical spirit matter more than dogma. "As Lessing saw in Judaism, Christianity, and Islam variations on a single theme, so Mr. Toynbee ... sees all universal religions ... as equally sharing in their great message to mankind, the message of unity beyond all ethnic divisions."[4]

For Toynbee history was a calling. He felt that all creative effort was ultimately barren if it did not enhance man's spiritual and social development, if it did not promote harmony and eliminate discord. Toynbee, who considered himself a survivor of World War I, felt a profound need to help his fellow man. He believed that in a world struggling for survival, he had an obligation to make a contribution to the understanding of the nature of the crisis that had afflicted the West and now the entire globe and to offer remedies.

Thus Toynbee wrote history didactically; he believed that from his study of the past he had gained certain insights into the human condition that could assist a foundering humanity. While historical precedents are not scientific blueprints, said Toynbee, they do allow man to under-

15

stand better and to cope more successfully with
contemporary problems.

     While maintaining that there were patterns to
the past, Toynbee rejected determinism. He did not
hold that past occurrences were inevitable or that
out of necessity the patterns of the past will repeat themselves in the future. Toynbee first read
Spengler's *Decline of the West* in 1920. He approved
of Spengler's inquiring into the histories of whole
societies, instead of national states, and of his
comparative approach to the study of civilizations.
He also employed Spengler's thesis that there are
patterns to the growth and decay of civilizations.
What he disliked about Spengler was his determinism,
his "arbitrary fiat," his dogmatic insistence that
"civilization arose, developed, declined, and
foundered in unvarying conformity with a fixed
timetable."[5] Unlike Spengler, Toynbee believed
that despite our knowledge of the past we cannot
predict with any certainty the course of history;
human affairs are amenable to regularities, but
these "laws" are not inexorable. The repetitive
element in history does not make man a slave to
fate but provides him with an opportunity for creative action; to a large extent man can shape his
own destiny. For Spengler, civilizations were organic bodies that are destroyed by necessity; rejecting the organic model, Toynbee attributed decline to man's own nature which he has the capacity
to remedy. Nor is man a helpless prisoner of the
past; he has it in his power to break with self-
destructive traditions and practices, but this requires a mighty effort. Toynbee insisted that he
was not a determinist. History reveals recurrent
patterns but there is no inevitability; man has the
freedom to shape his future.

     For Toynbee, man achieves freedom through
self-mastery and self-determination, when he is
able to break with tradition, overcome habit, and
meet new challenges. The highest form of freedom,
said Toynbee, is spiritual growth; when man guides
his conduct according to God's values he has successfully responded to the greatest challenge of
all -- that presented by his own nature. Man

thereby demonstrates he has freedom of choice. In rejecting God's law of love, man brings about his own disaster; he is overwhelmed by the irrationality, greed, and aggressiveness inherent in human nature. Freedom requires continuous acts of creation, for man must always transcend the limitations posed by human nature. In doing so, he not only performs an act of self-transfiguration that brings him closer to God, he also acquires the capacity to improve society.

CIVILIZATION: RISE, GROWTH, BREAKDOWN, DISINTEGRATION

Much of *A Study of History* deals with an analysis of the rise, growth, breakdown, and disintegration of civilizations. For most of human history, said Toynbee, man lived in primitive societies in which the younger generation acquired its outlook and habits by imitating its dead ancestors. A society ruled by custom remains static. The breakthrough to civilization came when creative personalities broke with tradition and attracted the following of the uncreative majority. The impulse that gave rise to civilization, stemmed neither from any special quality of race or from a favorable environment, but from a creative response to a challenge. The founders of Egyptian and Mesopotamian civilizations were heroic pioneers who made marsh lands give way to irrigation works, fields, and cities.

In *challenge-and-response*, Toynbee had a plausible explanation to account for the rise, growth, and decline of civilization. In accounting for the origin of civilization, Toynbee stressed not the environment in and of itself but the "human heroism" that enabled man to transform the environment for his own benefit. In the Nile valley man had to clear jungles and drain swamps before he could plant; he had to subdue and order the wantonness and formlessness of nature before he could create civilization. This point is central to Toynbee's analysis of civilizations. Man's great achievements stem from creative acts of the human spirit; conversely, spiritual and psychological defects ultimately cause a civilization's decline. Hence, for Toynbee, the essential problem confronting the modern West is not material but spiritual.

Man, said Toynbee, achieved a *tour de force* when he overcame physical and human challenges and created civilization. But if a civilization is to grow, it must move from "challenge through response to further challenge."[6] The creative spirit that enabled a civilization to rise must be preserved if the civilization is to avoid arrest and to continue its growth. A society in growth progresses toward self-determination, that is, it provides itself with fresh challenges that trigger a chain reaction of successful responses and still further challenges enabling it to move from strength to strength. It possesses an *élan vital*, an inner spiritual power, which enables it to face successfully one challenge after another.

It is creative personalities, men who "have succeeded in attaining self-determination through self-mastery,"[7] that propel humanity out of its inertia and enable a society to grow. Toynbee agreed with Bergson who held that "It is only the thrust of genius that has ever forced the inertia of Humanity to yield."[8] These pioneers break with custom, stir the inert and uncreative majority to follow their lead, and keep civilization in a healthy state of dynamic movement.

Growth for Toynbee stems from creative personalities who gain the mimesis of ordinary human beings. But when leadership fails, self-determination is lost and the harmony that society had shown during its period of growth ends. The once creative minority becomes impotent and cannot cope successfully with new challenges. During such times, the great mass of people, for whom civilization is only a thin veneer, revert back to their primitive humanity and society is in danger of breaking down.

Societies are not predestined to death, insisted Toynbee. Civilizations are not condemned by fate or by forces outside human control. Nor is breakdown the consequence of a mortal blow delivered by invading armies. Rather, civilizations break down for internal reasons, from wounds that are self-inflicted. "The most that the alien enemy has achieved has been to give the expiring suicide his *coup de grace* or to devour his carcass after it has already become carrion."[9] The truth is, as George Meredith said: "We are betrayed by what is false within." Suicide, not murder, is the reason why civilizations die. Civilizations break down when there is a deterioration within the social order, an inability to respond to challenges, and a subsequent loss of that self-determination that had once impelled growth; instead of variety and versatility, there is deadening uniformity and uninventiveness.

One aspect of the process of breakdown is "resting on one's oars." Becoming infatuated with its own achievement, a creative minority looks to the past, becomes senile, and loses the *élan* that had once enabled it to respond creatively to challenges. Resting on one's oars may take the form of idolizing an institution that has outlived its usefulness, as was the case with the Greeks whose infatuation with the polis eventually thwarted creativity; it prevented them from achieving the unity that alone could save Hellenic civilization from the suicidalness of internecine warfare.

Societies on the downhill slide from breakdown to disintegration, said Toynbee, are torn by social discord operating on two levels. First there is warfare among a number of parochial states within the same society until a single state delivers a knockout blow and creates a universal state. But a universal state established through violence, as in the case of Rome, cannot breathe new life into a disintegrating civilization. It can only provide a temporary reprieve.

Secondly, a disintegrating society breaks up into a dominant minority, an internal proletariat, and an external proletariat (barbarian warrior bands). The common consciousness that had bound together the different ranks of society during the civilization's growth falls apart. The creative minority that had once spurred the society to grow, loses its ability to create and becomes merely a dominant minority that "attempts to hold by force -- against all right and reason -- a position of inherited privilege which it has ceased to merit,"[10] and the internal proletariat, responding to the deterioration of the creative minority, executes its act of secession. The proletariat, feeling disinherited and unwanted, no longer follows a dominant minority that has lost its capacity for leadership.

This schism in the body social of a disintegrating society is the outward expression of a spiritual rift in human souls. In such a society human behavior and feelings are in turmoil. Some people demonstrate a loss of the creative faculty by giving free reign to their appetites; others go to the opposite extreme and become ascetics. A selfish individualism replaces a sense of duty to the community. Another conspicuous attitude of mind displayed by individuals living in disintegrating societies is the "hopeless feeling of being adrift in an uncontrollable, if not evil, Universe."[11] The sense of spiritual uncertainty leads many to find comfort by glorifying an earlier period of time (archaism) or by dreaming up utopias (futurism). Both archaism and futurism are signs of defeatism and therefore are uncreative responses to the spiritual crisis. The dominant minority in a disintegrating civilization adopts the cultural patterns of the proletariat; this results in a vulgarization of art, literature, and manners.

The dominant minority, resting on its oars, becomes rigid and ineffectual. Nevertheless it performs an act of creativity -- the establishment of a universal state. A universal state, according to Toynbee's scheme, emerges *after* a civilization has already begun to break down; it is the means by which the dominant minority checks for a time the process of disintegration. The universal state does not represent recovery from a Time of Troubles that might be centuries old; it is only a rally that enables the afflicted society "to enjoy a brief 'Indian Summer' before its final dissolution."[12] When the universal state comes too late and at too great a cost it will not endure, despite the expectations of its citizens who believe their earthly commonwealth is really immortal. However long it may last, it represents only the last phase of a civilization prior to its extinction.

For Toynbee, the ultimate significance of the universal state is that it provides a setting within which a universal church can grow in its tender infancy. But the universal state belongs wholly to the past. So too do the bevy of barbarian warrior bands that sprout on the universal state's borders. It is the universal church created by the seceding proletariat that will become the predominant force shaping the future.

The breakdown of a civilization makes possible a spiritual advance -- the emergence of a higher religion. A civilization fulfills its destiny when it ministers to the birth of a higher religion. Religion was at the core of Toynbee's historical consciousness. It provided him with a framework for assessing the essential meaning of Western Civilization and for explaining its near collapse in the twentieth century.

THE PRIMACY OF RELIGION

Toynbee maintained that in studying history as a whole we should "relegate economic and political history to a subordinate place and give religious history primacy. For religion, after all, is the serious business of the human race."[13] For Toynbee, the vocation of historian is a calling of a very special nature. It is "a call from God to feel after Him and find Him. ... History [is] a vision -- dim and partial ... of God revealing Himself in actions to souls that were sincerely seeking Him."[14] It leads us to a revelation of God and a hope of communion with Him. Toynbee believed that his craft was "ultimately a quest for the vision of God at work in History."[15] The facts of history, he maintained, are "clues to the nature and meaning of

21

the mysterious Universe and our place in it. ...
The spiritual reality behind the phenomena is, I
believe, the ultimate objective of all curiosity."[16]
This religious feeling pervaded Toynbee's historical consciousness.

Toynbee's view of history derived in part from
the biblical conception that it is through history
that man's will clashes with God's commands. God
showed man the way to righteousness, but man also
has the freedom to defy God. While God's hand was
at work in history, it was man who essentially made
his own history, for God's punishments were something that stubborn and rebellious man brought upon
himself. Thus for Toynbee history is filled with
spiritual meaning; it is a theodicy in which progress is measured by man's awareness of God.

Toynbee's conception of human nature was in-
separable from his religious outlook. Inherent in
human nature, he said, is "a vein of diabolical
evil," that manifests itself on an individual level
in self-centeredness and on the social level in
warfare and class antagonisms which have proved
fatal to civilization. Toynbee regarded as naive
the liberal belief in the essential goodness of
man; for him the atrocities of the twentieth century were sufficient proof of man's capacity for
evil. But Toynbee also believed that human nature
has an inherent capacity for goodness. In every
human soul a struggle is waged between these two
irreconcilable spiritual forces. This spiritual
division of the soul, said Toynbee, manifests itself in human society which is an arena of continual
warfare between good and evil. Human nature is out
of balance, said Toynbee. Man has demonstrated a
much greater talent for mastering inanimate nature
than for controlling his own emotions and for living in fellowship with others. If the individual
and society are not to be consumed by wickedness,
man must seek the support of higher religions --
Christianity, Islam, Judaism, Buddhism, Hinduism,
Zoroastrianism. Every human being, said Toynbee,
is disposed to behave as if he were the center of
the universe and to exploit everyone else in the
universe. The higher religions have tried to help

the individual to overcome an inherent self-centeredness and the community a destructive tribal-mindedness. As the center of human existence becomes the love of a Supreme Being, man treats his fellows with consideration and respect.

It was not a commitment to a particular theology that drew Toynbee to religion but an attachment to prophetic values. Higher religions, he believed, enable the individual to find a purpose in life and to deal with emotional distress; they promote better relations among human beings and facilitate social welfare. Belief in God makes the individual a better person and instills a social conscience in society. Only the values of higher religions can rescue man from a dehumanizing technology and totalitarianism; only prophetic values can prevent humanity from destroying itself in a nuclear holocaust.

Toynbee defined religion as a "human being's relation to an ultimate reality behind and beyond the phenomena of the Universe in which each of us awakes to consciousness."[17] Convinced that there exists a spiritual element within human nature, Toynbee then inferred the existence of an ultimate reality with which this spiritual element seeks communion, although he recognized that the existence of an ultimate reality is unverifiable.

Man has always demonstrated religious feelings, declared Toynbee, for it is through religion that he has tried to answer questions about the purpose of existence and the meaning of death. Toynbee classified the varieties of religions into three categories -- the worship of nature, the worship of man, and the worship of Absolute Reality, that is God. Primitive man expressed his religious feelings through the worship of nature -- animals, rain, moon, stars. Nature gods were for primitive man embodiments of the presence behind nature of forces to which he was at mercy. Nature worship receded, said Toynbee, because man had begun to exercise power over nature; man does not deify things that he has learned to control. While the primitive religion of nature worship persisted after the

rise of civilization, it was eventually superseded
by another lower religion -- the deification of a
human being (the god-like ruler) or a human institution (the sacrosanct state). In Greece, for example, the Greek goddess Athena, originally a nature divinity, came to represent the political
power of the human community, Athens. In idolizing
the collective power of their community, asserted
Toynbee, the Athenians still embraced a lower religion. By giving total commitment to their city,
the Greeks unleashed the dark side of human nature,
massacring and enslaving for their deified community. This transformation of the human community
into a virtual god lead to wars that ultimately
wrecked Hellenic civilization.

Toynbee defined the period from the eighth
century B.C. to the seventh century A.D. as an age
of spiritual progress. It began with the Hebrew
prophets and ended with Mohammed. Included within
the period were others of the world's great religious prophets: Buddha, Lao-tze, Confucious, Zara-
thustra, Socrates. Toynbee continually urged man
to return to the values taught by these prophets,
history's most inspired men. The higher religions,
insisted Toynbee, have given man the cure for his
spiritual malady; they have shown him how he can
transcend greed and aggressiveness and improve the
quality of social relationships. The higher religions have taught that man is not God, that human
power is limited, that love is the greatest good,
that man should never deify a human being or a human institution.

The human psyche, said Toynbee, will resist
all efforts of reason to eliminate religious sentiments; if the feelings are not directed toward the
higher religions, they will find other outlets, for
human beings cannot be without some form of religion. If the mind is not restrained and elevated
by higher religions, it will embrace myths that
give vent to the worst elements of human nature.
For Toynbee, the most dangerous expression of mythical thinking is the deification of the parochial
community (nationalism) which he saw as a principal
reason for the breakdown of civilizations.

24

Toynbee's conception of religion was personal rather than sectarian. Reared as an Anglican, Toynbee became an agnostic while an undergraduate at Oxford, concluding "that religion itself was an unimportant illusion."[18] Later, no doubt under the influence of the Great War, the rise of totalitarianism, and an impending second world war, he attributed an inestimable value to higher religions: they help man to overcome depression and anxiety, to conquer his destructive self-centeredness, and to assure him that in spite of his sinfulness he is redeemable.

While Toynbee admired the spiritual message of the higher religions, he rejected doctrines that lacked credibility. For example, he could not adhere to some essential Christian dogmas -- the Virgin Birth, the Resurrection, the Ascension -- for they are irreconcilable with what science tells us about the uniformity of nature. Nor did he regard Jesus as divine, but as a man inspired by a love of humanity unmatched by any other human being. To this extent, of all of God's children, Jesus came closest to fulfilling the ideals of the sonship of God. What is most valuable in Christianity is its precept that "self-sacrificing love is the most powerful of all the spiritual impulses known to us."[19]

While Christianity occupied a central place in Toynbee's thought, he came to believe that it was not a unique and final revelation. All the higher religions are alternate approaches to the mystery of existence. All the higher religions are variations on a theme; they all present some facet of God's truth. They all aspire to help the individual to attain the true end of life -- communion with a higher spiritual reality. They all liberate man by teaching that God alone, not man or his creations, is the supreme value in the universe and that only He is worthy of worship. They all help men and women to deal with life's misfortunes. They all hold the promise of salvation, a need which human beings feel more compellingly than the need for truth. They all help man to combat egocentricity and social discord. By addressing themselves to all mankind, not just a part of it, the higher religions enable man to overcome barriers between states and civilizations. The higher religions were revolutionary new departures for they all proclaimed a message of universalism -- the unity of mankind, a condition that Toynbee considered necessary for human survival.

Toynbee did not regard himself as an orthodox member of any of the higher religions, because he could not accept their exact and definitive answers to the riddle of existence, but he subscribed to their spiritual values -- love and compassion. Favoring "the maximum of religion with the minimum of dogma,"[20] he wanted all the historic higher religions to separate the essentials of their faith, a love of God and therefore a love of man, from doctrinal and ritual accretions.

He criticized religion's efforts to resist scientific truth by claiming authority "over other provinces of knowledge which were really Reason's legitimate domain."[21] While religion cannot compete with science in the attempt to understand and manipulate nature, science cannot provide answers to the most crucial questions of life -- man's relationship to himself, his fellows, and his God. For such spiritual insight, said Toynbee, we must turn to the higher religions.

Toynbee was a religious moralist who found rationalism intrinsically imperfect, incomplete and inadequate, and secularism a miserable failure. What gives unity to his thought is its spirituality and universalism -- a vision of the community of man united by a love of God. He held steadfastly that the Western liberal-rational tradition simply cannot bind men together in peace and fellowship, for it cannot permanently restrain man's evil nature which manifests itself in wars among peoples and in conflicts between classes. To be effective, liberalism and rationalism must draw inspiration from prophetic values. The inspiration of the Gospels must radiate widely into temporal society. For Toynbee, Christianity constitutes more than divine truth propagated by churches and structured by theologians. It is an historic force that is woven into the fabric of our existence; its values improve individual life and the social order.

But Toynbee was no simple-minded devotee. While displeased with the secularism of the modern West, he would not betray the heritage of intellectual freedom bequeathed by the Scientific Revolution and the Enlightenment. He would attempt to fashion a synthesis of reason and religion to fit the requirements of the modern age.

METHODOLOGY

Toynbee's historiography was a peculiar mixture of empiricism and mythical thinking. In the tradition of nineteenth-century positivists, particularly Buckler, Toynbee collected facts and statistics and searched for general rules and laws that govern human affairs. Toynbee felt that this empiricism distinguished his work from Spengler's. While Toynbee maintained that his method of inquiry was empirical, his critics have insisted that facts were forced to fit an arbitrary and rigid *a priori* framework. He tried to validate empirically preconceptions to which he had already committed himself. Consequently, said McNeill, "in the interest of fitting data into a pattern, he sometimes seems to cut and slice reality in an arbitrary and even fantastic fashion."[22] What Toynbee held to be logical conclusions deduced dispassionately from the facts were really personal value judgments and the facts themselves were often arbitrarily selected.

Moreover, much of Toynbee's history derived from mythology which Toynbee found a valuable assistance to the historian. From mythology Toynbee hoped to obtain an intuitive grasp of what is most essential to the human condition; he held that mythology expressed universal truths in a unique way. While the insights derived from mythological analogy are unverifiable, "mythology has a wider reach than science and a deeper penetrative power;"[23] it is a means of apprehending and expressing universal truth. By means of mythological analogy "the range of human intuition and understanding,"

27

could be extended "beyond the limits of the knowledge attainable through logical processes of
thought."[24]   For this reason he would drive "science and mythology in double harnass. ... the two
steeds, side by side, can carry us farther than
either steed can by itself."[25]   It is from Plato,
said Toynbee, that he acquired this approach.

> Plato taught me, by example, not to be
> ashamed of using my imagination as well
> as my intellect.   He taught me, when,
> in a mental voyage, I found myself at
> the upper limit of the atmosphere ac-
> cessible to the Reason, not to hesitate
> to let my imagination carry me on up
> into the stratosphere on the wings of a
> myth.   In never being either too proud
> or too timid to take a myth for the
> sake of reconnoitering regions of the
> Spiritual Universe beyond Reason's
> range, Plato was showing both the hu-
> mility and the audacity of a great
> mind. ... I have now lived to see the
> subconscious well-spring of Poetry and
> Prophecy restored to honor in the West-
> ern World by the genius of C.G. Jung.[26]

Like Plato, Toynbee relied on sudden flashes
of insight and resorted to myth and metaphor to
make a crucial point.   To elucidate his theory of
the rise, growth, and demise of civilization, he
summoned Goethe, Milton, Aeschylus, and the Bible.
Plato held that underlying the multiplicity of
phenomena were principles of unity; Toynbee,
Plato's disciple, also assumed that beneath the
multifariousness of historical experience lie principles of order.   There is form to the historical
process.

Toynbee was also greatly indebted to Bergson
whose works he avidly read during his student days
and to whom he often referred.   Originally attracted
to positivism, Bergson turned away from the positiv-
ist claim that science could explain everything and
fulfill all human needs.   Such an emphasis on the
intellect, said Bergson, sacrifices spiritual

impulses, imagination, and intuition and reduces the soul to a mere mechanism. The methods of science cannot reveal ultimate, reality, Bergson insisted. European civilization must recognize the limitations of scientific rationalism. The method of intuition, whereby the mind strives for an immanent relationship with the object, becoming one with it, can tell us more about reality than the method of analysis used by science. Entering into the object through an intuitive experience is the avenue to a truth that the calculations and measurements of science cannot obtain. Although not based upon scientific procedures, insisted Bergson, the method of intuition is a superior avenue to knowledge. Science is not the only avenue to truth and the mind is not a collection of atoms operating according to mechanical principles but a stream of consciousness with extraordinary intuitive capacities. Bergson's philosophy pointed away from science toward religious mysticism.

Like Bergson, Toynbee had a deep impulse to comprehend life directly and totally and toward this end he gave validity to extra-scientific knowledge. Like Bergson, Toynbee sought to complement the intellect with intuition, thereby arriving at a more complete understanding of personality and life. Also like Bergson, he yearned for communion with a transcendent reality of higher values and demonstrated some of the qualities of a religious mystic. Toynbee agreed with Bergson that men can never overcome their primitive tribalism and progress to ecumenical concord unless they demonstrate a common allegiance to God.

It is precisely this approach that aroused the ire of professional historians and made suspect Toynbee's claim that his conclusions were based upon an empirical study. Repelled by his religious-mythical orientation, many critics accused Toynbee of distorting the truth, undermining rationalism, and regressing to myth. "He is a man who believes ... in a strange mysticism about history. ... His is not the talent of science but of belief,"[27] said Ortega y Gasset. "For although Toynbee, in analyzing civilizations, claims to be dispassionate and scientific, in fact his whole analysis is governed by strong emotional prejudice,"[28] said H.R. Trevor-Roper. This is quite understandable, for professional historians are generally hostile to a religious world-view and are discomforted by religious explanations for social problems, especially when written in exalted tones and supported by long passages from the Bible, St. Augustine, Bishop Bossuet, and Bergson. Like G. J. Reiner, they are scornful of a methodology that uses myths and metaphors "not merely for the purpose of assisting thought, but as the basis for subsequent reasoning and classification. ... I dislike Toynbee's method, because it dwells in the sphere of myth and allegory, outside rationality."[29] Toynbee maintained that he aimed "to try out the scientific approach to human affairs and to test how far it will carry us,"[30] but ultimately he was a mythical thinker whose historical outlook was permeated with religious hopes and feeling. He praised Ibn Khaldun's *Universal History* "for bursting the bounds of this world and breaking through into an Other World," and St. Augustine's *City of God* for showing him "the tradition in which these two worlds stand to one another."[31] This attitude of mind repels both the professional historian and the liberal humanist. Critics agreed essentially with Pieter Geyl's assessment of Toynbee: "The problems ... which ... have to do with the health and prospects of survival of a civilization have always been tackled and will always be tackled on a different plane from that of religion."[32] Many of Toynbee's passages that seem to preach against the pagans offend the liberal-rationalist temperament; his pleas for spirituality and his analysis in religious terms of the ills of modern society are reminiscent of St. Augustine to whom humanists do not turn for inspiration or guidance. There are numerous parallels between the *City of God*, written when Rome was dying, and *A Study of History*, written when the West seemed near collapse. Like Augustine, Toynbee measured progress by spiritual advances -- man moving closer to God -- and held that doing without God ends in the undoing of man. Much of Augustinian pessimism pervades Toynbee's work. Most repulsive to liberal humanists was Toynbee's view that a civilization fulfills its historical mission by giving rise to a higher religion, that history is a progressive process with communion with God as the ultimate goal.

Toynbee's religious orientation provided him with a framework for comprehending the major stages of Western Civilization and for explaining the West's near collapse in the twentieth century. For Toynbee, Hellenism, the parent of the West, failed because it overvalued man and his creations. Hellenism's collapse prepared the way for a spiritual advance -- the Christian Middle Ages; the disintegration of medieval religious unity and the transformation of the West into a post-Christian civilization set the wheels of decline in motion.

NOTES

1. *Experiences*, p. 14.

2. William H. McNeill, "Some Basic Assumptions of Toynbee's *A Study of History*," in Edward T. Gargan, ed., *The Intent of Toynbee's History* (Chicago: Loyola University Press, 1961), pp. 31-32.

3. *Toynbee on Toynbee: A Conversation Between Arnold J. Toynbee and G. R. Urban* (New York: Oxford University Press, 1974), p. 16.

4. Hans Kohn, *Political Ideologies of the Twentieth Century*, pp. 269-70.

5. Arnold J. Toynbee, *Civilization on Trial* (New York: Oxford University Press, 1948; reprint edition published together with *The World and the West* (Cleveland: World, 1958), p. 20.

6. Arnold J. Toynbee, *A Study of History*, 12 vols. (New York: Oxford University Press, 1962-1964), 3: 128. The citation refers to the paperback edition. Volumes 1-3 were originally published in 1934, volumes 4-6 in 1939, volumes 7-10 in 1954, volume 11, an historical atlas and gazetteer, in 1959, and volume 12, a reconsideration of his theories and a discussion of his critics, in 1961. All references are to the paperback edition henceforth referred to as *Study*.

7. *Ibid.*, p. 234.

8. *Ibid.*, p. 237.

9. *Study*, 4: 115.

10. *Study*, 5: 26.

11. *Study*, one-volume edition, p. 243.

12. *Ibid.*, p. 228.

13. Arnold J. Toynbee, *Civilization on Trial*, p. 89.

14. *Study*, 10: 1.

15. *Study*, 10: 42.

16. *Experiences*, p. 90.

17. *Ibid.*, p. 125.

18. *Ibid.*, p. 127.

19. *Ibid.*, p. 135.

20. *Ibid.*, p. 143.

21. *Study*, 7b: 476.

22. Gargan, ed., *The Intent of Toynbee's History*, p. 41.

23. *Study*, 12: 40.

24. *Ibid.*, p. 250.

25. *Ibid.*, p. 40.

26. *Study*, 10: 228.

27. José Ortega y Gasset, *An Interpretation of Universal History*, trans. Mildred Adams (New York: W. W. Norton, 1975), pp. 251-52.

28. H. R. Trevor-Roper, "Arnold Toynbee's Millenium," *Encounter* (June 1957), reprinted in *Historical Essays*

(New York: Harper, 1957), p. 300.

29. G. J. Reiner, *History: Its Purpose and Method,* excerpted in Montagu, ed., *Toynbee and History,* pp. 74-75.

30. Toynbee, "What I am Trying to Do," in Montagu, *Toynbee and History,* p. 6.

31. *Study,* 10: 236.

32. Pieter Geyl, *Debates With Historians* (New York: The New American Library, 1958), p. 159.

HELLENISM AND CHRISTIANITY

Western Civilization is a confluence of two
traditions -- Graeco-Roman and Judaeo-Christian.
Toynbee's interpretation of these traditions is
crucial to an understanding of his philosophy of
history and his interpretation of the modern West.

HELLENISM

"Had Greek civilization never existed," said
the poet W. H. Auden, "we would never have become
fully conscious, which is to say that we would
never have become, for better or worse, fully human."[1] Breaking with the mythopoeic outlook of the
Near East, the Greeks conceived a world-view whose
focus was not mythic gods or priest-kings but man.
In Greece there arose a new conception of nature as
orderly and intelligible to reason and a new conception of the human being -- his capacity for rational thought, his need for freedom, his worth as
an individual.

In maintaining that nature does not behave
haphazardly, that it is not governed by blind
chance, that it is not manipulated by arbitrary and
willful gods, but proceeds according to general
laws, early Greek philosophers initiated the movement from myth to reason that came to characterize
every level of Greek cultural life by the age of
Pericles. From a rational inquiry into nature, the
Greek philosophical spirit turned to a rational investigation of man and the human community. Here
the decisive figure was Socrates who insisted that
man use his reason to make sense out of his own
life. Through reason the individual gains knowledge of ethical values and takes control of his
own life. Moral norms are not revealed to man in
the form of divine commandments, but must be discovered by the individual himself through critical
analysis. Socrates wanted to subject all human beliefs and behavior to the clear light of reason;

in this way ethics would be removed from the realm
of authority, dogma, superstition, and myth.

The Greeks were the first to define man by his
capacity to reason. It was the great achievement
of the Greek spirit to rise above magic, mystery,
authority, and custom and to discover the means of
giving order to nature and society. Every feature
of Greek civilization -- science, philosophy, art,
literature, politics, writing of history -- shows a
growing reliance upon human reason and a diminishing dependence upon divine guidance.

Political freedom also originated in Greece.
In Mesopotamia and Egypt man had no clear conception of his own individual worth; he had no understanding of political liberty. He was not a citizen but a subject who marched to the command of a
ruler whose power originated with the gods. As
such, royal power was not imposed upon an unwilling
population, but was religiously accepted and obeyed.
In contrast, the Greeks saw the state as a community of free citizens who made laws in their own interest. To them law was not an expression of whim
or divine commands but of reason, not of might but
of justice.

Underlying the Greek achievement was a humanist attitude toward life. The Greeks expressed a
belief in the worth, significance, and dignity of
man; they called for the maximum cultivation of human talent, the full development of human personality, the deliberate pursuit of excellence. By dis-
covering theoretical reason, by defining political
liberty, and by affirming the worth and potential
of the human personality, the Greeks broke with the
past and founded the rational and humanist tradition of Western Civilization.

It is precisely this tradition of secular humanism which the West has esteemed since the Renaissance that Toynbee questioned and challenged. For
Toynbee, Greek humanism was an expression of "man-
worship," that is, it glorified man and his works;
man not God was central to the world-view of Hellenism and this is what caused its downfall. The

great failing of the ancient Greeks, insisted Toynbee, was that they "saw in Man, 'the Lord of Creation' and worshipped him as an idol in place of
God."[2]

Toynbee's interpretation of Hellenism is crucial to his understanding of the nature, meaning,
and destiny of the West. Hellenism provided Toynbee with a structural model by which to examine the
breakdown and disintegration of civilization in
general. It also provided a moral lesson: modern
Western Civilization is a revival of the secular
humanism of the ancient Greeks and suffers from the
same defect -- an overvaluing and worshipping of
man's creations. Toynbee viewed Greek humanism as
"the most whole-hearted and uncompromising practice
of man-worship that is on record up to date."[3] It
was precisely this glorification of man and his
works, said Toynbee, that lead to Hellenism's
breakdown and disintegration, and it is a similar
attitude that is the principal threat to modern
Western Civilization. Because Toynbee derived his
patterns of growth and decline from Hellenic civilization and applied these patterns to the modern
West, we must examine in some detail his structuring of classical history.

Toynbee interpreted classical antiquity in the
light of the theory of challenge-and-response. The
Greek city-state represented a creative response to
the challenge of anarchy that burdened Hellenic society in its formative stage, the Dark Ages that
followed on the ruins of Minoan-Mycenaean civilization. Formed by the union of a number of smaller
communities, the city-state provided its inhabitants with a viable political unity that brought
security during an age of disorder. By engaging in
colonization when threatened by overpopulation and
food shortages, the city-states again responded
successfully to a challenge. In addition to enabling the Greeks to overcome the problems of anarchy
and stringency, the city-states stimulated cultural
creativity. For these reasons, said Toynbee, the
Greeks glorified their city-states, regarding them
as more worthy of devotion than the Olympian gods.
But the city-states did not deserve such devotion,

said Toynbee, for they were not capable of stimulating the individual to his best self. Toynbee saw two defects in the institution of the polis: warfare, which was endemic to Hellenic society, and injustice, for slavery was unchallenged, women had no political rights, and peasants, whose farms were too far removed from the civic centers, found it too difficult to participate in the political life of the city. Despite its considerable achievements, the city-state was still an imperfect human creation, and its undeserved idolization led to the decline of Hellenic civilization.

In the course of the sixth century B.C. the Greek city-states experienced an economic revolution, a change over from subsistence farming to the production of decorated pottery, wine, and olive oil for export that could be exchanged for cereals from Egypt, Sicily, and the Ukraine. This economic revolution, declared Toynbee, necessarily led to greater economic interdependence among the city-states, but this was not accompanied by political interdependence. The new economic circumstances demanded the creation of some form of Panhellenic unity, perhaps a voluntary federation. Could the Greeks meet this new challenge? Could they stop worshipping their city-states and transfer their political allegiance to a Panhellenic body politic? Only such a spiritual revolution could save them from disaster.

The advent of the Persian Wars gave the Greeks an opportunity to achieve the political unity that was made necessary by the accelerating economic unification of the Hellenic world. However, the cooperation displayed by Greek city-states in their victory over Persia did not endure. The half-century following the Persian Wars was a period of cultural flowering, but it also saw the Hellenic world heading toward self-inflicted disaster -- the Peloponnesian War.

Solon had performed a creative act by stimulating manufacturing of pottery and the cultivation of the vine and olives, thereby enabling Athens to overcome the limitations of its poor soil and to become a great commercial center. After the Persian Wars, Athens was in a position to push the Greek world in the direction of unity, but instead Athenian leaders transformed the Delian League into an instrument of Athenian imperialism. The price paid for this decline in the quality of statesmanship was the Peloponnesian War which started the Hellenic world down the path that leads from breakdown to disintegration. This fatal war broke out because Athens had proved unable to conquer the next challenge set by her own outstanding domestic successes -- the challenge of being called upon to create an Hellenic political world order. The Peloponnesian War, said Toynbee, was "the outward visible sign of an inward visible breakdown in the life of Hellenic Society."[4]

By forming the polis Hellenic society had responded creatively to the challenge of anarchy that existed during the Dark Ages; by establishing colonies the polis responded creatively to the challenge of over-population. But the institution of the polis was inadequate to cope with a society growing more complex. Because the Greeks idolized the polis, declared Toynbee, they could not create a Panhellenic political framework to halt fratricidal warfare. The rhythm of challenge-and-response was broken and there was a subsequent loss of self-determination.

The spiritual damage wrought by the Peloponnesian War, brilliantly described by Thucydides, was more significant than the material damage. The atrocities committed both on the international scene and in the civil wars that broke out within a number of city-states were evidence of this spiritual decline. The Peloponnesian War was the price paid for the Hellenic failure to achieve political unity peacefully, a unity required by new economic circumstances. The Time of Troubles was upon the Hellenic world which would be devastated by international and civil warfare with hardly a breathing space for the next four hundred years, until Octavian became master of Rome.

Ninety-three years after the disastrous

Peloponnesian War, the Macedonians imposed political unity upon the Hellenic society for a short period. Toynbee praised Alexander for rising above Greek ethnocentrism to the lofty ideal of a brotherhood of mankind, an ideal to which he himself aspired. However, the premature death of Alexander in 323 B.C. ended the brief period of Hellenic unity and dampened hopes for peace within Hellenic society. After Alexander's death, Hellenic society remained politically fractured, but now into contending kingdoms rather than warring city-states, and Hellenism continued its slide.

In the post-Alexandrian world, the deification of the king replaced the deification of the city-state. But god-kings or priest-kings could not fill the spiritual vacuum that existed in the Hellenic world as a result of the loosening of the bonds between the individual and his city-state.

Meanwhile, the problem of establishing an effective world-polity still remained, but now it was Rome that took up the challenge. By the middle of the second century B.C. Rome stood alone in the Mediterranean world. The Seleucid empire, the Ptolemaic empire, the kingdom of Macedon, and the Carthaginian empire had either been greatly weakened, broken up, or liquidated entirely. By subduing the Hellenistic states, Rome created a universal state that eventually brought order to the Mediterranean world, but she could not reverse the process of breakdown that had begun with the Peloponnesian War. Because the Roman Empire was created by force and much too late, said Toynbee, it could not redeem the afflicted Hellenic society. *Pax Romana* was only a temporary reprieve; coming too late and achieved after years of exhaustive warfare, *Pax Romana* was only a long rally, a peace of exhaustion, uncreative and impermanent, that could not halt the breakdown of Hellenism.

During *Pax Romana* the Hellenic world was no longer convulsed by war and revolution but it was not spiritually rejuvenated. The new cults that prevailed -- deification of the emperor and idolization of the Roman world-state -- were artificial and dull, unable to fill the vacuum left in human hearts that was caused by the decay of the worship of the city-states. The cults of the goddess Rome and the god Caesar, asserted Toynbee, were spiritually bankrupt, and the city-states, no longer centers of bustling political life, had lost their charm and fallen from the ranks of idols.

The Roman world-state, said Toynbee, could not breathe new life into a dying Hellenism. In the process of imposing peace upon the Mediterranean world, Rome had deepened the spiritual vacuum in human souls. While life was more secure, it was also duller, for there existed no ideal that could replace the lost devotion to the polis. The Roman Empire, too vast and impersonal, could not generate the same devotion that had once been extended to the city-state. Nor could the schools of philosophy stir the heart.

CHRISTIANITY

Into this spiritual vacuum, stepped Christianity whose strength, declared Toynbee, lay in its power to restore to Hellenic life some of the significance and enthusiasm that it had lost, and to provide an ideal of human brotherhood that could overcome cultural differences. Christianity offered man communion with a superhuman God of immense stature. Again man had a cause to which he could dedicate himself. The internal proletariat, resentful, alienated, and disinherited, seceded from the old society that was breaking down and gave rise to a higher religion in which gentleness triumphed over violence. A higher religion, said Toynbee, arises within a society that is far along the path of disintegration. It is a response to the challenge posed by disintegration. The internal proletariat seceded from the old order and turned to Christianity, for it treated people with consideration and love; it took care of orphans, widows, the sick, and the aged, and offered an ideal of human fraternity that drew no distinction between Italian, Greek, or Jew, between slave or freeman, between male or female, between rich or poor. As institutions of the disintegrating Roman

Empire atrophied, the Church became the most vital force in the Hellenic world. The old Roman dominant minority no longer possessed the creativity to lead and to inspire growth. From the ranks of the internal proletariat there emerged a new creative minority to perform in the drama of challenge-and-response. This new creative minority attracted to itself the mimesis of the uncreative masses. While the old society stubbornly fought its losing battle for survival, a new civilization was germinating in its womb; Christianity articulated itself into a universal church which survived the disintegration and collapse of the old society and carried the embryo of a new civilization.

The internal proletariat was the chief beneficiary of the universal state, for it used the peace, capital cities, legal codes, common language, and roads to spread a higher faith. But it was also the external proletariat, barbarians from beyond the Empire's borders, that benefited from the world-state, for under the peaceful conditions imposed by the universal state, the dominant minority lost its zest for combat and the ranks of the army were filled with barbarian recruits. Eventually the barbarian external proletariat overran the decaying world-state.

Neither Christians nor barbarians destroyed the Roman Empire, said Toynbee; they merely walked over a corpse. Hellenism had died before Christianity had become the official religion of the Roman Empire and before the barbarians had founded their successor-states on former Roman territory. Hellenism's death was due to its own failure to respond to a challenge that had confronted it in the fifth century B.C. Hellenic society never recovered from this failure to achieve political unity through peaceful means. Rejecting Gibbon, Toynbee maintained that Hellenic civilization had ruined itself long before the appearance of Christianity. Churches are not cancers but chrysalides; they do not destroy civilizations but preserve them by keeping alive "a precious germ of life through the perilous interregnum between the dissolution of one mortal representative of the species and the genesis of another."[5]

In the interregnum between the collapse of Hellenic society and the emergence of Western society, the barbarians established a number of successor-states. Unlike the Church, said Toynbee, these successor-states were not a creative prelude to Western society but merely an epilogue to Hellenic history. The barbarian states were short-lived, their contribution to Western Civilization insignificant. Both Church and barbarians shared the same stage during the interregnum, but only the Church had an enduring influence on the shaping of Western Civilization. The barbarian achievement was limited to an Heroic Age distinguished by epic poetry; the Church, on the other hand, born of the old society, survived the interregnum to become the soul of the new society -- Western Civilization. Thus the collapse of Hellenism was no disaster for it prepared the way for a spiritual advance; it ministered to the birth of Christianity which for Toynbee is the true soul of the West.

In Toynbee's system, a universal religion emerges after a civilization has entered its decline and it attracts a suffering and embittered internal proletariat. In times of prosperity man remains deaf to the call of the spirit, but during times of stress are found bursts of spiritual activity. The Graeco-Roman world had subdued the orient militarily and offered to orientals a secular way of life in which philosophy would take religion's place. This elevation of the intellect above the heart was not enough either for orientals or for Greeks and Romans themselves. In the form of Christianity the oriental world waged a counter-offensive. Christianity remained at war with the most formidable version of Hellenic man-worship, the worship of the world-state of Rome and its human emperor. "This question whether Man in one or other of his less ungodlike forms is God, or whether the True God is to be found neither in man nor in Non-Human Nature, was, and still is, one of the great issues confronting human souls."[6]

In the late Roman Empire, when classical

43

values were in decay, Christianity was a dynamic and creative movement. As the institutions of the disintegrating Roman Empire atrophied, the Church became the most vital force in the Graeco-Roman world. After the disintegration of Hellenic society the Church became the source for unity in the emerging Western Civilization. It became the integrating force of the medieval West. The creation of *Respublica Christiana*, declared Toynbee, marked an enormous spiritual advance over Hellenism. Its aim was to replace violence with a reign of spiritual authority and it demonstrated the immense power that religion exercises over human hearts, for devotion to the spiritual church exceeded the loyalty once given to a temporal Roman Empire.

The Christian Middle Ages were very dear to Toynbee. To him the "medieval Western Christian way of life still looks like one of Mankind's rare achievements."[7] The medieval genius lay in shaping a creative balance between papal authority and the secular requirements of princes and city-states, and between theological authority and Aristotelian philosophy and science.

In his earlier volumes, Toynbee regarded churches as links between a dying and an emerging civilization, i.e. Graeco-Roman civilization and medieval civilization. In his later volumes, Toynbee accorded churches a far higher status. Because they embody a higher religion, churches are on a spiritually, higher level than a civilization. Consequently, the breakdown of a civilization is no cataclysm at all if it ministers to the birth of a church, for this is the *raison d'être* of a civilization. A true catastrophe would be the birth of a civilization that emerges from a previously established church.

The emergence of a Christian society in the Middle Ages was a spiritual advance over the Hellenic world, and our current "post-Christian secular civilization might at best be a superfluous repetition of the pre-Christian Graeco-Roman one, and at worst a pernicious back-sliding from the path of spiritual progress."[8] Therefore we should

44

no longer regard our secular civilization as progress, and worthy of our admiration; rather, if we
were to think of it

> as one of the vain repetitions of
> the Gentiles -- an almost meaning-
> less repetition of something that
> the Greeks and Romans did before us
> and did supremely well -- then the
> greatest new event in the history
> of mankind will be seen to be a
> very different one. The greatest
> new event will then not be the
> monotonous rise of yet another sec-
> ular civilization out of the bosom
> of the Christian Church in the
> course of these latter centuries;
> it will still be the Crucifixion
> and its spiritual consequences.[9]

THE LIMITATIONS OF SECULAR HUMANISM

Toynbee's conception of the Hellenic and
Christian traditions is crucial to his understanding of the nature, meaning, and destiny of Western
Civilization. Toynbee, of course, was aware of the
immense achievement of the Greeks, but what impressed him more were the limitations of classical
civilization. For Toynbee, reason was not man's
finest achievement and freedom derived from a non-
spiritual source was tenuous. The history of Hellenism teaches what modern Westerners have forgotten or dismissed -- a secular and rational outlook
cannot hold society together or restrain man's
basest impulses. Unless he is guided by prophetic
values, man will deify his state or his leaders, an
act that unleashes the worst elements of human nature and causes civilization to break down. The
root cause of Hellenism's failure, Toynbee held,
was the deification of a human institution -- the
city-state and the Roman Empire -- and the deification of a human being -- a Macedonian king and a
Roman emperor. By idolizing man in place of God,
the Greeks and Romans ruined themselves.

Toynbee's dissatisfaction with Greek humanism was at the core of his critique of the modern West which he viewed as a depressing revival of Hellenic secularism and a repudiation of Christiantity, for him the true essence of Western Civilization. Toynbee maintained that since the Renaissance the West has revived the very practice that was at the root cause of Hellenism's ruin -- the deification of the state. Modern nationalism, he insisted, is the modern form of city-state worship; if it is not eradicated the modern world will suffer the same fate as Hellenism.

TOYNBEE AND THE TWO TRADITIONS

Christianity and classical humanism are the principal components of the Western tradition, but they represent two essentially different world-views. The triumph of the Christian outlook signi-fied a break with the essential meaning of classi-cism; it pointed to the end of the world of antiq-uity and the beginning of an age of faith, the Middle Ages. With the victory of Christianity the ultimate goal of life shifted away from achieving excellence in this world through the full and crea-tive development of human talent toward attaining salvation in a heavenly city.

Classicism held that there was no authority higher than human reason; Christianity taught that without God as the starting point knowledge is formless, purposeless, and error-prone. Classicism held that ethical standards were laws of nature discoverable by reason. Reason would instruct in-dividuals about what was best for them; it would enable them to govern desires and will, so that they might order their lives properly; it would show them where their behavior was wrong and teach them how to correct it. Because individuals sought what was best for themselves, they would obey the voice of reason. Christianity, on the other hand, main-tained that ethical standards emanated from the personal will of God. Without obedience to God's will men and women will remain forever sinful; only when they turn to God for forgiveness would they find the inner strength to overcome their sinful nature. Christianity contended that people cannot perfect themselves through scientific knowledge; it is spiritual insight and belief in God that they require and that must serve as the first principle of their lives.

It was the Christian outlook that pervaded Toynbee's philosophy of history. Man by himself cannot control his own nature or resolve the problems of the community; to be effective reason must be guided by Christian values. Toynbee considered philosophy an inadequate substitute for a higher religion and philosophers lesser figures than saints. He regarded the moral autonomy and self-sufficiency sought by Stoics and Epicureans as a largely selfish aim which forced them to neglect two emotions -- love and pity -- that are most vital for man's social existence and are the highest feelings that humans are capable of expressing. For this reason, Toynbee viewed Stoic and Epicurean sages as inferior to St. Francis. The whole-hearted feeling of love for a fellow human being can stem only from religious inspiration and not from the intellectualism of philosophy. Moreover, taught by an intellectual elite "in the scientific language of the Intellect and not in the poetic language of the Heart,"[10] philosophy cannot stir ordinary people. By itself the philosophic and scientific tradition that began in ancient Greece cannot rescue the modern West, which shows symptoms of decline. Not the humanist tradition that began in Greece but Christian spirituality was for Toynbee the most precious ingredient of Western Civilization.

But Toynbee did not reject reason. Like some of the Church Fathers and medieval scholastics, Toynbee, the student of Hellenism, was respectful of the rational tradition. Like Aquinas, who sought to synthesize Greek philosophy and Christian belief, Toynbee struggled to harmonize the spiritual values of higher religions with the requirements of the modern age. But unlike Thomas, Toynbee was a pluralist who held that all the higher religions are partial revelations of God's truth.

NOTES

1. W. H. Auden, ed. *The Portable Greek Reader* (New York: Viking, 1952), p. 38.

2. Arnold J. Toynbee, *Hellenism: The History of a Civilization* (New York: Oxford University Press, 1959), p. 10.

3. *Ibid.*

4. *Study*, one-volume edition, p. 171.

5. *Study*, 7b: 392.

6. Arnold J. Toynbee, *An Historian's Approach to Religion* (New York: Oxford University Press, 1956), p. 97.

7. *Ibid.*, p. 169.

8. *Civilization on Trial*, p. 207.

9. *Ibid.*, p. 208.

10. *An Historian's Approach to Religion*, p. 75.

CHAPTER FOUR

TRANSITION TO THE MODERN AGE

The centuries from the Renaissance through the Enlightenment saw the shattering of the medieval view of nature, society, and man and the emergence of the modern mentality. European thought moved away from the medieval division of the universe into a higher realm of perfection, the source of values, and a lower realm of corruption inhabited by man. From Copernicus to Newton there gradually emerged a universe whose laws the mind could grasp and explain in mathematical equations. To the philosophes nature was completely autonomous, neither requiring nor recognizing support or intervention from any higher source. Like nature, the intellect too was self-sufficient; it depended upon no transcendent realm, upon no power beyond itself in order to comprehend the natural world. What the mind did for nature it could do for society -- through reason alone uncover those general laws that govern the social world. Through its own powers the mind could interpret nature and society; it needed no divine assistance; it accepted no authority above reason; it insisted upon proof according to standards set by science. The monopoly of intellectual life by churchmen was ended and science became the great hope of the future. Rejecting the Christian concept that evil was intrinsic to human personality -- a consequence of the defiance of God by Adam and Eve -- the philosophes held that man was basically good and that evil resulted from faulty institutions, poor education, and bad leadership.

The shaping of the modern outlook from the Renaissance through the Enlightenment has been regarded as one of the great episodes in the history of mankind. But not by Toynbee. He lamented the decline of Christianity and the upsurge of secularism and regarded the modern West as a vain repetition of Hellenism. For him Christianity was more than a link between two secular civilizations, a parent Hellenic civilization and a daughter Western

Civilization. Higher religions are not just by-products of a disintegrating civilization or merely one element among many cultural components of a civilization but new departures. They belong to a distinctive species that is superior to a secular civilization. According to this view there can be no greater catastrophe than the withering of a higher religion.

THE BREAKDOWN OF THE MEDIEVAL WORLD

Toynbee, we have seen, admired the Middle Ages because it held the promise of a Christendom united by spiritual ideals. Such a society, he said, could have dealt creatively with war and politics, two traditions of Western Civilization that did not originate with Christianity but derived from ancient Greece, Rome, and the Germanic warriors. However, to succeed in unifying the West under a Christian banner, the medieval Church would have had to eschew force and remain dedicated to the ideal of God as love. It would have had to demonstrate the spiritual power of a St. Francis, "the greatest soul that has yet appeared in our Western World."[1]

The papacy had acted creatively, stated Toynbee, when it gave unity to a world burdened by feudal anarchy, when it substituted spiritual authority for physical force. But then the papacy soiled its spiritual mission by using force against its opponents; it set "upon a course which was to end in the victory of ... [its] adversaries the World, the Flesh, and the Devil over the City of God which ... [it] was seeking to bring down to Earth."[2] The tragedy began with Hildebrand, who, in seeking to rescue the Church from sexual and financial corruption, was drawn into the arena of power politics in which force was utilized for spiritual ends. This was a dangerous game. Intoxicated by the successful use of force, said Toynbee, the papacy carried it to extremes causing its own spiritual degeneration. The conflict with the Holy Roman Emperor eventually caused the papacy to lose its moral leadership and the devotion hitherto granted to a universal Church was transferred to emerging

50

secular states with disastrous consequences for the future of the West.

> ...this spiritual heritage from the Hildebrandine Church is the element in the constitution of our modern parochial states which has turned these once harmless and useful institutions into a grave menace to the welfare of our civilization. For the spirit of devotion which was a beneficient creative power in Western Christendom when it was directed through the gates of a *Civitas Dei* towards God himself, has degenerated into a maleficent destructive force in the process of being diverted from its original divine object and being offered instead to an idol made by human hands. Parochial states, as our medieval forebears knew, are man-made institutions, useful and even necessary in their place, which deserve from us that conscientious but unenthusiastic performance of a minor social duty which we render, in our time, to our municipalities and county councils. To idolize these pieces of social machinery, which have nothing divine about them, is to court a spiritual disaster; and this is the disaster towards which our modern Western World is heading today as an ultimate consequence of the spiritual spoilation of the Holy See by the secular principalities which were once kept in their place by the Papacy's moral authority.[3]

The establishment of *Respublica Christiana* would have fulfilled the mission of the Church; its miscarriage was "the most tragic of all the disasters that the Western Society has brought upon itself so far."[4]

The Renaissance contributed to the undermining of Christendom, for it revived not only Hellenic art and literary forms but also the Greeks' fierce devotion to their city-states. Modern man has remained infatuated with the Greeks and Romans, declared Toynbee, because the ancients taught him how to infuse citizens with patriotic fervor, organize armies, and build a powerful state. This deification of the parochial community was imitated by the citizens of Florence, Milan, Genoa, and the other Italian cities, who allowed loyalty to their local city to predominate over allegiance to *Respublica Christiana*. Machiavelli gave intellectual expression and moral approval to this new outlook. From Machievelli, said Toynbee, was derived the principle that the state was not subject to a transcendent moral law in its dealings with other states. In absorbing and surpassing Hellenic parochialism, the modern West has behaved according to the Machiavellian precept that the state is a non-moral institution. The revival of Hellenism, said Toynbee, ministered to Western man's "insatiable lust for power which was the inevitable ruling passion in hearts that had relapsed from Christianity into a pagan worship of a Collective Humanity," and he pushed "this resucitated political ideology of Hellenism to extremes that had never been approached by the Hellenes themselves in their self-immolation on the altar of an idolized Leviathan."[5] In elevating the state over Christian morality and universalism, the West expressed a defiance of its Christian heritage, conveniently forgetting that this parochialism was the chief cause of Hellenic civilization's downfall. And the same fate will befall the contemporary world, insisted Toynbee, if it fails to "exorcize this demon resolutely."[6]

Another shock to medieval Christendom was the Protestant Reformation which destroyed Europe's religious unity, strengthened the power of secular rulers, and ushered in the brutal Wars of Religion. In these conflicts, religion became a "tool for the furtherance of mundane military and political purposes ... a consequence of Religion's own unprincipaled attempt to use War and Politics as weapons in ecclesiastical struggles for supremacy."[7] Repelled by the violence and fanaticism of the Wars of Religion, seventeenth-century thinkers transferred their intellectual energies from a polemical theology to natural science.

The outbursts of violence and fanaticism during the Wars of Religion, declared Toynbee, alienated many Westerners from their ancestral religion and the new discoveries in science, which seemed incompatible with traditional dogma, intensified this estrangement. The Christian churches that had blundered morally during the Wars of Religion also discredited themselves intellectually by stubbornly retaining a Ptolemaic and Aristotelian science as if this natural philosophy was truly vital to Christian revelation.

The transference of interest away from theology to science was a revolutionary act, said Toynbee. The West would now push religion to the background and concentrate instead on science and technology. In the Middle Ages the inspired saint was the ideal; in the modern age the technician replaced the saint as Western man's ideal and the progressive conquest of physical nature became the overriding concern. As technology moved from triumph to triumph it came to be admired as a magic key that would unlock the door to an earthly paradise. Few recognized that science and technology, unrestrained by religious values, would pose enormous problems for the modern West.

The state system, nationalism, and technology, principal components of modern civilization, have made warfare more brutal than ever. With the breakup of the religious unity of Western Christendom in the sixteenth century, said Toynbee, war became infused with a sectarian religious fanaticism that magnified its evilness. But by the eighteenth century there had been achieved a divorce between war and religion, the immediate effect of which was to reduce the intensity of warfare to the lowest level ever attained in Western history. Warfare in the eighteenth century was relatively civilized -- "temperate and moderate," said Gibbon. Wars were waged for limited aims, casualty rates were low,

and the civilian population remained uninvolved.
The ferocity and mass emotions that had characterized the Wars of Religion had ended as warfare had
been transformed into the "sport of kings," a game
played for limited stakes and devoid of passion.
Armies were not recruited by conscription and they
did not live off the countryside; peace terms were
not crushing and countries were not wiped off the
map. Princes were forced to wage moderate warfare
for there existed no great passion that could rally
the nation to a total effort. In the eighteenth
century many people regarded war in much the same
manner as slavery -- an ancient curse that was
rapidly dissipating.

But, said Toynbee, the limited warfare of the
eighteenth century turned out to be only a brief
interlude between two bouts of fanaticism, the
earlier Wars of Religion and the later Wars of
Nationality. Once the people had become a "nation
in arms" fighting for national survival, warfare
could no longer remain temperate and undecisive.
During the French Revolution war became an ideological struggle and the flames of hatred fanned
by mass emotions could not be extinguished by the
rational and universal spirit of the philosophes.
The Wars of Nationality, reaching full fury in the
twentieth century, would outdo in fanaticism the
Wars of Religion.

THE FAILURE OF THE MODERN WEST

In Toynbee's structuring of Western history
the emergence of a modern secular civilization out
of the womb of *Respublica Christiana* was a "mon-
strous birth" that marked the beginning of the crisis of the West. A secularized modern Western Civilization, asserted Toynbee, has not transformed
human nature with its inherent capacity for wickedness. Indeed, modern technology and administrative
procedures have heightened man's criminal potential.
The crimes and failures of the modern West compel
us to be less complacent and enthusiastic about
secularism. Was it a mark of progress that the West
articulated itself into warring national states?
Did not the break with Christianity take the West

down a path that led to total war, genocide, totalitarianism, and nuclear weapons? Did not the rise of totalitarianism show that liberty loses its hold over men's hearts when it is divested of its religious foundation? Has a secularized Western Civilization succeeded in overcoming the two evils that have been the ruin of other civilizations -- warfare and class conflict? Have not profit obsessed Westerners ravished nature and exploited the world's poor? Has Western man's conquest of physical nature enabled him to overcome the spiritual and moral problems of dealing with himself, others, and God?

For Toynbee, Christianity, not Greek humanism or modern liberalism, is the essence of Western Civilization. The West's enduring achievement, he insisted, is not its science but its religion, Christianity, which "will continue to be a living spiritual force for thousands of years after our Western Civilization has passed away."[8] Consequently, the great act of treason committed by Western intellectuals was not the loss of confidence in the values of the Enlightenment, so evident in the twentieth century, but the earlier repudiatinn of the Christian essence of Western Civilization. This effort to "shift the rising edifice of our Western Christian Civilization from a religious to a secular basis ... was the original act of *hybris* which is being requited in our day by an *âtê* that has been accumulating for centuries at compound interest."[9]

NOTES

1. Arnold J. Toynbee, *Christianity Among the Religions of the World* (New York: Charles Scribner's Sons, 1957), p. 73.

2. *Study*, 4: 538.

3. *Ibid.*, p. 543.

4. *An Historian's Approach to Religion*, p. 117.

5. *Study*, 9: 3.

6. *Hellenism*, p. 253.

7. *An Historian's Approach to Religion*, pp. 171-72.

8. *Christianity Among the Religions of the World*, p. 63.

9. *Study*, 5: 411.

PROBLEMS OF THE MODERN WEST:
IDEOLOGIES AND TECHNOLOGY

Consistent with his philosophy of history, Toynbee viewed the problems of the modern West in religious terms. The modern West, he said, has become a post-Christian civilization in which the loyalty once given to Christianity has been transferred to ideologies. The three post-Chrisitan ideologies -- liberalism, communism, nationalism -- are all substitute religions that are in competition with Christian values. Liberalism, said Toynbee, has absorbed the Christian precept of respect for the individual, and communism has adopted the Christian ideal of social justice, but both have broken with the Christian roots of these ideals. A secularized version of social justice and individual liberty is intrinsically inadequate, declared Toynbee. The most pernicious of the ideologies for Toynbee is nationalism, which he regarded as a reversion to the deification of the local community as practiced in the city-states of Sumeria and Greece. Toynbee considered the essential question of our age to be whether the world's higher religions can regain the ground lost to ideologies.

LIBERALISM

The immediate historical roots of liberalism extend back to seventeenth century England, the Enlightenment, and the American and French Revolutions. The struggle for religious toleration by English Protestant dissenters established the principle of freedom of conscience, which is easily transferred into freedom of opinion and expression in all matters. The Glorious Revolution of 1688 set limits on the power of the English monarch and the natural-rights philosophy of John Locke declared that the individual was by nature entitled to freedom and justified revolutions against rulers who deprived citizens of their lives, liberty, or property. From Montesquieu, liberals derived the theory of the separation of powers and checks and balances that sought to guard against autocratic government. The philosophes had supported religious toleration and freedom of thought, expressed confidence in the capacity of the human mind to reform society, maintained that human beings are essentially good, and believed in the future progress of humanity -- all fundamental principles of liberalism.

The American and French revolutions were crucial phases in the history of liberalism. The Declaration of Independence gave expression to Locke's theory of natural rights; the Constitution of the United States incorporated Montesquieu's principles and demonstrated that people could create an effective government; the Bill of Rights protected the person and rights of the individual. In destroying the special privileges of the aristocracy and opening careers to talent, the French National Assembly of 1789 implemented the liberal ideal of equality under the law. It also drew up the Declaration of the Rights of Man and Citizen, which affirmed the dignity and rights of the individual, and a constitution that limited the king's power. Both the American and French revolutions explicitly called for the protection of property rights, another basic consideration of liberals.

In the long view of Western Civilization, liberalism is also an extension and development of the democratic practices and rational outlook that originated in ancient Greece and the value given to the individual by the Judaeo-Christian tradition. Christianity proclaimed the natural equality and inviolable worth of all humans; it insisted that rulers are God's stewards who must exercise their power for the common good; it taught the overriding value of love and charity and it instilled in man a thirst for justice; it held that man was responsible for his actions and must answer for them to God. All this flowed into the liberal-democratic tradition. However, liberals, identifying Christianity with the Old Regime, came to reject the Christian tradition as a barrier to political liberty and social progress. Toynbee called for a reconciliation of Christianity and liberal-democracy.

Toynbee valued the liberal tradition. He favored protection of individual rights, the rule of law, constitutional government, toleration, and social justice, and he respected the tradition of reason. But the liberal tradition, he said, cannot be a substitute for Christianity and cannot survive without retaining its link to the spirit of the Gospels. Divorced from Christianity, liberalism degenerates into selfish competiveness. Nor can a self-sufficient liberalism preserve individual liberty or compete successfully with totalitarian ideologies. To be effective, liberalism must be infused with spiritual values.

Like nineteenth-century conservatives, Toynbee held that the liberal stress on self-interest reduces society to a collection of self-seeking and disconnected individuals whose ighest ideal is profit. Also like nineteenth-century conservatives, Toynbee rejected the liberal view that evil is a product of a faulty environment and restated the Christian view of man's inherent sinfulness.

The tradition of reason, a crucial component of liberalism, gives man command over nature, said Toynbee, but this is much less significant than man's relations with himself, with his fellow men, and with God. Theoretical reason enables man to formulate rules that give unity to the phenomenal world; it does not enable him to enter into communion with the spiritual presence behind the universe or to recognize the Thou of his neighbor.

The liberal conception of personal liberty also suffers from an inherent weakness, insisted Toynbee. The idea of individual liberty originated in the Christian belief of the sacredness of the individual soul. However, liberalism removed the religious sanction from the ideal of individual rights. In separating freedom from its Christian context, liberalism could not fulfill its promised aim of promoting individual liberty. Conceived purely in secular terms the liberal ideal of liberty is powerless to contain human wickedness. Nor could liberalism capture men's souls the way Christianity had; with enlightened self-interest as its leitmotif liberalism was an uninspiring doctrine that could not compete with the totalitarian ideologies. Both communism and fascism offered a spiritually starved Western society an outlet for idealism that had once been channeled into Christianity. To this extent they resembled the theistic religions.

> The common gospel of Communism and Fascism was that, after a spell of unfruitful and ignoble sloth, Man was now at last waking up again to his true nature, which was to live dangerously for mighty ends that transcended the life of the individual. And a convert to this post-war pagan faith might perhaps persuade himself that the stirring times which had sunk into torpor towards the close of the seventeenth century ... were now returning, and that the new 'ideologies' which were the harbingers of this inspiring revolution in human affairs were destined to carry all before them.[1]

If Western liberalism is to maintain itself against the onslaught of totalitarian ideologies, declared Toynbee, freedom must mean more than just secular civil liberty; man must again feel with conviction the original meaning of liberty in the West -- respect for the individual because he has been ennobled by God.

COMMUNISM

An even more formidable ideological derivation from Christianity, said Toynbee, is communism. While Marxists may repudiate religion in general, and Christianity in particular, said Toynbee, their faith could have emerged only in a Christian setting. Marxism began as a Western Christian heresy that attacked a professedly Christian society for not adhering to the ideals of social justice proclaimed by early Christianity.

From Judaism, declared Toynbee, Marxism derived the apocalyptic vision of an inevitable and
irresistible revolution decreed by God himself and
designed to carry the Chosen People from its low
position to an exalted one. Post-Exilic Jews
dreamed of establishing through force and with
God's approval a great worldly kingdom that would
unite all Jews driven into exile. "Marx has taken
the Goddess 'Historical Necessity' in place of Yah-
weh for his omnipotent deity, and the internal proletariat of the modern World in place of Jewry; and
his Messianic Kingdom is conceived as a Dictatorship of the Proletariat."[2] Both Post-Exilic Judaism and Marxism conceived their messianic kingdom
as a material kingdom of this world; both expected
it to be achieved through violence. While the communists have dispensed with the belief in God they
have retained the Judaic belief of the Chosen
People, viewing the proletariat as the chosen class.
Perhaps this predestinarian aspect of communism can
be better understood, said Toynbee, by comparing it
with Calvinism, another predestinarian sect. Marxism supplied the proletariat of the nineteenth century with the same weapon that Calvinism supplied
the bourgeosie of the sixteenth century. The doctrine of historical materialism gave the proletariat confidence that they were favored by the forces
of the universe in the same manner that the doctrine of predestination gave assurance to the Cal-
vinist bourgeosie that they were the Elect.

Another Christian element in Marxism, declared
Toynbee, is a universalism that has led Marxists,
like Christians, to become missionaries of a
"Church Militant." "'Go ye into all the world and
preach the Gospel to every creature,' is an injunc-
tion which Marx feels to be laid upon himself and
which he lays in turn upon his followers. ... It is
not merely a revolution but a world revolution that
the good Marxian is in duty bound to strive for."[3]
Having dwelled in a Western society, Marx and En-
gels acquired the Christian precept, which they
never questioned, of converting others so that all
might be saved.

In addition to universalism and social justice, said Toynbee, communism has absorbed an unfortunate element of the Judaeo-Christian tradition -- fanaticism. In their conviction of the rightness of their cause, communists "had raised the emotional temperature of a political 'ideology' to a religious heat."[4] In becoming as fanatic as Christian zealots in the Wars of Religion, Bolsheviks displayed some of the worst qualities of human nature and soiled what had been a legitimate struggle for social justice. The Bolsheviks also acquired from Christianity (and from Russian tradition) an authoritarianism that dealt ruthlessly with deviation from orthodoxy. Whereas during the seventeenth century the West had revolted against the passive acceptance of authority, the authoritarian component in the Christian tradition had not eroded in the East, with the result that "a nineteenth-century Russian revolutionary who had rejected the tenets of Eastern Orthodox Christianity might not have shaken off the Christian tradition of authoritarianism."[5]

Communism's appeal, Toynbee believed, has stemmed from its religious nature. It fulfilled a spiritual need created by a declining Christianity; it appealed to man's idealism by giving him a noble cause to which he could dedicate body and soul.

> Man is spiritually frustrated if he
> cannot invest his petty transient
> personal life without abiding spiri-
> tual significance by devoting it to
> some cause that manifestly transcends
> it in spiritual value; and Communism
> proferred to Man an objective that
> might seem worthier than any that had
> been visible on his mental horizon
> since the latter-day eclipse of Chris-
> tianity. Communism called upon post-
> Christian Man to cure himself of a
> childish nostalgia for a justly dis-
> credited otherworldly Utopia by
> transferring his allegiance from a
> non-existent God to a very present
> Human Race to whose service he could

> devote all his adult powers by working
> for the attainment of an Earthly Para-
> dise.[6]

While both the reformist and universal features of
Marxism are rooted in Christianity, Marxism has
dispensed with a crucial Christian element. Early
Christian socialism, said Toynbee, taught that a
Christian's concern for another's welfare that
leads him to share his worldly goods, "is not a
mere love of Man for Man ... but is a spiritual relation to which God is a party as well as his human
creature."[7] Marx took a Christian principle and
applied it exclusively to the material plane of
life while he denied or ignored Christianity's
spiritual message. Consequently, communism, in contrast to Christianity, cares nothing for the individual human person, his dignity and his need for
spiritual consolation and uplifting. Because it
has dispensed with Christian spiritual values, communism cannot overcome differences between classes,
nations, and races and unify mankind.

NATIONALISM

For Toynbee, liberalism and socialism can be
integrated into the Christian tradition; nationalism cannot. Toynbee defined nationalism as a
"spirit which makes people feel and act and think
about a part of any given society as though it were
the whole of that society."[8] Because nationalism
induces man to deify his community, stated Toynbee,
it is a primitive form of religion. Nationalism
thwarts the vision of the unity of mankind held by
the prophets of all higher religions. Whereas a
higher religion emancipates man from his innate
self-centeredness, nationalism intensifies the brutal and selfish side of human nature. By provoking
fraticidal warfare amongst people that share a common civilization, nationalism hampers social progress. After studying all of man's civilizations
beginning with ancient Sumeria, Toynbee concluded
that nationalism has been responsible for "the
death of no less than fourteen civilizations for
certain, and perhaps of no less than sixteen, out
of the twenty-one civilizations that had come into

63

existence."[9] Although the spiritual message of
higher religions is infinitely superior to the
nationalist vision, higher religions have not been
able to break nationalism's power or appeal.

In Toynbee's spacious approach to history, nationalism exercises a powerful attraction because
it perpetuates age-old feelings inherited from a
hunting and food-gathering past when men lived in
small separated bands and acquired a tribal sense
of "insiders" and "outsiders." Since the food-
gathering stage constitutes ninety-nine percent of
human history, this tribal attitude toward outsiders became a deeply ingrained habit. The feelings that separated tribes and later villages endured with the creation of man's first civilizations. Impressed with his sensational victory over
nature that enabled him to build cities, man deified his own political community. The gods that
had previously represented the forces of nature now
came to represent also cities and states. The
wind-god Nanna became the god of the city-state
of Ur as later the olive-goddess Athena would become the deity of the city-state of Athens. An
element of religious devotion became injected into
a person's feelings for his city. Thus in ancient
times there already existed a relationship between
nationalism and religion and a potential for fanaticism. Deification of the parochial community,
raised the psychological temperature of city-state
warfare, a pattern that would be reproduced in
other civilizations and with a similar result --
breakdown and disintegration.

Modern nationalism, said Toynbee, sprouted on
soil fertilized by the wreckage of Latin Christendom during the era of the Renaissance and Reformation. The Renaissance's revival of classical culture, one of whose elements was a fierce devotion
to the city-state, raised nationalism to a new
pitch of intensity. The modern West, declared
Toynbee has admired not only the art and literature of Greece and Rome, but also their political
and military accomplishments. The Greeks and
Romans expressed a fierce loyalty to their community, organized effective armies, and engaged in

wars of conquest. In the fashion of the ancient Greek poleis, the citizens of Renaissance Italian city-states glorified the parochial community, thereby undermining loyalty to *Respublica Christiana*.

In addition to Hellenic parochialism, said Toynbee, modern nationalism has been aggravated by Christian fanaticism. While the nationalist has repudiated the Christian concern for mankind and its ideal of love, he has been driven by a fanaticism even worse than that demonstrated by Christians during the Wars of Religion. Convinced that they were in possession of the true faith, religious fanatics during the Wars of Religion sought to impose spiritual unity by force; regarding the nation as the highest good, nationalist fanatics have sought to impose national unity by persecuting minorities and regimenting the population. Nationalism transformed the human community into a god, warfare into a holy crusade, opponents into heretics, and citizens into true believers. That man has been willing to sacrifice himself for this modern cult is an indication that nationalism "was in truth a religious revival in the spiritual vacuum left in human hearts by the evaporation of a higher religion."[10]

Democracy is still another force that has increased the intensity of modern nationalism. At first glance, observed Toynbee, it appears that democracy represents universalism, not parochialism, the rights of man, not the special destiny of a people. But the parochial state has turned democracy into an agent of nationalism, thereby poisoning the political life of the modern world. The democratic state can mobilize all its human and material resources to wage total war. It can use all the instruments of propaganda to arouse the population to a total effort. Democracy has restored to warfare the ferocity of the Wars of Religion. It has transformed the "sport of kings" into *la guerre totale*.

Another force that has contributed to nationalism's "demonic dynamism," stated Toynbee, is industrialism. Like democracy, industrialism is universal in spirit, for it "will not work freely or effectively or beneficently except in so far as the World is organized into one single field of economic activity."[11] But when industrialism made its appearance, the Western world was already broken up into a multitude of petty political-economic units that erected barriers to economic integration. Entangled in the web of parochial states, industrialism, like democracy, has been unable to fulfill its essential nature. Instead of building a world order, industrialism, like democracy, has fortified the parochial state which seeks to promote its own economic interests at the expense of the rest of humanity.

The parochial-minded national state, created in a different social context, was not prepared to cope with the ecumenical forces of democracy and industrialism. The attempt to confine these new and dynamic forces within the framework of the national state, concluded Toynbee, resulted in the totalitarian state. Only a modification of parochial sovereignty could have dealt creatively with industrialism and democracy; perverted by their imprisonment within the national state, these two universal forces contributed to the power of totalitarian nationalism.

The dangerous tendencies in modern Western nationalism culminated in National Socialism which was a repudiation of "the moral and religious essence of ... Western Christian culture."[12] In rejecting Christianity for their human god, Hitler, and his goddess, the German state, declared Toynbee, the German people had adopted a neo-pagan religion. Toynbee believed that Nazism was not a peculiarly German phenomenon but a German expression of the crisis in Western Civilization -- the rejection of Christianity and the return to a primitive religion. The decline of Christianity had created a discomforting spiritual vacuum which was filled by post-Christian ideologies, of which nationalism was the most powerful, and Nazism its most malignant expression. The essential reason why Nazism won over the youth with astonishing ease, Toynbee believed, was not force or propaganda but latent idealism searching for a cause. German youth, no longer nurtured in Christian virtues and morality, embraced the cult of the state, the cult of the leader, the cult of the party, the cult of the race, and the cult of war. The spiritual vacuum that emerged with the decline of religion could not be filled by liberalism, for its stress upon self-interest, utilitarianism, and commercialism could not stir the spirit. To many people National Socialism was a new and inspiring faith.

The experience of National Socialism contains lessons for the West in particular and mankind in general, concluded Toynbee. The Nazi era demonstrated anew the precariousness of civilization and the immutability of human evil. A Germany disillusioned with Western Civilization was retreating into the darkness of the primeval forest where the German tribes had originated. The conversion of the barbarians to civilization had not rooted out barbarism from the Western midst; in the form of National Socialism barbarism "was taking its revenge by finding its way into the souls of its Western conquerors."[13]

Nazism, said Toynbee, was not merely a German response to defeat in World War I. "It marked the consummation ... of a politico-religious movement, the pagan deification and worship of parochial human communities which had been gradually gaining ground for more than four centuries in the Western world at large."[14] That a Western people could fall so low indicates that the West had not risen so high, that it is continually menaced by a perverse barbarism that it harbors within its own breast. For Toynbee, Nazism represented "one phase of the struggle between the spirit of Western Christendom and the spirit of a European barbarism which Christianity had sometimes charmed and had thereby partly tamed, but had never wholly exorcised."[15]

The moral catastrophe of Nazism, insisted Toynbee, demonstrates the inadequacy of liberal humanism. The secular values of the Enlightenment, unbuttressed by Christian spirituality, are insufficient to restrain man's basest impulses. After the Nazi experience it has become impossible to retain a "belief in the inevitable progress of a secularized Western Civilization and in the self-perfectibility of a graceless Human Nature."[16]

While Nazism emerged within Europe among a people that had been Christians for more than a thousand years, it was as much a human problem as it was a purely German or Western one, for within human nature there lurks a vein of wickedness to which Hitlerism makes a strong appeal. The Nazi experience reinforced Toynbee's belief that civilizations are still experiments in which man has sought to rise above the level of the primitive and that these experiments often end in failure.

> The moral is that civilization is nowhere and never secure. It is a thin cake of custom overlying a molten mass of wickedness that is always boiling up for an opportunity to burst out. Civilization cannot ever be taken for granted. Its price is eternal vigilance and ceaseless spiritual efforts.[17]

Toynbee has contributed to our understanding of nationalism. He was correct in regarding nationalism as the dominant spiritual force in modern Western society and he correctly assessed the destructive capacities inherent in modern nationalism. In particular, he called attention to a crucial development in the evolution of modern nationalism. In the process of feeding off democracy, nationalism destroys democracy's essential ideals. Liberalism nurtured nationalism and contributed to its success, but the momentum of nationalism could not be contained by liberal principles.

In the early nineteenth century, liberals identified nationalism with liberty, holding that a unified state free of foreign subjugation was in harmony with the principle of natural rights. They believed that love of nation was commensurate with the universalism and cosmopolitanism of the philosophes. Men must be liberated not only from tyrants and priests but also from foreign oppression.

But as nationalism grew more extreme, it clashed with liberal ideals. In the pursuit of national power, nationalists embraced militarist, imperialist and racial doctrines and lapsed into mythical modes of thought. They rejected the liberal stress on political liberty as an obstacle to national power, supported authoritarian leadership, persecuted ethnic minorities, and denied the ideal of human equality. They elevated loyalty to the nation above all other allegiances and interpreted politics with the logic of emotions. By the beginning of the twentieth century, an intolerant, mythic, belligerent, and racist chauvinism threatened the liberal ideals of reason and freedom. In 1902, the German philosopher Friedrich Paulsen analyzed the danger:

> A supersensitive nationalism has become a very serious danger for all the peoples of Europe; because of it they are in danger of losing the feeling for human values. Nationalism, pushed to an extreme, just like sectarianism, destroys moral and even logical consciousness. Just and unjust, good and bad, true and false, lose their meaning; what men condemn as disgraceful and inhuman when done by others they recommend in the same breath to their own people as something to be done to a foreign country.[18]

By regarding National Socialism as a lower religion, Toynbee has also contributed to our understanding of twentieth-century mass movements. Nazism was in intent a deliberate rejection of the core values of the West. Hitler understood his world-historical role better than did his adversaries:

> To the Christian doctrine of the infinite significance of the individual human soul and of personal responsibility, I oppose with icy clarity the saving doctrine of the nothingness and insignificance of the individual

69

human being, and of his continued
existence in the visible immortal-
ity of the nation.
....
Providence has ordained that I
should be the greatest liberator
of humanity. I am freeing man from
the restraints of an intelligence
that has taken charge; from the
dirty and degrading self-mortifica-
tion of a chimera called conscience
and morality and from the demands
of a freedom and personal independence which only a very few could
bear.[19]

Hitler intuitively grasped the problem of the
West: Western man found the liberal-rational tradition life-denying and political freedom burden-
some. National Socialism was much more than a political movement; it was a new religion, a beguil-
ing mystique, a saving faith. The Nazis shaped a
world-view in which myth was the centerpiece of existence. Hitler glorified the will and intuition
over the intellect and dispensed with objective
truth; Goebbel's cynically manufactured myths that
disarmed the intellect and made the individual vulnerable to manipulation. In typical mythopoeic
fashion the Nazis described the world as a battleground between divine and demonic powers, between
light and darkness. The German super-race, defenders of civilization and goodness, required for its
opposite a demonic race of subhumans with limitless
power for evil and conspiracy. In 1947 SS Captain
Dieter Wisliceny, soon to be executed for war
crimes, astutely analyzed the meaning of Nazi anti-
Semitism. He described it

as a mystical and religious view
which sees the world as ruled by good
and bad powers. According to this
view the Jews represented the evil
principle. ... It is absolutely impossible to make any impression on
this outlook by means of logical or

rational argument, it is a sort of religiosity, and it impels people to form themselves into a sect. Under the influence of this literature millions of people believed these things -- an event which can only be compared with similar phenomena in the Middle Ages such as the witch-mania.

Against this world of evil the race-mystics set the world of good, of light, incarnated in blond, blue-eyed people, who were supposed to be the source of all capacity for creating civilization or building a state. Now these two worlds were alleged to be locked in a perpetual struggle, and the war of 1939, which Hitler unleashed, represented only the final battle between these two powers.

The usual view of Himmler is that he was an ice-cold, cynical politician. This view is certainly wrong. In his whole attitude Himmler was a mystic who embraced this world-view with religious fanaticism.[20]

Reason employed in the service of myth stripped man of his dignity and relegated him to the world of things. It created a laboratory world of soulless technocrats and dehumanized victims. It forged assembly lines for murder and fashioned an attitude of mind that killed without conscience.

In his political behavior, twentieth-century man has demonstrated those illusions, fantasies, and deep emotional longings that have characterized the myth-making mentality since the dawn of man. Myth is a style of apprehending and believing that reason has never fully subdued. Particularly in times of stress, men have abandoned rational thought with its taxing demands for rigorous logic and objective truth and have reverted to myths whose simple explanations and simple solutions alleviate the anxieties and doubts of tormented souls and provide the certainty that men crave. In the twentieth century, myths have taken a new form;

political myths are not just the free play of the imagination, but as Ernst Cassirer points out, "are artificial things fabricated by very skillful and cunning artists"[21] in order to bend people to their will and to rouse the nation to a great effort. Twentieth-century myths of the class, the race, the state, the leader, the party, are all expressions of a perennial irrationality in human behavior, of an elementary layer of human existence that *logos* will never obliterate. They remind us that civilized man is never far removed from the attitudes of primitive man. Concludes Cassirer:

> In politics we are always living on volcanic soil. We must be prepared for abrupt convulsions and eruptions. In all critical moments of man's social life, the rational forces that resist the rise of old mythical conceptions are no longer sure of themselves. In these moments the time for myth has come again. For myth has not really been vanquished and subjugated. It is always there, lurking in the dark and waiting for its hour and opportunity. This hour comes as soon as the other binding forces of man's social life, for one reason or another, lose their strength and are no longer able to combat the demonic mythical powers.[22]

Toynbee understood the dangers inherent in mythical thinking and recognized the limitations of reason in confronting these volcanic eruptions of the irrational.

TECHNOLOGY

For Toynbee, the spiritual vacuum created by the West's turning away from Christianity was filled by ideologies, the most dangerous of which was nationalism. Still another idol, technology, attracted a Western soul that had broken with its ancestral religion. Toynbee regarded the rerouting of the intellect away from a traditional concern with religion to the domination of physical nature as "a

72

testimony to the strength and to the repulsiveness of Original Sin;"[23] it was man again behaving as if he were the highest spiritual presence in the universe. And because human nature remains as sinful as ever, man has misused his technological power. In the past three centuries technology has created an artificial environment fraught with danger to the human spirit.

> Man has now decisively overcome Nature by his technology; but the victor has been technology, not Man himself. Man has merely exchanged one master for another, and his new master is more overbearing than his former one. Man is still the slave of his environment; but this is now the environment that he has created for himself, not the environment with which Nature originally endowed him. Nature used to chastize Man with whips; Man's own technology is now chastizing Man with scorpions.[24]

This new man-made environment, said Toynbee, is less appealing than the older one and is a principal cause for world-wide unrest and violence.

Man is finding it increasingly difficult to adjust to the rapid cultural transformation caused by the momentum of technology. The emotions of urban man have been shaped by more than two million years spent as a food gatherer and hunter, said Toynbee, but the intellect has failed to comprehend these emotional needs. The mounting gap between what our intellect conceives and what our heart is capable of absorbing is causing a psychic catastrophe; we are finding it very difficult to adjust to the rapid and revolutionary upheavals resulting from the explosion of science and technology. The cultural change demanded by this ferocious march of technology is causing mankind to reel.

Technology has enabled man to vanquish inanimate nature, but in doing so man has become a slave to his own creations, for the factory hand works at tasks that are inherently impersonal, monotonous, and infantile. The middle class, which in the twentieth century has been abandoning private entrepreneurship, its traditional field of endeavor, in favor of public service or employment in large corporations, has also felt the pernicious effects of the industrial system. This change from self-employment to working for giant impersonal agencies has altered the mentality of the middle class, for tending "the machinery of a highly organized state administering many millions of subjects was, indeed, as soul-destroying a task as stoking a furnace, minding a power-loom or performing a repetitive act of scientifically managed physical movements in an assembly plant."[25]

Urban industrial workers and office workers, unlike skilled artisans of the pre-industrial age, take no pride in their work, asserted Toynbee. Having lost their enthusiasm for work, they live only for salaries and for recreation. The psychic strain resulting from the daily monotony of factory and office also leads people to turn to violence for relief. Urban violence is one of the consequences of work that is psychologically unfulfilling. In engaging in anti-social destructive acts, the bored worker is unconsciously taking his revenge on society.

The monotony of work is only one cause of the psychological distress that marks our lives in mechanized cities. Pollution, noise, traffic jams, dirt, ugliness, and the separation from nature also contribute to our distress. We earn our livelihoods in the cities but seek to escape from them. We live in suburbs, vacation in what remains of the countryside, and spend our retirement in distant regions. We are alienated not only from the work we do but also from the cities in which we labor. In 1969, Toynbee suggested that perhaps we have fashioned a new type of warfare, which may in reality be the Third World War, "a war not between states or peoples, but between personality and technology." Underlying student riots, separatist movements, black militancy, and the unrest of the poor, stated Toynbee, "is the effacement of the human personality by the 'brave new world' that has been conjured into existence"[26] by the advance of science and technology. For Toynbee, the Third World War in which we are now presently engaged is a revolt against depersonalization, an expression of rage against a tyrant technology that turns a person into a thing.

The mechanized city of the industrial age has replaced the kind of city that had been familiar to man for 5,000 years, declared Toynbee. Until the outbreak of the Industrial Revolution cities occupied only a small part of earth's surface. Industrialization has altered this pattern. The size and number of cities have increased. Mechanized cities are coagulating into megalopolies which themselves are spreading out and approaching each other. The megalopolies of the world are beginning to coalesce to form a new type of city, an Ecumenopolis -- a world encompassing city broken up only by "surviving remnants of greenery." The new wilderness will not be forests but something more fearful -- "a continuum of streets and buildings." Without intelligent planning the coming Ecumenopolis threatens to become a "world-wide shanty town."[27]

There is also the enormous psychological adjustment confronting uprooted peasants as they stream into the cities. "To be catapulted into megalopolis straight out of Arcadia is to be given a shock that may turn an innocent countryman into an urban criminal lunatic."[28] The new conditions of life and work are intolerable for a former farmer; they distort his human nature.

> Man is not a cipher, not a reference-number, not a computer-card; he is a living soul. To make his working conditions tolerable for him is necessary, and to achieve this is much, but it is still not enough. Man cannot live in a state of spiritual rootlessness; deracination threatens to drive him mad or to goad him into taking to criminal courses, and this threat hangs over all the hundreds

75

of millions of human beings who are
now streaming into the slums and
shanty-towns of the rising World-City
out of the villages in which they
and their ancestors have been living
since the invention of agriculture.[29]

Historically man has felt a close attachment
to his city, observed Toynbee, regarding it with
love and pride. Thucydides, Saint Paul, Cicero,
Machiavelli, Goethe all expressed warm sentiments
for their native cities. But inhabitants of modern
mechanized cities do not possess these feelings of
affection; a general *malaise* prevades our mechanized cities.

The triumphant march of physical science worried Toynbee more than it impressed him, for it was
moral and spiritual growth that he considered most
important. Moreover, human nature's capacity for
evil has been greatly heightened by placing at
man's disposal technical facilities of enormous
power. While man has expressed enormous pride in
his technology, he needs constant reminder that "it
is not the essence of humanity, and is not even the
feature of human nature that is the most crucial
for mankind's existence, survival, and well-
being."[30]

Man has demonstrated great skill in comprehending and mastering physical nature, said Toynbee, but he has not shown the same talent for spiritual and moral development. There is an imbalance
to man's nature; he has been endowed with much
greater ability for comprehending and mastering inanimate nature than for mastering his own nature
and for learning how to live in fellowship with
others. Since prehistoric times there has existed
a morality gap which is "growing wider as technology has been making cumulative progress while morality has been stagnating."[31] Man has not equip-
ped himself spiritually to handle his enormous
material power. And in the last three hundred
years the gap has widened. Because of our moral
backwardness, said Toynbee, we have turned technological advances into social calamities. The most

76

Nuclear weapons, pollution, and overpopulation, all products of technology, threaten mankind with extinction. By revitalizing our lives with prophetic values, Toynbee claimed, we can acquire the compassion needed to cope with the problems of an industrial age; by redirecting our intellectual energies away from machines toward human needs, we can acquire the knowledge and wisdom to deal effectively with these problems. A technological slowdown, a spiritual revival, and the entrance of our finest intellects into the liberal arts and social sciences offer mankind a hope for surviving the future. In the seventeenth century, according to Toynbee's scheme, man began to explore the universe from a mathematico-physical orientation, breaking with the spiritual world-view of Christianity. Now, three centuries later, we must wrench ourselves away from a singular attachment to mathematics and physics and make a fresh start with a spiritual approach.

We live in a world that is being increasingly united economically and culturally by the exporting of Western science, technology, administrative methods, and education. But the planet remains divided politically because of nationalism, another Western export. The problems posed by technology are not capable of piecemeal solutions, declared Toynbee, but require a world-wide effort. A prerequisite for this global effort is international cooperation on a political level -- some type of world-state.

NOTES

1. Arnold J. Toynbee, *Survey of International Affairs, 1936* (London: Oxford University Press, 1937), p. 23.

2. *Study*, 5: 178-79.

3. *Ibid.*, p. 179.

4. *Study*, 7b : 535.

5. Arnold J. Toynbee, et al., *The Impact of the Russian Revolution 1917-1967* (New York: Oxford University Press, 1962), p. 28.

6. *Study*, 8: 469.

7. *Study*, 5: 585.

8. *Study*, 1: 9.

9. *Study*, 9: 442.

10. *Study*, 7b: 521.

11. *Study*, 4: 169.

12. Arnold J. Toynbee, *Change and Habit* (New York: Oxford University Press, 1960), p. 18.

13. *Study*, 9: 450.

14. *Survey of International Affairs, 1933,* p. 111.

15. *Ibid.,* p. 202.

16. *Study*, 8: 289.

17. Arnold J. Toynbee, *Acquaintances* (New York: Oxford University Press, 1967), p. 294.

18. Cited in Friedrich Meinecke, *The German Catastrophe,* trans. Sidney Fay (Boston: Beacon Press, 1963), pp. 23-24.

19. Hermann Rauschning, *Voice of Destruction* (New York: G.P. Putnam's Sons, 1940), pp. 225, 232.

20. Norman Cohn, *Warrant for Genocide* (New York: Harper Torchbook, 1969), p. 180.

21. Ernst Cassirer, *The Myth of the State* (New Haven: Yale University Press, 1946), p. 282.

22. *Ibid.,* p. 280.

23. *An Historian's Approach to Religion,* p. 288.

24. *Experiences,* p. 326.

25. *Study,* 9: 573.

26. Arnold J. Toynbee, "A Substitute for War," *Long Island Press*, May 3, 1969, p. 13.

27. Arnold J. Toynbee, *Cities on the Move* (New York: Oxford University Press, 1970), p. 34.

28. *Change and Habit*, p. 208.

29. *Cities on the Move*, p. 245.

30. *Change and Habit*, p. 11.

31. Arnold J. Toynbee, *Surviving the Future* (New York: Oxford University Press, 1971), p. 41.

32. *Ibid.*, p. 43.

33. *An Historian's Approach to Religion*, p. 238.

PROSPECTS OF THE WEST

At the beginning of the twentieth century, recalled Toynbee, Westerners were certain that they
had created an orderly, rational, and satisfying
way of life that would endure. Most Westerners ad-
hered to Gibbon's view that what had befallen Rome
could never happen to the West, for the West had
experienced too much progress in knowledge and industry and the tenacity had been taken out of warfare. Brimming with confidence that they were different from other men, Westerners were certain that
the maladies that had ruined earlier civilizations
would not afflict them and that they would continue
to progress automatically. Toynbee recollected
that before World War I he and his parents

> expected that life throughout the
> World would become more rational,
> more humane, and more democratic,
> and that, slowly, but surely, polit-
> ical democracy would produce greater
> social justice. We had also expected
> that the progress of science and
> technology would make mankind richer,
> and that this increasing wealth would
> gradually spread from a minority to a
> majority. We had expected that all
> this would happen peacefully. In fact,
> we thought that mankind's course was
> set for an earthly paradise, and that
> our approach towards this goal was
> predestined for us by historical ne-
> cessity.[1]

World War I shook the complacency of Westerners and
the crimes of the Nazi era revealed a "criminality
... festering foully below the surface of life in
the Western World."[2] No longer believing in linear
progress, "we have awakened to the truth (how, one
wonders, could we ever have been blind to it?) that
Western man and his works are no more invulnerable

than the now extinct civilizations of the Aztecs and the Incas, the Sumerians and the Hittites."[3]

Does this mean that the West is in decline? To what extent is the West caught in the rhythm of breakdown and disintegration that ruined Hellenism the parent of the West?

THE DECLINE OF THE WEST?

In Toynbee's classification there have been twenty-six representatives of the species civilization. Sixteen of the twenty-six have died. Of the ten living civilizations, three are arrested (Polynesians, Eskimos, Nomads) and in danger either of being annihilated or assimilated by Western Civilization. Of the seven others -- Western Civilization, the main body of Orthodox Christendom in the Near East, the offshoot of Orthodox Christianity in Russia, Islamic society, Hindu society, the main body of Far Eastern society in China, and the offshoot of Far Eastern society in Japan -- "every one apparently, has already broken down and is now in the process of disintegration with the possible exception of our own."[4] But no doubt a Time of Troubles has descended upon the Western world and the West may "have passed its zenith for all that we know."[5]

A society in the process of breakdown falls into "bondage to some idol of its own making."[6] Like the ancient Hellenes, said Toynbee, modern Westerners have worshipped political communities as gods and have engaged in devastating fratricidal warfare. This infatuation with national sovereignty threatens to ruin the West as it had destroyed Hellenic society. If nationalism and world wars are signs of the breakdown of the modern West, what symptoms are there of disintegration?

In one respect the modern West is not confronted with the same situation faced by a disintegrating Hellenic civilization. There are no hordes of barbarians eager to penetrate the borders of a more advanced civilization, for primitive peoples are few and impotent. However, while the West "was conquering the barbarians in the flesh," barbarism, in the form of fascism and National Socialism,

> was taking its revenge by finding
> its way into the souls of its Western
> conquerors. ... and this evil had not
> been exorcized from Western souls by
> the military overthrow of Italian
> Fascism and a German National Social-
> ism; for this perverse Western mani-
> festation of Original Sin was an oc-
> cupational disease of a semi-educated
> urban lower middle class that was as
> ubiquitous as the Western Civilization
> itself, and there was perhaps no prov-
> ince of the Western World in which
> this class was not in some danger of
> succumbing to this malady.[7]

For Toynbee, human nature is the same today as it was for our ancestors, both primitive and civi- lized. While some superior personalities push civ- ilization forward, even in the most advanced civili- zations, the overwhelming majority of people demon- strate a primitive humanity. Thus the barbarism that threatens the West does not take the form of warrior bands beyond the frontiers; rather it mani- fests itself in a barbarous attitude of mind that has particularly afflicted the lower middle class. Disillusioned with the leadership of the West's dominant minority, the lower middle class embraced a lower religion, fascism. And the attraction of some variant of fascism, said Toynbee, remains an ever present danger in the West.

The ranks of the Western internal proletariat have been swollen, said Toynbee, by recruits drawn from the masses of the non-European world "that had been caught, like the last barbarians, in a world- encompassing Western net;"[8] from uprooted peoples, particularly American blacks; and from the intelli- gentsia, especially a university educated lower middle class that has no opportunity to use its ed- ucation. Also included in the ranks of the Western proletariat are ex-farmers forced to move to the cities in search of a livelihood:

> ...the transfer of population from the
> countryside to town has produced the
> same cancer in the Western as in the
> Hellenic body social: the cancer of
> an urban proletariat which has lost
> its roots in the country, has struck
> no roots in the town, and is reminded
> -- every time that it draws its dole
> -- that it is 'in' but not 'of' the
> society which has to serve as the un-
> willing 'host' of this unhappy social
> parasite.[9]

And this is a world-wide phenomenon because Western
Civilization has become global.

Aggravating the tensions between the Western
dominant minority and its global internal proletariat is a color bar. There is irony in the fact
that the Western dominant minority has "been recruited from the Teutonic-speaking descendants of
those White barbarians who had battered on the carcass of a dead Hellenic society some fifteen hundred years back in the past."[10] Uprisings of a
Western proletariat (Jacobins, 1793, Communards,
1871) have been dwarfed by insurrections of a Western proletariat of non-Western origins, so that "a
world-wide proletarian revolt against a world-wide
Western ascendancy had now become a possibility
with which the West had to reckon; and, for a Western Society at bay, this prospect was daunting."[11]
But, concluded Toynbee in 1939, the Western internal proletariat has been spiritually barren, unable
so far to lay "the foundations of a proletarian
universal church or even ... any strong-winged pro-
letarian-born higher religions."[12] In communism,
said Toynbee, a world-wide proletariat has found a
religion that promises it a new Jerusalem but communism cannot regenerate mankind spiritually, for
the Marxist Church Militant uses violence to
achieve its goal and creates a totalitarian state.

In still another way Western Civilization con-
forms to the pattern of disintegration. Hellenic

civilization had experienced two ruinous paroxysms
of warfare, the Peloponnesian War and the Second
Punic War. The West had its counterparts in the
Wars of Religion and the Wars of Nationality, principally the two world wars. The Wars of Religion,
symptoms of social breakdown, were followed by a
rally made possible by the spread of religious toleration. But the rally proved abortive, said Toynbee, for the principle of toleration, without a
spiritual anchor, could not succeed. "The spirits
that presided over its conception and birth were
Disillusionment, Apprehension, and Cynicism, not
Faith, Hope, and Charity; the impulse was negative,
not positive; and the soil in which the seeds were
sown was arid."[13] That the rally following the
Wars of Religion was terminated by the even more
destructive Wars of Nationality is the most distressing feature of Western Civilization that enables us to see a pattern of breakdown and disintegration. The "series of two paroxysms punctuated
by one rally ... had been the regular rhythm of a
Time of Troubles in the histories of civilizations
that had run through the whole disintegration process from breakdown to dissolution."[14] However,
even if the West is in the midst of a second bout
of warfare, what is more significant in terms of
its current and potential health is that a universal state has not been created by force, a condition that was avoided by the defeat of Germany in
two world wars.

While Toynbee saw signs of breakdown and disintegration in the West, he did not believe the
collapse of the West must follow, for man is not at
the mercy of an inexorable fate; he does have the
capacity to make intelligent choices and to root
out those malignancies that have ruined other civilizations. Even though sixteen civilizations have
perished and nine others seem in their death
throes, Toynbee did not believe that civilizations
are doomed inexorably; they are not living organ-
isms predestined to death. Westerners can remedy
the evils that afflict their society and breathe
new life into their civilization.

There is nothing to prevent our

Western Civilization from following
historical precedent, if it chooses,
by committing social suicide. But we
are not doomed to make history repeat
itself; it is open to us, through our
own efforts, to give history, in our
case, some new and unprecedented turn.
As human beings, we are endowed with
this freedom of choice, and we cannot
shuffle off our repsonsibility upon
the shoulders of God or nature. We
must shoulder it ourselves. It is up
to us.[15]

Rejecting determinism, Toynbee insisted that
the future cannot be predicted on the basis of historical patterns. While maintaining that a pattern
of breakdown and disintegration could be discerned
in the histories of dead and moribund civilizations,
Toynbee did "not believe that this pattern was predetermined or inevitable in any single past case."
Unlike Spengler, he did not postulate "a fixed pattern to which the history of every civilization is
bound to conform." Because "the course of human
affairs is not predetermined" Toynbee was unwilling
"to predict that the Western Civilization will go
the way that a number of its predecessors have
gone." The history of Western Civilization "is today still an unfinished story."[16]

SIGNS OF HEALTH

Although Toynbee saw symptoms of decline in
the West he also recognized signs of health that
make it impossible to predict whether the malady
afflicting the West is lethal. One principal sign
of health is the fact that the West has not yet entered into a universal state created by force. Another sign of health is that while the internal
proletariat might well secede there are "forces of
reconciliation and recuperation that were in the
field against the forces of schism and disintegration."[17] For example, the fact that Venetians and
Lubeckers had been able to transfer their loyalty
from their local city to a larger grouping, the national state, is an indication that Western man,

indeed all mankind, "might one day transfer their allegiance to a universal state between whose provinces war would be impracticable."[18] Toward this end, the movement for European integration is a hopeful sign. Another sign of moral health is the elimination of slavery, an evil that had been responsible for defeating civilizations in the past. Also encouraging for the West has been the compromise between free enterprise and socialism being worked out in a number of countries. Unbridled individualism, said Toynbee, leads only to the domination of the great masses by a masterful minority, whereas "a moderate dose of socialism was a prophylactic against the danger of the society's succumbing to a totalitarianism that would have imposed on human beings the social justice of the antheap and the beehive at the cost of forcibly depriving them of Man's distinctive birthright of freedom."[19] While the spread of education in Western lands is a positive sign, declared Toynbee, it also presents the danger that semi-educated masses would be manipulated by propaganda skillfully prepared by political parties, governments, and businesses; the hope lies in the possibility that an educated populace will acquire the intellectual capacity to detect propaganda. Another reason for encouragement is that Christianity, despite the efforts of Machiavelli, Hobbes, Voltaire, Marx, and Hitler, continues to retain some vitality in Western hearts. "This persistent vitality of a higher religion ... was an element in the Western situation in the twentieth century of the Christian Era that had been conspicuously absent in an otherwise comparable Hellenic situation in the last two centuries B.C."[20] For this reason the West may not succumb to the same fate as Hellenism. An apostate Western Christendom may yet be saved by being born again as *Respublica Christiana.*

SPIRITUAL REBIRTH

If the West is not to go the way of Hellenic Civilization it must return to its Christian roots, for neither our modern ideologies nor science can answer man's need for God or provide a spiritual conception of the individual. Toynbee likened late modern Western man to wanderers in the wilderness, "astray from their forefathers' One True God,"[21] who had succumbed to the temptation of "such devils as Nationalism and Fascism and Communism."[22] In its youth Christianity had fought against the worship of the Roman Empire and the Roman Emperor. Two thousand years later it was engaged in struggle with a modern form of Leviathan-worship, the post-Christian ideologies. That the West has awakened to the dangers of these ideologies is also a reason for optimism. Not only must Western man's spiritual rebirth enable him to overcome ideologies, it must also help him to end his obsession with technology, "his unduly prolonged child's play with clockwork."[23] Toynbee clearly stated his prescription for saving the West.

> In politics, establish a constitutional co-operative system of world government. In economics, find working compromises (varying according to the practical requirements of different places and times) between free enterprise and socialism. In the life of the spirit, put the secular superstructure back onto religious foundations.[24]

At the heart of Toynbee's remedy for coping with the crisis of a post-Christian West is the need for a spiritual reconversion, but this cannot be satisfied by conventional Christian orthodoxy. "The impulse to indulge in a second bout of traditional religion is, indeed, merely a manifestation on the religious plane of an Archaism, which, on all planes, we have found ... to be a bolt-hole that is always a trap because it invariably proves to be a blind alley."[25] The West cannot reverse history and undo the experience of intellectual enlightenment; it cannot dispense with the rationalism that has characterized late modern Western history. Christianity must not serve as an escape, a hiding place for lost Western souls who would forsake critical thought and make a virtue out of blind authority. Toynbee did not wish to revive the institutional power of churches, but to renew respect for Jesus' precepts of love and compassion.

This would be a true spiritual revolution, whereas a return to traditional orthodoxy would be a dead end. And if Western man "prayed God to grant him a pilot for the perilous passage, he would find the bodhisattva ... whom he was seeking in a Francesco Bernardo of Assisi, who was the most god-like soul that had been born into the Western World so far."[26]

While the kind of progress that men must aspire to is the "cumulative increase in the means of Grace at the disposal of each Soul in this world,"[27] Toynbee recognized that important reforms must be introduced in the secular sphere; without such reforms man might never have this opportunity for spiritual rebirth. However, he insisted that taking the salvation of the individual soul as the supreme aim of life also furthers social progress; there is no antithesis between following God and trying to help one's neighbor.

> In other words, the spiritual progress of individual souls in this life will in fact bring with it much more social progress than could be attained in any other way. It is a paradoxical but profoundly true and important principle of life that the most likely way to reach a goal is to be aiming not at that goal itself but at some more ambitious goal beyond it. ... Therefore, the replacement of the mundane civilizations by the world-wide and enduring reign of the Church Militant on Earth would certainly produce what today would seem a miraculous improvement in those mundane social conditions which the civilizations have been seeking to improve during the last six thousand years.[28]

All the higher religions teach us that our wants exceed our needs, that excessive self-indulgence is an obstacle to the pursuit of spiritual aims, and that man has a moral duty to consider his neighbor's needs -- attitudes which promote social progress.

In two ways Toynbee saw Western Civilization as unique. Firstly, of the seven extant civilizations only the West does "not show indisputable signs of being already in disintegration."[29] Secondly, Western Civilization has spread throughout the globe. Thus the destiny of the West has become tied to an emerging world civilization, the product of the outpouring of European ideas, institutions, and technology that began in the late fifteenth century. By adopting Western techniques and the Western state system, the non-Western world has become drawn into Western Civilization's spiritual crisis. But from this world-wide spiritual crisis, hoped Toynbee, there will emerge a universal state imbued with prophetic ideals. This is of critical importance in Toynbee's philosophy of history. From the beginning of human history mankind has been fragmented into different bands, tribes, states, civilizations. And now the West, without intending it, has become an agent of global unity, making it possible to realize the universalist visions of the prophets.

NOTES

1. *Surviving the Future*, pp. 106-07.

2. *Study*, 9: 433.

3. *Civilization on Trial*, p. 37.

4. *Study*, 4: 3.

5. *Ibid.*, p. 122.

6. *Study*, 9: 441.

7. *Study*, 9: 450-51.

8. *Ibid.*, p. 451.

9. *Study*, 5: 164-65.

10. *Study*, 9: 453.

11. *Ibid.*, p. 455.

12. *Study*, 5: 188.

13. *Study*, 6: 317.

14. *Study*, 9: 464.

15. *Civilization on Trial*, p. 45.

16. *Study*, 12: 519.

17. *Study*, 9: 461.

18. *Ibid.*, p. 446.

19. *Ibid.*, p. 448.

20. *Ibid.*, p. 461.

21. *Ibid.*, p. 450.

22. *Ibid.*, p. 449.

23. *Ibid.*, p. 629.

24. *Civilization on Trial*, p. 45.

25. *Study*, 9: 630-31.

26. *Ibid.*, p. 644.

27. *Civilization on Trial*, p. 229.

28. *Ibid.*, p. 216.

29. *Study*, 9: 411.

THE WORLD-STATE

All the strands of Toynbee's philosophy of history coalesced in his concept of the coming world-state. In this utopian vision he demonstrated again his hatred of nationalism, his fear of technology, and his concern for the individual.

The crisis of the West, said Toynbee, has now become part of a world-wide crisis; it is no longer a question of the West declining but of mankind perishing. For a humanity threatened with extinction by the lower religion of nationalism and the power generated by an idolized technology, Toynbee prescribed a universal state and a revitalization of spiritual ideals.

Because of war, maintained Toynbee, civilizations can only be regarded as experiments in which man has sought to rise above the level of the primitive. Just when it seems that man has pulled ahead, he again defeats himself by succumbing to war. And what has exacerbated warfare and wrecked civilizations more than anything else has been the absolute sovereignty and unqualified loyalty demanded by states; it is imperative that mankind break with the system of parochial states.

Toynbee believed that a political system's merit depends on its ability "to rid human social life of the violence that is the price of anarchy."[1] Judged by this standard, world-states have been considerably more successful than city-states or national states; they have succeeded in providing a large measure of domestic order and unity while engaging in relatively few wars with states beyond their borders as was the case of Rome in the two centuries after 27 B.C. To build a world-state is the great challenge facing mankind today, insisted Toynbee.

Toynbee maintained that humanity possesses the administrative and technological means to solve the problems of our industrial age, but there is a political barrier to effective action. Although the whole of mankind is being knit together economically and culturally by the outpouring of Western parliamentary government and industrialism, it remains divided politically and ideologically. But only a world government can deal effectively with the interrelated problems of the global age -- nuclear weapons, pollution, overpopulation; the survival of mankind depends on man's ability to create a global federation. But if it is to succeed and endure such a world-polity must rest upon a spiritual foundation, for purely human bonds cannot hold mankind together: "The only society that is capable of embracing the whole of Mankind is a superhuman *Civitas Dei*; and the conception of a society that embraces all Mankind and yet nothing but Mankind is an academic chimera."[2]

While political divisiveness is as old as the first hunting bands, declared Toynbee, world-mindedness is a relatively recent phenomenon making its appearance only after civilization had already established itself. A world-state was formed when one state delivered a knock-out blow to its competitors, but the age-old habit of divisiveness inherited from the early days of prehistory continued to persist. Conquered peoples often rejected the peace and stability imposed by the world-state and rose in nationalist revolt. In our own day, the subordination of the universal elements of communism to the demands of Russian nationalism demonstrates anew the greater attraction of parochial-mindedness. Yet world-states have not been without their appeal as evidenced by the loyalty Rome received from the different peoples that comprised the Empire. Historically world-states were established through conflict and conquest, but at a prohibitively high cost. While these world-states succeeded in imposing universal peace upon a war-stricken society, they could not cure the spiritual disorders caused by centuries of war; they could only temporarily arrest, but not reverse the society's downhill slide. For Toynbee, the solution for the problems posed by national sovereignty is the creation of a world-state by *consent*, not by force, before the process of breakdown and disintegration is well advanced. Modern weapons rule out the traditional way of creating a world-state, for atomic warfare would only unite mankind in death. Despite the persistence of nationalism, and even its growing intensity in some parts of the world, Toynbee believed that the creation of a global polity is not beyond man's capacity. A number of unifying tendencies exist today powerful enough to overcome formidable historical and psycholgical barriers to a world-wide state.

While tribalism is a deeply ingrained and formidable habit, said Toynbee, it is still a product of culture and not an ineradicable trait of human nature. Toynbee felt that man can be taught to regard a world-state as a superior form of political organization and he can learn to subordinate local loyalty to a world-wide loyalty. Since 1500 certain developments have served to push mankind together into the direction of a single society. The agent in this movement toward globalism has been the West. This is ironic, for while Western Civilization achieved cultural unity, it has been notoriously plagued with political parochialism.

Since 1500 the West has been spreading its technology, institutions, and ideas throughout the globe, bringing together the once separate societies into a common culture. This cultural unity, spurred by the annihilation of distance resulting from modern transportation and communication, might serve as the prelude to political unification. Spearheading the diffusion of Western civilization and the rise of world cultural unity is a world-wide intelligentsia comparable to the Hellenizers who served as the medium for the cultural unification of the ancient Mediterranean world. Perhaps the modern intelligentsia, many of whom already think and behave as world citizens and share a common Western Civilization, will provide the social and cultural bonds to hold together the world-state. The intelligentsia is producing Western style nation states throughout the globe that "are going to be uniform enough to serve as cells for the construction of a world-wide world-state, as the city-states standardized on the Hellenic pattern once served as cells for the construction of the Roman world-state."[3]

Another promising sign for future world unity, said Toynbee, is the growing economic and political consolidation of Western Europe since World War II and the discrediting of romantic nationalism. This radically new departure "is a good augury, considering how deeply ingrained is nationalism in the tradition of Western European peoples and how often one or another of them has tried to subjugate the rest by force. If the Western European peoples can unite with each other voluntarily, as they are now demonstrating they can, a voluntary unity of mankind, on a global scale is not a utopian objective."[4] Since World War II Western Europe has also displayed a distaste for militarism, a psychological revolution that reversed a tide that had been flowing since the opening of the modern era, except for one pause in the eighteenth century.

A world society requires that people share ideals and manners. Can mankind attain a stable political unity without at the same time achieving ideological and religious unity? Does a world political federation require uniformity of ethical standards and ideals? Toynbee did not believe that ideological and religious variety are incompatible with political unity so long as there is no accompanying animosity and competition for power. Is this possible? The answer to this question is related to the larger matter of Toynbee's vision of the coming world-state.

The future world-state will not be greatly centralized, said Toynbee, for the peoples of the world will only support world government reluctantly. Moreover, in an era of atomic weapons recalcitrant national states cannot be coerced into accepting world authority. States will not put themselves out of business, but will surrender some prerogatives for the sake of self-preservation. Realizing that the alternative may be self-destruction, declared Toynbee, mankind will choose a form of world government, but unlike the world-states of the past, which were unitary states imposed by force, the coming world-state will be a voluntary federal union. However, it must have the power to prevent local units, driven by parochial loyalties, from engaging in war. It is possible that over the years the loyalty that had once been directed to the national state may be transferred to mankind as a whole.

Toynbee feared that the coming world-state will be a dictatorship, for periods of social anarchy are often followed by autocratic rule as was the case of the Roman Republic in the first century B.C. In 1971, Toynbee speculated that by the year two thousand the world would be held together "by a atrociously tyrannical dictatorship," controlled perhaps by cliques of military men from different regions. This future dictatorship might "be imposed on the majority by a ruthless, efficient, and fanatical minority, inspired by some ideology or religion."[5]

While the lessons of history seem to indicate that the coming state will be a dictatorship imposed by a minority, Toynbee still held out hope that it would be created by voluntary agreement and would allow for participation in government which "is one of the natural human rights of every individual." But because self-annihilation looms if we fail to unite, "we cannot afford to wait till we can be sure of being able to build democracy into the world-state's original constitution."[6]

Ideally, Toynbee envisioned an eventual world government with sufficient power to abolish wars. National states would exist as federated units. To humanize Ecumenopolis, said Toynbee, it will have to be broken up into numerous small, self-contained, sub-units, the size of an ancient Greek city-state

or a medieval town. Each of these sub-units would
be adjacent to a country area that would remain
permanently undeveloped. Within these cities there
would be still smaller units, wards that would promote a sense of neighborliness. They would be so
designed that youngsters could go to school and
housewives shop without having to cross streets
travelled by autos. The intimacy of the rural vil-
lage will be transplanted to urban areas and men
will have a chance of feeling once more members of
a community. By decentralizing the world-city we
can cure the loneliness of city life and ease the
transition for the multitudes of new city dwellers
arriving from the countryside. By restoring a
sense of community to inhabitants of cities, by
treating them as persons and not as things, serial
numbers or ciphers, and by heeding their legitimate
grievances, we can reduce the level of violence.

Besides his affiliation to a local ward in the
coming world-city and his loyalty to the future
world-state in which he holds citizenship, there is
still another community to which the individual
could belong and from which he could derive grati-
fication -- a world-wide diaspora of people sharing
common professional interests. Russian physicists,
for example, have more in common with American scientists than they do with Russian farmers. Similarly, the world's doctors, mathematicians, musi-
cians, artists all form a community of their own
that crosses state frontiers. These people, meeting in international societies and communicating
by letter, telephone, and on television screens,
will serve as another bond of world unity.

To facilitate an attitude of world-mindedness,
schools will have to require fluency in at least
one foreign language and attempt to reduce race
consciousness. While race feeling is an obstacle
to the unity of mankind, there are many examples of
peoples -- Hawaiians, Mexicans -- who are relatively oblivious to racial differences. Toynbee believed that the bonds of common culture and common
religion are strong enough to overcome racial differences.

On the basis of historical experience, Toynbee did not want the future world-state to suppress completely local variety and autonomy for a standardized global culture and a centralized universal government. Such conditions tend to produce cultural deterioration and social stratification. "The Roman Empire prospered under the principate, when it was administered as a commonwealth of still autonomous, but no longer sovereign, city-states; it decayed with the decay of local autonomy and with the transformation of the world-government from an instrument for keeping the peace into an agency for the centralized bureaucratic administration of local as well as common affairs."[7] It will be the task of good statesmanship to create a harmony between the national and the universal. But if this is to endure and succeed, "the authority of the 'universal', and the loyalty paid to it, must be paramount."[8]

Toynbee hoped that religious or ideological variety will not be obliterated by future political unity. Through education, children will learn about all the world's ideologies and religions, and, hopefully, differences will become a stimulus for choice rather than a cause for irrational hate. Moreover, the problems confronting mankind -- "urbanism, pollution, psychological disorientation, and outbreaks of irrational violence ... transcend the traditional differences between ideologies."[9] And as both capitalism and communism become more flexible and pragmatic, ideological issues will seem less important.

SPIRITUALITY AND SOCIAL JUSTICE

Consistent with his interpretation of history, Toynbee believed that the coming world-polity needs a religious base. Only by embracing prophetic values can man overcome the limitations of parochialism and live in brotherly unity. Western technology is an inadequate scaffolding upon which to construct a world-state. Only by turning to the religious prophets of universalism -- Isaiah, Jesus, Buddha, Gandhi -- can man shape an enduring world order, for "there can be no unity of Mankind without the participation of God."[10] The leap from tribalism to ecumenicalism requires a religious revolution, but Toynbee recognized that man is still far from this stage.

According to Toynbee's world-view, fratricidal wars between states and conflicts between classes caused by injustice have been the principal reasons for the ruin of civilizations. The future world-state must not only be powerful enough to save humanity from committing suicide through nuclear warfare, it must also promote human welfare through a radical redistribution of the planet's goods. For the past five thousand years, stated Toynbee, the masters of the civilizations have terribly exploited the lower classes. The achievements of civilization have been built on the backs of peasants, but these unfortunates have continued to live at a starvation level. The favored few have defended their selfishness by insisting that they were trustees for all future generations. In a world of scarcity, the fruits of civilization had to go to a few or there would be no fruits at all and humanity would be deprived of its future. While this plea might have had some validity in the past, said Toynbee, our unprecedented progress in technology makes it invalid today. Yet some 3/4 of humanity currently live below the poverty line struggling for survival as did our early ancestors. In the past the exploited masses had docilely accepted poverty, but in the twentieth century this habit of resignation has been broken. For Toynbee, the world revolution of the peasantry for social justice is not only the dominant theme of the age, it is also "the most glorious *secular* revolution"[11] in world history. Throughout the world the poor are abandoning their fatalism and are demanding freedom from want; the cry for economic equality can no longer be silenced. This emancipation of the world's poor and oppressed, Toynbee was certain, will "stand out in retrospect as the epoch-making event of our age."[12] It is the West that deserves credit for this hopeful development "for it has not only conceived the ideal of social justice; it has also conjured up the material means for translating this ideal into practice."[13]

102

Toynbee found in the Judaeo-Christian tradition the source of the Western concept of social justice that is now becoming world-wide. Christianity has preached the dignity of every human being regardless of wealth or status; it has proclaimed that all men are entitled to spiritual justice. In the eighteenth century "the demand in Western Christendom for social justice overflowed from the religious into the secular province of social life."[14] The philosophy of the Enlightenment and the anti-slavery movement were secular applications of the Christian principle of social justice. But this secular demand for social reform would have been only utopian had not the Industrial Revolution simultaneously given man the tools by which he could realize the ideals of social justice. There has been a tragic facet to the movement for social justice, declared Toynbee. While it began within the bosom of religion and then overflowed into the secular arena, the established churches did not take an active part in this new orientation, but "stayed within their customary ecclesiastical bounds and left the cause of secular social justice to be championed by laymen who were indifferent to religion if not positively hostile for what seemed to them a callous betrayal of its mission."[15] If religion is to regain its former influence, concluded Toynbee, it will have to campaign more vigorously for social justice. For Toynbee, a religious society will be more successful than a secular one in achieving social reform. The spiritual progress that higher religions seek by having man draw closer to God will also result in an improvement in human material welfare.

How is the ideal of social justice to be realized in the future world-state? Certainly not by any dogmatic allegiance to either capitalism or communism. Toynbee rejected the doctrine that private profit is a sacred human right: "untrammeled freedom for economic private enterprise means freedom in this line for the small minority that commands the economic means for taking advantage of freedom here."[16] But for the great mass of ordinary people it does not mean freedom at all. Toynbee maintained that a mixed system of private enterprise and socialism offers the best solution. The proportion of the blend would be determined not *a priori* but according to experience and would be subject to modification.

On a political level, Toynbee sought a golden mean between the unrestricted sovereignty of national states and the unrestricted authority of a centralized world-state. On an economic level, he favored a mean between unrestricted private enterprise and unmitigated socialism. The American ideology, he said, stresses individual freedom but is not sufficiently concerned with social justice; on the other hand, the Russian ideology stresses social justice and dispenses with individual freedom. The middle way, which Toynbee saw developing in Western Europe, might prove to be the model for the non-Western world. Wise statesmanship, said Toynbee, should not attach itself to an ideology, capitalist or communist, that is regarded as a semi-religious faith; it should not turn to ideologies as panaceas for society's ills. Rather, it should strive for practical common-sense solutions to particular problems.

Toynbee valued individual liberty but felt that left uncurbed it leads to oligarchy, for it gives "a free hand to a minority who, in an unrestricted competition of all against all, are more than a match for the rest of the community in physical strength, mental ability, wealth, or political power."[17] By giving full scope to personal liberty, social justice is violated. But to pursue social justice with single-minded devotion is to suppress personal liberty which "is an indispensible condition for any human achievement."[18] In his hostility to fanaticism, in his opposition to doctrinaire thinking, in his stress upon balance and moderation, Toynbee displayed some of the qualities of British pragmatism.

Toynbee believed that the gap between rich and poor could be narrowed by a world-state sufficiently strong to tax the richer nations for the benefit of the poorer ones. As an immediate step, he urged the poor nations to form an international union that would emulate the militancy of labor unions: "If the poor majority of the World's countries were to strike collectively, by refusing to sell to the rich countries their labor, their raw materials, and their foodstuffs, except on more equitable terms, I believe that they could compel the richer countries to change the terms of trade to the poorer countries' advantage; and this would be a victory for justice."[19] Both developments -- the taxing of the rich and the growth of the power of labor unions -- had in Toynbee's life time helped to close the gap between the classes in England. He believed they now needed a world-wide application.

Toynbee's other proposals to promote social reform in the future world-state included government sponsored birth control, expanded education, and the redirecting of funds away from armaments and space exploration toward feeding and clothing the wretched of the planet. Toynbee regarded the space program as a great adventure, but likened it to the pyramids and the palace of Versailles -- masterpieces of human skill and cooperation built at the expense of the poor majority and therefore morally offensive. We should also stop manufacturing products that satisfy bogus wants conjured up by Madison Avenue and direct our productive capacities toward fighting a world-wide battle against poverty. To survive the future, said Toynbee, we shall have to alter the notion that the fruits of technology belong only to the immediate producers; instead we shall have to share with the whole of mankind the material wealth produced by technology.

The world-city must not only meet man's material needs, but it must also provide him with an outlet for his spiritual energies. Technology should assist man in achieving the true purpose of life, which is spiritual. Toward this end, we shall have to reeducate industrial man, enabling him to make proper use of his leisure so that he finds satisfaction in "thought and art, and religion ... the fields in which the spiritual side of human nature can find infinite scope. ... If we can succeed in doing this, we may see a new flowering of culture -- a second Renaissance -- instead of the development of a parasitic society, which, like the urban proletariat in the Roman Empire, lives for 'bread and circuses' and turns savage if it is not given to them."[20]

A heightening of spirituality will turn us away from idolizing wealth and power which we purchase "at the price of individual unhappiness for ourselves and of discord with each other."[21] It will lead to a rehumanizing of education stressing the study of man for the purpose of improving ourselves and bettering our relations with others. Toynbee considered it possible that a new generation of intellectuals, following the example of Socrates, will focus on narrowing the morality gap rather than pushing forward the frontiers of science and technology. He saw signs of such a reorientation occurring in the United States in the last third of the twentieth century. Guided by a renewed spiritual awareness and by new insights into human nature and society obtained by the transference of intellectual energy away from technology to the liberal arts, man may yet use technology and science to humanize the coming world-city. Particularly if we learn from Eastern religions, which unlike Christianity, do not regard nature as something that God gave man to exploit, we might treat the natural environment and non-human life with greater care and respect.

Toynbee warned that the struggle for social justice should not be accompanied by educational egalitarianism which stifles gifted children and reduces schooling to the lowest common denominator. The doctrinaire egalitarians damage the public interest, for exceptional individuals have always been civilization's pacesetters. Hopefully, the individual with unusual ability will recognize his "moral obligation to use his gifts, not in Napoleon's way, just for his own selfish advantage at his less gifted fellow men's expense, but, if he can rise to this height, in a bodhisattva's way -- that is to say, at his own expense for the benefit of all other sentient beings."[22] In this way he achieves self-transcendence.

Ultimately the solution to human problems requires a religious orientation, insisted Toynbee. That these problems could only be solved "by lifting them from the social to the religious plane was as true in a twentieth-century Westernizing world as it had been true always and everywhere since the transfiguration of Sub-man into Man."[23] God, as Saint Paul proclaimed, had "made of one blood all nations of men," and in the same spirit Saint James taught "that he who loveth God loves his brother also." It is in this spirit that man must approach the problem of social justice.

For Toynbee, the true end of human life can never be the accumulation of enormous amounts of consumer goods as dictated by advertising industry. What distinguishes man from non-human creatures with whom he shares the planet is that only he has a spiritual purpose in life. In pursuit of this spiritual end, said Toynbee, man needs only a small quantity of consumer goods. Man's wants have always exceeded his real needs even before advertising inflated them. Higher religions have consistently cautioned us "against excessive self-indulgence in the satisfaction of our material wants because they hold, and rightly hold, that this is an obstacle to attaining the true end of Man -- the true end of Man being the pursuit of spiritual aims."[24] All the higher religions have exhorted man to recognize his moral responsibility to his fellow man and to care not only for his own needs but also for those of his neighbor. In today's world, said Toynbee, this commandment is directed especially toward the rich Western minority. Toynbee urged Westerners to abide by the religious virtue of self-denial in order to care for the suffering poor throughout the globe. If Americans could take the lead the rest of the Western world would follow, guided "by the voice of religions."[25]

Future generations, said Toynbee, may look back upon the present materialism of the West with feelings of astonishment and even disgust and shame that so much energy was squandered trying to obtain immoderate amounts of material possessions. They will have arrived at a much healthier estimation of the amount of goods a man really needs in order to allow for spiritual development. Western man, who has sacrificed his soul by an over enthusiastic concentration upon material goods, can redeem himself by utilizing his technology for the good of all humanity.

If the future world-state manages to rid itself of war and class conflict that have traditionally wrecked civilizations and succeeds in coping with pollution and over-population, the next problem confronting mankind would be the role of leisure in a mechanized world. In the past only a minority had the self-discipline and self-education to utilize leisure creatively. This creative minority had given to mankind a priceless cultural treasure. The attitudes and interests of this creative minority are not easily transmitted. Toynbee feared that the lavishing of leisure on the unprepared masses would lead to cultural deterioration. What irony it would be if the reward for the elimination of war and class conflict turns out to be the wallowing for ages in a "commonwealth of swine." To prevent the coming world-state from becoming Huxley's "brave new world" or Plato's "commonwealth of swine," leisure must be utilized creatively. Technology is creating an abundance of leisure, but industrialized man "often positively dreads leisure because it confronts him with his own self, isolated terrifyingly in the 'lonely crowd.'"[26] Modern man spends his leisure in a "sub-human" way, principally as a passive spectator of television and sporting events. The society of the future must provide an educational system that stimulates aesthetic and intellectual growth. But while only a relatively few people possess the intrinsic gifts required for art or thought, religion provides "an infinite spiritual scope to Everyman."[27] It is the finest outlet for leisure.

Was Toynbee optimistic about the future? While granting that in the twentieth century material wealth has increased and in many instances conditions for the poor have improved, he noted that there has occurred, what nobody foresaw in 1914, a "great moral regression in people's treatment of each other." In the year 1971 the Western world was "much less humane than it was in 1913. We have to face the possibility that the World will become still more inhumane by the end of the present century."[28] Our Westernizing world in the twentieth century, said Toynbee, reveals extraordinary contradictions. At the same time that humanitarian feelings, as expressed in a concern for the human rights of all people, have risen to new heights, the cruelties of class warfare, nationalism, and racialism have shown man at his worst.

However, despite the difficulties burdening the world, Toynbee remained hopeful. We have the intellectual ability to cope with war, overpopulation and pollution, but the head must persuade the heart to renounce cherished and longstanding practices. Human beings have the capacity to choose life over death, good over evil, said Toynbee, and in the methods of Gandhi and Martin Luther King we have the proper guide. Toynbee felt that man, however reluctantly, tardily, or sulkily, will choose life over suicide by renouncing the institutions of sovereignty and war, so dear to human hearts. If humanity forsakes tribal-mindedness and false gods and becomes imbued with universalism and spirituality, from its sufferings it will have acquired wisdom.

NOTES

1. *Change and Habit*, p. 24.

2. *Study*, 6: 10.

3. *Change and Habit*, p. 155.

4. Arnold J. Toynbee, "For the First Time in 30,000 Years," *Worldview* 15 (March 1972), 9.

5. *Surviving the Future*, p. 113.

6. Arnold J. Toynbee, *America and the World Revolution* (New York: Oxford University Press, 1962), p. 67.

7. *Study*, 12: 618.

8. *Ibid.*, p. 619.

9. *Surviving the Future*, p. 142.

10. *Study*, 7b: 511.

11. *America and the World Revolution*, p. 86.

12. *Ibid.*, p. 40.

13. *Ibid.*, p. 41.

14. *Ibid.*, p. 161.

15. *Ibid.*, p. 199.

16. Arnold J. Toynbee, *Between Niger and Nile* (New York: Oxford University Press, 1965), p. 84.

17. *Study*, 9: 593.

18. *Ibid.*

19. *Surviving the Future*, pp. 134-35.

20. Arnold J. Toynbee, "Mankind's Moral Malady," in Larry Ng, ed. *Alternatives to Violence* (New York: Time-Life Books, 1968), p. 159.

21. *Surviving the Future*, p. 43.

22. *Experiences*, p. 347.

23. *Study*, 9: 594.

23. *America and the World Revolution*, p. 145.

25. *Ibid.*, p. 149.

26. *Surviving the Future*, p. 93.

27. *Ibid.*, p. 618.

28. *Surviving the Future*, p. 107.

CHAPTER EIGHT

ASSESSMENT

In many ways the thought of Arnold Toynbee seems strangely out of place in the twentieth century. While scholars in the various disciplines have been carving out still narrower areas of specialization, Toynbee chose to write a universal history. In an age of intellectual fragmentation, he suggested a comprehensive meaning behind the facts of history. In an era that strives for knowledge according to standards set by science, much of Toynbee's history was rooted in poetry and prophecy. In a secular age, he saw religion as the principal goal of life and the essential concern of the historian. Although he disclaimed the role of prophet, like the ancient Hebrew prophets, Toynbee, in a time of social distress and moral confusion, exhorted man to find certainty in God's ethical precepts. Like them he warned that when man forgets God and worships human creations he brings disaster upon himself and the social order. Such an outlook was most certain to arouse criticism.

TOYNBEE AND THE TRADITION OF LIBERAL HUMANISM

Historians have assailed Toynbee as an enemy of the liberal-rational tradition and have accused him of advocating and welcoming the decline of the West. H. R. Trevor-Roper held that Toynbee "is fundamentally anti-rational and illiberal. Everything which suggests the freedom of the human reason, the human spirit, is to him odious. ... To Toynbee the Renaissance was the beginning of the irreversible decline of the West, and every further manifestation of human reason is to him yet another milestone on the road to ruin."[1] Toynbee's "dismal prophecies" that the West was in decline, said Trevor-Roper, contributed to the spirit of defeatism with which Western countries first confronted Hitler in the 1930's. Trevor-Roper attributed to Toynbee an eagerness to see the West destroyed and for this reason was "even in 1939 ... blind or indifferent, to the particular threat of Nazi Germany."[2] Because Toynbee "hungers spiritually" for the defeat of the West and "seems to ... gloat over the extinction of our civilization," Trevor-Roper found his work "hateful."[3] Toynbee would sacrifice Western ideals of justice and freedom, Western rationalism, Western art and literature so long as Christianity, or at least its Catholic strand, survives as part of a syncretic religion of a universal state.

> Why should not our Western Civilization go to its doom, the sooner the better, carrying with it the rubbish with which human reason has by now fatally deformed it, provided that the valuable parts of it, its primitive pre-Reformation faith, can be preserved as one of the vitalizing ingredients of the new 'universal state'?
> ....
> Thus Toynbee is still the philosophic ally of any conqueror who will destroy the West. ... Such, I believe, is Toynbee's philosophy. It is a doctrine of messianic defeatism. Toynbee detests Western Civilization because it is basically liberal and rational. Detesting it, he wishes to see it destroyed, and he does not care who destroys it. On its ruins he envisages a new society, or rather the religion only of a new society. The new society itself, as far as he is concerned, can be the nightmare society of 1984, provided that the religion is the religion of Mish-Mash, of which he is the prophet and Messiah. And this he calls a great hope for the West.[4]

Pieter Geyl expressed somewhat similar sentiments. Toynbee "will have it that Western Civilization is in a bad way, and indeed, why should he care? Western Civilization means nothing to him."[5] Geyl dismissed Toynbee's assurances that he

believes in free will and considers the future
an open question. This assertion, insisted Geyl,
is as invalid as Toynbee's other often repeated
claim that his generalizations derive from an empirical study. By holding that only a return to
Christianity can save the West, an unlikely and un-
satisfying remedy indeed, said Geyl, Toynbee is
condemning all our efforts to futility; it is, in
reality, a death sentence. Despite his criticism
of Spengler, declared Geyl, an exacting determinism pervades Toynbee's system.

These early indictments by Trevor-Roper, Geyl
and many others have been echoed by more recent
critics. In 1968, Sidney Pollard concluded:

> Basically, Toynbee is opposed to
> rationalism. ... Toynbee is instinc-
> tively opposed to all that liberalism
> stands for: freedom to differ, a
> pluralist society, suspicion of
> authority, a belief in the values of
> this life, pursued by rational means,
> within ethical concepts justifiable
> on human rather than mythological or
> divine terms. Toynbee, on the con-
> trary, prefers feeling and intuition
> to analysis; a monolithic God to a
> pluralistic society; fixed, chartered
> course to chance or human initiative;
> and a miracle to partial, piecemeal
> reform.[6]

There is evidence to substantiate the view
that Toynbee was fundamentally hostile to the liberal-rational tradition of the West. His methodology belied the empiricism he claimed for it. By
imposing mythical conceptions of sin, *hubris*, and
Fate upon the course of historical events, Toynbee,
at times, seemed more a prophet or a mystic than
a sober-minded historian. Furthermore, Toynbee
barely acknowledged the accomplishments and the
worth of either Greek humanism or the Enlightenment
tradition. He rejected a secular definition of
freedom, insisted that reason, unguided by spiritual
values, has failed Western man, and stressed

communion with God as the prime aim of life. He praised the Middle Ages for striking a proper balance between religion and secularism and regarded modern Western Civilization as a vain repetition of a disintegrated Hellenic civilization. Like other twentieth-century intellectuals, Toynbee expressed a disillusionment with the Enlightenment conception of man and society. Even when the humanist creed encompasses non-religious spiritual values, as was the case with the philosophes, it will not succeed.

It can be argued that a pessimistic if not a defeatist attitude pervades Toynbee's thought. To be sure he denied that the West is doomed by necessity and insisted that man is free to shape his future. Yet he paraded before us dead and dying civilizations, none of which had succeeded in escaping from the cycle of breakdown and disintegration. Nor did he think that our modern Western Civilization is worth very much; it is just another meaningless repetition of the Gentiles. If an apostasy from Christianity has caused our decline and only allegiance to a revitalized Christianity or a new syncretic religion can reverse the process of decline, then indeed there is little hope for us.

And yet this view requires qualification and clarification. Toynbee tried to resolve a fundamental dilemma of the West -- finding a constructive place for the non-rational in a world that is being increasingly rationalized. For this reason, he rebelled against the reductionism inherent in the Enlightenment conception of reason; he wanted to rescue personality and feelings from reason which, in its relentless drive to make everything intelligible, degenerates into soulless mechanism, materialism, and technocracy. He held that reason is insufficient to protect man from himself; it is no match for individual self-centeredness and group tribal-mindedness that evoke the brutal side of human nature. It cannot compare with religion in awakening man's noblest sentiments -- love and compassion. Enlightenment values unbutressed by Christianity cannot restrain man's basest impulses nor contain the explosive energies of the non-rational. Liberalism divested of Christian love

degenerates into greed and competiveness that promote social injustice and the plundering of nature.
Nor can a purely secular statement of liberty safe-
guard individual rights against the claims of the
state; only when personal freedom is conceived as
God's intention for humanity will man have the
spiritual strength to resist totalitarianism. Because the ideals of the Enlightenment and of liberalism were divested of Christian spirituality, they
have failed and will continue to fail Western man.
Secular humanism, insisted Toynbee, is not sufficient by itself. It failed in Periclean Athens,
Medicean Florence, and Victorian England. It was
out of a concern for human dignity which has been
threatened by technology and totalitarianism that
Toynbee urged man to revitalize prophetic values.
When scientists and statesmen become inspired by
spiritual values, reason will be an instrument for
human betterment. Reason requires a spiritual ally,
otherwise all efforts at reform will be defeated by
human self-centeredness and all efforts to undo the
dehumanizing excesses of reason will fail.

But Toynbee was no enemy of reason. He was no
Nietzsche or Sorel glorifying primitive feelings.
What else was his hostility to nationalism and fanaticism but a recognition of the dangers of the
non-rational and a desire to control it? In recognizing and condemning the failings of institutional
religion and in refusing to accept dogma as truth,
Toynbee showed that he was not a simple-minded be-
liever or an obscurantist seeking security in the
orthodoxy of the Middle Ages. Nor did he negate
this world for an afterlife or espouse the withdrawal from the worldly life. He declared that
Christianity had erred grievously when it fought
the Copernican Revolution with theological doctrines derived essentially from Hellenistic thought
which had nothing at all to do with the essential
meaning of the religion of Jesus. But if Toynbee
would not deny reason, he was keenly aware of its
limitations.

> I would describe myself as ... a 'trans-
> rationalist'. I believe that one must
> follow reason as far as reason will

carry one, and that the findings
of reason ... must be accepted
without reservation. ... I also
hold, however, that reason has not
explained, and probably never will
explain more than a fragment of
the mystery of the universe, and
that the fragmentary picture that
reason gives has to be supplanted
by intuition. I believe that human beings cannot be without this
wider 'trans-rational' vision. At
the same time, I believe that intuition cannot give the verifiable
and demonstrable knowledge that
reason can legitimately claim to
give within its own limited field.[7]

In his humanitarianism, cosmopolitanism, and
concern for social justice, in his willingness to
accept the conclusions of science, in his insistence that man, through intelligent planning, can
utilize technology to improve the quality of life,
and in his hatred of totalitarianism, Toynbee was
heir to the liberal-rational tradition of the West.
Although he insisted that the values of liberal humanism are insufficient to protect man from fanaticism, irrationalism, and a persistent tribal-
mindedness or to give him the inner strength with
which to confront the anxieties and depressions
that burden every human soul, he nevertheless
sought to preserve much of the liberal-rational
tradition by buttressing it with prophetic teachings.

If by liberal we mean protection of individual rights, the rule of law, legitimate parliamentary government, freedom of thought, toleration,
social justice, then Toynbee must be adjudged a
liberal. "Toynbee *is* in many ways rather typical
liberal-democrat-socialist," concludes Roland
Stromberg. "He wants the welfare state and the
United Nations and racial equality and all the
rest."[8] The anonymous reviewer of the *Times Literary Supplement* was quite correct to describe *A
Study of History* as "a vision which expresses the

116

despair of a liberal who has seen the liberal dream
turn to ashes as well as the hopes of a liberal who
has turned again to God."[9]

Nor was Toynbee devoid of hope for Western
Civilization. He insisted that "we must not be defeatist, passive, or aloof in our reaction to the
current evils that threaten mankind's survival. If
these evils were caused by forces beyond human control, resignation and submission might be the only
course open to us. However, our present evils are
man-made and ought to be man-cured as well."[10]
Toynbee considered it "shameful, and therefore, de-
moralizing to allow ourselves to be destroyed by
refusing to make an effort that is manifestly within our power and that would manifestly save us if
we were willing to make it."[11]

LIMITATIONS

Toynbee was no enemy of reason and freedom and
he did not seek the destruction of Western Civilization. Nevertheless, he did blur the essential
achievements of the modern West and did champion an
orientation that could only weaken the liberal-
rational tradition. Toynbee paid scant attention
to the immense achievement of the modern West which
produced a new approach to the study of nature,
legal safeguards for the individual, constitutional
government, religious toleration, and intellectual
freedom.

> When I ask my fellow Westerners what
> the West stands for, and am told, as
> I usually am, that it stands for jus-
> tice, freedom and humanity, I ask if
> there is any civilization on record --
> not excluding those once represented
> by the Assyrians and the Aztecs --
> that has not also claimed to stand
> for the self-same virtues. Surely
> these are the virtues to which all
> human beings feel themselves con-
> strained to pay homage, but to which
> no human beings have ever succeeded
> in living up.[12]

To claim that the idea of freedom is universal is simply poor history and Toynbee should have known better. In creating democratic government the modern West brought to fruition an achievement that had its roots in the Greek polis, medieval representative institutions, the English Revolution of the seventeenth century, the natural rights philosophy of John Locke, and the French Revolution. No such comparable development existed in the East where the idea of political freedom and the institution of parliamentary government were alien. Because democracy was not native to the historical experience of Asia and Africa it has proven to be a fragile transplant. It is because of the spread of Western values that Chinese women no longer have their feet bound, that untouchability was abolished in India, that Muslim women are no longer compelled to wear the veil, that humanity condemns slavery as a violation of human rights, and that the poor of the world no longer regard poverty as their destiny. Only under prodding did Toynbee give recognition to the achievements of the modern West.

It is true that the expectations of the philosophes have not been fulfilled, that Condorcet's vision appears to us as an expression of naive optimism. But reason cannot provide that sense of certainty that derives from faith. What it offers is an independent and objective method of proceeding -- a method that welcomes and benefits from critical analysis and debate and rejects appeals to authority. And it is still this critical exercise of reason in the spirit of the Socratic dialogue that affords man the best means for achieving knowledge and with it self-liberation. Better than anyone Freud understood that against the power of instinctual life the intellect is often a feeble weapon. Yet Freud still urged the life of reason. "The voice of the intellect is a soft one," he wrote, "but it does not rest till it has gained a hearing. Finally, after a countless succession of rebuffs, it succeeds. This is one of the few points on which one may be optimistic about the future of mankind." And the same aims one expects from God, says Freud, "namely the love of man and the decrease of suffering," are the aims that the intellect will set for itself. Thus there may be no ultimate antagonism between the aim of the prophets of higher religions and the aim of Socrates, but "an illusion it would be to suppose that what science cannot give us we can get elsewhere."[13]

By treating history as a theodicy, by drawing inspiration from Augustinian pessimism and Bergsonian mysticism, Toynbee, whatever his intention, weakens respect for *logos* at a time when reason needs all the assistance the intellectual community is capable of providing. If the rational foundations of our civilization are eroded, we are more likely to experience an intensification of political myths that appeal to primitive feelings and a proliferation of irrational behavior patterns than we are to experience a reawakening of prophetic values.

To cope with the crisis of our civilization we shall have to renew our confidence in reason, enlarge our understanding of the non-rational, and affirm our commitment to freedom -- that means building upon the achievement of the Enlightenment. And toward this end the historian has a profound responsibility, even a calling as Toynbee holds. As to the nature of that calling the sentiments of J. H. Plumb seem preferable to those of Toynbee:

> Man's success has derived from his application of reason, whether this has been to technical or to social questions. And it is the duty of the historian to teach this, to proclaim it, to demonstrate it in order to give humanity some confidence in a task that will still be cruel and long -- the resolution of the tensions and antipathies that exist within the human species ... Hence the historian's opportunity is similar, although far from identical, to that of the philosophers of the Enlightenment. They too were slipping off the shackles of the past, destroying its pretensions and its

follies, but they also attempted to
create out of the debris a more extended, a more rational, a more detached sense of human destiny. And
so by his writings, by his thinking,
even by his example, the historian
today should be similarly engaged.[14]

Toynbee's religious orientation does not provide a sound basis for coping with the crises of
the modern West or with the world's problems in
this new age of globalism. Can a spiritual transformation be achieved when Western man's religious
world-view has been shattered, its dogmatic and institutional foundation subverted, when God's very
existence is doubted? Even if religion is socially
useful, even if it relieves psychic distress, can
Western intellectuals, in a mental climate shaped
by science and scepticism, return to what they no
longer accept as true? Can prophetic values un-
supported by the mystery and authority of theology
and the power of an institutional church sustain a
spiritual revolution? Higher religions have survived because the inspiration of their prophets was
transformed and hardened into dogma. Not Jesus'
Sermon on the Mount but the Pauline doctrine of a
resurrected savior-God became the centerpiece of
Christianity and made its triumph possible. A religion of love not rooted in dogma and protected by
priests may inspire sporadic outbreaks of spiritual
idealism but that is all. The religious revolution
that Toynbee seeks -- "a conversion of the soul
away from the World, the Flesh, and the Devil to
the Kingdom of Heaven"[15] -- cannot be achieved
through prophetic love alone, for without mystery
and authority, religion fades. And the modern West
is no longer receptive to the mystery and authority
of Christianity.

In a post-Christian scientific age in which a
religious world-view has crumbled and in which
Christianity has evidenced little ability to recon-
vert Westerners to their ancestral religion, Toynbee's hope for a contemporary St. Francis to lead
wayward Westerners back to the God of love seems an
expression of piety not reality. Perhaps this is

one of the reasons why Toynbee in his later works seemed increasingly more enamored of Eastern religions. The East, less scientific, industrialized and secularized, and traditionally more introspective, might prove more receptive to a religious revolution than the West. Even if the equation between an accelerating rationalization of nature and society and a decreasing adherence to traditional religious beliefs, can be upset, how could a religious reawakening take place? On this point the judgment of Hans Morganthau seems most perceptive:

> But even if it were true that the return to religious faith can save Western Civilization, can a civilization recover its religious faith by an act of will? ... Neither a teacher nor a whole civilization can by an act of will create the symbolic and ritualistic expressions of religiosity thus restored; least of all can they create them out of the fragments of religions, whose decline has made the restoration of religiosity necessary in the first place. What religions will grow from this new religiosity man must leave to fate. He must be content to be ready, and to make others ready, to see the signs and to read them aright when they appear.[16]

Toynbee's vision of the harmonization of the world's higher religions also seems doubtful, for it is based on the questionable assumption that these religions are spiritually equivalent, that their common concern for a higher reality outweighs disparities resulting from theological differences and separate histories. This is not the sober judgment of a historian but the faith of a mystic.

Toynbee also held out the possibility that twentieth-century man's "quest for the recovery of religion" may lead to new forms of religion "that will be so different from the traditional forms that, at first sight, man's new religion may hardly

be recognizable."[17] The very formlessness of Toynbee's religion of the future opens the door to all
forms of religious expression from futile mysticism
to violent eruptions of the non-rational, the very
thing that Toynbee was trying to guard against. A
religious revolution that calls for a return to
spiritual values but offers no institutional structure, no theology can degenerate into recklessness,
mindlessness, or even self-destruction; or it can
remain ineffectual.

There is also the reverse danger. A reawakening of religion might lead not to a heightening of
prophetic values but an intensification of fundamentalist dogmatism. Where this has occurred, particularly in the Islamic world, it has been accompanied by a reactionary social policy and an intensification of nationalism. Embracing a religious
frame of reference encompasses more than prophetic
values; it also invites the authority of priests
and the mystery of dogma. This is not what Toynbee
desired but it is certainly one of the lessons of
history. Nor does religion fulfill the expectations of its prophets. It promises ultimate knowledge and a way of living that is on the highest
ethical plane. "Yet its effect is the very opposite," says Ernst Cassirer. "In its concrete appearance it becomes the source of the most profound
dissensions and fanatic struggles among men. Religion claims to be in possession of an absolute
truth, but its history is a history of errors and
heresies. It gives us the promise and prospect of
a transcendent world -- far beyond the limits of
our human experience -- and it remains, all too human."[18] Thus the heightening of religious feeling
might well serve to impede the world-mindedness
that Toynbee sought, exacerbate the nationalism
that he hated, and thwart the social progress that
he advocated.

Religion can do many things, some of them inspiring of awe, but by its very nature it cannot
objectively and self-critically analyze and resolve
the problems of the human community. To the Socratic quest for knowledge of man, religion offers no
rational explanations; it does not clarify the

mystery of man but relates a story of sin and salvation that transcends objective knowledge. It must always take as its source and inspiration a standard that emanates from a higher realm and must always conceive this standard as ultimate truth whether or not it is a fruitful guide for intellectual enlightenment or social reconstruction.

The growing world integration in the modern era has not been the creation of religions but of business, science, and technology and it is doubtful that a religious revival will accelerate world-mindedness. Fundamentalist Hindus, Muslims, and Christians have less in common than scientists and technicians whatever their nationality. Science speaks a language of universal reason; while higher religions undoubtedly hold the ideal of universalism, they nevertheless are rooted in the concrete historical experience of a particular civilization. As such they might be a barrier rather than an aid to world unity.

THE ACHIEVEMENT

Of what value is Toynbee's immense effort? Will future generations admire *A Study of History* or will it only "be a curiosity in 20 or 30 years,"[19] as Bruce Mazlish suggested? Toynbee's work will always remain a profound expression of the torments and anxieties that have afflicted the West in the twentieth century. Future historians will also praise *A Study of History* for its innumerable stimulating and illuminating insights, for its wealth of data and extraordinary learning. Toynbee deserves credit for attempting a universal history, for stressing the value of all the world's civilizations and for eschewing Western ethnocentrism. If our planet does become increasingly unified then Toynbee will be heralded as a leading prophet and apostle of world unity. "To have stressed ... the fundamental oneness of mankind," says Hans Kohn, "will be a lasting merit of Mr. Toynbee's work and vision."[20]

Toynbee also deserves praise for daring to take a panoramic view of history in an age when historians are reluctant to venture outside their specializations. William H. McNeill is correct in holding "that there are insights attainable by taking large views of the past which cannot be had from close inspection of separated segments of history. ... It is passages,... when the free exercise of a synthetic imagination has succeeded in suggesting novel relationships and discerning new points of view, which ... make Toynbee a truly great historian."[21] There will always remain a need for historians to produce a comprehensive statement that attempts to give meaning to the many disparate elements that constitute human history in general and Western history in particular.

Perhaps the principal value of Toynbee's effort is that it forces us to reexamine the nature and central meaning of the Enlightenment tradition and to recognize the importance and enduring power of the non-rational in human affairs. Toynbee will ever remind us that theoretical reason, the great achievement of the Greek mind, is not the only component of Western Civilization; there is also the Christian tradition. For Socrates, knowing oneself meant that man's reason and will were autonomous; the human mind did not depend on forces outside itself for defining values and guiding conduct. Christianity represents an alternate and essentially opposing world-view. It teaches that man through reason alone cannot arrive at moral standards and cannot fully know himself, that the cause of sin, suffering, and sorrow is man's separation from God, that man cannot without God's grace overcome his sinful nature, and that the cure for an ailing humanity is communion with God. To regard this anthropology as ignorance or superstition is to misunderstand entirely the persistence and granite might of the non-rational, the well-spring of religious thought. Human nature will resist the complete rationalization of life; it will not discard every mythical explanation or reduce all belief to objective knowledge. To expect it to do otherwise is to misread the historical record and to oversimplify man's being.

The withering of traditional religion has not

meant the complete triumph of reason, the victory of *logos* over *mythos*. Surely the experience of the twentieth century teaches us that the vitality of myth endures, that when man ceases to believe in God he is capable of believing in anything and everything else. Herein lies the ultimate significance of Toynbee's effort. He forces us to confront the irrational, to find a constructive outlet for its creative energies and to cope with its destructive capacities. Who could deny his insight that man's religious sentiments have not been eradicated but have been rerouted into lower religions: the cult of the state, the cult of the race, the cult of the leader, the cult of the party, the cult of the machine? The non-rational is a permanent component of human nature that reason cannot obliterate; the human psyche will not submit to the total ratiocination of life. It is an axiom of Toynbee's thought that if man is deprived of higher religions that stress love and compassion he will embrace lower religions and dangerous myths whose capacity to destroy civilization has been historically demonstrated. On this point we have no assurance that Toynbee is mistaken. Toynbee compels us to consider if the source of evil is not within man himself, if human nature is not indeed afflicted with a vein of wickedness and aggressiveness, what religious thinkers call original sin. Toynbee agrees with Walter Lipmann that "men have been barbarians much longer than they have been civilized. They are only precariously civilized, and within us there is the propensity, persistent as the force of gravity, to revert under stress and strain, under neglect or temptation, to our first natures."22

Toynbee reminds us that religion is not something that we can simply reason away and forces us to reflect upon the meaning and utility of prophetic teachings for a secular but troubled age. By questioning the assumption that traditional liberal humanism offers the best defense against dangerous eruptions of the non-rational, Toynbee forces the humanist to reexamine, modify, and improve the instruments of reason.

Toynbee prods us to ask where is science

taking us and cautions us that our technical society, in the words of Jacques Ellul, manifests a
"raving rationalism." Faustian man in his determination to pursue truth and subdue nature, has
shaped an artificial world of imagined needs, a
Frankenstein technology and giant bureaucracies
that can depersonalize him and destroy the planet.
Like early nineteenth-century romantics, Toynbee
criticizes technicians for turning flesh-and-blood
man into a soulless thinking machine and a vibrant
nature into lifeless wheels, cogs, and pulleys.
Like adherents of eastern religions, he attacks
Westerners for their irreverent attitude toward
nature. By regarding nature as something that God
has given man to exploit, Westerners have plundered
and polluted the planet. Man can only survive,
says Toynbee, if he restrains greed, practices fru-
gality, and adopts a religious reverence for life
and nature.

Toynbee demands that we find meaning in what
many consider a meaningless universe, and cautions
us that science alone cannot provide this meaning,
cannot grasp life in its fullness. He warns us
that the bedrock of civilization is not man's domin-
ion over nature but the moral mastery of his own
nature and the quality of his relations with his
fellows. The ills of modern society, he insists,
cannot be cured merely by organizational or institutional changes. Mankind requires a change of
heart, a better spiritual orientation. To a stumbling Western Civilization he warns further that
civilizations break down from within, from a failure of leadership and a loss of élan. If a civilization is to endure it must be directed toward
something more inspiring than material gain. And
he admonishes those who would surrender to despair:
"We must strive to win the battle of life though we
have no guarantee that we will."[23]

Toynbee is more poet and artist than social
scientist. But his very subjectivity accounts for
his achievement. Many of the questions he asks are
not capable of empirical verification, but they do
awaken the historical imagination and provoke philosophic discourse. In an age that has seen reason

and optimism soar and collapse, Toynbee has raised the essential questions.

NOTES

1. H. R. Trevor-Roper, *Historical Essays*, pp. 300-01.

2. *Ibid.*, p. 305.

3. *Ibid.*, pp. 320-21.

4. *Ibid.*, pp. 309, 322-23.

5. Pieter Geyl, *Debates with Historians*, p. 185.

6. Sidney Pollard, *The Idea of Progress* (London: C.A. Watts & Co., 1968), p. 173.

7. Arnold J. Toynbee, "The Future of Religion," *Twentieth Century* 17 (Autumn 1961), p. 114.

8. Roland N. Stromberg, *Arnold Toynbee Historian for an Age of Crisis* (Carbondale, Illinois: Southern Illinois University Press, 1972), p. 82.

9. Montagu, ed., *Toynbee and History*, p. 110.

10. *The Toynbee - Ikeda Dialogue* (New York: Kodansha International Ltd., 1976), p. 55.

11. *Ibid.*, p. 57.

12. *Study*, 12: 626-27.

13. Sigmund Freud, *The Future of an Illusion*, trans. W. D. Robson-Scott, revised and newly edited by James Strachey (Garden City, New York: Doubleday Anchor Books, 1964), pp. 87-88, 90.

14. J. H. Plumb, *The Death of the Past* (Boston: Houghton Mifflin Co., 1970), pp. 142, 144-45.

15. *Study*, 3: 192.

16. Hans J. Morganthau, "Toynbee and the Historical Imagination," in Montagu, ed., *Toynbee and History*, pp. 198-99.

17. Arnold J. Toynbee, "The Challenge of Our Era," in
    New Frontiers of Knowledge, a symposium by distinguished
    writers, notable scholars, and public figures (Washing-
    ton, D. C.: Public Affairs Press, 1957), P. 24.

18. Ernst Cassirer, *An Essay on Man* (New York: Bantam
    Books, 1970), pp. 79-80.

19. Bruce Mazlish, *The Riddle of History: The Great
    Speculators from Vico to Freud* (New York: Minerva
    Press, 1968), p. 368.

20. Kohn, *Political Ideologies of the Twentieth Century*,
    p. 275.

21. Gargan, ed., *The Intent of Toynbee's History*, pp. 30,
    41.

22. Walter Lippmann, *The Public Philosophy* (Boston: Little,
    Brown and Co., 1955), p. 86.

23. *The Toynbee-Ikeda Dialogue*, p. 75.

BIBLIOGRAPHY

A complete listing of Toynbee's works and the secondary literature would cover scores of pages. A useful bibliography of Toynbee's writings is Monica Popper, *A Bibliography of the Works in English of Arnold Toynbee 1910-1954* (London: Royal Institute of International Affairs, 1955). A listing of works about Toynbee is found in John C. Rule and Barbara S. Crosby, "Bibliography of Works about Toynbee in Western Languages, 1946-1960," *History and Theory* 4 (1964): 213-33. Toynbee himself in volume 12 of *A Study of History* has compiled a bibliography of most of the reviews and articles dealing with his project. A recent and complete bibliography of both Toynbee's writings and critical secondary works is S. Fiona Morton, *A Bibliography of Arnold J. Toynbee* (New York: Oxford University Press), 1981.

SELECTED WORKS OF ARNOLD TOYNBEE

Toynbee, Arnold J. *A Study of History*. 12 vols. New York: Oxford University Press, 1934-1961. Oxford University Press has also published the paperback edition. A two-volume abridgement of volumes 1-10 was prepared by D. C. Somervell and published by Oxford University Press, 1947, 1957. There is also an abridged, illustrated, one-volume edition published jointly by Oxford University Press and American Heritage Press, 1972.

_____. *Survey of International Affairs*. London: Oxford University Press. Issued under the auspices of the Royal Institute of International Affairs. Toynbee was wholly or partly responsible for most of the volumes covering the period 1920-1950.

_____. "The Issue in British Foreign Policy." *International Affairs* 17 (May-June 1938): 307-337.

_____. "After Munich: The World Outlook." *International Affairs* 18 (January-February 1939): 1-28.

_____. "A Turning Point in History." *Foreign Affairs* 17 (January 1939): 305-320.

_____. *Civilization on Trial*. New York: Oxford

University Press, 1948.

_____. *The Prospects of Western Civilization*. New York: Columbia University Press, 1949.

_____. *The World and the West*. New York: Oxford University Press, 1953.

_____. *A Study of History, What the Book is For: How the Book Took Shape*. New York: Oxford University Press, 1954.

_____. *An Historian's Approach to Religion*. New York: Oxford University Press, 1956.

_____. *Christianity Among the Religions of the World*. New York: Charles Scribner's Sons, 1957.

_____. *Democracy in the Atomic Age*. New York: Oxford University Press, 1957.

_____. "The Writing of History." *Times Literary Supplement*, August 15, 1958. Special issue entitled "Books in a Changing World."

_____. *East to West*. New York: Oxford University Press, 1958.

_____. *Hellenism*. New York: Oxford University Press, 1959.

_____. "The Future of Religion." *Twentieth Century* 170 (Autumn 1961): 114-39.

_____. *Between Oxus and Jumna*. New York: Oxford University Press, 1961.

_____. *America and the World Revolution and Other Lectures*. New York: Oxford University Press, 1962.

_____. and Toynbee, Phillip. *Comparing Notes: A Dialogue Across a Generation*. London: Weidenfeld & Nicolson, 1963.

_____. *Janus at 75*. New York: Oxford University Press, 1964.

_____. *Between Niger and Nile.* New York: Oxford University Press, 1965.

_____. *Change and Habit.* New York: Oxford University Press, 1966.

_____. *Between Maule and Amazon.* New York: Oxford University Press, 1967.

_____. *Acquaintances.* New York: Oxford University Press, 1967.

_____. "A Substitute for War?" *Long Island Press*, 3 May, 1969, p. 13.

_____. *Experiences.* New York: Oxford University Press, 1969.

_____. *Cities on the Move.* New York: Oxford University Press, 1970.

_____. *Surviving the Future.* New York: Oxford University Press, 1971.

_____. "For the First Time in 30,000 Years." *Worldview* 15 (March 1972): 5-9.

_____. *Mankind and Mother Earth.* New York: Oxford University Press, 1976.

WORKS WHICH TOYNBEE CONTRIBUTED TO OR EDITED

Livingstone, Richard, ed. *The Legacy of Greece.* London: Clarendon Press, 1921; reprint ed. New York: Oxford University Press, Galaxy, 1969.

Toynbee, Arnold, et. al. *Frontiers of Knowledge.* A Symposium by Distinguished Writers, Notable Scholars, and Public Figures. Washington, D.C.: Public Affairs Press, 1957.

Meyers, Edward D. *Education in the Perspective of History.* New York: Harper & Row, 1960. A concluding chapter by Toynbee.

Toynbee, Arnold, ed. *Cities of Destiny.* New York: McGraw Hill, 1967.

Toynbee, Arnold, et. al. *The Impact of the Russian Revolution 1917-1967.* New York: Oxford University Press, 1967.

Toynbee, Arnold, et. al. *Man's Concern with Death.* London: Hudder and Stoughton, 1968.

Toynbee, Arnold, ed. *The Crucible of Christianity.* New York: World Publishing Co., 1969.

Ng, Larry, ed. *Alternatives to Violence.* New York: Time-Life Books, 1968.

SELECTED WORKS ON ARNOLD TOYNBEE

Africa, Thomas W. "The City of God Revisited: Toynbee's Reconsiderations," *Journal of History of Ideas* 23 (April 1, 1962): 282-92.

Aron, Raymond, ed. *L'histoire et ses interpretations: entretiens autour de Arnold Toynbee.* Paris: Mouton, 1961.

Brinton, Crane. "Toynbee's City of God." *Virginia Quarterly Review* 32 (Summer 1956): 361-75.

Christian, James Lee. "Arnold Toynbee's Concept of Man." Ph.D. dissertation. Boston University, 1957.

Collingwood, R. G. *The Idea of History.* New York: Oxford University Press, 1946.

D'Arcy, M. C. *The Meaning and Matter of History.* New York: Noonday Press, 1967.

Dawson, Christopher. *The Dynamics of World History.* New York: Sheen & Ward, 1956; reprint ed., New York: Mentor, 1962.

Donagan, Alan and Donagan, Barbara. *Philosophy of History.* New York: MacMillan, 1965.

Engel-Janosi, Friedrich. "Toynbee and the Tradition of Universal History, A Sketch." The McAuley Lectures, 1957. Saint Joseph College, West Hartford, Conn., 1957, pp. 221-47.

Frankel, Charles. *The Case for Modern Man*. New York: Harper & Row, 1955.

Gargan, Edward T., ed. *The Intent of Toynbee's History*. Chicago: Loyola University Press, 1961.

Geyl, Pieter, Toynbee, Arnold, and Sorokin, Pitrim. *The Pattern of the Past: Can We Determine It?* Boston: Beacon Press, 1949.

Geyl, Pieter. *Debates With Historians*. New York: Philosophical Library, 1956.

Hill, Christopher. "Dr. Toynbee's SNARK." *Spectator* 206 (May 12, 1961): 685.

Hunnex, Milton deVerne. "Toynbee's Idea of Etheralization as a Criterion of Progress." Ph.D. dissertation. University of Redlands, 1957.

Kahler, Erich. *The Meaning of History*. New York: George Braziller, 1964; reprint ed., Cleveland: World Publishing Co., Meridean, 1968.

Kirkwood, Kenneth P. "Arnold J. Toynbee Philosopher of History." An Address Given at the British Council. Karachi, March 1953.

Kohn, Hans. *Political Ideologies of the Twentieth Century*. 3d ed. New York: Harper Torchbooks, 1966.

Manuel, Frank E. *Shapes of Philosophical History*. Stanford, California: Stanford University Press, 1965.

Martin, Percival W. *Experiment in Depth: A Study of the Work of Jung, Eliot and Toynbee*. London: Routledge, 1955.

Mason, Henry L. *Toynbee's Approach to World Politics*. New Orleans: Tulane University Press, 1958.

Mazlish, Bruce. *The Riddle of History*. New York: Harper & Row, 1966; reprint ed. New York: Minerva Press, 1968.

Melko, Matthew. *The Nature of Civilizations*. Boston: Porter Sargent, 1969.

133

Montagu, M. R. Ashley, ed. *Toynbee and History*. Boston: Porter Sargent, 1956.

Nash, Ronald, ed. *Ideas of History*. 2 vols. New York: E. P. Dutton, 1969.

Perry, Marvin. "Arnold Toynbee: Nationalism as a False God." *Interpretation: A Journal of Political Philosophy* 4 (1974): 48-62.

Perry, Marvin. "Legacy of Arnold Toynbee." *Commonweal* 102 (December 19, 1975): 630-31.

Pollard, Sidney. *The Idea of Progress*. London: C. A. Watts & Co., 1968.

Stromberg, Roland N. *Arnold J. Toynbee Historian For An Age of Crisis*. Carbondale, Illinois: Southern Illinois University Press, 1972.

Sullivan, Richard E. "Toynbee's Debtors." *South Atlantic Quarterly* 58 (Winter 1959): 77-90.

Thompson, Kenneth W. "Toynbee and World Politics: Democracy and Foreign Policy." *The Review of Politics* 18 (October 1956): 418-43.

Trevor-Roper, H. R. "Arnold Toynbee's Millenium." *Encounter* 8 (June 1957): 14-28; reprinted in *Historical Essays*. New York: Harper Torchbooks, 1966.

Wagar, W. Warren. *The City of Man*. Boston: Houghton Mifflin, 1967; reprint ed. Baltimore: Penquin, 1963.

_____. *Good Tidings: The Belief in Progress From Darwin to Marcuse*. Bloomington, Indiana: Indiana University Press, 1972.

White, Hayden V. "Collingwood and Toynbee: Transitions in English Historical Thought." *English Miscellany*. Rome, 1957, pp. 147-178.

Woodward, C. Vann. "Toynbee and Metahistory." *The American Scholar* 27 (Summer 1958): 384-92.

Alexander the Great, 40
Alienation, 73-76
Aquinas, Thomas, 11,47
Archaism, 20,90
Augustine, St., 30,119
Barbarians, see external proletariat

Bergson, Henri, 18,28-30,119
Cassirer, Ernst, 72,122
Challenge-and-response, 17-18,37-39,42
Christianity, 8-9,25-27,41-43, 45-47,49,55,57-63, 65-67,89-90,103,124; see also religion and Middle Ages

Church, Roman, 42-44; see also Middle Ages

Civilization, rise, decline, and nature of, 17-21,68,80,87,95; see also Hellenism and Western Civilization

Communism, 60-63,86,96
Conservatism, 59
Democracy, 65,68; see also liberalism and freedom

Determinism, 16,87-88,113
Dominant minority, 19-20,42,85-86, 89,106
Education, 3-5,27,49,55,67, 113-114,119- 120,126
Enlightenment, Age of,

Ellul, Jacques, 126
External proletariat, 19,42-43,84
Francis, St., 47,91,120
Freedom, 3,6-7,16-17,36,58- 60,70,89,99, 103-104,117-118

Freud, Sigmund, 5-6,118-119
Futurism, 20
Geyl, Pieter, 30,112-113
Gibbon, Edward, 13,42,53,83
Hellenism, 11,24,35-45,62, 84,86-87,98

Hitler, Adolf,   66,69-70,111; see
                                      also National
                                      Socialism
Human nature,   17,22-23,68,76,85
Humanism,   36-37,45-47,55,
                                      67-68,111-117
Industrialization,   65-66,75; see also
                                      technology
Internal proletariat,   19,41-43,85-86,88
Irrationalism,   5-6,8,124-125
Judaism,   61
Kohn, Hans,   3,123
Liberalism,   26-27,57-60,68-69,
                                      111,113,116-
                                      117; see also
                                      freedom
Liberty,   see freedom and
                                      liberalism
Machiavelli, Niccolo,   52
McNeill, William H.,   14,27,124
Maritain, Jacques,   9
Marx, Karl,   see communism
Mazlish, Bruce,   123
Megolopolies,   75
Methodology,   27-30,113
Middle Ages,   31,44,49-51
Modernity,   49,55,117
Morganthau, Hans,   121
Nationalism,   24,46,51-52,54,63-
                                      69,84,98
National Socialism,   66-71,83,85
Ortega y Gasset, José,   29
Pax Romana,   40
Peloponnesian War,   38-40,87
Persian Wars,   38-39
Plato,   28,108
Plumb, J. H.,   119
Polybius,   14-15
Progress,   44-45,68,83,91
Reason,   3-7,26-27,35-36,
                                      45-47,59,71-72,
                                      114-116,118-
                                      119,124-125
Reformation,   52
Reiner, G. R.,   30

Religion,   8,15,21-27,49,63-
                                                64,77-79,90-91,
                                                101-102,106-
                                                108,120-125;
                                                see also Chris-
                                                tianity
Renaissance,   52,64-65,111
Rome,   40-44,90,96,98,101
Science,   26,29,49,53,76-77,
                                                125-126; see
                                                also technology.
Secularism,   44-45,54-55; see
                                                also humanism
Social justice,   60,102-108
Socialism,   89-90,104
Socrates,   24,77,106,119,124
Spengler, Oswald,   2,16,88,113
Technology,   53,72-79,90,101,
                                                105,126; see
                                                also science
Thucydides,   2,39
Totalitarianism,   8,60,66,89,115;
                                                see also commu-
                                                nism and Nation-
                                                al Socialism

Toynbee, Arnold J.,
    A Study of History, writing of,   13-14
    achievement of,   14,123-127
    alienation in modern society,   73-76
    Bergson, Henri, influence of,   28-29
    Christianity, history and nature of;
        attitude toward,   8-9,25-27,41-45,
                                                47,50-55,57,59,
                                                66-67,81-90,103
    civilization, patterns of,   17-21
    communism as a Christian heresy,   60-63
    criticism of,   27,29-30,111-114,
                                                117-123
    determinism, rejection of,   16,87-88
    education of,   11
    fanaticism, dangers of,   53-54,62,65
    Hellenism, rise and decline of,   37-44
    history as a calling,   15
    human nature, view of,   17,22-23,68,85
    humanism, view of,   36-37,45-47,55,
                                                67-68,113-114

leisure, view of, 108
liberalism, weaknesses of, 59-60,67-68
materialism, denunciation of, 107-108
methodology of, 27-30
Middle Ages, view of, 31,44-45
Modern West, failure of, 44-46,49-50,113-114
modernity, attitude toward, 49-55,117
mythology, use of, 27-28
nationalism, nature and dangers of, 24,46,51-52,63-68,84
optimism of, 88-89,108-109,117
pessimism of, 68,109,114
Plato, debt to, 28
progress, idea of, 44-45,68,83,91
reason, view of, 26-27,45,47,59,114-116
religion, view of, 11,15,21-27,44,77-79,90-91,101-102,106-108
social justice, view of, 60,102-108
synthesis, need for, 13
technology, impact of, 53,72-29,90,101,105
universalism of, 14-15,26,123
war, nature and effects of, 12,15,52-54,65,87,99
Western Civilization, prospects of, 83-92
world-state, toward the creation of, 95-109
World War I, impact on, 1-2
Trevor-Roper, H. R., 29-30,111-112
Universal state, see world-state
Universalism, 13-15,26,61,100-101,123
War, 1,12,15,52-54,65,87,99
Western Civilization, 2-9,37,43-47,54-55,57,66,83-92,95,97-98,111-114
World-state, 20-21,88-89,92,95-109
World War I, 1,12,15,83